NIGHTINGALES UNDER THE MISTLETOE

NIGHTINGALES UNDER THE MISTLETOE

by

Donna Douglas

Magna Large Print Books
Long Preston, North Yorkshire,
BD23 4ND, England.

British Library Cataloguing in Publication Data.

Douglas, Donna
    Nightingales under the mistletoe.

    A catalogue record of this book is
    available from the British Library

    ISBN   978-0-7505-4221-0

First published in Great Britain by Arrow Books in 2015

Published in Large Print 2016 by arrangement with
Random House Group Ltd.

Magna Large Print is an imprint of Library Magna Books Ltd.

Printed and bound in Great Britain by
T.J. (International) Ltd., Cornwall, PL28 8RW

Acknowledgements

I usually leave them till last in my acknowledgements, but this time I feel my husband and daughter should come first in my list of thanks. Writing *Nightingales Under The Mistletoe* was hard for various reasons (not least me coming up with a new plot two weeks before the deadline!) and even though I was the one at the keyboard, they suffered every word and every page with me. Ken was a true hero, supplying endless cups of tea, listening to my frustration and leaving packets of Fruit Gums hidden around the house to cheer me up. Harriet gave tons of encouragement, read every page with her usual perception, and thankfully didn't once tell me it was rubbish. I love you both, and I don't know how you put up with me in deadline mode, but I do appreciate it...

And my friends frequently came to my rescue, too. Thank you to Maureen Clark for making sure I actually stepped outside the house occasionally, and for turning up with fabulous cupcakes (is everyone getting the impression I respond best to food-based rewards? If so, you're right). Thank you also to June Smith-Sheppard for sending masses of cyber love, and for still being my friend even when I disappear off the radar for weeks on end. And thank you also to Rachel Diver and

Fiona Coleman for allowing me to vent and drink Singapore Slings, and to my author friends Jessica Gilmore and Pamela Hartshorne for allowing me to vent and drink fizzy wine (are you also getting the impression I respond to drink-based rewards? Right again).

Finally, a big thank you to my agent Caroline Sheldon, and to the wonderful team at Arrow, especially my editor Jenny Geras (welcome back!), Kate Raybould, boss lady Selina Walker, Philippa Cotton in publicity and Sarah Ridley in marketing, and all the amazing sales team, especially Aslan Byrne and Chris Turner. Thank you so much for making the Nightingales what they are, and for throwing me a very nice lunchtime party when I didn't expect it!

To Becki Ward

Chapter One

It was a cold, foggy November night when Jess Jago arrived on the last train from London.

She was the only passenger to get off the train at Billinghurst, a deserted rail halt in the middle of nowhere. Jess dumped her suitcase and gas-mask case on the ground and peered around her, trying to get her bearings. The fog was so dense she could almost feel it, like ghostly damp hands pressing on her face.

She laughed nervously. You're imagining things, girl! It was just a bit of fog, no worse than the gritty, yellowish pea-soupers that regularly en-shrouded the East End.

She took a deep breath, annoyed with herself for being so twitchy. Honestly, she'd lived all her life in Bethnal Green, grown up among rogues and thieves and God knows what else, and now she was scared because she was in the country-side, with nothing around her but a few trees – and deathly silence...

'Are you the new nurse?'

The low, gravelly voice came out of the gloom, making her jump out of her skin.

Jess fumbled in her coat pocket for her torch and aimed the beam into the fog. She swung it slowly left and right, then flinched as it suddenly picked out a grizzled old face under a shapeless hat.

'Turn that thing off, for God's sake,' he growled.

'You'll have the ARP out, thinking we're bloody Germans.' He gave a rattling cough. 'Well, what are you standing there for? I ain't got all night, you know. It's nearly ten and some of us have beds to go to. Besides, this fog plays hell with my chest.'

Jess heard the faint jingling of a harness, and the clomp of heavy hooves on the iron hard ground. As she lowered the beam of her torch, she saw a cart and a fat grey horse, its head curved wearily downwards.

'Who are you?' she asked.

'Father Christmas, who do you think?' The old man sighed impatiently. 'My name's Sulley – Mr Sulley to you – and I've been sent to fetch you to the Nurses' Home. Now are you coming or not? You're welcome to walk if you want, but it's more than five miles, and I doubt if you'd find your way on a night like this, especially since they took all the signposts away.'

Keeping her torch beam low, Jess carried her suitcase round to the back of the cart and threw it on, then went round to the front and climbed up on to the wooden seat beside the man.

'At last!' Sulley muttered. He cleared his throat noisily, spat at the ground, shook the reins and they shifted forward slowly, the heavy wheels rolling beneath them as they started up the lane. The cold night air smelled of dung and damp earth.

The lurching motion lulled her, and Jess felt her eyelids growing heavier, her head nodding towards her chest. She was bone weary after her journey. The train had been crowded as usual and seemed to inch down the line, stopping every five minutes to allow another troop train to pass.

12

Jess had found herself crammed into a carriage with a dozen army boys, all in tearing high spirits. She had shared her sandwiches with them, and they'd made her laugh with their jokes and singing. They reminded her of Sam, full of fun, refusing to take life seriously.

But Jess had seen enough sorrow and nursed enough wounded soldiers at the Nightingale to know the kind of fate that might befall them. Even as she laughed with them, she found herself looking at their bright, smiling faces, wondering how many of them would come home again.

Once again, a picture of Sam came into her mind, and she pushed it away out of habit. She couldn't allow herself to give in to the fear that prowled in the shadows of her mind, waiting to pounce if she once allowed it.

Beside her, Sulley had started talking. 'The village is full of Londoners now,' he grumbled. 'What with you lot from the hospital and all the evacuees, it's worse than hop-picking season. Hardly feels like it's our home any more.'

Jess bristled. 'It's not our choice to come down here,' she said sharply. 'We have to go where we're sent.'

She certainly wouldn't have left London if she'd had any choice in the matter. The Blitz had torn the heart out of both the East End and the Nightingale Hospital, and it felt disloyal to abandon it in its hour of need.

But Matron had been insistent. Most of the patients had been evacuated from London to the Nightingale's temporary hospital in Kent, and more nurses were needed there.

'It may only be for a few months,' she had said. 'But until we can re-open the wards here, you'll be of more use down there. And I'm sure you'll welcome the chance of some country air,' she had added with a small smile. 'A change might do you good.'

She had made it sound as if she was doing Jess a favour. But if she thinks that then she doesn't know me at all, Jess thought. She had been born and brought up in the back streets, with the tang of smog in her lungs from the moment she was born. She was used to the shouts of costermongers and street vendors, the smell of the docks and the glue factory, the rumble of trams and buses. After two years of war, she was even used to the wail of the air-raid sirens, the crump of falling bombs and the reek of cordite and choking dust that followed an attack. She had no time for the country, or the people in it.

An eerie screech came out of the fog. Jess started out of her seat in terror.

'What the bleeding hell was that?' she yelped.

Sulley chuckled. 'It's only an owl! Bless me, it ain't going to hurt you.' He dug in the depths of his pocket for a dog end, clamped it between his teeth and lit it with one hand, the other controlling the fat old horse. Not that she needed much controlling. Jess could have walked faster than the mare's steady plod.

Once again, the motion lulled her. This time Jess must have drifted off, because the next thing she knew the cart had jerked to a halt.

'Here we are,' the old man said. 'Home Sweet Home.'

Jess peered into the foggy darkness. 'I can't see anything.'

'The Nurses' Home is through that gate and up the track a way. There was no room for you lot from London at the hospital home; so they had to convert some old farm buildings.'

Jess sniffed. A strong odour of manure hung in the air. 'It smells like a pigsty!'

'That's right.' Sulley chuckled. 'I daresay it's what you Londoners are used to.' His laughter turned into a wheezing cough, and he spat at the ground.

Jess glared at him. At least I don't stink like an old goat, she thought. That coat of his reeked of cigarettes and sweat.

She climbed down from the cart and retrieved her suitcase from the back while the old man watched her, drawing on his thin dog end.

'I'll be here tomorrow morning first thing to collect you,' he called after her as she walked away, dragging her case behind her.

Jess turned to face him. 'You what?'

'I have to take you and the other nurses down to the hospital. It's a two-mile walk otherwise.' He jiggled the reins and the old horse clopped off into the darkness before Jess could reply.

The Nurses' Home, such as it was, stood at the end of a deeply rutted farm track. It was a long, low building with rough whitewashed brickwork, and a bucket by the front door to catch the drips from the rickety tin roof.

Jess squared her shoulders. Oh, well, in for a penny, she thought, and knocked at the door.

It was opened by a tall, elderly woman in a stark

grey dress and linen bonnet. Jess recognised her at once as Miss Carrington, one of the Nightingale Hospital's most fearsome ward sisters. Jess's heart sank to her shoes. As Sister of the Female Chronics ward in London, Gertrude Carrington had regularly reduced students to tears. Jess couldn't imagine what she would be like as a Home Sister, tasked with looking after the nurses' welfare.

She looked down her long nose at Jess. 'You were expected over an hour ago, Nurse Jago,' she greeted her coldly.

And good evening to you, too, Jess thought. 'The train was late, Sister.'

Miss Carrington narrowed her eyes. 'You'd better come in,' she said. 'And take off those shoes. I don't want you trampling filth all through the place.'

Inside the building was just as bad as outside. The air was sharp with cold, and reeked of damp. Jess's breath curled upwards in a feathery plume as she followed the Home Sister down a long, straight passageway with doors leading off to either side.

'As you can see, our surroundings are somewhat basic,' Miss Carrington said matter-of factly. 'But there is a war on, so we must make the best of it.' She fixed Jess with her steely gaze. 'May I remind you that even though you are not in London, you are still a nurse of the Nightingale Hospital, and will be expected to adhere to the standards of your training.'

'Yes, Sister.'

'The rules in this Home are the same as in

London. No male visitors at any time, and lights out at half-past ten. The door is locked at ten o'clock, and you are expected to be in by then unless you have been given a late pass by Matron. Is that understood?'

'Yes, Sister.' Jess looked down at her stockinged feet so that Miss Carrington wouldn't see her smile. She didn't know a nurse who hadn't flouted those rules at least once. Most of them managed to lead very lively social lives right under the noses of their superiors. As she walked down the passageway, she was already thinking how easy it would be to slip in through an open window after lights out. She wouldn't even have to risk her neck shinning up a drainpipe.

Then she remembered. She was stuck in the middle of the country, miles from anywhere. What would be the point of sneaking out when there was no dance hall, or picture house, or anywhere else to go?

Not only that, she had scarcely been out since Sam was called up. It didn't feel right to go out and enjoy herself.

They reached the end of the passageway, and Miss Carrington flung open the very last door. 'This will be your room,' she announced.

It was so small, there was barely enough room for the two narrow iron bedsteads, separated by a chest of drawers. Each bed had a small pile of starched, pressed bed linen sitting squarely on the bare mattress. Over one of the beds, close to the ceiling, was a thin strip of window, shrouded by a heavy blackout curtain. Jess frowned up at it. Perhaps she'd been wrong about sneaking in after lights out. Getting through that tiny gap would be like squeezing through a letterbox.

'We are expecting another nurse from Ireland next week, but you will have the room to yourself until then,' Miss Carrington said. 'The bathroom is down the passageway, the fourth door on the right. There is a nurses' common room at the other end of the building, should you wish to use it.' Her lip curled with disapproval. 'However, it is next to my room, and I don't expect to be disturbed. That means no music, no dancing, loud laughter or high jinks.'

'Yes, Sister.'

'The driver will pick up you and the other nurses at half-past six in the morning, and take you up to the hospital,' Miss Carrington continued. 'You should report to Matron's office straight away, and she will assign you to a ward. As you know, we are having to share the hospital building, so you will report to the matron of the infirmary, Miss Jenkins.' She sniffed the air above Jess's head, her nose wrinkling. 'And please make sure you have a bath before you go to bed. I can see I will have to speak to Mr Sulley yet again about transporting manure in that cart of his!' She gave a final roll of her eyes and then left.

Jess listened to the Home Sister's footsteps squeaking back down the passageway, then sat down on the bed. The thin horsehair mattress barely yielded under her weight. She could already feel the springs of the ancient bedstead poking through. She could only imagine what it would be like to sleep on.

She took off her gloves and massaged the life

back into her frozen hands. Her fingers throbbed as the blood flowed painfully back into them. It made her think longingly of the accommodation in London. At the height of the Blitz, all the nurses, sisters, doctors and students had taken to sleeping down in the basement. It had been hot, cramped and frightening at times as the bombs rained down on them, but Jess would rather endure that discomfort than this freezing cold room.

Keeping her coat on, she set about making up the bed. The thin blanket and sheets looked as if they would barely keep her warm.

She eyed the empty bed beside her for a moment, then grabbed the blanket from the neatly folded pile and added it to her own bed. When her new room-mate arrived she would give it up, but until then her need was greater.

She unpacked her belongings. She hadn't brought much with her. She lined up her books and propped the photograph of Sam on the windowsill. She paused for a moment, her fingertip tracing the curve of his handsome face. He looked so serious in his uniform, she barely recognised the cheeky young man who had joked his way into her heart four years ago.

She could imagine how he'd laugh at her now. 'Look at you, making such a fuss,' he'd say. 'Life could be a lot worse, believe me!'

And he'd be right, thought Jess as she lay back on the hard bed, her eyelids already drooping. As Miss Carrington had said, there was a war on and they had to put up with it.

After all, how bad could it be?

Chapter Two

Even with an extra blanket and most of her clothes on, it was far too cold for her to sleep that night, so Jess was exhausted the following morning when Mr Sulley arrived in his horse and cart to take her and a dozen other bleary-eyed nurses to the hospital. At half-past six it was still pitch-dark and they huddled together in the back of the cart, their cloaks pulled around them for warmth.

'At least it's not raining,' said the girl next to Jess, a pleasant-faced staff nurse called Alice Freeman. 'That's much worse. Especially when Mr Sulley won't put the cover up.'

'You mean he leaves you to get wet?' Jess said in disbelief.

'Soaked to the skin, sometimes.' Alice nodded. 'We've all got colds, and Nurse Owen was sent to the sick bay with pneumonia last week.'

The other nurses joined in with their own horror stories of life away from London, so by the time they arrived at the hospital gates Jess was feeling thoroughly depressed.

She clambered out of the cart after the others and found herself standing outside high walls and an imposing pair of wrought-iron gates. Dawn was starting to break, and against the dull pewter sky she could make out the solid black bulk of a building at the end of a long sweep of drive.

'That's the infirmary. Grim, isn't it?' Alice whis-

pered beside her. 'Apparently it used to be a luna-
tic asylum, until they closed it down and turned it
into a hospital. We all reckon it's haunted.'

It didn't look very welcoming, that was for sure.
Now her eyes were getting used to the gathering
light, Jess could make out a forbidding three-
storey building with straight rows of windows that
seemed too small for such a large place. They
seemed like dozens of blank eyes, staring down at
her.

'I don't believe in ghosts,' she said.

'Probably just as well,' Alice replied.

They hurried up the drive, and Alice pointed
her in the direction of the main building, and
Matron's office.

'Be warned,' she said. 'She'll probably be awful
to you. She's awful to all the London nurses.'

'Why?'

'I don't know. We think she's a bit upset that
we've taken over her hospital.' Alice rolled her
eyes. 'As if it's our fault we're here.'

'Is she that bad?'

Alice gave her an enigmatic look. 'She's nothing
like our darling Miss Fox, that's for sure.'

There was already a sorry-looking line of
nurses waiting outside Matron's office when Jess
got there. One carried the evidence of her crime,
a broken thermometer in a receiving dish.

As Jess joined the end of the line, the two nurses
beside her were whispering between themselves.

'What did you do?' she heard one say to the
other.

'Helped myself to the leftovers from a patient's
plate. I couldn't help it, Sister had cancelled my

dinner break and I was starving. Now I'm going to lose half a day's leave over a wretched potato!'

All too soon it was Jess's turn to be summoned to Matron's office. Miss Jenkins sat behind her desk, all dressed in black. She was older than Miss Fox, more solidly built and a great deal grander. Her face was unsmiling beneath her elaborate starched linen headdress as she regarded Jess over the rim of her spectacles.

'Who are you?' she demanded.

'Jago, Matron. I've been sent from London.'

'Another one?' Miss Jenkins tutted. 'We're already quite overrun as it is. Honestly, doesn't Miss Fox need any nurses? She seems very keen to send you all down here.'

'I'm sure she just wants to help you, Matron.'

Jess realised it was the wrong thing to say as soon as she saw Miss Jenkins's pale blue eyes harden.

'Are you suggesting I need help?' she snapped. 'Perhaps you don't think my nurses are up to the job?'

'No, I didn't mean–' Jess started to say, but Miss Jenkins cut across her.

'That's the trouble with you London nurses, you think you know everything. I daresay you've come to teach your country cousins a thing or two, have you?'

Jess again tried to protest, but Miss Jenkins was still speaking.

'Let me tell you something, Jago. I have been running this hospital for thirty years, and I think I know what I'm doing. And I must say, I'm rather sick and tired of outsiders coming down here and telling us our business. As if your London training somehow makes you better than everyone else!'

She stopped abruptly, her cheeks flushed pink. 'Very well,' she said, more calmly. 'Since you're here, I suppose you should make yourself useful. Report to Sister Allen on Female Medical, I daresay she'll know what to do with you. Send in the next girl on your way out, please.'

And that was it. Jess was still in a daze as she headed out of the front door and back down the stone steps.

She hadn't expected Matron to clasp her to her bosom and thank her for coming to the rescue. But it would have been nice to feel she was actually wanted.

'Watch out!'

Jess swung round to see a bicycle hurtling towards her. The rider was pedalling furiously, gathering speed, almost as if he wanted to knock her down. Jess barely managed to spring out of his path as he flashed past.

'Look where you're going!' she called out. 'You could have sent me flying.'

'You shouldn't be dawdling, should you?' the young man shouted back over his shoulder as he barrelled past.

'And you shouldn't be riding on the path. You're a menace!'

But he was already gone, his scarf fluttering behind him like a pennant in the dawn light.

She found the Female Medical ward on the top floor of the main building. Like the wards at the Nightingale in London, it was a vast, high-ceilinged room, smelling of polish and disinfectant. Forty beds faced each other in two rows running along its length. In the middle of the ward stood a long table and the ward sister's desk.

Sister Allen was as pleased to see her as Miss Jenkins had been.

'And Matron sent you to me, did she?' she sighed. She was in her late twenties, sandy-haired and freckled. 'Well, I suppose she had her reasons. You can start by helping Maynard with the baths. Then do the beds and get the patients ready for the doctor's round at half-past ten. Do you think you can manage that?'

'Yes, Sister.'

'Hmm.' Sister Allen looked as if she very much doubted it. 'Well, ask Maynard if you get stuck. Don't come to me, I'm far too busy.'

Jess found Maynard in the bathroom, warming towels on the radiator. She was a lively, green-eyed blonde of about Jess's age.

'Oh, hello,' she greeted Jess over her shoulder. Maynard was the first person to smile at her since she'd walked through the hospital gates. 'Where did you spring from?'

'I'm Nurse Jago. I've been sent down from London.'

'Have you? Poor you.' The girl looked sympathetic. 'I'm Nurse Maynard, but you can call me Daisy.'

'What do you want me to do?'

'Mrs McCready needs an emollient bath. She's a diabetic and her skin is itching like mad. Do you think you could prepare the linseed bag for me? You'll find everything you need in the prep room next door.'

'I'll do it now.' As Jess turned away, she happened to glance at the contents of the bath tub. 'Is the water supposed to be that colour?' she asked.

'Oh, yes, it's always brown, unless you run the taps for ages and ages,' Daisy replied cheerfully. 'I think it's rust in the pipes, or something.'

'Shouldn't Sister get someone to look at it?'

'Oh, she's tried. But finding a decent plumber is nigh on impossible since they've all been called up. We just have to put up with it.'

Jess eyed the mucky brown water dubiously. It didn't look at all safe. 'What about when you want to make a hot drink for the patients?'

'Sister says it's all right as long as we boil it properly. And if it tastes foul most of the patients are too ill to complain anyway!' She gave Jess an apologetic smile. 'I daresay it's not what you're used to in London, is it?'

Jess thought about working in the bombed-out hospital, sweeping fallen masonry from the floors every morning and boiling instruments for hours over spirit stoves when the power went off. Once she'd even assisted with an operation by shining a torch over the surgeon's shoulder.

'I dunno about that,' she said. 'We had to make do in our own way.'

'I'd love to go to London,' Daisy said, unfolding another towel. 'I suppose you'll find it all very dull down here. All we get are old ladies with diabetes, heart problems and bronchitis.'

Jess went off to the prep room. It was a tiny space lined with shelves and glass-fronted cupboards containing a variety of preparations in jars and bottles. Two other cupboards were filled with equipment and dressings. In front of her was a counter with a sink and a stove top.

Jess found a pan in the cupboard, filled it with water and set it on the stove. As she went to pick up the sack of linseed from the floor, a scurrying motion caught her eye.

'Bloody mouse!' She went to catch it but it had already disappeared down a hole in the skirting board.

'I know. They're everywhere unfortunately,' sighed Daisy Maynard behind her. 'But they're not nearly as bad as the rats.'

'Rats?' Jess swung round in horror.

'Not many,' Daisy assured her hastily. 'And we hardly ever see them up here. They're mainly in the Fever Wards,' she said, as if that would make Jess feel better.

She examined the nibbled corner of the hessian sack and hoped she'd never see the damage a rat could do.

As she set about weighing out the linseed into a bag and boiling it up, Daisy stood in the doorway and chatted. Jess found out she was twenty-one years old, her parents were dead and she lived with her brothers and sisters. One of her brothers was in the army, and her elder sister was a house-maid at Billinghurst Manor. They lived in one of the workers' cottages on the castle estate.

She also found out that Sister Allen was bitter because her naval officer boyfriend had jilted her, and the previous staff nurse on Female Medical had had to leave quickly for 'family reasons'.

'And we all know what that means, don't we?' Daisy gave her a sidelong look.

'Do we?'

'You know!' Daisy mimed a pregnancy bump on the front of her apron. 'Although frankly, I'm amazed she managed to get into trouble since there are no men in the village any more. Not a single one. Not one you'd want to be seen with anyway. If you want to find a decent one, you have to go all the way in to Tunbridge Wells, and there's only one bus a day there and back.' She sighed again. Jess strained the bag from the boiling water, then held up the pan. 'I'll take this through for you, shall I?' she said, before Daisy could say any more. She'd already made up her mind that Daisy Maynard was a terrible gossip, and Jess had a feeling it wouldn't be long before she herself was being discussed around the hospital.

Eventually, Jess managed to escape Daisy's chatter long enough to get some jobs done. She made and straightened beds, cleaned false teeth, combed hair, sponged faces and applied liberal amounts of methylated spirit to backs and shoulders.

And then it was time for the doctor's round. Jess had pulled down her sleeves and was fastening on her starched cuffs as she joined Daisy and Sister Allen at the doors outside the ward.

'Really, Jago, your appearance is very sloppy,' Sister Allen hissed. 'I don't know what kind of standards you had in London, but it really won't do here. Make sure you're properly presented in future.'

'Yes, Sister.' Jess looked down at herself. She couldn't see anything wrong with her appearance, but she knew better than to contradict a ward sister.

The next moment the doctors came striding up the corridor. There were two housemen, both young men in their twenties, one dark and good-looking, the other gawky and bespectacled with untidy brown hair. Jess instantly recognised the awkward one as the young man who had nearly knocked her down on his bicycle that morning.

If he recognised her he didn't show it. His serious gaze skimmed straight over her towards Sister Allen.

'Dr Drake,' Daisy whispered. Her downturned mouth told Jess all she needed to know. 'And the handsome one is Dr French.'

Dr French was much more friendly. He greeted Sister Allen and Daisy, then turned to Jess.

'And who have we here?' he said, his eyes twinkling. His dark hair was swept off his high, noble brow and his upper lip was outlined with a thin moustache, making him look like Errol Flynn.

Jess cleared her throat nervously. 'Er – Jago, sir.'

'It's very nice to meet you, Nurse Jago.' His charming manners confused her. The last time a doctor had spoken to her directly was when Mr Prentiss, the Nightingale's Ear, Nose and Throat consultant, had lambasted her for handing him the wrong forceps.

Dr Drake gave an impatient sigh. 'May we get on?' he said. 'We've a great many patients to see.'

'Yes, yes of course. We all know you're a very busy man, Dr Drake.' Dr French pulled a mocking face at the nurses behind his fellow houseman's back. 'Lead on, Sister. After you, Dr Drake.'

They couldn't have been more different, Jess thought. Dr Drake was whip thin and radiated

28

impatience, while Dr French preferred to take his time. He would stop to chat to each patient in turn, holding their hands and offering them cigarettes. The women swooned as if he was a visiting movie star.

All the while, Dr Drake would sigh and fidget at the end of the bed. Jess could see a pulse beating rapidly in his neck.

'Does Dr French always take so long to do his rounds?' she asked Daisy.

'It depends. Sometimes it takes even longer. Except when Dr Drake is doing the rounds, and then it's over in five minutes. But Dr French is much more patient, which is why everyone adores him. He is divine, isn't he?' she sighed.

'If you like that kind of thing.' Jess glanced at her watch. It was almost time for lunch, and they weren't nearly ready. Once again, she desperately missed the city, where people didn't know each other's business. Where there were proper routines and things were done with speed and efficiency, and taps didn't belch out rusty water.

She didn't think she would ever get used to country life.

Chapter Three

'What do you think you're doing?'

If the girl hadn't been so young and pretty, Stan Salter of the RAF Works Squadron might not have given her the time of day. He'd already got it in the ear from the CO for not getting the job done quickly enough. Added to which it was freezing cold and he wanted to finish work before his fingers dropped off.

But he'd always had a weakness for blondes, and this one was a real peach.

He allowed his gaze to travel the length of her body, from her polished riding boots to the fair curls that framed her face. She reminded Stan of a china doll, with those wide blue eyes and perfect Cupid's bow lips. He'd bet she had a beautiful smile.

But she wasn't smiling now as she stood a few feet away from him, holding on to her horse's bridle. The other hand twitched a riding crop against her slim thigh.

Not that Stan was afraid. His RAF overalls gave him a feeling of power, as well as making him attractive to women in a way he never was in civvies. 'I'm measuring up,' he told her. 'What does it look like?'

'Why?'

He leaned against the tree trunk and took a packet of Craven 'A's out of his pocket. Since he'd stopped work anyway, he might as well enjoy himself. 'It's got to come down to make way for the airfield.'

'What airfield?'

'You ask a lot of questions, don't you?' He lit his cigarette, cupping his hand around the end to shield it from the cutting November wind. 'The one they're building on this land.'

'Since when are they building an airfield?'

'Since the RAF requisitioned that big house over

30

there.' He nodded towards the manor house that could just be seen beyond the trees. 'By this time next month, this whole area is going to be full of aircraft hangars and runways. Reckon you'll have to find somewhere else to ride your horse then, eh?'

'We'll have to see about that, won't we?' The young woman scowled.

'Oh, don't be like that, sweetheart. Look on the bright side. In a few weeks this place will be swarming with RAF boys. You'll enjoy that, won't you?'

The girl frowned. 'I don't think I will,' she said.

'You mean to tell me you wouldn't fancy a pilot for a boyfriend?'

Her horse shied a little. As the young woman went to steady it, Stan caught the flash of gold on her left hand. Typical, he thought. The pretty ones were always taken.

But that didn't mean anything these days. With so many men away fighting, their lonely wives often enjoyed a bit of company.

'You play your cards right and I could get you an invitation to the big house,' he said. 'They're going to be having a high old time up there, I expect. Parties and dances and all sorts. We RAF boys know how to have a good time.'

'Do you indeed?' The girl turned away and swung herself up into the saddle in one nimble movement. 'Well, it's very kind of you, but I don't think I'm going to need any invitations to that house from you.'

'Oh?' Stan took a long drag on his cigarette. 'And what makes you say that?'

'Because it's my house,' the girl said over her shoulder, as she dug her heels into her horse's flanks and galloped off into the trees.

Mr Rodgers the land agent was in the estate office just behind the stable yard. He jumped up from behind his desk when Millie strode in.

'Lady Amelia! I'm sorry, I wasn't expecting you–'

'What's all this about the RAF taking over my house?' Millie interrupted him.

Colour rose in his face. 'Ah.'

'Well? Is it true?'

He cleared his throat. 'I'm afraid it is, my lady. The letter came three days ago.'

Millie stared at him, astonished. 'Why didn't you tell me about it immediately?'

'I – I didn't want to worry you.'

'Worry me?' she echoed in disbelief. 'I'm not a child, Mr Rodgers! Would you have kept this news from my father?'

'No, of course not. But–'

You're not your father. The words hung unspoken in the air between them.

Millie forced herself to stay calm. 'When were you going to tell me?' she asked. 'Or did you think I wouldn't notice when the RAF moved in to my house?'

Mr Rodgers stared down at the papers on his desk. 'I was trying to sort something out,' he said quietly. 'I hoped it wouldn't come to anything...'

'And in the meantime you decided to keep me in the dark,' Millie said. 'You had no right to do that, Mr Rodgers. I am responsible for Billinghurst now, and you cannot make decisions without consulting me.'

'I apologise, my lady. I – I was only trying to help.'

Seeing Mr Rodgers's hangdog expression, Millie was instantly sorry she'd snapped at him. She had come to rely on her land agent in the six months since her father had died. She knew nothing about estate management and Mr Rodgers had been the voice of experience, offering her sound advice and guiding her gently but patiently when she had been too dazed by grief to make a single decision.

It couldn't have been easy for him either, she reflected. He had been her father's land agent for as long as Millie could remember. It must have been difficult for him to suddenly find himself taking orders from a young woman he'd known since she was a little girl.

'So what exactly is going to happen?' she asked quietly.

'According to the letter I received, the RAF wants the land at the south-east corner of the park for an airfield.'

'I know,' Millie said. 'They've already started measuring it up.'

Mr Rodgers winced. 'I'm sorry, my lady.'

'It doesn't matter now,' Millie said. 'Go on – what else do they want?'

'Perhaps it's best if you read their letter?' Mr Rodgers handed it over.

Millie scanned the letter, barely taking in the details, discussion over a fair rent, etc. All she could see was that the RAF and Royal Canadian Air Force planned to take over her house as an officers' billet and training centre for a bomber squadron.

At least they weren't fighter pilots, Millie thought. She wasn't sure she could bear the sight of Spitfires from her window. Not after what had happened to Seb.

'As I said, I'm trying to prevent it,' Mr Rodgers said. 'I've been writing letters, making telephone calls...'

'Why would you want to prevent it?' Millie asked, passing the letter back to him.

He looked perplexed. 'Pardon me, my lady, but I assumed... I didn't think you'd want to have your home taken away from you?'

'Billinghurst Manor is a big place, Mr Rodgers. I'm sure we can find room for a few RAF officers.'

'But the RAF, my lady? Surely under the circumstances–'

'There is a war on, Mr Rodgers, and we all have to play our part,' Millie interrupted him before he could mention Seb's name. 'I would have liked to be informed, that's all. Does my grandmother know about this?'

Mr Rodgers looked pained. 'No, my lady.'

'Then I suppose I'll have to tell her, won't I?'

'Would you like me to break the news to her, my lady?'

Once again, Millie saw herself through his eyes, as a child who needed to be shielded. 'I'm sure it would be better coming from me.' She gave him a grim smile. 'Wish me luck, won't you?'

'I'm sure you won't need it, my lady.' But the glint in his eyes told a different story.

She found the Dowager Countess in the drawing room, taking tea with Mrs Huntley-Osborne. Millie's heart sank at the sight of the village worthy. Elizabeth Huntley-Osborne's visits to Billinghurst seemed to be all too frequent these days, usually when she wanted something.

What was it now? Millie wondered impatiently. Another salvage drive? Or more fund-raising for the Russians?

'Ah, there you are, Amelia.' Her grandmother put down her cup. 'Mrs Huntley-Osborne is collecting clothes for refugees in Europe.'

'I wondered if you had anything to spare, Lady Amelia?' their visitor said. She was dressed in her usual no-nonsense uniform of a tweed overcoat and sturdy brogues. A thin strip of fox fur draped around her wide shoulders was her only nod to fashion. But she still managed to look overdressed beside the austere elegance of Millie's grandmother Lady Rettingham.

'Yes, of course. I'll get one of the maids to look for something.'

'There's no need. I've already asked my maid to go through your wardrobe,' her grandmother put in.

'How – thoughtful of you.' Millie sent her a frowning look, which her grandmother completely ignored. She turned back to their guest. 'If you don't mind, I need to speak to my grandmother in private?'

Mrs Huntley-Osborne's brows rose. 'Oh, well, I'm sure I don't want to be in the way...' But her sizeable backside remained firmly glued to her seat.

'Nonsense, my dear, you must stay and finish your tea,' Lady Rettingham said smoothly. 'I'm sure whatever Amelia has to discuss with me can wait.'

'Of course.' Millie retreated to the window seat, trying to suppress her annoyance as Mrs Huntley-Osborne settled back in her chair. Millie was mistress of Billinghurst and yet she felt like a child, dismissed into a corner to play by the adults.

She stared out of the window, her attention drifting out over the grounds to the front of the house, where a group of land girls were busy turning the formal front lawn into a vegetable patch.

Their raucous laughter made Millie smile. Once upon a time she had been that young and fancy-free herself. As plain Millie Benedict, she had defied her grandmother's wishes and taken herself off to London to train as a nurse. Those three years, sharing an attic room with two other students, had been some of the happiest of her life.

But when she looked back now, she could hardly believe she was the same person. Sometimes she wondered what had happened to the light-hearted girl she once was.

At last, Mrs Huntley-Osborne put down her cup and roused herself to leave. 'I mustn't take up any more of your time,' she said. 'Besides, I have a meeting of the prisoner-of-war committee in an hour, and then I have to talk to the WVS about another salvage drive. Busy, busy, busy!' she trilled.

'You leave us all feeling quite exhausted, my dear.' Lady Rettingham's voice was laced with double meaning. Millie glanced at Mrs Huntley-

Osborne, but luckily she didn't seem to notice.

Millie forced herself to stay patient as her grand-mother made a great show of saying goodbye to their guest. Then, once she had left, Lady Rettingham turned on Millie.

'Really, Amelia, you could be more gracious. I hardly knew what to do with myself when you came rushing in here like a hoyden.'

'She's very tiresome,' Millie said.

'Of course she is,' Lady Rettingham dismissed. 'Her sort always are. But she's also a very useful woman to have on your side if you want to get anything done. You should remember that.' She sat down in her chair and smoothed her skirt over her knees. 'Now, what is it that's so important you had to rush in here dressed like a farmhand to tell me?'

'We've had a letter from the Air Ministry.'

'Whatever do they want?'

Millie met her grandmother's gaze as steadily as she could. 'This house.'

Lady Rettingham sat ramrod straight in her chair as Millie explained about Billinghurst Manor being requisitioned. Her grandmother's eyes narrowed, but she didn't lose a fraction of her outward composure. As she was always telling Millie, it was vulgar for ladies to display their emotions.

'Strangers?' she said, when Millie had finished. 'Here? In our home? But where are we supposed to live?'

'I don't know. I imagine they'll leave us a few rooms. Or we could move into the Lodge?'

'The Lodge is not big enough to swing a cat in!'

'It's big enough for you and Henry and me.'

'And what about the staff?'

'We'd keep on as many as we could. But I expect most of them will be called up soon.' All the footmen, the grooms and most of the estate workers had already enlisted, and now they were calling up the women, too.

The Dowager Countess looked horrified. Poor Granny, Millie thought. She was an indomitable woman, but since the war began she had gradually seen her whole way of life disappear. And all on top of the grief of losing her only son six months ago.

Lady Rettingham roused herself. 'This cannot be allowed to happen,' she said flatly.

'But there's nothing we can do,' Millie said.

'Nonsense, there must be something. They're trying to bully us, to take advantage. We must fight it. I'll talk to Rodgers, have him write a letter–'

'He's already done that, and it didn't work. Besides,' Millie said, 'I'm rather glad the house is being requisitioned.'

Her grandmother stared at her blankly. 'Are you quite mad?'

'Think about it, Granny. These men are fighting for our freedom. The least we can do is offer them somewhere to live.'

'Let's see if you're so glad when we have aircraft landing on the lawn,' her grandmother said darkly. She shook her head. 'Your father would never have put up with it.'

'Actually, I think Father would have been proud to do his bit,' Millie said, but her grandmother ignored her.

'Not that this would have happened if he were

still alive,' she murmured. 'They wouldn't have dared come up with such a plan then. He would never have stood for it.'

'Yes, well, Father isn't here, is he?' Millie said. 'There's only me.'

'More's the pity,' her grandmother muttered.

Millie ignored the barb. 'As I said, I'm all for the idea,' she said. 'And I shall be doing everything I can to make the RAF welcome.'

Lady Rettingham's jaw tightened. 'We'll see about that.'

Millie thought about her grandmother's words as she went upstairs to the nursery. She hoped the Dowager wouldn't take it upon herself to fight the requisitioning of the house. She could be very stubborn when she wanted to be.

But it was more than that. It upset Millie that her grandmother didn't trust her to do what was best. *More's the pity.* The words still stung, even though she was used to her grandmother's harsh tongue. As if Millie wasn't painfully aware every day that her father was dead, and that she was a poor substitute. She was doing her best to run the estate as he would have wanted, but it wasn't easy.

Nanny Perks was sitting in the chair by the nursery fire, doing some mending. She looked up with a frown as Millie entered.

'Lady Amelia.' She put down her sewing and stirred herself reluctantly. She was a sturdy middle-aged woman with thick dark eyebrows set low over disapproving black eyes.

'Hello, Nanny. Where's Henry?'

'I've put him down for his afternoon nap.'

'I'll just peep round the door...' Millie started

39

towards it but Nanny Perks stepped into her path, blocking the way.

'You can't,' she said. 'He's sleeping.'

No sooner had she said the words than a small voice called out, 'Mama?'

'It sounds as if he's awake to me.'

Millie made to move past, but Nanny Perks stepped into her path.

'You can't disturb his routine,' she insisted. 'You'll spoil him.'

They eyed each other for a moment. There was a steeliness in the nanny's manner that unnerved Millie. Sometimes she had to remind herself that she was Miss Perks's employer and not a naughty child herself.

'Mama?' Henry's voice rose, plaintive and hopeful, from the other side of the door. Millie brushed past Nanny Perks and opened it.

Henry was already out of bed by the time she opened the door. He launched himself at her, wrapping his arms tightly around her waist. Millie ruffled his hair, all her anxieties melting away. 'Hello, my angel.'

'Have you come to play, Mummy?' He looked up at her with imploring eyes.

'No.' Nanny Perks's voice was firm. 'It is not playtime, Master Henry, as you well know.'

Millie gave him a conspiratorial wink. 'Perhaps just a little game,' she said. 'What will it be? Snakes and Ladders?'

Behind her, she could feel disapproval coming off the nanny in waves. 'Please try not to be too lively with him, Lady Amelia,' she said, tight-lipped.

Henry rushed to fetch the game, and they seated themselves at the small table beside the window, overlooking the park. Millie watched her son as he carefully set out the counters and the dice. His cheeks were bright pink, his fair curls standing up in unruly tufts. He looked so like his father it was heartbreaking. Every time Millie looked at him she saw Sebastian in those steady grey eyes and wide smile.

'I have something very exciting to tell you, darling,' Millie told him. 'We're going to be moving to a new house soon. And you'll have a new nursery and a new bedroom. And guess what else?' She leaned forward confidingly. 'There will be aeroplanes in our park.'

Henry's face lit up. 'Real aeroplanes?' He looked out of the window, pressing his nose to the glass. 'Where?'

'They're not here yet. They have to build a special place for them first, called an airfield. It'll be just beyond those trees.' She pointed out the spot to him.

'Can we see them when they come?' Henry asked.

'I'm sure we can.' Millie smiled at his enthusiasm. If only her grandmother had been so keen! 'That's why we have to move out of the house, you see. So the pilots have somewhere to live.'

'Pilots?' He tilted his head to one side. 'Will Daddy be coming home?'

The sudden shaft of pain caught her unawares. 'No, darling,' she said patiently. 'Daddy is dead, don't you remember?'

Henry nodded, but Millie knew he hadn't

taken it in. He wasn't yet four years old, he didn't understand what death meant. He had attended his grandfather's funeral, but he still wandered the house sometimes, looking for his 'grumps' to play ball with him.

Millie wasn't sure if he truly remembered his father. Henry had been barely three years old when Sebastian's plane was shot down over the English Channel. Millie did her best to keep his memory alive in her son's mind, telling Henry stories and showing him pictures. But as the months went by, she feared that Sebastian was slipping further away from Henry's thoughts. Soon he would be nothing more than a face in a photograph, no more real than one of the characters in his favourite fairy story.

Sometimes Millie almost wished Seb would fade from her memory, too. Then perhaps she wouldn't miss him so desperately.

'Mama!' Her son's impatient cry made her look up. Henry had set up the board and was waiting for her to start. Millie smiled and picked up the dice, but her thoughts were still elsewhere, out there with her husband.

She didn't like to think of the way he died. She preferred to remember him in life, before the wretched war took him away from her, before he joined the RAF and put on his slate-blue pilot's uniform. She remembered their first meeting during her coming-out season. She was a reluctant debutante and he was her best friend's brother. As the younger son of a duke, he could have had his pick of the society beauties, but he had never left her side, gallantly squiring her to the various dinners and dances. At the time, Millie thought he was doing it out of the kindness of his heart, and as a favour to her friend Sophia. It was only years afterwards he admitted he had been in love with Millie since the moment they'd met.

For her, love had come more slowly. She had spent three years in London training as a nurse. During that time there had been several flirtations, but through it all Seb had been there, waiting patiently for her, and his steadfast love had finally won her over.

They had married after Millie finished her training, and those two years were idyllically happy. She was a young wife and mother, living a charmed life on her family estate where the sun always shone and she didn't have a worry in the world.

Even when war broke out and Seb joined the RAF, it hadn't dawned on Millie that anything could happen to threaten her perfect existence. Until that awful morning in September 1940 when the telegram had arrived.

'You've landed on a snake, Mama! Look! Now you've got to go right back and start again.'

'So I have.' Millie moved her counter, her thoughts still elsewhere.

That day had changed everything. By the following spring, her father had died of a heart attack, leaving Millie to look after her grandmother, her son and the estate.

'I've won!' Henry gave a shout of joy. Almost immediately, Nanny Perks swooped in.

'It's time for your nap now, Master Henry.'

'But I want to stay with Mama!'

'Let him stay–' Millie started to say, but Nanny Perks already had Henry firmly by the arm.

'I'm sure your mother is far too busy,' she said sternly. 'She has work to do, just as I have.'

Her message wasn't lost on Millie. This was Nanny Perks's domain, not hers. She didn't belong there.

So where did she belong? Millie wondered as she walked away sadly, Henry's cries of protest ringing in her ears. Mr Rodgers and her grandmother didn't think she was capable of running the estate, Nanny Perks didn't think she had any place looking after her son. Everyone insisted on treating her as if she were a hopeless child.

Please, she prayed silently, don't let them be right.

Chapter Four

'An airfield? Here, at Billinghurst?'

'That's what I heard,' Grace said.

'And there'll be airmen staying at the house? Actual RAF officers?'

'A bomber squadron, so they tell me.' Grace ladled stew on to a plate and passed it down the table. 'And make sure you eat plenty of those vegetables, Walter,' she warned her younger brother. 'They're good for you, don't forget.'

He pulled a face. 'But I don't like carrots.'

'They'll help you see in the dark. All the fighter pilots eat them.' Grace smiled as Walter reluctantly reached for the spoon and added a few carrots to his plate. He was a growing boy, but too scrawny for twelve years old

Daisy poked at the meat on her plate. 'What's this?'

'Stew, what does it look like?'

'What's in it?'

'Rabbit.'

Daisy pulled a face. 'Not again! If I eat any more rabbit my nose will start twitching!'

'You'd better have some of these carrots, then.' Walter grinned, pushing the dish towards her.

'Pack it in, you two.' Grace pointed the ladle at them. 'Beggars can't be choosers, you know. I can't just march into the butcher's for a pound of rump steak.'

'I've forgotten what a steak looks like,' Daisy moaned.

'I promise when this war's over, I'll buy you the biggest, juiciest steak you've ever seen,' Grace said. 'But until then you'll have to get what you're given. Anyway, cheer up,' she said as her sister picked disconsolately at her food. 'We've got apricot flan for pudding.'

Walter looked up hopefully. 'Real apricot flan?'

'What do you think?' Daisy muttered.

Grace smiled. 'You tell me when you've eaten it.' She hoped her brother wouldn't notice it was made with yet more of his loathed carrots, along with some almond essence and a dollop of plum jam.

'So what will you do when Lady Amelia moves out of the big house?' Daisy asked through a mouthful of food. 'They won't need all those servants any more, surely?'

Grace shot a quick look across the table to where Walter and their youngest sister, ten-year-old Ann, were eating. 'Actually,' she said in a low voice to Daisy, 'this arrived earlier.'

She took from her pocket the letter she had been carrying around with her all day, and slid it across the table towards her sister.

Daisy stared at the envelope then back up at Grace, her green eyes round. 'Your call-up papers?' she whispered.

Grace nodded. 'Maggie the second housemaid got the same letter yesterday.'

Both their gazes dropped to the letter on the table, as if they had conjured up a malevolent spirit.

'What are you going to do?' Daisy asked.

'Not much I can do, is there?' Grace shrugged. 'I'm going to have to go down to the Labour Exchange and see what they say.' But a gnawing feeling of dread in the pit of her stomach betrayed the worry she felt.

Daisy bit her lip anxiously. 'They won't send you away, will they?'

'Shhh!' Grace glanced at Walter and Ann. They were bickering between themselves, oblivious to their sisters' whispered conversation. 'I don't know,' she replied honestly. 'That's what I'm worried about. Maggie says we're what they call mobile because we haven't got kids.'

'What about Walter and Ann?'

'I'm their sister, not their mum.' Although she might as well be, as she'd been looking after them ever since she was thirteen years old.

Grace pushed her plate away, her appetite gone. The thought of having to leave them all was too much for her.

'There must be something you can do,' Daisy said.

'I've been trying to think. I don't have many skills, do I? All I know is being in service, and I don't think scrubbing floors would help the war effort!'

'But you can't leave! Who'll look after us?'

The distress in her sister's green eyes touched Grace's heart. It reminded her of the day their mother had died, and the other children had all looked to her to take care of them.

'I'm sure it will be all right,' she reassured Daisy, just as she had on that sad day. 'I'll think of something, don't you worry.' She stood up, automatically clearing away the dishes as she did so. 'Now, will you be all right to serve up the pudding? Only I've got to get to the village hall for the WVS meeting at six.'

Daisy grinned, her fears forgotten. 'What's Mrs Huntley-Osborne got you doing now? Another salvage drive, or knitting socks for soldiers?'

'I think we're supposed to be sorting out clothes for the refugees in Europe.'

'Rather you than me. I wouldn't fancy going through Mrs Huntley-Osborne's cast-offs!'

'Lucky you don't have to do it, then.' Grace scraped leftovers into the pig bin. 'Now, I'll feed the chickens and put them away for the night before I leave. Make sure Walter has a wash before he goes to bed, will you? You could grow spuds behind his ears.' She pulled a face at her brother.

'I'm going to have a nice long soak myself.'

'As long as you only fill the bath up to the line, remember?' Grace reminded her.

'Have a heart! I ache all over. Sister Allen had us cleaning the ward for hours today.'

Grace laughed. 'And you're complaining! I do that every day at the manor.'

'Yes, but you're used to it. I'm supposed to be nursing, not cleaning...' Daisy stopped suddenly. 'That's it!' she cried. 'That's the answer.'

'What?'

'You could come and work at the hospital!' Daisy's face was eager. 'They're crying out for VADs to help on the wards.'

'VADs?'

'Voluntary Aid Detachment. They're like assistant nurses. You'd have to do some training classes, but I'm sure–'

But Grace was already shaking her head. 'I couldn't,' she said. 'What if it was too difficult? I haven't got your education, remember?'

'Being a VAD isn't difficult. All you have to do is clean the ward, and make beds, and fetch and carry for the nurses. You've been doing that for his lordship and Lady Amelia for years!'

'I suppose so...' Grace frowned, considering it. 'But I'm a bit nervous, thinking about it. I mean, I've never worked anywhere but up at the house.'

'You'd soon get used to it,' Daisy said. 'Go on, it'll be fun working together!'

Grace wished she had her sister's confidence. Daisy might be two years younger, but she was far more self-assured. 'And you really think I'd be able to manage it?'

'Of course. And I'd be there to help you, wouldn't I?' Daisy stood up, and started to help with the empty dishes. 'Promise you'll think about it, anyway?'

'I will,' said Grace.

By the time she'd finished talking to her sister and feeding the chickens, Grace was late for the WVS meeting. Sorting was already underway in the village hall, with groups of women seated at long trestle tables, each one piled with clothes and cardboard boxes.

Grace had hoped she might be able to sneak in unnoticed, but Mrs Huntley-Osborne bore down on her immediately.

'Ah, there you are, Grace. We were beginning to think you weren't coming.' Her smile was fixed. 'We did say six o'clock?'

'Sorry,' Grace mumbled, taking off her coat.

'Well, at least you're here now. Go and join your friend Mrs Kemp over there, will you? I think she's been keeping a space for you.'

Pearl Kemp was Grace's oldest friend. They had gone to the village school together and then into service at Billinghurst Manor until Pearl married when she was eighteen. Now she was a plump, happy farmer's wife with two children.

'Did you get a lecture from Mrs Huntley-Osborne?' she asked, as Grace joined her. 'Was she very cross?'

'Not too bad. I only got the smile, not the eyes.' She did a quick impression of Mrs Huntley-Osborne's rictus grin. Pearl snorted with laughter, which earned them both another disapproving look from the woman herself.

49

Grace sat down. 'What are we doing?'

'Sorting through this lot, and putting aside anything that needs to be mended.' Pearl nodded to the table at the far side of the room, where Mrs Huntley-Osborne was sitting with her closest cronies, Miss Pomfrey, Miss Wheeler and Mrs Urquart. 'Look at them. I bet they're keeping all the best stuff for themselves.'

'I know Lady Amelia contributed some lovely clothes,' Grace said.

'There you are, then. I expect Mrs Urquart has already helped herself to anything worth having, the greedy old witch.'

'They'd never fit her. Unlike these...' Grace held up a pair of voluminous pink silk bloomers.

Pearl shrieked with laughter. 'Oh, no! They're not sending those to the poor refugees, are they? As if they didn't have enough unhappiness in their lives, without having to wear Mrs Huntley-Osborne's drawers!'

'Do you think they're hers, then?'

'Well, they're not Miss Pomfrey's, are they? She's as thin as a rake.'

'We should put them aside,' Grace said. 'We could send them to the RAF to use as a parachute!'

They both wept with laughter, and Grace mopped her eyes with the bloomers then realised what she'd done and they laughed even harder. They were still giggling helplessly when Mrs Huntley-Osborne called over.

'Is something amusing, ladies?'

'No, Mrs Huntley-Osborne,' they chorused solemnly.

'Blimey, it's like being back at school!' Pearl complained, when she'd gone. 'It's bad enough we have to give up our spare time, without being glared at for having a laugh!'

'I could do with a laugh,' Grace sighed, tucking a lock of sandy hair behind her ears.

'Why? What's wrong?'

'My call-up papers arrived in the post this morning.'

'No! Oh, you poor thing. What are you going to do?'

'I don't know. Daisy said I should think about getting a job at the hospital, but I'm not sure I've got the brains for it.'

Pearl didn't reply for a moment as she inspected the seam on a skirt. Then she said, 'You know, it might be good for you if you did have to leave the village.'

'Oh, yes? How do you work that out, then?'

'It might be just what you need. The chance to spread your wings, do something for yourself.'

Grace stared at her, shocked. 'But what about my family?'

'They're not babies any more, Gracie. Ann's what – ten years old? They're more than able to manage. Besides, Daisy could help out, couldn't she?'

Grace shook her head. 'Daisy's got enough on her plate with her nursing.'

'She could still help you out a bit more.'

'She does her fair share.' Grace ignored her friend's old-fashioned look. She knew Pearl didn't approve of Daisy. 'A proper little madam' she'd called her on more than one occasion. Grace knew

Daisy could be a bit thoughtless at times, but she had a good heart underneath it all.

Besides, if she did have grand ideas about herself, then Grace had encouraged them. Daisy had a good brain in her head, and Grace had been happy for her to stay at school and better herself instead of leaving early and helping to support the family. It had been a strain, but it was worth it when she qualified as a nurse. Grace was very proud of her clever sister.

At the end of the evening, Mrs Huntley-Osborne thanked them for their efforts, and reminded them that there was another paper salvage drive the following week.

'I expect everyone to take part and do their bit,' she warned, her gaze sweeping the village hall like a searchlight.

Pearl rolled her eyes. 'She's never satisfied, is she?' she whispered.

'May I also remind you that Miss Wheeler will be giving a talk on thrifty cookery next Thursday,' Mrs Huntley-Osborne continued. 'I think it's something we will all benefit from.'

'What does Miss Wheeler know about thrifty cookery?' Pearl said. 'Her maid does everything for her, she hasn't had to boil an egg in years.' She turned to Grace. 'You should do that talk,' she said.

'Oh, no, I couldn't.'

'Why not? Everyone knows you're the best cook in the village. And I bet they'd rather listen to you than to Miss Wheeler.'

Grace shook her head. 'I wouldn't know the first thing about standing up in front of all those people. I'd be a bag of nerves.' She could feel herself turning crimson at the very idea.

'You shouldn't be so modest,' Pearl said. 'You're capable of a lot more than you think, Grace Maynard. It's about time you started having a bit more confidence in yourself.'

Perhaps she was right, Grace thought to herself as she made her way home later. Not about the cookery talk – she would rather sort through a thousand pairs of Mrs Huntley-Osborne's bloomers than do that! But perhaps she was capable of more than she thought. Perhaps she might even be able to do that VAD's job, if it was as easy as Daisy made out...

Chapter Five

'I'm so sorry, ducks. I'm being a terrible nuisance, I know.'

Hilda Reynolds looked up at Jess. She was sixty-three years old and a gentle little woman. Even though pernicious anaemia had taken all the strength from her body, her true cockney spirit still shone in her bright eyes.

Jess had a soft spot for her, and not just because they came from the same back streets of Bethnal Green. The poor old girl was very ill, and very far from home.

'I wouldn't have said anything, but I've felt that bad since I woke up this morning,' Hilda went on, looking wretched.

Jess laid a cloth over the receiving dish and set it aside, then gently wiped Hilda's chin with a damp flannel. 'You should've told us earlier you felt sick.'

'I mentioned it to Sister, but she didn't take much notice. I s'pose she's right, ain't she? I mean, a bit of sickness is to be expected.'

Jess put a comforting hand on Hilda's back, feeling the knobbled arch of her spine through her flannel nightgown. She was barely skin and bone because she couldn't keep any food down. It was all Jess could do to get her to take her liver extract.

'All the same, that's what we're here for,' she said.

'You're very kind, love, but I didn't want to be any trouble. I can see how busy you are. I noticed a couple more arrived this morning?'

Late November had brought an epidemic of broncho-pneumonia to the Female Medical ward. Suddenly every bed was full, with extra beds arranged down the middle of the room to accommodate the patients who seemed to arrive every day, either from the village or on one of the Green Line buses sent down from London.

Jess and Daisy spent their working hours in a flurry of changing beds, applying poultices, tepid sponging and setting up steam kettles.

'Anyone from London?' Hilda enquired hopefully.

'Mrs Briggs is, I think. But she's so poorly I haven't had a chance to chat to her.'

'It'll be nice to have a bit of company.' Hilda smiled weakly up at Jess. 'I miss the old Smoke, y'know.'

'So do I, Mrs Reynolds.' A week had passed, and

although Jess had settled into the new routine, she still hadn't settled into her surroundings. She loathed the countryside, with its unearthly quiet and strange smells. People reckoned London stank, but Jess would have swopped the reek of manure for the smell of the tanning works and the glue factory any day.

'I miss my family, too. I wish my Jean could get down to see me, but it's so difficult for her, with the kids. Did I tell you, she's working part-time on the buses now? I'd like to see that, my Jean driving a bus–'

'Nurse Jago!' Sister's voice rang out across the ward. 'Come here immediately.'

Jess glanced at Hilda. The poor woman looked terrified.

'Oh, lor', that's done it,' she whispered. 'You ain't in trouble, are you, love?'

'Of course not, Mrs R. How could I be in trouble for doing my job?' Jess smoothed down her apron. 'I'll be back in a minute. Shout out if you feel sick again.'

Sister Allen was waiting for her at the desk, a thunderous expression on her face.

'I thought I told you to prepare the new patient … Miss Pomfrey?' she snapped.

'I was on my way, Sister, but Mrs Reynolds called out that she felt sick, so I thought I'd better attend to her first.'

'Oh, you did, did you?' Sister Allen's eyes were pinpricks of venom. 'When I give you an order, I expect you to carry it out immediately, do you understand? Not when you have a moment, or when you feel like getting around to it!'

'Yes, but Mrs Reynolds–'

'Mrs Reynolds is always complaining about something!' Sister Allen cut her off. 'The Londoners do nothing but moan, in my experience. They want everyone's attention all the time.'

The muscles in Jess's jaw ached from the effort of not answering back.

'I'll get on and prepare Miss Pomfrey,' she said tightly.

'See that you do,' Sister said. 'And remember what I said, Jago. The next time I give you an order, I expect it to be carried out immediately. Do you understand?'

'Yes, Sister.'

'I'll be watching you.'

Miss Pomfrey was to occupy a bed at the far end of the ward. She was sitting upright in the bedside chair, her bag at her feet.

'You took your time,' were her first words to Jess as she pulled the screens around them.

Good morning to you, too, Jess thought. 'Yes, well, I'm here now, aren't I?' She fixed on her brightest smile. 'Let's get you into bed, shall we?'

Jess was surprised that Phyllis Pomfrey had been admitted with her varicose veins when they were crying out for beds. But even though she was by no means the most seriously ill patient on the ward, she still had a great deal to say for herself. As she told Jess, she was a retired nurse, and she knew how things should be done. And she didn't hesitate to point out where Jess was going wrong. She was too rough, too quick, the water she used to wash her was too cold, the pillows weren't arranged properly and Miss Pomfrey's leg wasn't propped up high enough.

Never mind moaning Londoners, Jess thought. Miss Pomfrey could give Hilda Reynolds a few lessons in complaining.

Miss Pomfrey was taking her to task about putting her belongings too far out of reach on her locker when Jess heard Mrs Reynolds calling out for help.

'Excuse me a moment,' she cut Miss Pomfrey off in mid-complaint and stuck her head out of the screens. Almost immediately, Sister Allen bore down on her.

'Is something wrong, Jago?' she asked.

'I thought I heard Mrs Reynolds calling out...'

Sister's brows arched. 'And why should that be any concern of yours?'

'I—'

'Go back and attend to your patient, Nurse.'

Jess just managed a quick, helpless look at Daisy before she retreated back behind the screens.

Miss Pomfrey scowled at her. 'Well?' she said. 'Are you going to move my spectacles, or do I have to fall out of bed and break my neck trying to reach them?'

Don't tempt me, Jess thought, snatching up the glasses and putting them down again.

She was fetching a bedpan when she met Daisy in the sluice, rinsing out a bed sheet under the tap.

'Bother, this rusty water is just making the stain worse,' she complained. 'This is all your Mrs Reynolds's doing, by the way, vomiting everywhere.'

'Don't blame me. I tried to go to her when she first called out, but Sister wouldn't let me.'

'She wouldn't let me go either. Said Mrs Reynolds has to learn to wait her turn.'

Jess frowned. 'Have you ever noticed how Sister treats the patients from London different from everyone else?' she asked.

'What do you mean?'

But before Jess could answer they were interrupted by a voice bellowing down the corridor outside.

'Hello? Is anyone there?'

Jess went to the door of the sluice, just in time to see a stately-looking woman swathed in a tweed coat go sailing past.

'Can I help you?' Jess called after her.

The woman turned around slowly, and Jess found herself looking into a pair of steely eyes.

'I'm looking for my friend Miss Pomfrey,' she announced.

'And you are?'

The steely eyes narrowed to slits. 'I beg your pardon?'

'Mrs Huntley-Osborne! What a pleasant surprise.'

All at once Sister Allen descended on them, wearing an expression Jess hadn't seen on her face before. The corners of her mouth were pinned upwards in what looked oddly like a smile. Except it couldn't be, because Sister Allen never smiled.

'How delightful to see you,' she gushed. 'You're here to visit Miss Pomfrey, I imagine? How very thoughtful. I'll take you to her, shall I? I expect she'll be pleased to see you.'

Jess was still watching them walking down the corridor together when Daisy came up behind her. 'I see you've met Mrs Huntley-Osborne?'

58

'Who is she?'

'The village busybody. She and Miss Pomfrey are on the WVS committee together.'

'She can't just turn up. It's not a visiting day.'

Daisy sent her a pitying look. 'You don't know Mrs Huntley-Osborne,' she said. 'The rules never apply to her. Besides, she and Sister Allen are very thick together.'

'I can see that.' Jess craned her neck. At the far end of the ward, Sister was fawning over the woman in the tweed coat. She couldn't have looked more excited if King George himself had turned up for a visit.

They were still chattering away behind the screens when Jess went to check on the other new patient, Elsie Briggs.

She was in her thirties, with untidy brown hair and a strong-featured face. She was suffering from endocarditis, a disease of the heart that required absolute bed rest.

'Hello, ducks. How are you feeling?' Jess lifted her wrist and checked her pulse. It skipped and fluttered under her fingers.

'Not good, Nurse.'

'Oh, dear, I'm sorry to hear that. Anything I can do?'

'Yes. You can stick me on a bus and send me back where I came from!'

Jess smiled as she marked the pulse rate on the chart. 'I'm afraid I can't do that, Mrs Briggs.'

'But I shouldn't be here! It's all wrong. I've got an old man and five kids at home. I should be there with them, not down here on a bleedin' holiday!'

59

Jess looked at her, pale and fighting for breath. She hardly looked as if she were on holiday.

'What if a bomb drops on them while I'm not there? What'll I do then, eh? Answer me that.'

'I'm sure nothing will happen to them, Mrs Briggs. Now, you mustn't upset yourself. Can I get you a nice warm drink? It might make you feel better.'

'The only thing that'll make me feel better is going home to my kids.' Her voice was jagged with emotion. 'It's no good, Nurse. I want to go back to London.'

'Jago! Come here at once!' Jess jumped at the sound of Sister Allen's voice ringing out.

Oh, Mrs Briggs, I know how you feel, she thought.

It was a long day, and she was relieved to go off duty at eight o'clock. But Sister Allen couldn't resist one last act of vindictiveness, and forced Jess to stay and give the report to the night nurse while she herself sloped off early. As a result, Jess missed the last cart and had to walk the two miles back to the Nurses' Home.

The other girls had gathered in the Common Room, but Jess went straight to her room. She slipped off her shoes, enjoying the blessed relief after fourteen hours on her feet, then wrapped herself in a blanket and curled up on her bed to write a letter to Sam. She spilled out all her frustration about being stuck in the country, and about the ill treatment she and the other London nurses received at the hands of the spiteful Matron and senior staff. It felt good to get it all off her chest.

She had just finished the letter when there was a commotion outside. Jess hurried down to the Common Room where the other nurses were all crowded at the window in the dark, peering round the blackout curtain.

'Who is it, can you see?'

'I can't see anything, it's all pitch black. But it sounds like a lorry.'

'Why has it stopped here?'

'What is going on?' Miss Carrington stood at the door to the Common Room.

Alice Freeman spoke up. 'Please, Sister, I think we have visitors.'

'Visitors? Don't be absurd.' Miss Carrington went to the front door and flung it open. 'Hello?' she called out into the darkness. 'Who's there?'

She flashed her torch into the blackness and it illuminated an army lorry at the end of the path, with at least a dozen soldiers in the back of it.

Alice squealed. 'Soldiers! Oh, my goodness, there are soldiers!'

'Are they coming here? Quick!'

The other girls started smoothing down their clothes and running their fingers through their hair, still in darkness. Jess went on staring out of the window, trying to make sense of what she was seeing.

Two of the soldiers jumped to the ground, then turned to lift another figure out of the back of the lorry. Miss Carrington's torch beam caught a pair of long, coltish legs as they were lowered to the ground.

Jess heard a shriek of laughter, than saw the mane of unruly black curls, and felt a rush of blood to her head. No, it couldn't be...

'It's a girl!' Alice Freeman was back at the window, her nose pressed to the glass. 'And she's got a suitcase with her.'

Not just any girl. Jess watched her turn and give the soldiers a cheery wave as they clambered back into the lorry.

'Thanks, lads!' she called out.

'Who is it, do you know?' the other nurses were asking amongst themselves.

'Never seen her before in my life.'

'I know her,' Jess said. Even in the pitch-dark, she would have known that sing-song Irish voice anywhere.

Chapter Six

She hurried to the front door and called out, 'Effie O'Hara!'

The girl swung round.

'Jess?' A grin lit up her face. 'Jess Jago! Of all people – what are you doing here?'

'Excuse me!' In her excitement, Jess had forgotten all about Miss Carrington who was standing beside her. She was puce-faced and looked as if she might explode. 'Am I correct in thinking that *you* are the new nurse from Ireland?'

Effie recovered her manners and bobbed a funny little curtsey, wobbling like a baby giraffe on her long legs. 'That's me, Sister. Euphemia O'Hara. Do you remember me?'

'How could I possibly forget you, O'Hara?' Miss Carrington's lips tightened. 'And you arrived here – in that?' She pointed towards the army lorry as it pulled off.

'It was the only way I could get here, Sister. There were no more trains until tomorrow, and those boys were kind enough to offer me a lift down from London, so...' She shrugged expressively.

Effie hadn't changed, Jess thought. She was extraordinarily pretty, with her milky Irish skin and wide blue eyes surrounded by a cloud of untamed black curls. She was also just as scatty and hopeless as she had been when they'd trained together. She hadn't even stepped over the threshold and already she was in trouble.

Miss Carrington's face turned from puce to deathly white. Words seemed to fail her. 'Come in immediately, and stop making an exhibition of yourself!' she finally managed to say.

The Home Sister turned to Jess. 'She'll be sharing your room, Jago,' she said shortly. 'Get yourselves washed and straight into bed, if you please. And that goes for the rest of you. We've had quite enough disturbance for one night. We will speak again in the morning,' she warned Effie ominously.

Effie made a face at Jess. 'That's done it,' she whispered. 'If I'd known Miss Carrington was Home Sister I would have asked them to drop me up the lane!'

Jess stared at Effie as she struggled out of her coat. She still couldn't quite believe Effie was here. The last time she'd seen her she was being packed off to Ireland to finish her training, just after the war started.

'Why didn't you write and tell me you were coming to England?' she asked as she led the way down the passage.

'I did, but the post is so slow these days. My letter probably got lost. Anyway, I didn't know you'd be here, did I? I thought you were in London.'

'Miss Fox sent me down.'

'Me too. I was hoping to stay in London, but now I know you're here, I'm glad I didn't.' Effie seized Jess's hand. 'This is grand, isn't it? It'll be like old times, sharing together...' She followed her into their room and stopped dead. 'Is this it?' she asked, looking around.

'I'm afraid so. It's a bit small, isn't it? And freezing cold.'

'Ah, I don't care. I'm so tired I could sleep anywhere.' Effie dumped her suitcase on the floor and flopped down on the bed, her legs hanging off the edge of the mattress. 'God, I'm exhausted!' She stifled a yawn with the back of her hand.

'What made you decide to come back to the Nightingale?' Jess asked.

'You know me. I like a bit of excitement.' Effie grinned, irrepressible as ever. 'As soon as I finished my training, I wrote to Miss Fox asking if I could come back to the Nightingale.'

'And what did your mother have to say about that?' Jess had heard stories of the formidable Mrs O'Hara, and how protective she was of her girls. Especially Effie, her youngest.

'Oh, you know...' Effie's voice trailed off, then she sat up straight. 'I nearly forgot, I've brought

64

something with me.' She rolled off the bed and kneeled down in front of her suitcase. Unfastening the straps, she said, 'We've been hearing all about the rationing over here, and how hard it is to get anything decent to eat, so–'

She flung open the case and took out a tin. Inside was a fruit cake, a box of chocolates, and some cheese. 'There was a bottle of whisky too, but I gave that to the army lads. Come to think of it, I might give the cheese to Miss Carrington as a peace offering, what do you think?' she said.

Jess didn't reply. She was too busy staring at the food, speechless. It had been so long since she'd seen such wonders, she could feel her mouth watering just looking at them.

'I think I must be dreaming,' she murmured. 'First you being here, and now all this...'

'I didn't want to turn up empty-handed!' Effie grinned. 'I thought it would help me make friends with the other nurses.'

'I'm sure it will.' Although Jess didn't think Effie would ever need to bribe anyone with chocolate. She had such a warm, cheerful nature, people were instantly drawn to her.

'Why don't we go and fetch them in now?' Effie said. 'We could have a midnight feast.'

'Aren't you too tired?'

'I've woken up again now. It must be all the excitement.'

The other nurses were only too happy to leave their beds and creep into Jess's room, especially when they heard there were chocolates and cake to be had. They ooh-ed and ah-ed over the treats, passing them round.

In the middle of the party Jess noticed Effie had gone very quiet. She looked over to see her friend had fallen asleep on her bed, still fully dressed and wearing her shoes.

She smiled to herself. Now Effie O'Hara had arrived, Jess had a feeling the country wouldn't be so quiet any more.

Effie jerked awake, her heart racing. For a moment she lay in the chilly darkness, trying to remember where she was. Then she heard Jess snoring softly in the next bed, and felt herself relax.

She had made it. She was really here.

Effie stared up at the ceiling. She couldn't believe she'd really done it. Even as she was boarding the ferry to take her away from Ireland, she'd kept expecting someone to come after her, to try and stop her. It wasn't until she saw the houses of Dun Laoghaire receding into the distance that she had allowed herself to breathe.

Jess shifted in the darkness and turned over. Effie stared across at her friend's outline. She couldn't tell anyone, not even Jess, what had really happened.

She had been disappointed when she'd found out she wasn't staying in London. Living in the big city had been part of the attraction of leaving Ireland for her. But now she thought about it, coming to the country wasn't such a bad idea. Effie also knew that it would be harder for anyone to find her buried down here in the heart of the Kent countryside.

If anyone came looking for her. She closed her eyes and sent up a silent prayer that they would all forget about her. But even as she said her final amen, she knew it was a forlorn hope.

Sooner or later, someone would come.

Chapter Seven

On a damp Tuesday in December, two days after the Japanese bombed an American airbase in a place called Pearl Harbor, the men from the Office of Works arrived at Billinghurst Manor to dismantle the house.

Millie threw herself into the task of supervising them. All day she went around the rooms making sure that the paintings and precious ornaments were carefully packed for storage and the polished wooden floors covered with linoleum. Curtains and chandeliers were taken down, fireplaces and carved cornices were boxed in, and decorative panels covered with sheets of hardboard. By late afternoon, the house had a strange, blank look to it.

All the while, her grandmother roamed around like a tragic wraith, staring at the bare walls and sighing over the cheap blackout curtains that had been put up in place of the silk brocade.

'Such a pity,' she kept saying, until Millie didn't think she could bear to hear the words any more. 'Such a terrible, terrible pity. I really don't know what your father would say about it.'

'I'm sure he'd want to help the war effort as much as I do,' Millie replied briskly.

'We should be preparing for Christmas,' her grandmother said, ignoring her. 'Billinghurst always looked so beautiful at Christmas, don't you think? With an enormous tree in the hall, and holly and ivy festooned everywhere. And candles. Hundreds and hundreds of them, everywhere you looked...'

'We could have candles at the Lodge,' Millie pointed out. It wasn't like her grandmother to be so sentimental. She had barely paid any heed to holly and candles and suchlike in the past. But Lady Rettingham had taken to sighing a great deal, and sniffing back tears when she thought Millie was within earshot. Millie had been upset by it at first, but now she suspected her grandmother was putting it on.

Lady Rettingham shook her head. 'It won't be the same,' she said sadly.

Millie took a deep breath. No, it won't be the same, she wanted to say. But nothing was the same. Seb was dead and her father was dead, and it was their loss, not that of a few dusty ornaments, that had taken the life out of Billinghurst for her.

'Yes, well, we all have to make sacrifices, don't we? Anyway, the Quartering Commandant should be here soon.' She changed the subject rather than have the same pointless argument with her grandmother again.

'Quartering Commandant! It sounds like he's in charge of some ghastly ancient torture.' Lady Rettingham drew herself up to her full height, as if mentally preparing for battle. 'I daresay he will try to bully us. But we must stand up to him.'

'Yes, Granny.'

'I mean it, Amelia. You mustn't allow these people to make too many demands. Heaven knows, we have given in to them enough already.' Lady Rettingham shook her head. 'If only we had a man here,' she sighed.

Millie bristled. 'I'm sure I'm capable of talking to them, Granny.'

'Yes, but they'd take more notice of a man, don't you think?' Lady Rettingham paused for a moment, then said, 'You know, I really think you should consider marrying again.'

Her voice was almost lost under the sound of hammering, and for a moment Millie wasn't sure she'd heard her correctly. 'I beg your pardon?'

'Oh, don't look at me like that, Amelia. We have to be practical. You need someone to help you run the estate.'

'I have Mr Rodgers,' Millie pointed out.

Her grandmother gave a tsk of irritation. 'That isn't what I meant, as you well know,' she said. 'I'm only thinking of you, Amelia. You're twenty-six, far too young to be widowed. You shouldn't be alone.'

'I'm not alone. I have Henry. And you,' she added.

'You can't spend the rest of your life locked up here with an old woman and a small boy!' Lady Rettingham replied dismissively. 'It isn't fair on you or Henry. He needs a father.'

'And I need someone to run the estate for me, do I, because I'm not capable of doing it on my own?' Millie said.

Her grandmother's silence spoke volumes.

Millie was saved from answering by a knock on

69

the door. 'I expect that will be the Quartering Commandant,' she said, moving past her grandmother. 'I'd better go and see him, since I don't have a man to do it for me!'

But it wasn't the Quartering Commandant. Their housemaid, Grace Maynard, stood in the hall. From her embarrassed expression, Millie guessed she must have heard their argument.

'I just wanted to say goodbye, your ladyship,' she mumbled. 'It's my last day today.'

'Oh, yes, of course. You're joining the VADs, aren't you?'

'That's right, your ladyship.' Grace's face lit up with pride. She was a solidly built girl, with wide hazel eyes and thick sandy hair scraped back off her broad, smiling face.

'We'll miss you,' Millie said. Grace's resignation had caused her grandmother much consternation, especially as they couldn't seem to find a replacement maid. It was yet another of the Dowager Countess's grievances against the war.

'I'll miss this place too, your ladyship.'

'How long have you worked here?'

'Ten years, your ladyship. Since I was thirteen years old. It's all I've ever known...'

The girl's eyes were filled with apprehension, and Millie rushed to reassure her. 'But I'm sure you'll have a wonderful time at the hospital,' she said. 'It's such worthwhile work, although it can be very hard.'

'I don't mind hard work,' Grace said stoutly.

'I know that, Grace.' As far as Millie was aware, the girl had never missed a day's work in her life. She was there first thing in the morning, cleaning out the grates, and last thing at night. No wonder Grandmother was so devastated at the prospect of losing her.

'Wait there a moment,' said Millie. She left Grace in the hall while she went to fetch her purse. 'I want you to take this, as a token of our appreciation for all your years of service...'

She went to hand her the five pound note, but Grace shrank back from it as if Millie was offering her a venomous snake.

'Oh, no, your ladyship, I didn't come for that—'

'I know you didn't, Grace. But I want you to have it anyway. Call it an early Christmas present, to buy yourself something nice.'

'Thank you, your ladyship.' Grace couldn't meet her eyes as she took the money reluctantly. 'It'll come in very useful, I'm sure.' Millie walked her through the hall, past three men from the Office of Works who were setting up ladders to take down the pictures hanging there.

At the front door Grace stopped abruptly, like a horse refusing a fence.

'It's not right, your ladyship.' She shook her head in confusion. 'Servants never use the front door...'

'Yes, but you're not a servant any more, are you?' Millie smiled at her. She opened the door. 'Goodbye, Grace,' she said. 'And good luck.'

'Thank you, your ladyship.'

Grace hesitated for a moment, then took a step through. As she did, she lifted her face to the sky and smiled, and suddenly it was as if the sun had split the grey clouds, bathing her in golden light.

Millie watched her springing down the steps, so full of joy and hope. How she envied the girl her freedom. She was starting a new life, doing a job where she would be truly useful and valued. Millie envied her.

She turned back to see the men about to take down the portrait of her mother that hung over the fireplace facing the front door. One was up the ladder, while the other two stood below him, waiting to take the painting's weight.

'Wait!' Millie left the front door open and hurried towards them. 'Are you taking that down, too?'

'We were told it was to go into storage,' one of the men spoke up.

Millie stared at the portrait. Her mother, Lady Charlotte, smiled back at her, calm and beautiful. People always said they looked alike, but Millie couldn't see it. Lady Charlotte was far more composed and graceful than Millie would ever be, her fair hair arranged in waves around a heart-shaped face, with clear blue eyes that seemed so full of life.

The thought of putting her into a cold, dark storage room made Millie sad. This was more than just paint on canvas to her. It was the only connection she had to the mother who had died giving birth to her. She often stood in front of it when she felt sad or alone, and tried to imagine her mother offering her words of solace and comfort.

But as she'd told her grandmother, they all had to make sacrifices.

She turned to the men, who were waiting expectantly for her instructions. 'Take it down,' she said.

As she turned away, she was suddenly aware of another man standing in the open doorway. Tall, dark and slimly built, even in his unfamiliar RAF uniform Millie knew him instantly.

She stared at him, stunned. Surely it couldn't be ... could it?

'Hello, Millie,' he said.

Chapter Eight

'William?'

She stared at him, stunned. The last time Millie had seen Dr William Tremayne was the day after her State Finals. She'd left the Nightingale behind to start her new life with Sebastian, never expecting to see the hospital or William again.

But here he was, standing in her hall, large as life.

He looked rueful. 'I'm sorry, I should have let you know I was coming. But when I saw the name of the house on the requisitioning letter ... well, you know I could never resist springing a surprise.'

He grinned, and in spite of the unfamiliar uniform Millie suddenly saw again the handsome, boyish young housemen who'd stolen her heart when she was eighteen years old.

'I don't understand. Are you the Quartering Commandant?'

'Good lord, no, he's just having a snoop around outside. I'm attached to the squadron that's going to be stationed here. We're going to be neighbours.'

While she was still taking this in, another man

73

strode in. He was fair and stockily built, with a thick moustache.

'Plenty of grounds at the front for the vehicles, sir,' he reported, 'and there are some outbuildings that could be useful...' He saw Millie and stopped dead. 'Oh! I beg your pardon.'

'Millie, may I present our Quartering Commandant, Flight Sergeant Ellis? Bob, this is our hostess, Lady Amelia Rushton.'

'Pleased to meet you, your ladyship.' Colour crept up from Ellis's collar.

'Sergeant,' Millie greeted him, aware all the time of William's dark eyes on her. 'If you'll excuse me, I'll let my grandmother know you're here.'

'There's no need.' Lady Rettingham appeared in the doorway to the drawing room.

It amused Millie to watch the two men freeze like rabbits caught in the sights of a gun. The Dowager Countess was a formidable figure, and her hauteur could reduce the temperature in a room by several degrees.

'Granny, this is Flight Sergeant Ellis, the Quartering Commandant I told you about. And this is—'

'Squadron Leader Tremayne,' William finished for her. 'I have been appointed as your liaison officer. Pleased to meet you, Lady Rettingham.'

She looked frostily at the hand he offered, but didn't deign to take it.

'And what, pray, is a liaison officer?'

William let his hand drop to his side. 'It's my job to ensure you're satisfied with the arrangements, and to deal with any problems as they occur.'

Lady Rettingham's brows arched. 'Then I suspect, Squadron Leader, you are going to be a very busy man.'

William cleared his throat. 'I do sympathise, Lady Rettingham,' he said. 'This is a difficult situation for everyone.'

'Is it?' the Dowager replied icily. 'Tell me, have you been turned out of your home?'

William looked nonplussed by the question. 'I—'

'Shall we make a start?' Millie broke in desperately.

'Sergeant Ellis and I can look around the house by ourselves, if it would be more convenient?' William said, recovering himself.

Millie opened her mouth to reply, but her grandmother got in first.

'Certainly not,' she replied with asperity. 'This is still our home. For now, at least.'

William inclined his head. 'As you wish, Lady Rettingham.'

It was odd for her to listen to the two men, walking from room to room of her home, coldly discussing how each one could best be used. The dining room was to be the officers' mess, the library their briefing room, Millie's father's old study the Wing Commander's office. Other rooms were to be used for training, communications and intelligence, recreation and equipment storage. Millie tried to remind herself it was all for the war effort, but it was difficult to see her home torn apart before her eyes.

All the time, she kept her gaze fixed on William's tall, dark figure. She could hardly believe he was here, in her house. It was as if a tiny fragment of time had dislodged itself from the past and drifted into the present.

As they went out to inspect the stables and outbuildings, William fell into step beside her.

'I must say, you're being extraordinarily good about this,' he said. 'I've seen peers of the realm in tears at the prospect of leaving their homes. Grown men sobbing over the loss of their orangerie or billiard room.'

Millie shrugged. 'It has to be done, doesn't it? Besides, it seems rather unfair to have such a large house for the three of us, and not put it to some good use.'

William paused, and Millie braced herself, knowing what was to come.

'I heard about your husband,' he said. 'I'm sorry. I understand he was a fine officer.'

'I don't know about that, but he was a fine man,' Millie replied quietly.

'You must miss him?'

'Of course.' She changed the subject. 'So you fly bombers?'

'Not at the moment. I took a bit of a battering a while back, so–'

'You were hurt?'

'Not too badly. I'm fit to fly again, but they've put me in charge of training the raw recruits for the time being.'

'And you'll be billeted here?'

'That's right.' He glanced sideways at her. She caught the look in his dark eyes and realised that he was testing her, silently sounding out her reaction to him.

She was an eighteen-year-old girl, enjoying her first taste of freedom in London, when William

Tremayne first came into her life. He was her room-mate Helen's elder brother, a sweet and charming rogue, and all the nurses loved him.

William had set his sights on Millie and for a while it looked as if she might be the one to tame him. But their romance, such as it was, had fizzled out when Millie fell in love with Sebastian. And when they married and she returned to live at Billinghurst, she left her old, girlish life – and William – behind her.

She was pleased and relieved to discover that she didn't react to him the way she used to, that she was no longer the hopeless little eighteen-year-old student whose heart skipped a beat whenever he walked on to the ward. It might have made life very awkward for them both if she had been.

As it was, having a familiar face around might actually make things easier for all of them, she decided.

'Then I hope you'll be very happy here,' she said.

The tour ended, and they returned to the entrance hall. As Sergeant Ellis attended to his list, William thanked their hosts.

'You have been most accommodating,' he said to Millie.

'Hasn't she?' Lady Rettingham said, tight-lipped.

Millie ignored her. 'When do you think you'll move in?' she asked William.

'In the next week or two, I think.'

'So you'll be throwing us out before Christmas?' her grandmother said.

Embarrassed, Millie said, 'Granny, please! You

make it sound positively Dickensian.'

'And what would you call it? Two defenceless women and a child turned out of their own home. As if we haven't lost enough.' The Dowager Countess fished in her pocket for her lace-edged handkerchief.

Millie glanced sideways at her grandmother. She was putting on the sentimentality again. She must have conveniently forgotten that it was vulgar for a lady to show her emotions in public.

William seemed to understand what she was doing. He stared at her, unmoved. 'I assure you, Lady Rettingham, that given the choice most of the men in the squadron would rather be in their own homes than yours this Christmas. I know I would.'

Touché, Millie thought, glancing at her grandmother. There was a combative light in her eyes as she dabbed at her non-existent tears.

The men left and Millie braced herself, waiting for what was to come.

'Well, I must say, you didn't put up much of a fight,' Lady Rettingham said, immediately recovering herself. 'Offering them the outbuildings without a murmur.'

'I'm just being practical,' Millie argued. 'The men have to sleep somewhere.'

'Hmm.' Millie could feel her grandmother's keen gaze upon her. 'You seemed rather friendly with Squadron Leader Tremayne, too.'

Millie hesitated, wondering if she should tell her. There was no point in hiding it, her grandmother would find out sooner or later. Lady Rettingham found everything out in the end.

'William was a doctor at the Nightingale while I was training.' She saw her grandmother's wince of distaste. Lady Rettingham preferred to draw a veil over Millie's brief career as a nurse. As far as she was concerned, those three years were a kind of temporary madness that was never to be spoken of. 'But don't worry, Granny, those days are well and truly gone.'

'I hope you're right, Amelia.' Lady Rettingham's comment was laced with meaning.

'Well, that seemed to go well. Better than I'd been expecting at any rate.' Bob Ellis sat behind the wheel of the car and shook a cigarette out of his packet. 'The old girl was a bit of a battleaxe, but that's nothing unusual.' He lit his cigarette and took a long drag. 'Lady Amelia seemed nice, though.'

William's attention was fixed on the mellow honey-coloured stone façade of the house. It was a stunning place, with its gables and mullioned windows. He hoped it wouldn't be ruined.

'Millie's a lovely girl,' he replied absently.

'Millie?'

'I used to know her. She was a nurse at the hospital where I used to be a doctor.'

'Oh, yes?' The Quartering Commandant sent him a questioning sideways look. 'Bit of romance, was there?'

William laughed. 'Not in the way you're thinking! As a matter of fact, it was all very innocent and chaste.'

Although not for want of trying on his part. He'd been captivated by Millie from the first moment he saw her. Not just attracted, but entranced. Millie Rushton was the closest he had ever come to falling in love.

'Well, that could work out very well for you, couldn't it? Having her living next door. Chance to renew old acquaintances, if you see what I mean?'

'I don't think so, Bob.' If he was honest, that had been on William's mind when he'd arranged to come down and see her. But he'd hardly recognised Millie when he'd walked into the house. The sweet, lively, fun-loving girl he'd known had been replaced by a sombre, brittle young woman. 'She's changed,' he said.

'Hardly surprising, is it? The bloody war's changed all of us, one way or another.'

'I suppose you're right,' William agreed heavily. In a way, he was relieved that he hadn't felt an attraction to her. It would make life a lot easier, he decided.

Chapter Nine

'How do I look?' Grace turned away from the mirror to face her sister.

'Let's see...' Daisy inspected her closely. 'Your collar could be a bit straighter. And you're going to need some more pins in that cap.'

Grace turned back to her reflection and reached for a hairpin, but her hands were shaking so much it slipped from her grasp.

'Here, let me.' Daisy worked busily, pinning the

starched linen into place and tucking stray strands of Grace's hair underneath it.

Grace watched her in the mirror, marvelling at her skill. 'You're so quick,' she said. 'I'll never be able to do it as well as you.'

'You will, once you've practised it enough times.' Daisy stood back to admire her handiwork. 'There, that's better.'

Grace admired her reflection shyly. She hardly recognised herself. The blue VAD's dress was so smart, with its stiff starched collar and cuffs, she didn't think she would ever want to take it off.

'Come on,' said Daisy, throwing her navy blue cloak over her uniform. 'You don't want to be late on your first day, do you?'

She moved to the door but Grace stayed rooted to the spot. She had been looking forward to this moment for weeks, but now it was here she was suddenly filled with apprehension.

'I wish we were on the same ward, Dais,' she said.

Her sister smiled. 'I know, Gracie, but Matron would never allow it because we're so busy on Female Medical. Anyway, you'll be all right on the Military Ward, I'm sure. Miss Wallace the ward sister is meant to be an angel. And think of all the handsome soldiers you'll meet!'

She nudged her, and Grace smiled reluctantly. Her sister's lively spirits could cheer up anyone.

'I suppose so,' she said.

They walked down to the hospital together. It was a crisp, cold morning, and on the horizon streaks of pink and gold had started to lighten the indigo sky. As they neared the gates, Daisy turned to her and said, 'It's probably best if we don't talk to each other much once we get inside. It's all right if I speak to you first, but VADs and juniors aren't supposed to address seniors and staff nurses.'

Grace nodded. 'I understand. It's like at the big house, where the second parlourmaid isn't allowed to speak to the first parlourmaid.' There had been some real jealousies in the servants' hall, with kitchen maids lording it over scullery maids, and lady's maids lording it over everyone. 'So who am I allowed to speak to?' she asked.

'No one, I'm afraid. The VADs are right at the bottom of the heap.' Daisy looked apologetic. 'But as long as you keep your head down and only speak when you're spoken to, you should be all right. And whatever you do, don't try to be too chummy with the ward sister. Miss Wallace is nice, but she'll still bite if you push her.'

'I'll try to remember that,' Grace said.

Her nerves must have shown, because Daisy squeezed her hand. 'You'll be fine,' she said.

Grace had been assigned to the Military Ward, on the top floor of the building. The patients were having their breakfast when she arrived, and the smell of fried bacon was mixed with the strong scent of disinfectant. Most of the men were sitting up in bed with trays, but some were seated around the big table in the middle of the ward. A couple of the fitter men were busy pushing a trolley and handing out cups of tea. Young and old, big and small, all the men wore identical striped hospital-issue pyjamas.

When Grace entered through the double doors, the murmur of conversation ceased and every face turned to look at her. Her heart jumped into her mouth, and it was all she could do not to turn tail and flee.

A woman came down the ward to greet her. She was wearing a sister's grey uniform, with a linen bonnet tied in a bow under her pointed chin. She was in her forties, slim and attractive, with dark hair and a smile that made her brown eyes sparkle.

'You must be Maynard?' she greeted Grace with relief. 'We were told we were getting a new VAD. I'm Miss Wallace, the ward sister.'

She seemed friendly enough, but Grace remembered her sister's warning.

'How do you do, Sister?' she said warily.

'All the better for seeing you, I must say! There's only Nurse Freeman and myself on the ward at present, so as you can imagine we're quite busy. We could certainly do with some help.'

'What would you like me to do first, Sister?'

Miss Wallace's smile widened. 'That's what I like to see, someone who's ready to get straight to work! Go and put your apron on, then you can wash up the breakfast dishes and put them away.'

It was a relief for Grace to be able to hide away in the kitchen, even if she did have a mountain of greasy plates and cups to wash up.

'Oh, dear, bad luck!' Nurse Freeman said as she pushed a trolley laden with dirty dishes into the kitchen. 'You've only been here five minutes, and you're already up to your elbows in hot water.'

'I don't mind,' Grace said. 'I like to keep busy.'

'Oh, I expect you'll enjoy it here, then,' Nurse Freeman said. 'We'll keep you very busy!'

And she was right. After she'd dried up and put

away all the dishes, Miss Wallace set Grace to cleaning the ward. She got stuck in, pleased to be doing something she was familiar with. Starting from the top of the room, as she'd been taught in service, she took down the light fittings and washed them, then damp dusted all the surfaces and the bedsprings, washed down the lockers, sprinkled tea leaves on the floor to settle the dust, then swept and polished every inch.

She was on her hands and knees, scrubbing the wheels of the beds with a wire brush, when a cheeky voice said, 'I've got a good view from here!'

Grace looked over her shoulder at the young man sitting in the bed above her. His left leg was dressed and propped up with a drain tube coming from it, and he was leaning over to eye her rear end appreciatively.

She held up the brush. 'Do you want me to wash your mouth out with this?'

The man in the next bed laughed. 'Take no notice of him, Nurse. He only arrived last night and he's already making a nuisance of himself. Too cocky for his own good, if you ask me.'

'No one is asking you, are they?' the young man replied. He was just a kid, no more than eighteen. 'They're just jealous of my good looks and charm,' he said to Grace.

She regarded him, his shorn hair sticking up at angles around his lively, freckled face, and tried not to laugh.

'My name's Terry Thompson, but my mates call me Tommo. What's yours?' he asked.

'None of your business,' Grace replied, going back to her scrubbing.

'Ooh, playing hard to get, eh? I like that in a girl.' He leaned back against his pillows, hands behind his head. 'Not a very lively lot here, are they? Most of 'em look half dead to me.'

'That's why we're in hospital, you daft git,' the man in the next bed retorted.

Tommo nodded towards the curtains surrounding the bed on his other side. 'Psst, Nurse,' he hissed to Grace. 'Who's in there?'

She glanced at the screens. 'I'm not sure,' she said. 'It's my first day too.'

'His name's Alan Jones,' Tommo's other neighbour explained. 'Young Welsh lad. Got shot up bad in North Africa, he did. Terrible head injury.' He ran his hand down the side of his face to indicate the damage.

'Sounds as if he's lucky to be alive,' Grace said.

'I dunno about lucky, Nurse,' the man said grimly. 'You should hear him scream at night. During the day too, sometimes. The slightest thing sets him off, and then he's crying for hours, unless someone manages to calm him down.' He shook his head. 'Horrible to listen to him, it is. I'll tell you what, I wouldn't like to know what goes on in that poor beggar's head.'

Grace stared at the screens. She couldn't imagine what Alan Jones must look like, but she hoped she wouldn't have to come face-to-face with him too soon.

'Want to know why I'm in here?' Tommo piped up, not to be outdone. 'I was shot in the leg. Blasted away half the muscle, so the doctor said. You can't imagine the mess–'

'I'm sure Maynard has no wish to hear about

your war wound, Mr Thompson.' Grace heard Miss Wallace's voice just as a pair of well-polished black shoes appeared in front of her. 'She has quite enough to do, so please stop bothering her.'

Afraid Miss Wallace might think she was slacking, Grace scrambled to her feet and said, 'I've finished, Sister.'

'Have you? That was quick.' Miss Wallace's brows arched. 'Let's see what you've done shall we?'

Grace was nervous as she followed Miss Wallace down the ward. She kept her fingers crossed in the folds of her dress, praying silently that the ward sister wouldn't find a speck of dust as she ran her hand along the bed rails and round the light fittings.

Finally, Miss Wallace said, 'Well, that all seems to be perfectly in order. Well done, Maynard. You've worked very hard.'

Grace felt the blush rising up from under her starched collar. 'Thank you, Miss – I mean, Sister.'

'Run along and take your dinner break now, and then come back at twelve and help Nurse Freeman serve the patients.'

Grace was so happy she almost skipped down to the dining room. Her first morning was over, and Sister had actually praised her. Wait until Daisy heard about it!

The dining room was on the ground floor, a vast room the size of a tennis court, laid out with rows of long tables. Grace spotted Daisy at a table on the far side of the room. She was sitting with two other nurses, a tall, slender girl with curly hair and a smaller, sharp-featured girl. Grace was about to go over and join them when she caught her sister's eye and suddenly remembered what Daisy had told her about not mixing. She veered off to the right instead and joined a table of other VADs.

By the time she'd hurried through her meal and got back to the ward, the patients' food had been delivered from the kitchen on big trolleys. Miss Wallace dished it out on to plates, and Grace and Nurse Freeman handed them out one by one to the patients. Most of them needed a bed tray, but some gathered around the central table again.

Some of the men were on particular diets and Miss Wallace had ordered special food, like plain boiled fish or a milk pudding, to be sent up for them. Grace marvelled at how the ward sister managed to remember all the men and what they needed. She even took the time to dress up some of the trays with lace cloths and tiny buds of flowers taken from the vases on the table.

'For the men who've lost their appetites,' Alice Freeman explained to Grace. 'Sister says if the food looks appetising, they're more likely to eat it.'

Grace was given the job of delivering Tommo's meal to him. She reached the young man's bed, but there was no sign of him. Grace stared at the empty bed. 'Where is he?' she asked his neighbour.

'Dunno, Nurse,' he shrugged.

'That's odd. I'm sure he's not supposed to move with that leg–'

Suddenly she felt something shoot out from under the bed and grab her ankle. She screamed in panic, the tray went up in the air and landed with a crash. Kidney pudding, gravy and mashed potatoes went everywhere, all over the bedclothes and her clean floor, so beautifully polished that morning.

Tommo's face appeared from under the bed, his hand still circling her ankle. 'Gave you a proper fright, didn't I?'

Grace was just about to reply when an ear-splitting scream rang out from behind the screens around the next bed. It seemed to go on for ever, getting louder and louder like the ghastly wail of an air-raid siren.

Suddenly everyone was hurrying towards her. Nurse Freeman dumped the tray she'd been holding and pushed her way behind the screens, with Miss Wallace following. Several of the men also got up from the table and stood around on the other side of the curtains, watching anxiously.

'That's torn it,' Tommo said, hauling himself out from under the bed.

'I expect the noise of that tray crashing down brought on one of his nightmares.' The man on Tommo's other side stared at him accusingly.

'I wasn't to know, was I?' he grumbled. 'It was only a bit of fun.'

The screams slowly subsided into heart-rending sobs. Grace had just started to pick up the fragments of smashed crockery from the floor when the screens parted and Miss Wallace appeared.

'What's happened here?' she demanded.

Tommo started to speak, but Grace got in first. 'It's my fault, Sister,' she said. 'I dropped the tray.'

'Well, that was very clumsy of you, I must say.' It was the mildest of rebukes, but it still stung like a barb. 'Get it cleared up, then clean the floor, and strip this bed. And please try to be more careful in future,' she sighed. 'We're busy enough without you making extra work for us.'

'You didn't have to take the blame, you know,' Tommo whispered when Miss Wallace had gone.

'I didn't. I only told the truth. I dropped the tray, not you.'

'Only because I frightened you.' Tommo looked uncomfortable. 'Cheers, anyway.' he said. 'I reckon I'm in enough trouble with this lot, without getting into any more.'

'Perhaps this will teach you a lesson?' Grace said, collecting up the last of the pieces. But as she stood up and saw the mischievous glint in his eye, she wasn't sure it would.

Chapter Ten

'When can I go home, Nurse?'

Jess paused, the spoonful of rice pudding half-way to Mrs Briggs's mouth. She didn't know why the patient continued to ask the question when the answer was always the same.

'You know what the doctor said, Mrs B,' she explained patiently. 'You have to have complete rest.'

'Yes, but how long for?'

'Until your heart recovers.'

'Well, I ain't going to be here at Christmas, that's for sure!' Mrs Briggs declared.

Jess sighed. Nursing Elsie Briggs was proving to

be a real trial, She was a salt of the earth cockney and a lovely woman, but stubborn with it. With her serious heart condition, she was supposed to rest in bed and refrain from exerting herself. But bed rest didn't come naturally to a woman who had brought up five kids.

Jess didn't blame her. No mother wanted to be apart from her children, especially at this time of year.

'I'm not spending Christmas away from my kids, bad heart or no bad heart!' Mrs Briggs repeated. 'I'm going back to London, even if it's the last thing I do.'

It probably will be! Jess bit back the retort. 'Look, Mrs B, you've got to understand your heart is very weak,' she explained. 'You've seen how we have to feed and wash you? That's because you're not allowed to do anything for yourself. How do you think you'll manage in London? The journey alone could kill you.'

Mrs Briggs was silent for a moment. 'All the same, I want to go,' she said, her mouth set in a tight line.

Jess looked at her, doing her best not to cry, and felt a surge of pity.

She discussed it with Daisy later as they made the beds.

'She's very difficult, isn't she?' Daisy agreed. 'I caught her trying to get out of bed the other day.' She shook her head. 'Sister was furious with her.'

'Sister's always furious with someone. Except Miss Pomfrey,' Jess added.

'Perhaps Mrs Briggs's family will come to visit today?' Daisy suggested.

'I doubt it. Hardly any of the London patients get visitors.'

At least Hilda Reynolds was getting a visit today. She was so excited when Jess went to tidy her up.

'That's it, love. Make me look nice. Don't want to give my Jean a scare, do I?' She smiled weakly.

'You'll look a picture, Mrs Reynolds,' Jess promised. She'd given Hilda a good wash and dressed her in a freshly laundered nightdress for her daughter's visit, knowing how much Hilda was looking forward to it.

But in spite of her outward smile, inside Jess's heart ached. She knew the old lady didn't have very long left. The pernicious anaemia was killing her slowly but surely. Her skin was a waxy yellow, speckled here and there with ugly brown patches over her emaciated body.

Even her cockney spirit seemed to be deserting her. She was too fatigued to do anything but sleep most of the time, although she was trying to rally herself for her daughter's impending visit.

Jess hoped Jean's visit would cheer Hilda up. There was no hope for her, but Jess desperately wanted her to have some happy memories for her last days.

'Do you think Jean will bring your grandkids?' she asked, as she carefully arranged Hilda's hair in fine white strands over her bony shoulders.

'I hope so, love. I'd like to see them once more before...' Her voice trailed off. 'But it's a long way for them to come. I told Jean not to come herself, but she would insist...'

'Of course she wants to see you,' Jess said. 'I bet

91

she'd be here every day, if she could.'

'Bless you, love, I wouldn't ask her to do that. She's got far too much on her plate already. But I'm looking forward to having a little chinwag with her, to catch up on what's happening at home.'

Poor Hilda, Jess thought. She wondered if she would be so brave in her position. 'There, you're all done.' She put down the brush. 'You look like a film star.'

'Oh, I dunno about that.' Hilda ducked her head modestly. 'Just so long as I don't worry my Jean too much.'

Jess pushed the screens back and almost collided with Mr Sulley. As well as ferrying nurses to and from the hospital in his horse and cart, he also worked at the hospital as an odd job man. Although he never seemed to be around when there was a job that needed doing.

This time he was coming down the ward, dragging an enormous Christmas tree.

Jess fell into step beside him, pushing the trolley of wash things. 'Where did you get that?' she asked. 'I thought there was a shortage of Christmas trees this year?'

'Not if you know where to look, there isn't.'

'Where did you get it?'

Sulley tapped the side of his nose. 'Ask no questions and I'll tell you no lies. Let's just say a local gamekeeper I know owed me a favour.'

Daisy was waiting for them at the far end of the ward. 'Is that our tree? Where did you get it?'

Sulley glared at her. 'Don't you start!'

'He pinched it,' Jess said.

'I did not!' Sulley looked offended. 'And I'll

thank you not to go around spreading stories like that, young lady. We're respectable people down here, not like you light-fingered London lot!'

'They don't call it pinching down here,' Daisy said. 'They call it poaching.' She nodded towards the tree. 'I've never heard of anyone poaching a tree, though.'

Sulley's fist closed around the tree trunk, snatching it away from them. His grizzled face was almost hidden behind the foliage. 'If you two are going to carry on besmirching my good name, I'll take the blessed thing away.'

'No, don't,' Daisy said. 'What shall we decorate it with?'

'There are some old boxes of decorations down in the store room, so I'm told. But don't think I'm fetching them for you,' Sulley replied, still disgruntled.

Sister reluctantly gave them permission to decorate the tree once all their chores were done. Effie came on duty at one o'clock, just as Jess and Daisy were arguing about who should go down to the basement for the decorations.

'I'm not going down there,' Daisy declared. 'It's full of spiders and cadavers and rats and all sorts. Besides, I went last time, when I took the soiled dressings down to the incinerator.'

'The incinerator is not nearly as bad as the basement,' Jess said. 'Besides, you didn't take those soiled dressings down. I did.'

'You didn't!'

'I did!'

Effie emerged from the cloakroom, fastening up her apron. She was humming under her breath.

'Hello, girls,' she greeted them cheerfully.

Daisy and Jess looked at each other, then as one they both turned to Effie.

'You have to go down to the basement and collect the box of Christmas decorations,' Daisy told her.

Effie shrugged. 'If you like.'

Jess regarded her cautiously. 'Are you sure you don't mind?'

'Why should I?'

As she went, Daisy said, 'No one would go down to the basement willingly. Is she sickening for something, do you think?'

'Love sick, probably, if I know her,' Jess said. 'She didn't come home until after midnight last night, so I expect there's a man involved.'

Sure enough, when Effie returned with the dusty box of Christmas decorations, she declared, 'Well, girls, I'm in love!'

'Not again!' Jess sighed. The RAF had arrived a week ago and Effie had been out with a different man every night since. Once or twice Daisy had gone with her, both of them dressed up to the nines. And every time Effie returned sighing to the Nurses' Home and woke Jess up to tell her she'd met the man of her dreams.

'It's different this time,' Effie insisted. 'This time it's real.'

'Let's hear all about it,' Daisy urged. 'Who is he? What's his name?'

'His name's Kit, and he's a pilot.'

'Aren't they all?' Jess muttered, rooting gingerly through the box. If she unearthed a rat, she would scream the ward down.

'He's very handsome,' Effie went on, ignoring her. 'And so dashing. He talks like Leslie Howard. I've always liked men who talk nicely.'

'He sounds smashing,' Daisy sighed. 'Does he have a friend?'

'As a matter of fact, he does,' Effie said. 'I've arranged for us all to meet up in the Keeper's Rest on Friday night.'

'Ooh, I can't wait!' Daisy squealed with excitement.

'You can count me out,' Jess said.

Effie pulled a face. 'Why?'

'I don't fancy it.'

'You mean you want to stay in and write another one of your letters to Sam?' Effie teased. 'Can't you miss one night? The poor lad won't get a chance to read them all! Go on,' she said. 'Why don't you come out with us, just once?'

'I told you, I don't fancy it. I'd rather stay at home with a good book. But if you're going out, you might want this.' Jess pulled a sprig of mistletoe out of the box. It had been fashioned out of paper and wire, with cotton-wool berries.

Daisy laughed. 'Let's put it up over the door to the ward and see if we can get anyone to kiss us!'

'Knowing my luck, I'll probably get old Sulley!' Jess said.

Daisy twirled the sprig thoughtfully between her fingers. 'Perhaps we could get someone to kiss Sister?' she said.

Jess laughed. 'I doubt it! It'd take a mallet on the head, not mistletoe, to get anyone to kiss her...' She broke off, seeing Effie's and Daisy's horrified expressions. She didn't need to turn round to

95

know that Sister Allen was standing just behind her.

'Jago, Miss Pomfrey needs your attention,' she said shortly.

Had she heard? Jess wondered. Sister was always so angry with her, it was hard to tell.

Miss Pomfrey was sitting up in bed with an embroidery frame propped in front of her.

'Thread this for me, would you?' She handed Jess the needle and thread. 'I'd do it myself but I can't be bothered to keep taking my glasses on and off.'

Are you sure you wouldn't like me to do that for you, too? Jess thought. A please or thank you would have been nice, at least. In the two weeks Miss Pomfrey had been there, she had proved herself a real nuisance. She treated Jess and the other nurses like maids, sending them here and there to do her errands.

What a contrast to poor Mrs Briggs, Jess thought. She was supposed to rest but she couldn't bear to watch the nurses fussing around her.

And as if Miss Pomfrey wasn't unbearable enough, there were the frequent visits from her equally ghastly friend, Mrs Huntley-Osborne. She turned up most days, whenever she felt like it, and stayed for as long as she pleased. It was a terrible nuisance, but Sister said nothing about it.

Jess gritted her teeth, determined not to let her irritation get the better of her. 'That's beautiful work you're doing,' she admired the embroidery in Miss Pomfrey's lap. 'Are you making anything special?'

'I'm embroidering tray cloths for the prisoners-of-war.'

'And is there much call for tray cloths in prisoner-of-war camps?' Jess joked. Miss Pomfrey glared at her, stony-faced.

'Being a prisoner-of-war is no laughing matter,' she snapped. 'But since you ask, we will be selling them to raise funds for sending packages out to the POWs. Would you like to buy one?'

'Um...'

'You could send it to your mother as a Christmas gift?'

Jess had never even seen her sluttish stepmother Gladys pick up a broom except to hit someone with it. She couldn't imagine her knowing what to do with a tray cloth. Perhaps Sam's mum might like one, though...

Dr Drake appeared like a whirlwind in the doorway to the ward.

'Sister has asked me to check on a patient.' As usual, he addressed a spot just above Jess's shoulder.

'I'll fetch her for you, Doctor.' Jess started to walk away, then an impulse seized her and she turned back again. 'But while you're here, I wondered if you could have a word with Mrs Briggs? The endocarditis patient in bed six.'

Dr Drake stared at her blankly. He couldn't have looked more shocked if his stethoscope had started speaking to him.

'What about her?' he snapped. 'Has there been a deterioration?'

'Oh, no, Doctor. It's just—'

'What? Spit it out, Nurse!'

Jess took a deep breath. 'She wants to go home, sir.'

He frowned. 'What on earth do you mean?'

'Back to London, sir. She misses her family.'

'But she's very ill. It's out of the question.'

'I know, but she misses them so much, I wondered if it might be doing her more harm than good to keep her down here away from them?'

Dr Drake was silent. Jess wasn't sure if he was taking in what she'd said, or working out what to tell Matron when he reported her.

They were interrupted by a sudden snort of laughter from the corner. Jess turned to see Effie and Daisy hiding behind the linen cupboard, giggling helplessly.

A terrible sinking feeling overcame her, and she cast her eyes upwards. There was the sprig of mistletoe, dangling precariously a few inches above their heads.

Dr Drake followed her gaze upwards. He saw the mistletoe, and his angular face suffused with colour.

'Of all the ridiculous–' He snatched the mistletoe down and stuffed it in his pocket. 'I suppose you think this is funny, do you? Keeping me talking here while your friends make fun of me?'

Jess's mouth fell open. 'What? No, sir, I knew nothing about this...' she started to say, but Dr Drake wasn't listening.

'You might have time to waste, Nurse, but I assure you, I don't!' he bit out, brushing past her.

'Well!' Daisy said, when he'd gone. 'Someone can't take a joke.'

'He's the rudest man I've ever met,' Effie agreed.

Jess said nothing. She had seen the stricken look on his face, and couldn't help feeling sorry for him. 'He thought we were playing a prank on him,' she said.

'What if we were? He deserves it,' Daisy declared. 'You could give me a whole bunch of mistletoe and I still wouldn't kiss him!'

Chapter Eleven

At least Dr Drake didn't run to Sister as Jess had feared he might. By the time visiting hour arrived at two o'clock, she had started to feel that she might escape punishment.

As the visitors lined up outside, Sister instructed Jess to wait at the door and issue them with tickets as they came in.

'Remember, only two tickets per patient,' she said, as she always did. 'If a patient doesn't have a spare ticket, the visitor must wait outside. I will not have my ward overrun with strangers.'

As she handed out the tickets, Jess searched all the visitors' faces for a woman who might be Hilda Reynolds's daughter. She recognised most of the people from their regular visits, but couldn't pick out any strangers in the crowd, let alone any who might be Jean.

The last of the visitors trickled through, and Jess glanced over her shoulder. Hilda was sitting up, craning her neck to see the doors. Jess looked away as she closed them, unable to bear the look of disappointment on the old lady's face.

She went over to Hilda's bed. 'Can I get you a cup of tea, love?' she said. Jess knew she would be in trouble with Sister but she didn't care. She felt she had to offer some comfort, even if it was only a weak cuppa.

'No, thank you, love. I don't have much of a taste for it these days.' Hilda's brave smile wobbled. 'Don't look like she's coming, eh?'

'You never know,' Jess said. 'It's still early.'

'I expect it was too difficult for her to get away,' Hilda said. 'Yes, that'll be it. It's such a long way to come, you see, and she might not have been able to get the time off work.' She shrugged her thin shoulders. 'It's a pity, though. I would've liked to see my girl.'

Jess pressed her hand. She desperately wished she could say the right thing to comfort Hilda. 'Are you sure you wouldn't like that cup of tea?'

'Ta, love, but I'd rather go to sleep, if it's all right with you?'

'Of course. Here, I'll sort your pillows for you so you're more comfortable.'

By the time she'd finished rearranging the pillows and straightening the bedding, Hilda had already drifted off to sleep. Jess watched her for a moment, the fine blue veins of her eyelids standing out against the creamy yellow of her skin.

Four o'clock came, and Sister rang her bell to announce the end of visiting time. Just as Jess was ushering the last of the visitors out, a woman came running up the passageway, red-faced and breathless, dragging two children behind her.

'Come on, kids!' she snapped at them. 'Get a

move on, we're late enough as it is!'

She saw Jess and hurried towards her. 'Excuse me, love, is this Female Medical Ward? Only I'm looking for my mum.'

The woman looked untidy and harassed, but there was something instantly familiar about her warm smile and bright eyes. 'You must be Jean?' Jess said.

'That's right, love. You know my old mum, then? How is she?'

'She'll be all the better for seeing you, I expect. We didn't think you were coming?'

'I know! It's been bleedin' murder all the way down. First the train dropped us miles from anywhere, then we found out the buses weren't running.' She rolled her eyes. 'On my life, I ain't never setting foot outside Stepney again if I can help it!'

'Well, at least you're here now.' But as Jess stood aside to let Jean and her children in, Sister approached.

'What's going on, Nurse?' she demanded. 'Who are these people?'

'Mrs Reynolds's daughter, come to visit,' Jess explained.

'How d'you do, Sister?' Jean said, but Sister Allen ignored her.

'You're too late,' she said. 'Visiting time finished five minutes ago.'

Jean stared at her. 'You're having me on, ain't you?'

'I assure you, I'm not.'

'Have a heart, love. I've come all this way to see my mum. It ain't my fault if the trains ain't working, is it?'

'Then you should have set off earlier and got here on time, shouldn't you?'

'But I–' Jean started to say, but Sister held up her hand.

'I'm sorry, but rules are rules,' she said.

'So what am I supposed to do?' Jean looked helpless.

'You'll have to come back on Sunday.'

'But I can't! The trains hardly run on a Sunday. And besides, I've got to work. It's taken me two weeks to sort out my shifts so I could come down today.'

'That really isn't my problem, is it?' Sister turned on her heel and walked away.

Jess followed her. 'Sister, please–'

'Rules are rules, Jago,' Sister Allen cut her off. She turned round to face Jess, eyes narrowed to slits. 'I do hope you're not thinking of disobeying my orders?'

'No, Sister,' Jess said quietly.

'Good. Now see that person and her children off the premises.'

Jean was doing her best to console her whimpering children.

'It ain't no use crying, kids. There's nothing we can do about it.' She looked near to tears herself. 'We'll try and come down another day, eh?'

'I'm sorry,' Jess said helplessly.

'It ain't your fault, love. You ain't the one with the heart of stone.' Jean glared past her towards Sister Allen.

'I know, but I wish there was something I could do.'

Jean shook her head. 'I wouldn't want to get

you into trouble. Anyway, I s'pose I'd best leave these with you.' She handed over a bag to Jess. 'It's just a few bits and pieces I've been putting by for Mum. Christmas presents, y'know.'

'I'll make sure she gets them,' Jess promised.

'Tell her I'll try to get down and see her before Christmas, if I can. And I'll telephone every day.' Jean reached out and grabbed Jess's hand. 'You will tell her we were here, won't you? Make sure she knows we didn't let her down.'

'I will.'

Hilda was still sleeping peacefully when Jess placed the gifts beside her locker.

'It's such a shame,' she said to Daisy. 'Poor Mrs Reynolds will be so disappointed.'

'At least she'll have the presents. They'll be a nice surprise for her when she wakes up,' Daisy replied.

'Not as nice as seeing her daughter.' Jess frowned. 'I don't understand it. Back in London when a patient was nearing the end, Matron always allowed visitors to spend as much time with them as they could. She reckoned it made things easier for everyone.'

Daisy smiled grimly. 'I couldn't see Sister Allen wanting her ward cluttered with visitors at all hours!'

'It's not about what she wants, is it? It's about what's best for the patients.'

Jess looked down at Mrs Reynolds's frail figure, looking like a doll under the bedclothes.

'Perhaps you should talk to Matron, if you feel like that about it?' Daisy suggested archly.

'And get my head bitten off? No, thanks. Besides, I know what she'll say – "I know you London nurses think you know everything, Jago, but this is my hospital and I'll run it in my way!"' She mimicked Miss Jenkins's hoity-toity tone.

Daisy laughed. 'That's just like her!'

'Isn't it?' The voice made them spin round. Jess's mouth turned to sandpaper at the sight of Miss Jenkins herself, standing behind her. Sister Allen was with her, barely able to keep the smile of malicious satisfaction off her face.

'Was there something you wanted to say to me, Nurse Jago?' Miss Jenkins's voice was frosty.

Jess hesitated. She glanced sideways at Daisy, who was watching her expectantly, then at Mrs Reynolds's sleeping form. She took a deep breath.

'Please, Matron, I wondered if Mrs Reynolds's daughter could come to see her out of visiting hours? It's so difficult for her to get down from London, you see, and it'd do Mrs Reynolds so much good to see her, especially as...' she lowered her voice '...she doesn't have much time left.'

Miss Jenkins's eyes bulged like steel ball bearings. 'Do you hear that, Sister?' she addressed the woman at her side. 'Once again, Nurse Jago thinks she knows better than the rest of us.'

'I didn't say that, I just–' Jess was silenced by a sharp nudge from Daisy.

'And she thinks it's acceptable to answer back to her superiors!' Matron's eyebrows almost disappeared into her starched headdress. 'That tells you something about the way things are done in London, doesn't it?'

'Indeed it does, Matron,' Sister Allen agreed smugly.

'But you are correct about one thing, Nurse Jago,' Miss Jenkins said. 'This is my hospital, and I will run it in my own way. And if you don't like it, I'm sure Miss Fox can find something for you to do in London.'

Jess stared down at her shoes. 'Yes, Matron.'

Miss Jenkins narrowed her gaze. 'I've got my eye on you, Jago,' she warned. 'Please don't give me cause to speak to you again.'

Daisy stifled a giggle as they watched her walk off towards Miss Pomfrey's bed, Sister Allen still at her side. 'Oh, dear,' she said. 'You had a lucky escape there.'

Jess's mouth firmed. 'I don't know about that,' she said.

Chapter Twelve

'When can we go and see the planes again, Mama?'

Millie smiled at her son over the breakfast table. 'Would you like to go this morning?' she asked.

Nanny Perks cleared her throat. 'Excuse me, your ladyship, but we're leaving for Lyford after luncheon,' she reminded her.

'I know, Nanny, but there's still plenty of time, isn't there?' Millie ignored Miss Perks' scowl and turned to her son. 'I have to go up to the house first, but I'll be back soon. We'll go then.'

Henry jigged up and down in his chair with excitement. 'Can we go and see the pilots?' he asked, his grey eyes shining.

'No, darling, we can't disturb them when they're busy. But we can ride up to the top of the hill and look down. You'll have a good view then, won't you?'

'But only if you're a good boy and eat all your breakfast,' Nanny Perks put in, thoroughly disgruntled.

After breakfast, Millie went up to the house to see William. She made a point of meeting him a couple of times a week, to find out if there were any problems there. If a pipe burst or a roof tile came loose, she would rather know about it before the rot set in to the timberwork.

This time she had to tell him they were spending the weekend with Seb's parents, the Duke and Duchess of Claremont.

Millie couldn't feel enthusiastic about the prospect. Even though she was the daughter of an earl herself, she always felt like a poor country cousin visiting her in-laws. They were so frightfully grand, and Millie had got used to living such a simple life, that she wasn't sure she would even know how to conduct herself in sophisticated company any more.

But she knew her grandmother couldn't wait to stay in a 'real' house again. Lady Rettingham loathed the Lodge, with its cramped rooms and only one part-time maid to order about. But Millie quite liked it. The rooms were nothing like as splendid as those in the main house, but they were a great deal more practical to look after, and a lot easier to heat, too. On cold winter nights, it was an absolute luxury for her to go to bed in a cosy bedroom instead of suffering the damp and draughts of her old room, with its inadequate fireplace and high ceilings. She didn't envy the RAF officers at all, struggling with the ancient plumbing and inadequate heating system.

As she walked up the drive, a pair of pilots passed her and nodded in greeting. Millie could tell from their leather jackets and flying suits that they had been out on a mission that morning and were now heading up to the house to debrief and enjoy some much-needed breakfast and rest.

It astonished Millie how quickly their presence had become familiar to her. She had got used to the guards at the gates, the rumble of cars and lorries on the drive, and the drone of the planes swooping over the roof. She had got used to the people, too, the airmen and the ground crews and the female WAAFs in their smart slate-blue uniforms. She even knew some of them by name, as she had hosted a tea party to welcome them all to Billinghurst.

She went up the stairs into the house. The entrance hall had been transformed into a reception area and office. Two WAAFs sat at desks on either side of the hall, tapping away on their typewriters. Millie had met them both several times before. The dark-haired one was called Jennifer Franklin, and the blonde was a girl from Lancashire called Agnes Moss.

They both looked up and smiled at her. 'Good morning, Lady Amelia,' Franklin greeted her.

'Good morning. Is Squadron Leader Tremayne free?'

'I'm afraid he's down at the airfield at present.

107

Can someone else help you?'

'Oh, no, it's not important. I only wanted to let him know we're going to be away for the weekend. Just in case anyone needs me for anything.'

'I'll be sure to let him know, Lady Amelia.' Franklin jotted it down on the pad next to her.

'Thank you.' As Millie left, Agnes Moss said, 'Are you going somewhere nice, your ladyship?'

Millie paused in the doorway. 'We're spending the weekend with my husband's parents.'

'Do they live in a house like this?'

Franklin frowned at her, but Millie didn't mind. It seemed like a fair question. 'Actually, Lyford is a lot grander than Billinghurst.'

'All right for some! Have a smashing time, won't you?' Agnes Moss was smiling when she said it, but there was a glint in her eye that Millie didn't understand.

'Thank you.'

As Millie closed the front door, she heard laughter explode from inside.

'Moss!' she heard Franklin cry. 'How could you? You nearly made me laugh out loud.'

'I couldn't help it,' Moss said. 'Did you hear it? "In case anyone needs me for anything." As if the war couldn't go on without her!'

'Don't be cruel!' Franklin said, but she was still laughing.

'Who does she think she is?' Moss went on. 'Swanning around here as if she's part of the war effort. What's she going to do if Hitler invades? Throw him a tea party?'

Millie stood rigid with shock. She wanted to run away but her legs wouldn't move.

'It's William I feel sorry for,' Moss continued. 'She's obviously got a thing for him, which is why she's here every five minutes. It's embarrassing.'

'Poor woman,' said Franklin.

'Poor William, you mean! He can't escape her. She's everywhere you look.'

'I feel rather sorry for her,' Franklin said. 'She's obviously keen to make herself useful.'

'Then she should find herself a proper job to do, and leave us to ours.'

'You never know. Perhaps the novelty will wear off soon and she'll go and play somewhere else. Where's the tea trolley, by the way? I'm parched.'

The typing started again, rapid as machine-gun fire. Still Millie couldn't move. She was so mortified, she wanted to melt into the doorframe so she couldn't be seen.

She had thought she was being helpful by getting involved. She'd had no idea that everyone felt she was in the way.

Shame washed over her. Did William really think she had a thing for him, as Moss said? The very thought made Millie cringe.

She managed to get down the steps, hurrying as fast as she could to put as much distance between herself and the house as possible. She got as far as the walled garden, and sat down on the stone bench around the ornamental fountain. The stone felt cold and rough, but the gentle burbling of the water relaxed her.

A couple of the ground crew went past and waved to her. Millie turned away to stare into the murky green depths of the pool. She couldn't face them. Did they think the same as Moss, that she was just a silly, interfering woman with nothing better to do with her time? She'd thought they liked her, but now she could see they were just barely tolerating her, smiling to her face while all the time wishing she would go away and mind her own business.

Well, she would. From now on, she would keep herself to herself.

As she stood up, she realised what her fingers had been tracing in the rough stonework. She had thought the stone was crumbling away from age, but now she realised that the indentations were actually letters. She peered closer, trying to make out the words. KF, RD, FC... Not words, but initials. And dates, too, all of them within the last month.

Anger raced through her. Someone had defaced her property! Not only did they think she was a joke, they had vandalised her home, too.

She wanted to storm back to the house and have it out with them there and then, but she couldn't face Agnes Moss's sneering expression or Franklin's quiet pity.

Millie stared back at the house behind her. What else had they done? she wondered. Played darts in the plasterwork and whittled their names in the oak staircase, she shouldn't wonder. And to think she had worried that the house might seem unwelcoming, with its bare walls and boarded-up fireplaces. Now she wished she had boarded up the doors, too, so they couldn't get in.

Her grandmother was right. Her father would never have stood for it. He would have resisted any attempt to have his house taken over. He certainly wouldn't have tried to befriend the interlopers like Millie had, rushing around after them like a puppy waiting to have its tummy stroked.

But not any more.

She went back to the Lodge, still steaming with anger. Henry rushed to greet her, Nanny Perks following close behind.

'I'm ready!' he cried.

Millie stared at him blankly. It was only when she saw his riding clothes that she remembered her promise.

'We're not going,' she said.

'No!' Henry cried.

'But you promised the child,' Nanny reminded her.

'I know what I promised, but we can't go.' Her mind was already elsewhere, racing ahead. She would write a letter, she decided. Not to William, but to the Wing Commander, telling him exactly what she thought. Or even to the Air Chief Marshal...

Henry's lip stuck out. Seeing him hovering on the edge of tears, Millie tried to placate him.

'Don't cry, darling, please.' She crouched down so her face was level with his. 'We can do something else. I could teach you a new card game...'

'Don't want cards!' Henry shouted. 'I want to see the aeroplanes.'

'Well, we can't,' Millie snapped. 'We're not going to see those wretched planes again, do you understand? It's bad enough that we have to have them here at all.'

Henry's face crumpled. He had never seen his mother lose her temper before, and Millie could see at once how much it frightened him.

'Henry...'

She reached for him but he fled. Millie went to go after him, but Nanny Perks stopped her.

'It's better if I see to him.' Her disapproving look said it all.

Millie sank down on the window seat, utterly wretched. Now her own son was frightened of her. She was a stupid, hopeless mother as well as everything else. Nanny Perks was quite right to treat her with contempt.

Her grandmother came in. 'What on earth is all the shouting about?'

'Nothing, Granny.'

Her grandmother peered at her. 'Are you quite well, Amelia? You look as if you've been crying.'

She fished out her handkerchief and blew her nose. 'I think I might be getting a cold, that's all.'

Lady Rettingham's inquisitive expression turned to one of dismay. 'Please tell me you're well enough to go to the Claremonts'?' she said. 'I don't think I could bear it if we had to cancel our arrangements. I can't wait to get away.'

Millie looked out of the window, at the landscape filled with slate-blue uniforms. 'Neither can I, Granny,' she said.

Chapter Thirteen

Hilda Reynolds died late on Friday morning.

Jess was in the middle of scrubbing the bathroom just before lunch when Sister Allen summoned her and announced matter-of-factly that Mrs Reynolds had been moved to one of the private rooms off the ward corridor, and that Jess would have to perform last offices.

'I can't spare anyone else to help you as it's almost time for the midday meal,' she said briskly. 'And please be quick about it. I am off duty this afternoon, and I don't want to be delayed.'

'Of course, Sister. Heaven forbid you should be inconvenienced!' Jess muttered as she vented her temper on stripping Mrs Reynolds's bed, attacking the iron rails with Lysol and a scrubbing brush, as if she could scrub away her anger and sadness.

Poor Mrs Reynolds. And her poor daughter, too. Jean would be devastated that she'd missed her chance to say goodbye to her mother.

Hilda Reynolds looked perfectly peaceful, the blinds drawn so that the side room was filled with murky shadows. In spite of what Sister had said, Jess took her time, washing Hilda carefully, combing out her long, fine strands of hair and arranging them into two plaits, tied with white ribbon. It took her several attempts to get them right, as her hands were shaking with rage.

How she detested Sister Allen and this wretched hospital! She could never have imagined any ward sister in London, no matter how spiteful, denying a dying woman the joy of seeing her family for the last time. Especially when they'd travelled all day to see her. Miss Fox would never have allowed it, Jess decided.

But Miss Fox wasn't here. Instead they had to put up with Miss Jenkins, who was every bit as vindictive as Sister Allen.

Jess had learned to put up with the rough treatment that all the London nurses received. But to make the patients suffer through no fault of their own was too much...

She dressed Hilda in a clean nightgown, and rolled white stockings up over her stick-thin legs. At least the poor woman was at peace from her dreadful illness now, although that wouldn't be any consolation to her family. Jess wondered if she should write to Jean, to let her know that her mother hadn't suffered? She knew the hospital would contact her, but felt as if she wanted to add her own condolences.

She was busy mentally composing a letter in her head when she heard Mrs Huntley-Osborne's braying voice passing the door. She was on her way down the corridor.

Jess looked at the watch on her bib. It was nearly one o'clock. Sister Allen would have gone off duty by now.

She came out of the bathroom, rolling down her sleeves, and met Daisy.

'Oh, hello,' the other girl greeted her cheerfully. 'Have you finished with Mrs Reynolds? Such a

114

shame, isn't it? We've just finished serving the meal, and Sister's just gone off duty so...' Daisy must have seen the light of combat in Jess's eyes because she stopped and said warily, 'What's wrong?'

She nodded in the direction of Mrs Huntley-Osborne's broad rear, disappearing through the double doors to the ward. 'What's she doing here?'

'Come to visit Miss Pomfrey, I expect. Now, shall I put the kettle on, or will you?'

'In a minute. I'm going to have a word with Mrs Huntley-Osborne first.'

'What? No, you can't! Jago–' But Daisy's words were lost as Jess marched down the corridor.

Mrs Huntley-Osborne was already at Miss Pomfrey's bedside when Jess caught up with her.

She cleared her throat. 'Excuse me,' she said. 'I'm going to have to ask you to leave.'

Mrs Huntley-Osborne turned to her. She was even more formidable up close, with that square jaw and her bulky body encased in tweed. The fox stole around her neck stared at Jess, glassy-eyed.

'I beg your pardon?' she said.

Jess stood her ground. 'Visiting hours are Wednesdays and Sundays, from two until four. It is now–' she looked at her watch again '–twenty-past one on a Friday afternoon. You shouldn't be here.'

Ensconced in bed, Miss Pomfrey let out a little yelp of outrage. 'Do you know who you're talking to?' she spluttered. 'This is Mrs Huntley-Osborne!'

'I don't care if it's the Queen of Sheba, she ain't allowed here outside visiting time. Rules are rules,' Jess parroted Sister Allen's words firmly.

115

Mrs Huntley-Osborne drew herself up to her full height. 'I will talk to Sister about this. Where is she?'

'She ain't here. Now, if you don't leave immediately, I will call a porter to have you removed,' said Jess.

She and Mrs Huntley-Osborne stood toe to toe, eyeballing each other. Jess barely came up to the other woman's shoulder, but she refused to be intimidated. She was an East End girl, and she'd faced down tougher types than this old windbag.

But all the same, she was relieved when Mrs Huntley-Osborne turned away and snatched up her bag.

'Very well,' she said. 'But, believe me, you haven't heard the last of this. I shall be speaking to Matron.'

Daisy was hiding in the corridor, watching the scene unfold. She hurried after Jess as she returned to the bathroom.

'What do you think you're doing?' she hissed. 'You can't talk to Mrs Huntley-Osborne like that!'

'Why not? I don't think it's fair to have one rule for one person, and another for everyone else.' She took off her cuffs and rolled up her sleeves. 'If Mrs Reynolds's daughter can't come in five minutes late, I don't see why an old witch like that can turn up whenever she feels like it.'

'Yes, but all the same ... you do realise she's going to go straight to Matron, don't you?' Daisy said.

'What can she do?' Jess shrugged.

A moment later, the ward telephone rang.

116

'I think you're just about to find out,' Daisy replied.

Jess was still reeling from her bruising encounter with Matron as she left the hospital with Daisy and Effie after their shift finished at eight.

'So she's putting you on nights on the Fever Wards as punishment?' Daisy laughed. 'She must be utterly furious with you!'

'She wasn't best pleased,' Jess said.

It was an understatement. Miss Jenkins had been so incandescent with rage, Jess thought she was going to hurl herself across the desk that separated them.

'Is this true, Nurse?' she had demanded, her pale eyes bulging. 'You had the temerity to eject Mrs Huntley-Osborne from the ward?'

'It was out of visiting hours, Matron,' Jess tried to defend herself, but Miss Jenkins was having none of it.

'It is not for you to decide who should be where and when in this hospital. Mrs Huntley-Osborne happens to be Chair of the Hospital Fund-Raising Committee, as well as a dear personal friend of mine. I will not have her spoken to in such an offhand manner. I can only put it down to the fact that you have not been properly trained in how to deal with people. I could never imagine one of my own nurses...'

And so it went on. And all the while, Jess was aware of Mrs Huntley-Osborne standing behind Matron's shoulder, a smug expression on her square-jawed face.

'Poor Mrs Huntley-Osborne,' Daisy giggled. 'I

don't think anyone's ever said no to her.'

'Then it's about time someone did,' Jess muttered. 'Nasty old busybody, thinks she's better than everyone else.'

'Oh, no, I've just had a thought,' Effie cried. 'You do realise that you'll probably be on nights over Christmas?'

Jess pulled a face. 'I hadn't thought of that.'

'That's a shame,' Daisy said. 'Christmas is always such fun on the wards, isn't it? There's the carol singing, and the presents, and the Christmas show...'

'All right, you don't have to rub it in!' Jess said irritably.

'Well, that settles it, then. If you're going to spend the next few weeks in isolation, you've definitely got to come out with us tonight,' Effie said. 'No, don't argue.' She held up her hand as Jess started to protest. 'You've got to have some fun, my girl. Go on, please? I'm sure Sam would not want you to shut yourself away for his sake.'

Jess considered it for a moment. 'You're right,' she agreed.

'Then you'll come?' Effie's blue eyes lit up with excitement. 'Oh, that's grand!'

'But I don't want you trying to fix me up with anyone,' Jess warned.

'Of course not.'

'I mean it. I'm not interested.'

'I won't, I promise,' Effie said solemnly.

Back at the Nurses' Home, Miss Carrington appeared in the hall as they were taking off their cloaks. 'There's a letter for you, O'Hara,' she said.

'A letter, Sister?' Effie looked up, shock written

all over her face.

Jess nudged her. 'Don't look so surprised, I expect your mother's written to you at last.'

Miss Carrington held the envelope at arm's length and squinted at it. 'It was originally sent to London, and it's been redirected here.' She looked at Effie over her spectacles. 'You silly girl, why didn't you give your family your new address?'

Effie's face turned pink. 'I thought I had. She must have forgotten it.'

'Well, it looks as if she's found you anyway,' Miss Carrington said.

'Yes,' Effie said slowly. 'She has, hasn't she?'

Jess noticed her friend's expression as Miss Carrington handed over the letter. She looked so wary, it might have been a hand grenade she was taking.

'I'll read it later,' she said, shoving it into her pocket.

Jess didn't think any more about it as they got ready for their night out. It was so long since she had gone out, it felt strange to be dressing up. Not that she had anything very fancy to wear, just her usual skirt, blouse and cardigan.

Effie was dressed up to the nines as usual, in a blue dress that perfectly matched her eyes. Her dark curls were swept up and fastened at the back of her head with a matching ribbon.

'What did your mother have to say?' Jess asked Effie as she watched her putting on her shoes.

'What?'

'Your letter? It was from your mother, wasn't it?'

'Oh ... yes, it was. But I haven't had a chance to

119

read it yet.' Effie stood up and grabbed her bag. 'Come on, we'll be late.'

The Keeper's Rest was a sea of slate-blue, with RAF and Canadian Air Force uniforms everywhere they looked.

'I can't see Kit anywhere...' Effie scanned the crowd, craning her neck to see.

'Perhaps he isn't here?' Jess edged aside to allow a pair of WAAFs to squeeze past. The crush of so many bodies around her was making it difficult to breathe.

'Oh, he'll be here ... yes, look, there he is. Kit! Kit!' Effie waved madly, her voice carrying across the noisy bar.

He pushed his way through the crowd to greet them. He was just as Effie had described him, tall and good-looking with sleek fair hair and an aristocratic, high-cheekboned face.

'Darling!' He swooped Effie up in his arms and gave her a long, extravagant kiss. Daisy and Jess looked at each other, embarrassed.

Finally they separated, and Effie said, 'These are my friends, Jess and Daisy.'

'Pleased to meet you, ladies.' He spoke in a lazy, upper-class drawl. 'Come over and meet the others.'

He led them to a corner table, where two young men sat with beers in front of them. One was a handsome giant, with thick fair hair and clear blue eyes. The other was small, wiry and very dark, with a lively face that didn't seem able to stop smiling.

Jess grabbed Effie's sleeve. 'You promised you wouldn't try to fix me up!' she accused.

'I didn't know there were only going to be two

of them, did I?' Effie said. 'Besides, we're having a drink with them, not getting engaged!'

'Who's getting engaged?' Kit swung round.

'No one, but Jess has a boyfriend and she doesn't want your friends to get the wrong idea.'

Jess glared at Effie, embarrassment washing over her. She could cheerfully have killed her.

'Did you hear that, boys? Jess here is out of bounds.' She caught the wink Kit gave the other two men, and her unease grew.

Kit introduced the blond giant as Max, and the smaller man as Harry. 'They're Canadians, but don't hold that against them,' he said.

Daisy made a beeline for Max, leaving Jess to squash herself on to the bench next to Harry. He was a bit too close for comfort, his wiry body pressed into her side.

'Can I buy you a drink, Jess?' he offered.

She looked at him sharply. 'A drink?'

'Yeah. Like this.' He held up his glass of beer. 'I'm told it's the custom to have them in these places.'

'I'll have a lemonade, please,' Jess replied stiffly.

His dark brows rose. 'Sure I can't get you anything stronger?'

'No, thank you.'

'You really are determined to hold on to your honour, aren't you?' Kit squinted mockingly at her through a plume of cigarette smoke. Effie was perched on his knee, her arms around him.

'It's a free country,' Jess shot back.

'Shut up, Kit. I'll get the lady whatever she wants.' Harry edged past her and headed for the bar. Jess watched him go, strutting on short,

121

slightly bowed legs. He wasn't remotely her type, she was relieved to realise.

Daisy, on the other hand, was staring up at Max as if she wanted to eat him. 'Are you a pilot?' she asked, wide-eyed.

Max nodded. 'Kit and I fly together.' His voice was deep and so quiet Jess could hardly hear him across the table.

'Does it take two of you to fly a plane?' Daisy asked.

'Depends how much Kit's been drinking the night before,' Max joked.

Kit grinned and raised his glass in a mocking toast.

'How about you, Harry?' Effie asked, as he returned with the drinks. 'Do you fly planes, too?'

Kit laughed loudly. 'I'd like to see that!'

'I'm the rear gunner,' he said. 'It's my job to keep the plane – and these two – safe.'

'Otherwise known as Tail End Charlie!' Kit put in.

'You may mock, my friend, but you won't be laughing when I'm all that's standing between you and a BF-107,' Harry said solemnly.

'So you're all in the same crew?' Effie said.

'That's right.' Kit threw his arms around his friends' shoulders. 'You're looking at the crew of the good ship D-Dragon. Us and a couple of others, of course,' he added.

They were all so different, Jess noticed, as the conversation flowed around her. Max was the quietest, although between Kit's showing off and Harry's wise-cracking there wasn't much chance for him to speak.

Not that it seemed to put Daisy off. She was flirting like mad, laughing and touching his arm and batting her eyelashes at him like there was no tomorrow.

'Looks like your friend's taken a real shine to my pal Max,' Harry commented next to Jess.

'It looks like it.'

'She'll have her work cut out for her. He's a real shy guy. Not like Kit over there. He's what you'd call a fast worker.'

Kit certainly seemed to be getting on well with Effie. They were talking and laughing, their heads close together, Kit's arm firmly encircling Effie's waist.

Jess felt Harry shift in his seat beside her. Thinking he was going to do the same, she edged away.

'Calm down, I'm not going to ravish you!' he laughed. 'If it makes you feel better, I've got a wife at home.'

Jess recoiled from him. 'You're married?'

Across the table, Kit laughed. 'Oh, dear, that's torn it!'

'Relax.' Harry lowered his voice. 'I'm not looking to play around or anything like that. To be honest, I didn't even want to come out tonight, but Kit talked me into it. He reckons I spend too long stuck in the billet, writing letters home.'

Jess smiled reluctantly. 'That sounds like me.'

Harry took out his wallet and showed her a photograph of his wife and plump toddler son. Kit laughed.

'You're never going to woo a girl by showing her photos of your wife and kid, old chap!' he mocked.

'Who says I want to? There's only one girl for me. Unlike you,' he muttered under his breath.

Jess looked at the photo, feeling comforted. Harry obviously adored his family, and she could relax knowing he wasn't going to expect anything of her except friendship.

'You must miss them?' she said, handing him back the photograph.

'I do,' he sighed. 'Especially at this time of year. Do you know, I haven't spent a single Christmas with my little boy? He'll be three next month, and I haven't seen him since he was a baby.' He stared mournfully into his glass.

'You will do soon, I'm sure,' she tried to comfort him.

Harry shook his head. 'Not the way this war's going.' He gave her a twisted smile. 'Listen to me, feeling sorry for myself! How long is it since you saw your boyfriend?'

Now it was Jess's turn to stare into her glass. 'Two years,' she said quietly.

'It doesn't get any easier, does it?'

She shook her head. 'No, it doesn't.'

'Stop feeling sorry for yourselves, you two!' Kit's voice rose. 'I refuse to allow anyone to wallow in self-pity. Life's too bloody short!'

'Especially if *you're* flying the plane,' Max said.

Kit roared with laughter. 'It speaks! I bet you never expected that, did you, Daisy?'

Daisy smiled up at him. 'I like the strong, silent type.'

'I reckon you've found the man of your dreams, in that case,' Kit said.

Harry and Jess glanced at each other. 'Your

friend really has got it bad, hasn't she?' he said.

An hour later they left the pub and spilled out on to the deserted village green.

'Brr, it's cold!' Daisy shivered extravagantly and huddled against Max.

'Here, take this.' He took off his jacket and put it around her shoulders.

'Thank you.' Daisy gave him a tight-lipped smile, but Jess could tell that wasn't quite what she'd had in mind.

'That's not how you keep a lady warm, old chap!' Kit laughed, and immediately wrapped Effie in his arms for a long, passionate kiss.

'Are you cold?' Harry asked Jess. 'I mean, I'm only offering you my jacket, nothing else,' he added hastily.

Jess smiled. 'I'm warm enough, thanks.'

'Are you glad you came in the end?'

She nodded. 'Are you?'

'Very. Maybe we can do it again sometime? Just as pals?'

Jess smiled. 'I'd like that.'

A distant roar filled the sky above them. Max and Harry looked at each other, and Kit dropped Effie like a stone and rushed into the middle of the green to look up at the sky.

'Can you see them?' Harry asked, following him.

'Not from here...' Kit craned his neck. 'Oh, wait ... yes, I can see the first of the stream heading in now ... over there, at two o'clock.'

They all went to join him, their faces tilted up to the inky sky. Jess could just about make out the shifting shapes of planes against the blackness of the sky. A number were approaching, the

125

rumble of their engines growing louder as they came in to land.

She glanced at the three men. Only a few minutes earlier they had been laughing and joking, but now they were all concentrating, their faces upturned, eyes fixed on the aircraft. Jess saw Harry's lips moving, and realised he was counting them as they passed overhead.

They passed over until there was nothing left but a distant drone.

The three men seemed to relax. 'All present and correct,' Kit said, relief in his voice.

The girls said goodnight to the young men, and Effie and Jess headed back to the Nurses' Home. Max gallantly offered to walk Daisy back to her cottage.

'I wish Kit had offered to walk me home!' Effie was disgruntled as they made their way down the lane, their arms linked so they wouldn't lose each other in the blackout.

'It's a four-mile round trip,' Jess reasoned. 'Max only walked Daisy home because she practically lives on their doorstep.'

'That's true, I suppose.' Effie sighed. 'I wish we lived closer to the village. It's miserable having to walk all this way. And I'm so cold!' She pulled her coat tighter round her.

'We won't get there any faster if you keep complaining!' Jess said.

'Your Harry seemed nice,' Effie remarked as they trudged along.

Jess sighed. 'He's not my Harry!'

'You seemed to be getting on like a house on fire.'

'So did you and Kit.'

'Do you think so?' Effie sounded pleased. 'He is grand, isn't he?'

And so it began. Jess listened patiently as Effie went through the evening in fine detail, repeating every single word Kit had uttered, and analysing what it all meant. Did he like her? Was she being too forward? Should she have pushed him away, instead of letting him kiss her like that?

Jess knew better than to join in, or to try to give her advice. Effie wouldn't listen, anyway.

What with the cold, the dark, and Effie droning on and on, the journey seemed to take even longer than usual. It was a relief when they reached the rutted farm track that led to the Nurses' Home. It was almost midnight and the place was locked up and in darkness. Luckily Effie had become an expert in finding her way back in after lights out.

'I asked Freeman to leave the bathroom window open round the back,' she whispered. 'If we climb onto the dustbin we should be able to squeeze in.'

'What bin?' Jess asked. 'There's no bin here.'

'Isn't there? Oh, dear, it must be round the side. Let's go and look.'

They tiptoed around to the side of the building. Jess turned on her torch and slanted the beam downwards, shielding it carefully with her hand so the light could barely be seen. Finally they found the bin, just under their own window.

'Right, let's carry it back round,' Effie instructed in a whisper. 'But careful, mind. We don't want to drop it and make a racket.' She put her arms around it. 'It's too heavy for me. Give

127

me a hand, will you, Jago? Jago...'

But Jess's attention had been caught by something else. The stray beam of her torch had picked out something in the dirt. Something lying white and crumpled, underneath their window.

It was Effie's letter, the one Miss Carrington had given her earlier that evening. And it hadn't been opened.

Chapter Fourteen

Millie's in-laws the Duke and Duchess of Claremont lived at Lyford, a breathtakingly beautiful Georgian house thirty miles to the south-west of Billinghurst, just over the county border.

'No gun turrets, I see,' her grandmother commented, craning her neck to look out of the car window as they entered by the gateway to the estate. 'Claremont is such a wily old fox, I expect he's found a way to avoid this beastly requisitioning business.'

Her meaning was plain, even though she didn't say it out loud. Millie had failed to protect Billinghurst.

But for once she didn't even try to argue. Her grandmother was right, she *had* failed. Thank God Granny didn't know about the damage the RAF had caused. Millie would never hear the last of it if so.

She jammed her foot down on the accelerator pedal in a sudden burst of anger, making the car

128

lurch forward. Lady Rettingham grabbed the edge of her seat dramatically.

'Gracious, Amelia, you're not at Brooklands!' she cried. 'It's bad enough we don't have a chauffeur to drive us any more, without you trying to kill us all.'

'Sorry, Granny.'

They drove up the long avenue of beeches and parked on the broad sweep of gravel in front of the house. Immediately, the door opened and a butler came out, flanked by a pair of footmen.

'I see they still have staff at Lyford,' her grandmother observed stiffly.

'Only because they're too old to be called up.' Millie peered out of the car window. The ancient butler looked decidedly unsteady on his legs, and the footmen weren't much better.

Lady Rettingham sent her a withering look. 'Nevertheless, they are still staff.'

The Duke and Duchess were waiting for them with tea in the library. Their daughter, Millie's old friend Sophia, was with them, heavily pregnant and radiant.

'I watched you coming up the drive,' she said, moving forward to embrace Millie. She smelled divinely of Guerlain perfume. 'My dear, how thrilling that you drove yourself. What an adventure! Don't you think, Mama?'

'Very modern, I'm sure,' the Duchess replied with a tight smile. She was a brittle beauty in her fifties, elegant in a cashmere twinset and tweed skirt.

'And here's little Henry! Goodness, hasn't he grown? And he looks so like...' Sophia stopped, biting her lip to hold back Seb's name.

Millie caught her friend's sorrowful look and quickly said, 'Say hello to your aunt, darling.'

Henry shook his head and buried his face in the folds of Millie's dress. 'He's very shy, I'm afraid,' she said apologetically, ruffling her son's hair.

'I expect he'll come out of his shell with his cousins. Billy and Eliza are simply dying to see him.' Sophia turned to Nanny Perks, who was waiting by the door. 'Take Henry up to the nursery, would you? Wright will show you the way.'

Millie watched Henry go, his hand trustingly in Nanny Perks's. He had forgiven his mother for her outburst of temper that morning, but she still hadn't forgiven herself.

'I can't tell you how pleased I am to see you,' Sophia said, taking Millie's arm and leading her to the window seat. 'I've been so looking forward to this weekend.'

'Me too.' Millie hoped her friend wouldn't hear the lack of enthusiasm in her voice. Coming to Lyford was always a strain for her, bringing back painful memories of happier days there with Seb.

And if she was honest, it was difficult to see Sophia, too. Happily married with two beautiful children and another on the way, she was living the life Millie had had until Seb was taken from her. She didn't begrudge Sophia her happiness, but it was difficult not to envy her.

Millie pulled herself together. It wasn't Sophia's fault that Seb was dead. She shouldn't forget her friend had lost a very dear brother, too. And Sophia's own husband David was a captain in the Guards, so she had to live with daily anxiety herself.

The butler served them tea, and Millie asked Sophia about her pregnancy. 'It can't be too long now, surely?'

Sophia groaned. 'Another two months. But honestly, it feels as if I've been pregnant for ever!' She laid her hand across her swollen belly. 'There was something I wanted to ask you actually. David and I have decided, if it's another boy we'd like to call him Sebastian. Would that be all right?' She eyed her sister-in-law anxiously.

Millie smiled. 'I think that would be wonderful,' she said.

'Are you sure? I don't want to upset you—'

'I'd be honoured. And I'm sure Seb would be, too.'

'I'm glad.' Sophia looked relieved. 'Do you remember, we named Billy after your friend – you know, that doctor you worked with, William – what was it?'

'Tremayne,' Millie stared into her teacup.

'Yes, that was it. Dr Tremayne. Gosh, he was a hero, wasn't he? Dashing in to deliver Billy when I suddenly went into labour at that party. And you helped too, of course,' she added. 'Honestly, I can't imagine there was ever a birth like it. Thank God for Dr Tremayne, stepping in to rescue me.' Sophia smiled at the memory. 'I wonder where he is now?'

Millie was about to tell her, then changed her mind. The last person she wanted to discuss at that moment was William Tremayne.

On the far side of the room, the Duke was holding forth to Lady Rettingham.

131

'Yes, well, I had a word with some pals in the War Office, got them to agree to letting me store the contents of a couple of museums here,' he was saying. 'Quite a good show, isn't it? I look after a few Rembrandts and whatnot, and we don't have any unwanted house guests.'

Millie couldn't bring herself to glance at her grandmother. She could only imagine the look on her face.

'By the way, I forgot to tell you,' Sophia said, distracting her. 'Guess who'll be joining us for the weekend?'

Millie risked a glance at her grandmother. She was looking at the Duke, an expression of utter loathing on her face. 'Who?'

'Teddy Teasdale!'

Millie forgot her grandmother instantly. 'Teddy Teasdale? But I thought he was in the army?'

'He is, but he has an office job. Not far from here actually. He's doing something frightfully clever with the Intelligence Corps. Well, he always was rather a brain, wasn't he?'

'Was he? I don't remember that.' Millie's most vivid memory of Lord Edward Teasdale was of him riding one of his father's prize hunters down the staircase at Teasdale Hall during a particularly rowdy house party. He was utterly, adorably feckless, and one of her dearest friends. But they had lost touch over the past year or so.

'And that's not all.' Sophia leaned in confidingly. 'I haven't told you the most delicious bit of gossip yet. He's coming with Georgina Farsley!'

'No!' Millie's mouth fell open. 'Surely she hasn't got her hands on him now?'

'It seems so,' Sophia said. 'Just think, Teddy and that ghastly American girl! She's after his title, obviously. You know what a dreadful social climber she is. But the question is, what's he doing with her?'

'Perhaps he's in love?' Millie said.

'More like in debt!' Sophia laughed. 'Anyway, I'm surprised you're so calm at the prospect of seeing her again. Have you forgotten how appallingly she used to treat you when we were debs together?'

'Of course I haven't forgotten. But perhaps time has mellowed her?'

'I very much doubt it.'

'Anyway, it's all in the past,' Millie said. 'I'm prepared to let bygones be bygones.'

Sophia laughed. 'You won't be saying that by the time this weekend is over!'

'I'm sure she's changed,' Millie said.

She was proved wrong the minute Georgina swept in, dark and glamorous in a daring Schiaparelli trouser suit. She greeted the Duke and Duchess and the other guests, but ignored Millie entirely.

'Not ready to let bygones be bygones, then?' Sophia breathed in Millie's ear.

'Apparently not.'

'She looks beautiful. I hate her already.'

'But where's Teddy?' Millie asked.

He, as they overheard Georgina telling their hosts, had been delayed on important war business. She was tight-lipped as she said it, and Millie had the feeling that so far as she was concerned, no war was more important than being at her side.

'I bet they've had the most furious row,' Sophia whispered to Millie as they sat down for dinner that evening. 'This should be very entertaining!'

They were going in to dinner when Teddy finally turned up.

'I'm so sorry, everyone,' he said. 'A couple of Germans got washed up with the tide at Whitstable, and I had to have a quick chat with them.'

He greeted the Duchess, Millie and the other guests, but when he went to kiss Georgina she turned her face sharply to present him with her cheek. Millie caught Sophia's eye across the table.

There was a place set for Teddy beside Millie. She glanced at him sideways as he took his seat. He looked different, she thought. Two years in the army had transformed his soft, overindulged body to lean muscle. His light brown hair was cropped close to his head, revealing a surprisingly good bone structure. She could see why Georgina was attracted to him, and it wasn't just for his title.

'Oh, dear,' he said as he sat down. 'I rather think I may be in the dog house.'

'Quite right too. It was unforgivable of you to abandon poor Georgina like that.'

'I couldn't help it, could I? I could hardly tell the coastguard to send the Germans off for another trip around the bay.'

He looked up the table towards Georgina. She was staring rather hard at her plate.

'Well, I think she's going to sulk for the rest of the evening, so I might as well talk to you,' he said with a touch of defiance. 'How are you, Millie?'

'Very well, thank you.'

'And the baby? Henry, isn't it? How is he?'

Millie blinked in surprise. She was impressed Teddy had remembered her son's name. From what she recalled, he often had trouble remembering his own. 'Not such a baby any more.' She smiled fondly. 'He's three years old now.'

'Good heavens, really? Time does fly, doesn't it?' Teddy lowered his voice. 'I was so sorry to hear about Seb, by the way. I wanted to come back for the funeral, but I was stuck in France with the Intelligence Corps and it was rather difficult to get away.'

Millie was silent for a moment. She never quite knew what to say when people talked about Seb's death. No response seemed appropriate somehow.

She changed the subject. 'On second thoughts, I think perhaps we should stop speaking for a while,' she said lightly. 'I don't think your girlfriend likes it.' Georgina was throwing her looks like knives down the length of the table.

'In that case, I think we should flirt wildly,' Teddy said, glaring back at Georgina. 'She's got to learn I'm not her pet dog.'

'I don't think it's all your fault,' Millie said. 'She's never forgiven me for marrying Seb when she had her eye on him.'

'Georgina Farsley has had her eye on every eligible bachelor in England at some point,' Teddy said.

Millie was shocked. 'What an ungallant thing to say!'

'It's true, isn't it? She's so desperate for a title, it was only a matter of time before she got round to me.'

Millie looked from one to the other. There was definitely something going on between them, and she didn't want to get involved with it. She turned to her other side and started talking to her neighbour, an elderly magistrate with a hearing problem. It was frustrating, having to shout at him constantly, but at least it stopped Georgina scowling at her.

The following morning neither Georgina nor Teddy surfaced until after luncheon. But when they did finally appear, things were still frosty between them.

The Duke and Duchess had organised a shooting party, but Millie disliked shooting and Sophia cried off because of her pregnancy. She retired to her room for a nap, leaving Millie and her grandmother to entertain themselves in the drawing room.

'Thank heavens everyone has gone,' Lady Rettingham sighed. 'I know house parties are supposed to be entertaining, but the constant presence of other people can be rather wearing.'

'I think I might go up to the nursery to see Henry,' Millie said.

Her grandmother stared at her blankly. 'Whatever for? I'm sure Nanny Perks is looking after him perfectly well.'

'Yes, but I want to see him.'

'Nanny won't appreciate it.'

I don't care what Nanny thinks. Millie opened her mouth to argue when Teddy suddenly appeared.

'Oh, I'm sorry,' he said. 'I didn't realise this room was occupied.'

136

'It's perfectly all right, Edward. Do join us.' Lady Rettingham was suddenly animated, her earlier fatigue forgotten. 'Amelia and I were just about to have some tea. Weren't we, Amelia?'

'Were we?' Millie stared at her grandmother.

'Thank you.' Teddy flopped into the armchair opposite them.

'I thought you'd gone shooting with the others?' Millie said.

He shook his head. 'To be honest, I don't trust Georgina around me when she has a gun in her hands.'

Millie laughed. 'Haven't you two kissed and made up yet?'

'I would say the chances of a reconciliation are almost nil.'

'Oh, dear, I'm sorry to hear that.'

'Are you? I'm not.'

Out of the corner of her eye, Millie saw her grandmother rise from her chair. 'If you'll excuse me for a moment,' she said, 'I thought I might go and visit my grandson in the nursery.'

Subtlety wasn't her grandmother's strong suit, Millie decided, as she watched her slip from the room. But fortunately Teddy didn't seem to notice.

Millie turned her attention back to him. 'Surely she hasn't given up on you just because you were late yesterday?'

'Oh, no, we've been on the rocks for a long time. Yesterday was simply the straw that broke the proverbial camel's back.' He sighed. 'I wish all girls were as uncomplicated as you, Mil.'

She laughed. 'What an insult! Edward Teasdale,

am I so desperately uninteresting?'

'I didn't say you were uninteresting, I said you were uncomplicated. The most uncomplicated and delightful girl I've ever met. Which is probably why I've never fallen in love with you.'

Her grandmother would be so disappointed, Millie thought wryly.

'That's the trouble, you see,' Teddy continued. 'I only ever fall in love with complicated women. Either they're too old, or too young, or too mad or too married.'

'Which is Georgina?'

'Oh, she's none of those. But she's very rich, and my parents have told me that I have to marry before I'm thirty or they'll cut me off without a penny.'

'They can't do that!' Millie said. 'You're their son and heir.'

Teddy shook his head. 'You don't know how desperate they are to see me married. I've played the field for too long, as far as they're concerned. Now I have to do the decent thing in the next year, or face the consequences.'

'Poor you,' Millie sympathised. 'But I know the feeling. My grandmother is keen for me to marry again.'

His brows rose. 'But you've done your bit, haven't you? Produced an heir?'

'Yes, but my grandmother doesn't think I should be alone for the rest of my life.'

'She's got a point,' Teddy said. Then a thought occurred to him. 'I say, you don't think we...'

'No, Teddy!' Millie cut him off firmly. 'Definitely not. I'm not your type, remember?'

'I suppose not,' he sighed.

'Anyway, don't even hint about it in front of my grandmother,' she warned him. 'I don't want her getting ideas about us.'

'I hate to tell you this, Millie, but you're too late.' Teddy grinned. 'She already asked me last night if I would like to call on you after Christmas.'

'She didn't?' Millie's shoulders slumped. 'Oh, dear. She could have asked me first.'

But what was the point of that? she thought. Even if her grandmother had asked, she would never have listened to Millie's answer.

'Should I make an excuse not to come?' Teddy asked, watching her anxiously. 'I can, you know, if it will make things awkward?'

'Oh, no, you might as well come,' Millie shrugged. 'But don't bring Georgina, will you?'

Millie spent the rest of Sunday avoiding being alone with Teddy. Between her grandmother's speculative looks and not so subtle attempts to push them together, and Georgina's furious accusing stares, it was a relief when Monday morning came and they could return to Billinghurst.

But as Millie approached the house, the feelings of anger and humiliation that she had left behind on Saturday came flooding back.

As they passed the men in the makeshift guard house, her grandmother sighed heavily and said, 'Well, here we are again. I must say, I'm rather sorry to be back.'

Me too, Millie thought. She wasn't sorry to have left Lyford, but Billinghurst didn't feel like her home any more. It had been taken over by strangers and she was no longer welcome there.

She stopped the car at the Lodge to allow her grandmother, Henry and Nanny Perks to get out, then drove it up to the house and parked in the stable block.

As she was heading back down the drive, she heard someone calling her name. She turned to see William running down the steps of the house towards her.

'I've been watching out for you at the window.' He smiled at her. 'I'm sorry I didn't have a chance to say goodbye before you left.'

Are you? Millie thought. She could hardly bring herself to look into his face, she was so mortified. All she could remember was Agnes Moss's sneering tone.

It's William I feel sorry for... She's obviously got a thing for him... It's embarrassing.

'Did you have a good time?' William asked.

'Yes, thank you.' She started to walk away, but he called out to her again.

'Millie? Is something wrong?'

She swung back to face him. There was so much she wanted to say, but she couldn't find the words. Instead all her frustration crystallised on the one thing she could say.

'Your men have vandalised the ornamental fountain.'

He looked taken aback. 'I beg your pardon?'

'They've carved their initials in the stone. It's ruined.'

'Ah.'

There was something about the way he said it. 'You knew!' Millie accused.

'Yes, I'd noticed. I meant to talk to you...'

'How could you?' she cut him off. 'How could you let them do it?'

'I can explain–'

'I trusted you. I welcomed you into my home and this – this is how you repay me!'

'Millie, please.' He spoke quietly, but there was something about the firm way he said it that silenced her. 'You're right, I did notice what had happened to the fountain, and I was going to talk to you about it. It's become a bit of a tradition, you see. When one of the men doesn't come home, the others carve his initials in the stone and the date so they can remember him. It's supposed to be a mark of respect, not vandalism.'

'I–' Millie opened her mouth to speak, then closed it again.

'But I do understand how you feel,' William went on. 'I promise I'll tell the men to stop doing it. And I'll get someone from the Works Squadron to come and replace the stonework.'

No, she wanted to say. Just leave it. I'm sorry. But instead the words that came out were, 'See that you do.'

She started to walk off. She heard William call out her name again, but she ignored him, trying to put as much distance between herself and her scalding embarrassment as possible.

She'd done it again. Stupid, stupid Millie, getting everything wrong...

There was a commotion coming from the Lodge. As she drew closer, Millie could hear Henry's voice, shrieking in excitement, and Nanny Perks's stern tones as she tried to calm him down.

'What's going on?' she called out as she opened the door. Henry escaped Nanny Perks's clutches and rushed to greet her. 'Mama, look! Look!'

He dragged her into the sitting room. 'Careful, darling,' Millie laughed, 'you'll pull me over...'

She stopped dead. There, in the corner of the sitting room, was the biggest and most beautiful Christmas tree she had ever seen, its branches weighed down by baubles and decorations. It was so tall it scraped the ceiling, filling the drawing room with the fresh scent of pine needles.

Millie stared at it. 'Where did it come from?'

'The airmen brought it, Your Ladyship,' the maid told her quietly. 'Squadron Leader Tremayne said they wanted to do it, to thank you for being so kind and welcoming to them.'

Henry swung from her hand, unable to stay still in his excitement. 'It's magic, isn't it, Mama?'

'Yes, darling. It is magic.' Millie smiled at him automatically, but her thoughts were elsewhere.

Stupid, stupid Millie had got it wrong again.

Chapter Fifteen

Jess heard the children screaming in the darkness, long before she reached the ward.

The Fever Wards were situated on the far side of the hospital, beyond the other outbuildings, so far from the main building they might as well have been in the next village.

Jess had been put on the children's whooping

cough ward. She had got used to her solitary life; snatching a few hours' sleep at the Nurses' Home if the circling planes overhead and Home Sister's strict housekeeping routine allowed, then tramping the two miles to the hospital along blacked-out country lanes. Occasionally Sulley might give her a lift in his horse and cart, if he was feeling charitable.

Once or twice she had managed to snatch a few hours with her friends, if one of them had the morning or afternoon off duty. They had even been to the pictures in Tunbridge Wells with Kit, Max and Harry. But most of the time, Jess lived in a twilight world of poorly children.

And they were all desperately poorly. For the whole of her twelve-hour shift Jess had to cope alone with twenty sick children, none of whom slept for more than an hour at a time. As she hurried from bed to bed, comforting them, cleaning up vomit and changing wet and dirty beds, she lived in fear of one of them convulsing or choking during a severe bout of whooping.

Each night was an endless vigil of loneliness and anxiety, ending with exhaustion and a pile of stained linen to rinse for the laundry.

Not surprisingly, the day nurse looked at the end of her tether as she handed over to Jess.

'We had a new one in today, a baby,' she said. 'Whooping cough and gastro-enteritis. He needs to be barrier nursed, so I've hung up an overall for you by the bed. Be really careful, won't you? The last thing we need is for the rest of them to get infected.'

'I will,' Jess promised.

143

'Dr Drake said he'll check on him in a couple of hours, but of course you know to telephone him at any time if you're worried. I have to say, I'm not sure the poor little mite will last the night.' She spoke in a flat, matter-of-fact way. They lost too many children on the Fever Wards to allow themselves to mourn them. 'You're supposed to be sharing a runner tonight, but I haven't seen her yet so I expect one of the other wards has already nabbed her. Do telephone the Night Sister if you need any help, won't you?'

Much good it will do me, Jess thought. The Night Sister would just tell her to get on with it, as usual. Miss Tanner did her best to help, but she couldn't magic spare nurses out of thin air.

After the day nurse had gone off duty, Jess went round all the beds, checking on everyone, cleaning up vomit and changing beds while all around her children screamed and retched and made the terrifying whooping sound that seemed to turn their little bodies inside out.

Then she went to attend to the baby, remembering to put on the overall and cap that hung beside his cot. She did it carefully, pushing her arm through one sleeve then the other, fastening the button and tying the tape around her waist.

The baby's name was Stephen Cope. He was a tiny, feverish little thing, clammy with perspiration. Strands of fine hair clung damply to his scalp. Jess checked him over and gave him a few drops of boiled, cooled water from a sterilised pipette.

She was changing his nappy when the runner appeared. She was a pro, a local girl called Julie Todd.

'Ugh, that looks nasty.' She flinched from the livid green contents of the nappy.

'It is.'

'Poor lamb.' Julie peered past Jess's shoulder at the baby in the cot. 'Will he do, do you think?'

'The day staff nurse didn't seem to think so, but you never know.' Jess hoped he would. Losing a baby was awful enough, but it was particularly cruel so close to Christmas. She could only imagine what Stephen's poor parents must be going through, ragged with worry for their little boy.

Julie took the soiled nappy out to the incinerator, but she didn't come back. Runners were in short supply, and Julie had either been nabbed by another ward or she had dallied by the Furnace Room for a sneaky cigarette. Being warm and isolated made it a popular spot for exhausted night nurses.

Either way, her absence irritated Jess as she rushed around, trying to deal with all the children's needs at once. A three-year-old girl struggling to breathe who needed a steam tent. A frightened eight-year-old evacuee who woke up in tears after a nightmare. All his friends had gone back to London for Christmas, but his mum hadn't sent for him. Now he was terrified that the bombs had got her or, that she had forgotten about him.

Jess did her best to console him, all the while aware that at the other end of the ward at least two more children were coughing themselves sick.

And then baby Stephen started screaming.

He was in a terrible state by the time Jess reached his cot, feverish and almost black in the face. As Jess went to put on her overall and gown, he suddenly started to convulse violently, his tiny body jerking and twisting like a puppet.

For a moment she froze, utterly terrified. Then, forgetting her cap and gown, she scooped Stephen up into her arms and ran with him to the sluice.

She could hear the other children screaming out for her but she was deaf to them as she filled a sink with cold water and immersed the baby in it as gently as possible. She had never done it before, it was something she'd only heard about in lectures while she was training. She wasn't even sure it would work, or if the shock of the cold water would kill him. But if it didn't, she knew the convulsions would.

She closed her eyes, praying fervently, until she felt the twitching and jerking stop. Stephen went very still in her arms. Jess hardly dared to open her eyes, terrified that the poor little mite would be dead.

But, thank God, he was staring up at her with his bright little button eyes. Jess took him out of the water and undressed him quickly, put him in a clean nappy and laid him back in his cot. Then she telephoned to let Dr Drake know what had happened.

She put the telephone receiver down and slumped back in Sister's chair. It was just turned midnight, and she felt as if she'd already lived through a lifetime.

Dr Drake arrived on the ward five minutes later.

'How is the child?' For once Jess was so thankful to see him she didn't mind his abrupt manner.

'He's a lot better, Doctor. His temperature is

still high, but not dangerously so. And he's taken some more water.'

She waited tensely while Dr Drake examined the baby. 'And he was convulsing, you say?'

'Yes, Doctor. I tried to cool him down as best I could. It seemed to work.'

She didn't mention what had happened afterwards, how she had sat in the darkness at Sister's desk and cried quietly with relief.

'Indeed. Indeed,' Dr Drake muttered. For the first time he looked properly at Jess, and she felt herself pinned by a pair of sharply intelligent eyes. 'How did you know what to do?' he asked.

'I only did what any other nurse would do, sir.'

'Hmm.' He went on staring at her for a long time, until Jess started to feel uncomfortable. Then he looked away and scribbled a few lines on the baby's notes. 'Well, he seems to be doing well at the moment,' he said, hanging up the chart on the end of the cot. 'Telephone me immediately if there is another crisis.'

'Yes, Doctor.'

As he took off his overall, he said quietly, 'Well done, Nurse.'

'Thank you, sir.'

He went to walk away, then stopped. 'By the way,' he said. 'I thought you should know, I arranged for Mrs Briggs on Female Medical to be transferred back to London today.'

Jess blinked at him. 'Thank you, sir,' was all she managed to say.

She watched him as he strode off down the ward, letting the doors swing shut behind him without looking back. Had she really just had a few kind words from Dr Drake? Effie and Daisy would never believe it, she decided.

She was right, Daisy didn't believe it.

'You're making it up,' she declared, when Jess met her the following afternoon. They were going to a WVS sale of work in the village hall where Daisy was hoping to find some Christmas presents for her family.

'I'm telling you, it happened.'

'You mean to say Dr Drake was actually nice to someone?' Daisy grinned. 'You don't think it was that mistletoe giving him ideas, do you?'

'Don't!' Jess still blushed to think about it.

The village hall was set out with long tables, each neatly arranged with all kinds of items for sale. There were peg dollies and teddies made from fabric scraps, home-made cakes, Christmas puddings and jars of jam, knitted scarves, gloves and hats, as well as all kinds of second-hand toys and clothes.

Jess spotted Miss Pomfrey, her varicose veins now on the mend, sitting behind a long table laden with her precious embroidered tray cloths and antimacassars.

Mrs Huntley-Osborne moved briskly amongst them, exhorting everyone to buy.

'It's all in a good cause,' she boomed. 'All proceeds to the Prisoners-of-War Fund.'

'I could do with some mistletoe, to give Max some ideas,' Daisy said, examining a painted wooden car. 'He's so shy, it's all I can do to get him to hold my hand!'

'You should take it as a good sign, that he

148

respects you,' Jess said. 'It's better for a man to be a bit reserved than out for what he can get.'

'I suppose so,' Daisy said but she still looked wistful. 'I just wish he was a bit more keen. You know, like Effie's Kit?'

He's a bit too keen, if you ask me, Jess thought. Going to the pictures in Tunbridge Wells, she had sat chastely in the front of the stalls with Harry, Daisy and Max, while Effie and Kit wrestled in the back row. Jess was worried that her friend was getting into a situation she might not be able to control. But as usual when Effie was in love, there was no telling her anything.

'Anyway, I've invited him to spend Christmas Day with us, so hopefully that will give him a bit of a push,' Daisy said.

Jess sent her a sideways look. 'What does your sister say about having an extra mouth to feed at Christmas?'

'Oh, I haven't told her yet – but I expect she'll be all right about it,' Daisy replied airily. 'Grace never makes a fuss about anything. What do you think about a jigsaw puzzle for my brother? On second thoughts, he probably wouldn't sit still long enough to do it!' she answered her own question.

In the end, Daisy bought a bow and arrow for her brother, and a knitted doll for her younger sister.

'Now I've got to find something for Grace,' she said, sorting through a pile of second-hand clothes.

'How about some scented soap?' Jess suggested.

Daisy shook her head. 'Grace doesn't like anything fancy. How about this?' She held up a knitted scarf in a dull brown colour.

'It's very – practical,' Jess said tactfully.

'It's perfect for her.' Daisy was searching in her purse for the money when there was a commotion behind them.

'I'm telling you, I was going to pay for it!'

'What the–?' Jess looked around to see a heavily pregnant, red-haired girl arguing with one of the WVS helpers. She was holding a baby's knitted matinee jacket.

Daisy nudged Jess. 'Oh, dear, there's going to be trouble now,' she said, a hint of glee in her voice.

'Who is she?' Jess asked.

'Her name's Sarah Newland. She used to be Mrs Huntley-Osborne's maid, until–' She nodded towards the girl's swollen belly. 'Mrs Huntley-Osborne gave Sarah her cards and told her never to darken her door again.'

The woman behind the table snatched the matinee jacket from the girl's hands. 'Clear off! We don't want any trouble from you,' she snapped.

'I haven't come to make trouble, I just wanted to buy some baby clothes.'

'Well, they're not for sale to the likes of you. These are for respectable mothers.'

'I am respectable!'

The woman sneered. 'You don't know the meaning of the word, Sarah Newland! Now be on your way.'

The girl looked near to tears but utterly defiant. 'You can throw me out, but you can't make me leave this village,' she declared. 'I'm staying whether you like it or not.'

She directed her comment to Mrs Huntley-

Osborne, who was standing as rigid as a statue, watching the scene.

As the girl turned to leave, Jess hurried over.

'How much for the jacket?' she asked the woman behind the table.

'Sixpence, but...'

Before the woman knew what was happening, Jess thrust a coin into her hand and snatched up the jacket. Then she turned and offered it to Sarah.

'Go on, take it,' she said. 'It's for you.'

Sarah Newland looked warily from the tiny knitted jacket to Jess's face and back again.

'No, thanks,' she spat out. 'I don't want anyone's charity.'

Then she turned on her heel and walked out, her head held proudly high.

Daisy came up behind Jess as she stood, frozen with shock. 'I wouldn't get involved, if I were you.' She took her friend's arm to steer her away. As Jess went to follow her, the knitted jacket still in her hand, she glanced up and caught Mrs Huntley-Osborne's eye. She was staring straight back.

Chapter Sixteen

It felt strange to be in a hospital again.

Breathing in the disinfectant-scented air, Millie was transported to her training days. Except now she was no longer a pro trying to escape the eagle eye of the ward sister. She was the lady of the manor, come to dispense some festive cheer to the patients at the behest of the Hospital Fund-Raising Committee.

Even so, when she saw Matron waiting for her with the rest of the committee members, it was all Millie could do not to stand to attention.

Matron stepped forward to greet her but Mrs Huntley-Osborne got there first. 'Lady Amelia, how wonderful to see you,' she took charge of the situation, almost elbowing Miss Jenkins out of the way in her rush.

'I'm so thankful that you have given up your Christmas Eve to visit *my* hospital,' Miss Jenkins joined in, with a pointed look sideways at her friend.

'If you'll come this way...' Mrs Huntley-Osborne stepped neatly in front of her.

'After you, Mrs Huntley-Osborne.' Matron smiled through clenched teeth.

It was comical to watch the pair of them jockeying for position as they led the way down the corridors. At any moment, Millie expected their ample backsides to become wedged in the double doors as they tried to pass through at the same time.

They visited each ward in turn so Millie could hand out gifts. Each ward was bright and cheerful, decorated with a Christmas tree and paper chains looped across the high ceilings. As they entered each ward, the sister in charge would be waiting to greet them. Millie recognised some faces from her days at the Nightingale. And judging from the puzzled looks several of the ward sisters gave her, they knew her, too. She could almost see the consternation on their faces as they tried to place where they had met Lady Amelia Rushton before. It made her smile to think what they would say if they knew she was the same Nurse Millie Benedict who had often featured so unfavourably in their ward reports.

'It seems very busy,' she commented to Matron. 'I would have expected most of the patients to go home for Christmas, yet you seem to have extra beds in every ward?'

'I'm afraid we are rather overcrowded,' Matron agreed. 'It generally happens during the winter months, when we're overrun with bronchial complaints. But we've also had to turn two of our wards over to military patients. And we have to find room for all the patients they keep sending down from London. As if we didn't have enough sick people down here.' She heaved a sigh.

'I'm sure it must be in the patients' best interests to send them?'

'I daresay it is.' Miss Jenkins sniffed. 'But I must say, Lady Amelia, between you and me, I don't like it one bit. Of course I didn't object when I was told that the Nightingale was moving down here. I had hoped their Matron and I could work together. But she has completely taken over in a most unwelcome manner.'

'Our delightful hospital has been quite overrun with sick people from London, bringing their nasty diseases with them,' Mrs Pomfrey put in.

'And the London nurses leave a great deal to be desired,' Matron finished. 'Honestly, I don't believe I've ever met such a shabby, ill-disciplined group of young women as those Nightingale nurses.'

'Really?' Millie said. 'How interesting.'

The Nightingale nurses certainly didn't seem shabby or ill-disciplined to her as they moved around the wards purposefully in their familiar blue uniforms, going back and forth with trolleys and trays, plumping pillows, straightening bedclothes and consoling the patients. It made Millie long for the days when she had been one of them, giggling and gossiping with her friends in the sluice when Sister wasn't looking.

On the Military Ward, Millie was pleased to see another familiar face. She remembered Miss Wallace, the ward sister, from her days in training. She had always been the most delightful of the sisters, friendly and caring to even the humblest of pros.

Miss Wallace seemed just as pleased to see her. 'Why, Nurse Benedict,' she greeted her, a wide smile lighting up her face. 'Have you come to work?'

'Unfortunately not, Sister.'

'That's a pity. We could do with some more good nurses here.' She flicked the slightest of glances in Matron's direction.

'I'm not sure how good I was,' Millie said ruefully.

Matron broke in, looking puzzled. 'I didn't know you were a nurse, your ladyship?'

Millie smiled at Miss Wallace. 'Oh, yes,' she said. 'As a matter of fact, I trained at the Nightingale.'

She didn't want to look at Miss Jenkins's face,

but she was sure it was a picture.

Matron was rendered speechless for the rest of their tour. Afterwards, when Millie joined the other trustees for tea, Matron excused herself from the festivities. Millie thought she might have offended her with her jibe about the Nightingale, until Miss Jenkins explained that she had to go and rehearse for the Christmas show.

'Oh, the Christmas show!' Mrs Huntley-Osborne trilled. 'What fun! I must say, I am looking forward to it this year. Tell me, Matron, will you be performing another of your memorable arias?'

'I will indeed,' Miss Jenkins beamed. '"Let The Bright Seraphim", if all goes well.'

But Millie was hardly listening. The Christmas show. Just those three words brought all kinds of wonderful memories rushing back, of scurrilous songs and sketches composed in bedrooms, rehearsals that left them aching with laughter and poor Miss Wallace trying to keep control of it all. 'You're putting on a Christmas show?' she said.

'Well, I'd hardly call it a show,' Matron dismissed. 'Just some of the doctors and nurses performing for the patients. Most of it is rather juvenile, actually, but some of us try to raise the tone if we can.'

'Why don't you stay and watch it?' Mrs Huntley-Osborne enquired. 'It's hardly Glyndebourne,' she added, ignoring a glare from Miss Jenkins, 'but I'm sure our performers would be delighted to have such a distinguished audience. Isn't that right, Matron?'

'Quite right, Mrs Huntley-Osborne,' Miss Jenkins replied through gritted teeth.

Millie was just about to refuse, but then she stopped herself. Could there be any harm in stepping away from her duties and reliving the old days, just once?

'I'd love to,' she said.

William saw Millie straight away, sitting in the front row of the audience beside a large woman in a tweed coat. Before them a makeshift stage had been set up, with a lopsided curtain draped across it.

He fixed his gaze on the back of her blonde head as he and the other men took their seats at the back of the dining room. Even from the other end of the room, he could see her back and neck were rigid with tension. Did she ever relax, he wondered.

The last time they had seen each other was three days ago, when they'd had that stand-off over the wretched fountain. He'd waited to see her again, but all he'd had was a chilly little note the following morning, thanking him for the Christmas tree and informing him that no further action should be taken over the ornamental fountain. The men could go on carving into the stonework if they wished.

At least she still had a heart somewhere inside that frozen exterior, William thought. After their last meeting, he had begun to doubt it.

He was disappointed that he hadn't been there to see her face when she saw the Christmas tree for the first time, though. He had so wanted to see her smile again.

Or perhaps he'd just wanted to see her, full stop.

'So what is it we're watching, Tremayne?' the flying officer beside him interrupted his thoughts.

'Oh, it's just a piece of nonsense the hospital puts on every year,' he said. 'Songs, sketches, a few monologues, you know. The main point is to poke fun at your superiors, take revenge for everything you've suffered over the past year.'

He'd always enjoyed his involvement in the show, even though he generally got into serious trouble with his consultant afterwards.

'Will there be pretty nurses?' another officer asked. 'I'll sit through anything so long as there are pretty nurses.'

'You've already got a pretty nurse!' someone reminded him.

'More than one, from what I hear!' another joined in.

'It doesn't hurt to look though, does it?' the officer said. 'Look but don't touch. Isn't that right, Squadron Leader?'

'Quite right, Phillips.' William's gaze sought out Millie's blonde head again, sitting in front of him. 'Look but don't touch, that's the motto.'

Millie was certainly untouchable these days. He'd thought as time went on she might start to thaw slightly, to become more like her old self. He had looked forward to her visits, watching her as she sat in his office or as they walked the grounds together, waiting for a smile or a look, something to tell him that she was still the Millie he had remembered. But as fast as she'd started to come out of her shell, she had suddenly withdrawn again. The shutters had come back down, and he finally had to admit that the Millie he'd known,

157

the girl he had once adored, was gone for ever.

Of course he couldn't blame her. The poor girl had been through so much, he wasn't surprised she'd toughened up, developed a hard shell to cope with it all. But all the same, he couldn't help missing her.

The lights dimmed, and the show began, and all around him the men began whooping and clapping. Millie glanced around and William hunkered down in his seat so she wouldn't see him.

The show was all exactly as he had expected. Lots of cobbled-together sketches and monologues, well-known tunes with new lyrics about different aspects of hospital life, poking fun at various characters. The London nurses did a very funny song about life in the country, with lots of references to a particularly bad-tempered black and white cow. Having seen the matron deliver a trembling aria, a fearsome sight in her black and white uniform, William had no doubt who they were singing about.

Meanwhile, the airmen around him seemed to be making their own entertainment, guffawing with laughter every time someone forgot their words or a piece of scenery fell down. And whenever a particularly attractive nurse appeared on the makeshift stage, the catcalls were deafening.

But William barely noticed what was happening on-stage. His attention was fixed on Millie. She was laughing, he noticed. All the tension had left her and she was throwing herself into the show, clapping and singing along with the rest of the audience. Seeing her, William felt a stirring of attraction to the girl he had once known. This was Millie as he remembered her, carefree and happy, her face suffused with so much joy it was as if she was lit from within.

After the show, he left the rest of the men and fought his way towards her as she was leaving.

He thought he'd lost her in the crowd, until he spotted her by the doors. She was saying goodbye to the woman in the tweed coat.

She turned to leave and he called out to her. 'Millie?'

She looked over her shoulder at him, and her smile disappeared like the sun behind a cloud. Her eyes darted to the doors, then back to him.

'William,' she greeted him warily. 'What are you doing here?'

'We were invited to see the show.' Why did he suddenly feel like a tongue-tied schoolboy? he wondered. 'I got your note,' he said.

A delicate blush coloured her cheeks. 'Thank you for the tree,' she said. 'It was very thoughtful.'

'I thought you and Henry might like it. The men wanted to do something to thank you. You've been so helpful and accommodating to us.'

He saw her expression change and wondered how he'd managed to say the wrong thing again.

'May I give you a lift?' he offered.

'No, thank you. I have my car outside.'

'A drink, then?' He knew he sounded desperate, but he didn't care.

Panic filled her eyes. 'I have to go home,' she muttered. 'It's Christmas Eve, Henry will be waiting for me...'

As she pushed open the door, William blurted

159

out, 'Have I done something wrong?'

She glanced back at him, but said nothing.

'I might be imagining it, but you seem rather distant,' William went on, stumbling over his words. 'I wondered if I'd offended you in some way. That fountain business, perhaps? Because if it is...'

'It isn't,' Millie said shortly. 'I've told you, I don't want the fountain replaced.'

She paused for a while and William waited for her to speak again. They stood like two stones in a stream, with the rest of the world flowing around them.

'It has come to my attention,' she said finally, 'that I may have been rather – over enthusiastic of late.'

'I don't understand. What do you mean?'

Millie stared at the ground, and he could see it was difficult for her to speak. 'I spend far too much time at the house,' she said.

'It's your house.'

'That's the point. It isn't my house any more.' She looked up at him. 'I should have left you to it, and not got involved so much. But I just wanted to do my bit, you see. To be useful for once...'

He saw the vulnerability in her blue eyes, and felt himself melt.

'Can we have that drink? Please?' he said.

It was early evening, and the Keeper's Rest had just opened its doors so it was very quiet, save for the landlady polishing glasses behind the bar and a couple of diehard regulars who supped their pints in the corner.

Millie looked up at William as he put her drink in front of her. 'What's this?'

'Port and lemon,' he said. 'Don't you remember?'

'The first drink you ever bought for me.' The faintest trace of a smile touched her lips. 'Gosh, I was so naïve in those days, I'd never even been into a pub before. I had no idea what to drink.'

'You soon got a taste for these, as I recall. You drank so much, I practically had to carry you back to the hospital.'

They were both silent for a moment, and William could tell they were sharing the same memory. He had almost kissed her that day. She had asked him to, but he'd turned her down because he didn't want to take advantage. He'd cursed himself for it afterwards, of course. Why hadn't he kissed her while he had the chance?

His gaze dropped to her soft pink lips. He'd kissed many girls since then, but she was the one he remembered.

The girl who got away.

Millie sat upright, suddenly brisk and business-like again. 'Hopefully that won't happen this evening,' she said stiffly.

Not a chance, he thought. How could he kiss her with that mask in the way?

'Did you enjoy the show?' he asked, changing the subject.

'It was very entertaining.'

'Very,' William agreed. 'I particularly enjoyed it when that elderly doctor nearly toppled off the stage.'

'Lord, yes. Poor man, I felt so sorry for him. Do you think he was ill?'

William laughed. 'I think he was tight!'

'Really?'

'I could practically smell the whisky on his breath from where I was sitting.'

'You're a fine one to talk. I seem to remember you used to partake of some Dutch courage during the Christmas shows at the Nightingale,' Millie reminded him.

'You're right,' William agreed ruefully. 'Do you remember that year we did a duet and I forgot all the words?'

'You left me standing there, absolutely mortified—'

Once again she stopped abruptly, remembering herself.

'I miss those days,' William said.

'So do I,' she agreed. 'It was the one time in my life when I actually felt as if I belonged somewhere.'

He frowned at her. She was gazing down at her glass, a sad, lost look on her face.

'Don't you feel as if you belong at Billinghurst any more because we're there?' he asked.

Millie shook her head. 'No, it isn't that. I'm glad you're here. At least the house can be useful, even if I can't be.'

There it was again. That word. Useful. Every time she said it her face clouded over, he noticed.

'Surely you must feel useful, running the estate?'

'My land agent runs the estate. Between you and me, I'm rather hopeless at it. At least, my grandmother thinks so.'

William thought about the formidable Lady Rettingham. She would not be an easy woman to please, he decided.

'What about your son? You take care of him, don't you?'

'When his nanny allows me near him.' Millie lifted her slim shoulders in a shrug. 'So you see, Squadron Leader, I'm not really needed anywhere.'

She looked up and gave him a sweet, sad smile. In that moment he desperately wished he could do or say something to help her.

'Perhaps you should go and ask Matron for a job?' he suggested.

A glint of humour lit up her eyes. 'I would love to see my grandmother's face if I did that!'

'I'm serious,' he said. 'You said yourself you felt as if you belonged as a nurse. And I'm sure they would love to have you back.'

She shook her head. 'I couldn't. It's been so long I'm sure I don't have the skills any more.'

'It's only been four years since you qualified. I'm sure there are women nursing who have been out of the profession for far longer than you. Besides, your skills will come back to you.'

A strange expression came over Millie's face. She was already considering the possibility; he could tell by the sparkle of hope in her eyes.

'At least think about it,' he urged.

'I will. Thank you.'

They finished their drink and headed back to their cars. William wasn't sure if he was imagining it, but Millie seemed to have more of a spring in her step.

'Well, goodbye,' she said, as he opened her car door for her. 'I hope you have a good Christmas.'

'You, too.' On impulse, he added, 'You could

163

come to the Officers' Mess tomorrow for a drink, if you like? Bring your grandmother and little Henry,' he added quickly, sensing she was about to refuse.

Millie smiled. 'I'm sure Henry would love to meet the pilots!'

'I expect they'd like to meet him, too. Especially as so many of them are away from their own families.'

The smile faded from Millie's face, and once again he saw the guard go up. 'As long as you're sure I wouldn't be in the way?'

William sighed. 'Millie, I don't know where you've got this absurd idea from, but you should put it out of your mind straight away. You could never be in the way. I'd see you every day if I could–'

He hadn't meant to say it, and as soon as he saw Millie's startled expression he wished he could take back the words.

But then she smiled again. 'I'll remember that,' she said. 'Happy Christmas, Squadron Leader Tremayne.'

'Happy Christmas, Lady Amelia,' he replied.

Chapter Seventeen

'Happy Christmas, Nurse! How about a Christmas kiss?'

Tommo was the first person to greet Grace when she came on duty on Christmas morning.

164

He was with the other men at the table, eating his breakfast, sitting awkwardly sideways with his bandaged leg propped up on a chair beside him.

'You'll get a punch in the kisser if you don't shut up!' The man next to him rolled his eyes at Grace. 'Talks all day from morning till night, he does. Never gives anyone a minute's peace.'

'You're all boring, that's your trouble, Grand-dad!' Tommo snarled back. 'I'm telling you, Nurse, I can't wait to get out of here.'

'And so say all of us!' the men chorused around the table.

Tommo ignored them and turned back to Grace. 'Can I have my kiss, then?' He craned forward, his eyes closed, lips puckered in readiness.

'Look at him!' his neighbour said. 'As if anyone would want to kiss that ugly mug.'

Grace was still smiling as she went into the kitchen, where Alice Freeman was spreading margarine on to slices of bread.

'Good morning, Nurse Freeman. Merry Christmas,' Grace said.

'Morning,' Alice mumbled. She had her back turned, but Grace could see from the rigid line of her shoulders that something wasn't quite right.

'Is everything all right, Nurse Freeman?' she asked.

Alice glanced over her shoulder at her. 'Yes, thank you,' she replied, but her smile was strained as she handed the plate to Grace. 'Will you take this to Mr Jones?'

The screens had been removed from around Alan Jones's bed a few days earlier, as Dr Drake had decided that it might benefit him more if he could see what was going on around him.

Not that he seemed to take much notice of anything. He lay listlessly in bed, propped up against his pillows, staring mournfully at the world from his single unbandaged eye.

He barely registered Grace's presence as she drew up a chair beside him.

'Good morning, Mr Jones,' she greeted him. 'I've got your breakfast for you.'

No response. Grace started to feed him his porridge, patiently coaxing the spoon past his slack lips. He was like an empty husk of a man, she thought, the spark of life had departed.

'It's a bloody miracle, ain't it?' Grace looked round to see Tommo standing at the foot of the bed, leaning heavily on his crutches. 'A bullet like that to the head – it's enough to kill anyone, ain't it?'

Grace looked down at Alan. 'He's lucky to be alive,' she said.

'Is he?'

'What do you mean?'

'You should hear him, screaming and crying in his sleep. What must there be in his head to make him go on like that? Those doctors might have taken a bullet out of his head but they can't take out all those memories, can they? They're still in there, all those fears and horrible sights he saw, and he's trapped in there with them.' He tapped his temple to make his point. 'That's no way to live, is it?'

Grace glanced at Alan Jones. His face registered no emotion. She scraped her spoon on the rim of the bowl and held it up to his lips. There was no reaction. All the time she was aware of Tommo, still watching her with interest. His presence made her nervous.

'Don't you want to finish your breakfast?' she asked pointedly.

'I ain't hungry.' Tommo looked over to where the other men were sitting, laughing and joking together. 'Besides, I don't want to sit with that lot. They're all too boring.'

As if to prove him wrong, a shout of laughter went up from the table. 'They look as if they're having a good time,' Grace commented.

'Not with me.'

'Perhaps if you made more of an effort to fit in, instead of trying to get on everyone's nerves all the time, you might get on with them better?' she suggested kindly.

'I don't want to get on with them. I want my mates.'

'They could be your mates.'

'I mean my real mates. In the regiment.' Tommo looked like a belligerent child, teetering on the edge of a tantrum.

Miss Wallace came on to the ward at eight o'clock. She quickly did her rounds, wishing all the men Happy Christmas, and handing out small gifts to each of them.

'Writing paper!' Tommo stared at his present in disgust 'What am I supposed to do with that?'

'Write to your family?' Grace suggested.

'I ain't got any family. And I can't read nor write neither.'

The man in the bed next to him, a kindly sergeant called Jefferson, sighed. 'Give it here, I'll swap with you,' he said. 'Your writing paper for a half a packet of Craven A's, how about that?'

'I suppose so.' Tommo handed the paper over with bad grace. 'But I'd rather have a whole packet,' he added.

Sergeant Jefferson grimaced. 'Don't push your luck, mate!'

Once they had finished their chores, Miss Wallace called Grace and Alice into her office for coffee and a nip of brandy from the locked cupboard she kept for medicinal purposes.

She gave them both a gift, too. Grace's was a small, leather-bound book.

'It's one of my old nursing textbooks,' Miss Wallace explained. 'It's rather out of date now, I'm afraid, but it might be of interest to you, since you seem keen to learn more about nursing.'

'Thank you, Sister.' Grace studied the tiny print on the tissue-fine pages.

'I thought it might even inspire you to consider training yourself one day.'

Grace looked up at her. 'Me, Sister?'

'Why not? You have a real talent for it.'

Grace looked down at the book again so Miss Wallace wouldn't see her face. No one had ever said she had a talent for anything, except cooking and keeping house. Wait until Daisy hears about this, she thought. Her sister would be so proud.

Before Grace could reply, Alice Freeman burst into tears beside her.

'Why, Nurse Freeman, whatever is the matter?' Miss Wallace asked.

Alice looked up at her with swollen, red-rimmed eyes. 'Oh Sister, my mother telephoned this morning. My father's in hospital.'

'Oh dear, I'm sorry to hear that. Is it very serious?' Miss Wallace asked.

Alice nodded, fishing for a tissue in her pocket. 'It's his heart. The doctors have told my mother they don't know if he'll recover, or...'

'Then you must go to him at once,' Miss Wallace said, interrupting her. 'Go and see Matron, and tell her you need to leave immediately.'

'I – I did, Sister. She ... she said I had to stay and work a week's notice.'

Miss Wallace's eyes narrowed to dark slits. Grace didn't think she'd ever seen her so angry.

'Nurse Freeman, may I remind you that you are a Nightingale girl, and as such you are under Miss Fox's control, not Miss Jenkins's.' Sister's voice shook as she spoke. 'I will telephone Miss Fox immediately and inform her what's happened.' She patted Alice's arm. 'Don't worry, my dear. You will be able to go back to London and see your father.'

Alice was still subdued, but a bit more cheerful as they went about their morning's work. At noon, it was time for Christmas dinner. All the men were excited as the turkey was brought on to the ward and set down in the middle of the table with great ceremony.

All except Tommo. 'Is that it?' he mocked. 'I've seen bigger pigeons in Trafalgar Square!'

He jeered at Dr Pearson when he came to carve the bird, too. 'Blimey, look at him, hacking about with that knife!' he whispered, loud enough for the whole table to hear. 'And he calls himself a surgeon!'

No one laughed. 'If it wasn't for Dr Pearson,

half the blokes on this ward wouldn't be here, so shut your trap!' someone growled at him.

When the rest of the men were tucking into their Christmas dinner, Miss Wallace gave Grace a plate of food to take to Alan Jones.

'He probably won't manage all of it, but see what you can do,' she said. 'And if he wants a drink, make sure you measure it carefully and mark off the amount on his chart. It's very important he doesn't have more than twenty fluid ounces in a twenty-four-hour period, otherwise it could be very harmful to him.'

Grace took her position at Mr Jones's bedside. But as Miss Wallace had predicted, he didn't want to eat. He ignored her attempts, even though she cut the turkey and vegetables into the tiniest pieces. No matter how hard Grace tried to coax him, he wouldn't take a single mouthful.

She sat back in her seat, the fork still in her hand, and stared at him in despair. 'Oh, Mr Jones. What am I going to do with you?' she sighed.

'Can I have a go?'

She looked around. There was Tommo, watching them as usual.

'You?' Grace frowned.

'I dunno, he might take it better from me than from you.' He shrugged diffidently. 'Us both being soldiers, and that.'

Grace hesitated, then said, 'I'll ask Sister.'

Miss Wallace was surprised, but she said, 'I don't see why not. Anything's worth a try, I suppose.'

Tommo pulled up a chair and Grace handed him the tray and showed him what to do.

He brushed her off irritably. 'It's all right,' he

said. 'I know I'm from Bermondsey but I have used a fork before.'

'Suit yourself.' Grace walked away and left him to it. But she stayed close by, plumping up pillows and straightening bedclothes, so she could check what was going on.

'Go on, mate,' she heard Tommo urging softly. 'Get it down you. You heard what the nurse said – the sooner we get better, the sooner we can get out of here.'

Alan rolled his single good eye to look at Tommo. Then, to Grace's astonishment, his lips parted a fraction, just enough for Tommo to put the fork in.

Tommo grinned. 'That's it, mate. You've got the idea. Let's try another one, shall we?'

'Will you look at that?' Sergeant Jefferson said. 'Now, there's a Christmas miracle if ever I saw one.'

'Isn't it?' Grace stared at the unlikely pair. Miss Wallace came up behind her.

'It looks as if our Mr Thompson might have found one friend at least,' she observed.

After Christmas dinner had been cleared up and the dishes washed and tidied away, Miss Wallace sent Grace home.

'Good gracious, you're already late as it is,' she said. 'You should have reminded me of the time.'

'That's all right, Sister,' Grace said. 'Besides, I don't like to leave while there's work to be done.'

'Then you'll never leave this place!' Miss Wallace smiled wryly.

It wasn't that bad, Grace reflected as she hurried home. Cleaning a ward and looking after the patients wasn't nearly as hard work as cleaning out grates, setting fires and hauling buckets of coal up endless flights of stairs. And she enjoyed her work, too. At Billinghurst Manor she wasn't supposed to be seen by the family, let alone speak to them. She'd had to sneak around the house, using the back stairs and hidden doorways and praying that she wouldn't accidentally come face to face with anyone. Lady Amelia had always been kind and polite, but the Dowager Countess treated her as if she was part of the furniture, no more human than the coal scuttle.

But at the hospital Grace could chat and be friendly, and she felt appreciated.

Even though it was only mid-afternoon, dirty grey clouds were gathering ominously overhead, heavy with the promise of snow. The wind had a bite to it, and Grace wound her new knitted scarf tightly around her neck to keep it out.

At least she was going home to a nice warm home, and her Christmas dinner cooked for her. And what a Christmas dinner it would be! She had spent every spare moment she had queuing at the grocer's and carefully hoarding whatever food she could find. Yesterday she had managed to buy a goose from Mr Sulley. It had cost every penny of her savings, and she didn't dare ask the old man where it had come from. But it meant she wouldn't have to kill one of the chickens. Grace hadn't been looking forward to the prospect.

And Daisy had the day off, so Grace had given her strict instructions to put the bird in the oven that morning, so that it would be ready for when she got home. All she would have to do was prepare the vegetables and cook the potatoes, and...

'Sorry I'm late,' she called out as she let herself in through the back door. 'I hope you've put that goose in the oven, Daisy?'

She sniffed the air. There was no delicious smell of roast bird. Still in her coat, she bent down and opened the oven door. It was empty.

'Daisy Maynard!' Grace thrust aside the curtain that led to the kitchen. 'I thought I asked you to–'

She stopped dead. They had a visitor.

Chapter Eighteen

'This is Max,' Daisy said.

He had been sitting at the table, playing cards with Walter and Ann. But he rose to his feet instantly and came to greet Grace. He was so tall, his fair head almost touched the low-beamed ceiling.

'Max McLennan. How do you do, ma'am?' he greeted her in a deep Canadian accent, extending his hand. 'Thank you for inviting me to your home.'

Grace looked sharply at Daisy. She stood there, wearing her best butter-wouldn't-melt expression. 'I'm sorry, Mr McLennan, but I wasn't aware I had invited you,' she said.

She would never have said it if she hadn't been so tired. But she'd been working hard all morning, and she wasn't in the mood for her sister's nonsense. Especially as Daisy hadn't even laid

173

the table or put the dinner in the oven.

Max's smile faltered. 'I don't understand... I thought it was all arranged?' He glanced at Daisy, who in turn looked back at Grace.

'I thought I'd told you?' she said. Faint colour crept up her throat. Daisy always blushed when she was lying.

'Perhaps it's best if I go?' Max broke the tense silence.

'No!' Daisy protested. 'You mustn't go. Tell him, Grace. Tell him it's all right if he stays?'

'If it's not convenient...'

'It is! Tell him, Gracie!'

Grace looked from her sister's pleading face to Max's crestfallen expression. Poor man, it wasn't his fault her sister was so thoughtless.

'Of course,' she said, forcing a smile. 'I'm sorry, I didn't mean to sound ungracious. You just caught me unawares, that's all.' She glared at her sister.

'Are you sure?'

'Honestly, I'd like you to stay. Besides, I don't think Walter would forgive me if I turned a real-life airman out of the house!' She ruffled her brother's hair affectionately. 'Anyway, I'd better get that goose in the oven or none of us will be eating until Boxing Day!'

She went into the back yard, and Daisy followed. 'Don't be cross, Grace,' she pleaded.

'Do you blame me? How could you invite a stranger and not tell me?'

'I was going to ask you, but I thought you might say no.'

'So you thought you'd just bring him anyway?'

Grace stared at her sister, dumbfounded by her logic. 'What if we didn't have enough food to go round? There is a war on, you know!'

'But you always have enough for visitors! Besides, he's brought his own rations,' Daisy said. 'And he's brought some chocolate, and a tin of ham.'

'Even so, you should have warned me, instead of embarrassing us all,' Grace said, heading for the shed. 'The poor man didn't know where to put himself, and neither did I. And why didn't you put the bird in the oven, as I asked?'

'I forgot.'

'Too busy making eyes at your boyfriend, I suppose? Honestly, it's going to take hours to cook it. We'll be lucky if–' Grace went to lift the latch on the shed door and realised it was already undone. 'Who's left this open?'

'Not me,' Daisy said. 'Walter was the last one in there, I think.'

'I thought I said to keep it–'

As she opened the door, there was a loud crash from inside and a streak of red flashed past her.

Daisy screamed, and the chickens started squawking in their coop. A second later Max and Walter came running out of the house, with Ann on their heels.

'What is it?' Max said, as Daisy launched herself into his arms. 'What's happened?'

'I'll tell you what's happened!' Grace emerged from the shed with the savaged remains of their goose in her hands. 'A bloody fox has had our Christmas dinner!'

'Oh, Max, it was horrible!' Daisy buried her

face in his broad chest.

'How did it get in there, that's what I want to know?' Grace glared at Walter.

He shuffled his feet. 'I only went in to get my bike. I'm sorry, Grace.'

She sighed. 'It's a bit late for that, now.'

She looked down at the shredded carcass in her hands. It was such a beautiful bird too, so plump and rounded. They could've feasted on it for days.

'Can't we cook what's left?' Walter asked hopefully.

Daisy lifted her face from Max's chest. 'Ugh, no! I'm not eating a fox's leftovers, thank you very much!'

'She's right,' Grace sighed. 'All we can do now is give it a decent burial.'

Anger and disappointment welled up inside her, and suddenly all she wanted to do was cry. She caught Max's gaze over her sister's head. His face was straight, but there was a glint of mirth in his blue eyes.

'It's not funny,' she muttered. But as Grace said it, she felt her lips begin to twitch. She looked down at the remains of the goose and laughter bubbled out of her.

Max started laughing too, as did Walter and Ann. Soon they were all roaring.

All except Daisy, who looked blankly from one to the other. 'Well, I don't see what's so funny,' she retorted. 'A fox has had our Christmas dinner, and all you can do is laugh!' She turned to Grace. 'You'll have to kill one of the chickens,' she declared.

Grace sobered instantly. 'I can't.'

'Why not? That's what we were going to do before we got the goose, isn't it?'

'I know, but...' She looked towards the coop. 'I don't think I'd have the heart,' she said.

'I'll do it, if you want?' Max offered. He moved towards the coop but Grace stepped in front of him, still nursing the goose's remains to her chest.

'You can't,' she said. 'I wouldn't know which one to choose. They've all got names, you see. I'm attached to them.'

Daisy tutted. 'Oh, for heaven's sake! What are we going to eat, in that case?'

They all looked at one other for a moment. Then Max said, 'I have an idea. There's a British restaurant in Tunbridge Wells. I'm sure it'll be open today.'

Ann and Walter looked excited, but Grace said, 'How would we get there?'

'I could borrow a jeep from the base?'

Walter looked fit to burst. 'Can we go, Gracie? Please?'

'Well, I'm going, even if you lot aren't,' Daisy declared.

Grace shook her head. 'I'm sorry, kids, we don't have the money.'

'It doesn't cost much. And I'd be happy to treat you,' Max said.

'Oh, no, I couldn't let you do that...'

'Please?' His eyes met hers. 'It's the least I can do. I feel as if I ruined your Christmas.'

Grace smiled reluctantly. 'Why? Was it you who sneaked into our shed and stole our goose?'

'Well, no, but I'm sure my presence didn't help. Please?'

Grace looked at Walter and Ann's pleading faces. 'Well, I suppose it'll be better than a tin of ham for our Christmas dinner. If you don't mind us all joining you?'

'It'll be my pleasure,' Max said. Daisy didn't reply.

Grace had never been to a British restaurant before, and she was entranced. It was little more than a basic, self-service canteen, but it was clean and they managed to get a full Christmas dinner, with pudding to follow, for just ninepence each.

'It's cheaper than I could make it at home,' she said. 'And there's plenty of it too. Not like the horrible little bits of meat we get on the ration.'

'I wish I could have taken you somewhere fancier,' Max said.

'Oh, this is fancy enough for Grace!' Daisy put in, laughing. 'She never goes out, do you, Gracie?'

Grace felt herself blush. It was the truth, but she still felt embarrassed.

Throughout the meal, Walter kept Max occupied with endless questions about his training, and the planes he'd flown, and whether he liked the new Halifax design, or preferred the Stirling.

Max was very patient with him, explaining the pros and cons of the various craft, and the intricacies of mine-laying expeditions. Grace watched her younger brother's rapt face and was glad he had another man to talk to. He missed his older brother Albie now he was away fighting.

But Daisy didn't seem to feel the same. 'Honestly, can't you shut up for a minute?' she snapped at Walter. 'You've been going on at poor Max for hours.'

'I don't mind,' Max started to say, but Daisy cut him off.

'That's not the point,' she said sulkily. 'The rest of us can't get a word in edgeways.'

Grace couldn't help feeling the remark had been aimed at her, too. She wasn't sure why, when she was just being polite.

After the meal, Max took them all home in the jeep and dropped them at their front door.

'Thank you for a lovely day, Miss Maynard,' he said.

'You can call me Grace, if you like?' She smiled. 'And really, we should be thanking you for going to all that trouble for us.'

'I enjoyed it. It was good to have some civilised company.'

'That's the first time I've ever heard Walter called civilised!' Grace laughed. She held out her hand for Max to shake. 'You'll have to come back and have a proper dinner with us another time,' she said.

'I'll look forward to it.' Max's grip was firm and warm, his aquamarine eyes meeting hers directly.

As he shook her hand, Walter suddenly gave a shout of laughter. 'Look what you're standing under!' he said.

Grace looked up. There, hanging above the front door, was a sprig of mistletoe.

'How did that get there?' she said.

'I put it up,' Daisy muttered.

'You'll have to give Gracie a kiss!' Walter called out.

'Shut up, Walter!' Daisy hissed, glaring at him.

Grace let go of Max's hand and stepped away.

'I think you've got the wrong sister,' she said, forcing a laugh.

Max's face was serious. 'I guess I have,' he murmured.

Chapter Nineteen

'Have you quite taken leave of your senses, Amelia?'

Lady Rettingham sat back in her chair and regarded her granddaughter, her expression aghast. Millie sat opposite her, hands locked together, determined to stay calm.

'I'm quite sane, thank you, Granny,' she replied evenly.

'Are you? I very much doubt it, since you've come up with such an absurd notion.' Lady Rettingham's mouth pursed in disapproval. 'Really, child, I do wish you would forget this obsession you have with being Florence Nightingale. It's most tiresome. I thought you'd finished with all this nonsense years ago?'

'So did I. But things change, don't they?'

Millie's life had certainly changed, that was for sure. A year or even a month ago, she would never have dared suggest such an idea to her grandmother. But now...

'And what makes you think they'd even want someone like you?' Lady Rettingham tried a different tack.

'They're crying out for nurses, Granny. So many

have joined up, there aren't enough to go round.'

'I see. You've clearly looked into this, haven't you?'

Millie had been thinking about little else for three days, all over Christmas. Ever since her visit to the hospital on Christmas Eve, and her conversation with William, the idea had been taking root and growing in her mind. And the more she thought about it, the more perfect it seemed.

But not to her grandmother.

'And who is going to run the estate, if you're off being a nurse?' Lady Rettingham asked.

'Mr Rodgers, of course. He's been running the estate perfectly well since Father died anyway.'

'Yes, but he still needs guidance from you.'

'Why?' Millie said. 'As you've told me on several occasions, the estate is far better run by a man.'

She wondered if she'd gone too far when she saw her grandmother's lips turn white. 'Yes, but Mr Rodgers isn't family, is he? And what about Henry?' she changed the subject again. 'Have you thought about what this might do to him?'

'I don't know what you mean?'

'You're going to be bringing all kinds of terrible diseases into the house, aren't you? What if Henry catches dysentery or diphtheria? What will you do then?'

'He won't, Granny!' The idea was so absurd Millie couldn't help smiling.

Her grandmother stiffened, back straightening even more. 'I'm glad you find this so amusing, Amelia.' She shook her head. 'No, I can't agree to it. You are the mother of the heir to Billinghurst, and your place is here, looking after your son's birthright, not running about emptying strangers' bedpans.' She shuddered delicately at the thought. 'I'm sorry, but you must forget all about this ridiculous notion.'

She started to rise from her chair, as if that was an end to the matter. Millie stared into the dying flames of the fire.

'No, Granny, I won't forget it,' she said quietly.

'I beg your pardon?'

'I know you've never approved of my nursing, but it was something I loved,' Millie said. She went on staring into the fire, unable to meet her grandmother's stern gaze. 'When I was working at the hospital, for the first time I felt as if I had a purpose in my life. I wasn't just Lady Amelia, a silly debutante waiting to marry well. I was actually doing something useful, helping people.'

Her grandmother froze, still standing over her. Millie wasn't sure if she was listening, but at least she hadn't walked away.

'I just want to feel that way again,' she said. 'I know everyone says I have a purpose now, running the estate and doing charity work. But I'm really just dabbling, playing at doing something worthwhile when everyone knows I'm just silly Lady Amelia again.' She steeled herself to look up at her grandmother. 'I want to feel as if I'm really making a difference. Is that such an absurd notion?'

Her grandmother was silent for a long time, her expression unreadable.

'And I suppose if I say no, you'll do it anyway?' Lady Rettingham said shortly.

Millie dropped her gaze again. 'I telephoned my old matron Miss Fox this morning. She'd like me to start next week.'

'I see.' Her grandmother was tight-lipped. 'Well, I don't know why we're even discussing it, since it's clearly all done and dusted.'

'Because I want your approval,' Millie said. 'I want you to tell me you're happy for me.'

Her grandmother was silent for a long time. 'Then there is nothing more to be said, is there?' she snapped.

'Come with me. I want to show you something.'

Kit took Effie's hand and started to lead her off the dance floor, but she hung back. The band had just started playing an Andrews Sisters song, one of her favourites. 'Can't we just dance to this one, please?' she begged.

Kit laughed. 'You've danced to every song so far!'

'I know. Isn't it wonderful?' She had barely left the floor for hours, and was breathless with all the whirling and spinning. But she was having the time of her life.

And to think she'd imagined that life in Billinghurst would be dull! Ever since the RAF had arrived, it had been one long round of nights out, trips to the pictures, going out to dinner and now to a Christmas party in the Officers' Mess.

And of course there was Kit. Effie had never imagined she would find someone as handsome, witty and worldly wise as he was. No wonder she was head over heels in love with him.

He tugged on her hand. 'Are you coming, or not?'

'Where are we going?'

'You'll see.'

Effie saw the challenging look in his eyes. For all she adored him, she wasn't sure how wise it was to go out into the night with Kit. She was all for a bit of kissing and canoodling, but he could be quite passionate when they were on their own, and Effie had struggled to keep him at bay.

'I promised not to leave Daisy...' She looked across the dance floor at her friend, who was spinning around in the arms of a handsome pilot officer.

'She'll be all right,' Kit said. 'She probably won't even notice you're gone. She's too busy trying to make Max jealous.' He grinned.

Effie looked again at Daisy. Kit was right, she did keep glancing over at Max. But he was laughing about something with his friend Harry and hardly seemed to notice.

She followed Kit out into the cold night air, and down the steps. 'Where are we going?' she asked.

'It's a secret. Close your eyes.'

'Kit...'

He put his hands over her eyes.

'Trust me,' he said softly.

She felt herself being guided away from the house. At some point they turned off the drive, and the crunch of damp gravel under her feet gave way to soft wet grass that brushed against her legs. Behind her, the sounds of the dance receded until all she could hear was the wind whispering through the trees and the eerie hoot of an owl.

She started to panic. 'Kit, I don't like it,' she said. 'Let me see...'

Almost immediately he released her and she

blinked. He might as well have kept his hands over her eyes because she could see nothing in the dense, cold blackness.

'Where are we?' she asked.

'Do you like it? It's a little private spot I found this morning while I was taking a walk around the grounds,' Kit sounded pleased with himself. 'It's our own personal hideaway, somewhere we can be alone together.' He smiled, and his teeth flashed white and wolfish in the darkness.

Effie was instantly wary. 'I want to go back inside.' She shivered. 'It's too cold.'

'I'll soon warm you up, darling.'

His arms went round her, crushing her to him, his mouth closed on hers, greedy and plundering. At the same time, his hand came up to cup her breast through the thin fabric of her dress. Effie pushed him away.

'Kit, don't. I want to go back inside, this wet grass is ruining my shoes... I said, don't!' She slapped his hand away.

He broke away from her, looking hurt. 'What's the matter? Don't you love me?'

'You know I do.'

'Then why don't you prove it?' He started to nuzzle her neck, gently nibbling away at her earlobe. This was much nicer than the rough ravishing he usually tried, and Effie felt a warm sensation uncurling in the pit of her belly.

'You see, you like it, don't you?' he coaxed her, his voice husky with desire. He kissed her again, his tongue insinuating itself into her mouth, almost choking her. Effie turned her head away sharply.

'Kit, don't–'

And then, suddenly, a voice came out of the darkness.

'You heard the girl. Leave her alone!'

Chapter Twenty

The next thing she knew, Kit was lying flat on his back in the long grass.

'Kit!' Effie dropped to her knees beside him, damp seeping through her skirt, as a figure separated itself from the shadows and loomed over her.

'Leave him,' he said curtly. 'It serves the eejit right for bothering you.'

The sound of his voice was like an electric shock, bringing her back to her feet. 'Connor?' she whispered.

'Hello, Euphemia.' She couldn't see his face in the darkness, but she could hear the smirk in his voice.

Kit groaned, and Effie bent to help him to his feet.

'How did you find me?' she asked.

'I went to the hospital in London and asked. You're not that hard to find, you know.'

Now her eyes were getting used to the dark, she could make out the tall, broad-shouldered figure, a mane of dark curls framing his rugged features.

'I suppose Mammy sent you?' she said.

'She didn't send me, I offered to come. You didn't answer her letter. She was worried sick about you.'

Kit, who had been brushing himself down, now stepped in. 'Who is this person, Effie?'

She glanced at Connor. He stared back at her expectantly. The moon appeared from behind a cloud, casting cold light on the planes and angles of his face.

'His name's Connor Cleary. He's–' she searched for the rights words '–someone I knew in Ireland.'

She saw Connor's lip curl at the introduction, but he said nothing.

Kit squared up to him. 'Well, Mr Cleary, you can jolly well get lost!'

Connor didn't move a muscle. Only a slight hitch of his eyebrow showed he'd heard what was being said to him.

'Did you hear me?' Kit took a step closer.

Connor looked at Effie. 'Is this why you ran away from Ireland?' he said pityingly, nodding towards Kit. 'Is this really the best you can do?'

Incensed, Kit took a swing at him. Without even looking at him, Connor's hand flashed out and grabbed Kit's arm, pinning it effortlessly behind his back.

'I've got no argument with you, friend,' he growled. 'Just stay out of this, all right?'

'I'm not your friend – ow!' Kit yelped in pain as Connor twisted his arm further up his back.

'Leave him alone!' Effie shouted.

Connor paused for a second, Kit dangling use-lessly at the end of his arm. He released him with a shove. Kit staggered a few steps then found his feet, massaging his shoulder where Connor had twisted it.

'Are you all right?' Effie hurried over to him. 'Let me see–' She tried to examine Kit's arm but he shrugged her off irritably.

'I barely touched him. It's just his pride that's hurt,' Connor said, unconcerned.

Effie scowled at him over her shoulder. 'Now you've seen me, you can go home and tell Mammy I'm perfectly well,' she said.

'You can tell her yourself. I've booked us both on a boat back to Ireland tomorrow afternoon.'

'What?' Effie and Kit spoke together.

'We'll catch the first train up to London tomorrow morning,' Connor went on, ignoring them. 'Be ready at eight o'clock.'

'But I'm not going back to Ireland,' Effie said. 'I've decided, my life is here now.'

'You've decided?' Connor gave a derisive snort. 'You can't make decisions for yourself until you're twenty-one.'

'I am twenty-one. Well, nearly, anyway. My birthday's in two months.'

'And I daresay in two months you'll be catching the boat back here. But until then you're coming home with me.'

Effie folded her arms across her chest. 'You can't make me do anything.'

It was a dangerous thing to say. Even in the darkness, she could see Connor's eyes glint with the light of battle. 'You're getting on that boat, Euphemia, if I have to pick you up and carry you on to it myself.'

He took a step towards her and Effie jumped back with a squeal. He was strong enough and just about mad enough to do it, too.

'Now, look here–' Kit broke in. 'You can't go round making threats to her like that.'

Connor turned slowly to face him. Kit wasn't short by any means, but Connor's powerful height seemed to dwarf him. 'Haven't I warned you not to get involved? This is a private conversation.'

'Stop it, both of you.' Effie stepped between the two men. 'I'm sorry you had a wasted journey, Connor. But I've made up my mind, I'm staying here.'

'We'll see about that.' He turned to go. 'I'll be back for you tomorrow morning at the Nurses' Home. Be ready at eight.'

He headed off into the shadows, as quickly and as silently as he'd arrived.

'Bloody thug!' Kit shouted after him. He made sure Connor was a safe distance away before he spoke, Effie noticed. 'Lucky he left when he did, or there really would have been trouble.'

Yes, Effie thought. And Connor would have been the one causing it, she was sure of that.

'Are you certain you're all right?' she asked. 'He didn't hurt you?'

'Nothing I couldn't give back, if he hadn't taken me by surprise.' Kit was the picture of injured pride. 'Although perhaps we should go back to the house?' he added, looking about him nervously.

As they walked back together, Kit said, 'Who is he, anyway?'

'I told you, someone I knew in Ireland.'

'A boyfriend?'

'God, no!' Effie laughed. 'He's a neighbour. His father owns the farm next to ours. We grew up together.'

189

'What's he doing here?'

'You heard him. He's come to fetch me home.'

'It's a long way to come for a neighbour?' Kit observed.

Effie grimaced. 'Believe me, Connor Cleary would travel to the ends of the earth if he thought he could aggravate me by doing it!'

It had been the same since they were kids, growing up together on neighbouring farms. Whether he was dropping worms down her back during Sunday Mass, or throwing mud at her on the way to school, Connor had made it his mission to infuriate and upset her.

'Did you really run away from home?' Kit asked.

Effie hesitated, then nodded. 'I had no choice,' she said. 'My mammy would never have let me go otherwise. And I so wanted to come back to England. You can't imagine how dull Kilkenny was after being in London.' She sighed. 'Much good it's done me. I suppose I'll have to go back to Ireland with Connor now.'

Kit frowned at her. 'No one is going to make you do anything, darling,' he said. 'I'll see to that.'

Effie looked at him pityingly. He was so gallant, it made her heart break for him.

'You don't know Connor Cleary,' she said.

Chapter Twenty-One

By the time the following morning came round, Effie was terrified.

She left the Nurses' Home early, before Sulley's cart came to collect them all, and tramped the two miles to the hospital in the dark rather than run the risk of meeting Connor.

She was on duty on Female Medical, but spent most of her time checking her watch and looking nervously out of the windows, half expecting to see him marching up the drive like an avenging angel. She knew Connor Cleary too well to put anything past him. He was more than capable of slinging her over his shoulder and carrying her out of the ward if he felt so inclined.

'Are we keeping you from something, Nurse O'Hara?' Sister Allen asked finally.

'No, Sister.'

'Only you keep looking at the time. I thought perhaps you had an urgent appointment?'

'No, Sister.'

'Then perhaps you'd get on with charting those samples? And stay away from the window,' Sister Allen warned.

From then on Effie tried to be more subtle about looking at her watch, and only glanced out of the window when she was hidden behind the screens, out of Sister's line of sight.

As lunchtime approached and nothing happened, Effie began to allow herself to relax. Connor wasn't coming. He'd caught the train without her, and now he was on his way back to Ireland.

And good riddance, she thought.

But even as she tried to convince herself she was safe, the dread crept in. That wasn't the way Connor went about things. Once he'd made his mind up, nothing would stop him.

Sure enough, as she left the hospital after her duty at eight o'clock that evening, he was waiting for her by the gates. Effie had spent so long dreading his appearance, it was almost a relief to finally see him.

He was standing by the cart, chatting to Sulley and patting Delilah as if they were old friends. The nurses waiting in the back of the cart were craning their necks, watching with interest.

Effie didn't blame them. With his height and lean muscled body, Connor Cleary could seem quite attractive, if you didn't know him the way she did.

She squared her shoulders and forced herself to walk towards the cart, feigning a lack of concern. He was so deep in conversation with Sulley, she didn't think he'd noticed her at first. But as she went to move past him, he suddenly said, 'You didn't turn up.'

Effie stopped. 'Did you really expect me to?'

'I suppose not.' He shrugged.

'Well, then.'

Effie started to climb on to the cart, but Sulley shook his head and said, 'Your brother says he's walking you back to the Nurses' Home.'

'My brother?' Effie turned to Connor as Sulley

jingled the reins and headed off.

Connor gave her an infuriating wink. 'I had to tell him something. Besides, we're practically family, aren't we?'

Effie sent him a scathing look. They might be physically alike, both tall, black-haired and blue-eyed, but as far as Effie was concerned, that was where any similarity ended. 'Just because my sister married one of your cousins doesn't make us flesh and blood.'

'Thank God!'

'At least we agree on something.'

Effie set off down the lane, intent on leaving him behind. But Connor's long strides caught up with her easily.

'I waited for you,' he said. 'I called at the Nurses' Home this morning, like we agreed.'

'I didn't agree to anything,' Effie reminded him, still looking ahead of her. 'And you shouldn't have called at the Nurses' Home,' she added. 'Now I expect I'll be in trouble with Miss Carrington.'

'Is that the old biddy who runs the place? Aye, she didn't seem too pleased, to be honest with you.'

Effie turned on him. 'You have no right to come here and spoil everything.'

'And you had no right to go breaking your mother's heart!' he shot back.

Guilt lanced her, and she turned and started walking again. 'I didn't meant to upset her,' Effie said over her shoulder. 'But I wouldn't have had to run away if everyone had listened to me and let me do what I wanted in the first place.'

'Oh, yes, because you're so capable of looking

after yourself, aren't you, Euphemia?' Connor mocked. 'You've got such a level head on your shoulders, you'd never get into any trouble.'

'I know how to look after myself. I lived in London for two years, didn't I?'

'And if last night was anything to go by, we can all see what good that did you!'

She stopped again, so abruptly Connor almost slammed into her. 'What do you mean by that?'

Connor flicked his curly hair off his face, fluttered his eyelashes and mimicked her in a breathy voice, 'Ooh, Kit, stop ... don't...'

Scalding colour flooded her face. 'You were listening to me! How long were you standing there?' she demanded.

'Long enough.'

'That is not what I sound like,' she said huffily.

'Yes, it is. And if I'd waited another minute you would have had your knickers off.'

Effie gasped as if he'd struck her. 'How dare you!'

'I'm only trying to talk some sense into you. You're out of your depth with him, Effie.'

'You know nothing about him.'

'I know his kind. And he's not the sort you should be getting involved with. You're so easily flattered, you can't see what men like him are really after. And once he's had it he won't want to know you. The next thing we know you'll be coming back to Kilkenny six months gone and no sign of the father!'

'Connor Cleary! How dare you speak to me like that!'

'Someone's got to talk some sense into you. You

seem to have lost any that the Good Lord gave you, that's for sure.'

'Oh, and you're so wise, aren't you? What do you know about the world? At least I've seen a bit of it. The furthest you've ever been is Cork!'

'I'm here now, aren't I? It doesn't take a lot of sense to get on a ferry.'

'Then why don't you do us all a favour and get one home?'

He folded his arms across his powerful chest. 'I promised your mother, I'm not going anywhere unless you go with me.'

'You'll be here a long time, then.'

'That's what I thought,' he said.

She narrowed her eyes. 'What do you mean?'

'I had a feeling you'd decided to be stubborn as usual, so today I went and found myself a job, right here in Billinghurst.'

She felt the blood drain from her face. 'You didn't?'

Connor nodded. He looked so pleased with himself, it was all she could do not to slap him. 'I don't know if you've heard this but they're crying out for strapping lads like me, since everyone joined up. And you'll never guess where I'm working?'

She didn't trust the glint in his blue eyes one bit. 'Where?' she asked cautiously.

'At the hospital. I'm going to be working as an orderly, so I'll be able to keep an eye on you,' he grinned.

Effie glared at him. She would not give him the satisfaction of seeing her riled, she decided. 'I don't care,' she declared, turning away. 'It's a free country, you can stay as long as you like. You'll get bored with it before I do.'

Connor smiled maddeningly. 'We'll see, shall we?' he said.

Chapter Twenty-Two

On New Year's Eve, Jess decided to pay a visit to Sarah Newland. Daisy Maynard gave her the address.

'But I don't think you should go,' she advised. 'You saw what she was like at the WVS sale. She's trouble.'

'From what I saw, she wasn't the one making the trouble,' Jess replied. 'Besides, I make up my own mind about people, thanks very much. I don't need the likes of Mrs Huntley-Osborne and her cronies telling me what to think.'

'Please yourself.' Daisy shrugged. 'But don't blame me if you don't receive a warm welcome. That girl's got a temper to match her red hair!'

Sarah Newland lived in a drab one-roomed cottage on the far side of the village. Daisy's warning was on Jess's mind as she walked up to the front door and knocked. Perhaps she shouldn't have come? It wasn't like her. She preferred to mind her own business, and leave other people to get on with theirs. But at the same time, there was something about Sarah that intrigued her. She couldn't forget the image of the girl, proud and defiant as the other women circled her like a pack of hyenas.

It took a long time for Sarah to open the door.

She looked tired, her red hair hanging limply around her freckled face.

She frowned when she saw Jess. 'Yes?'

Her abrupt manner took Jess aback. She cleared her throat. 'I'm Jess,' she said. 'We met–'

'The girl from the village hall,' Sarah finished for her sharply. 'I remember you. What do you want?'

'To give you this.' She took the matinee jacket out of her bag and handed it to the girl. Sarah glared at it, then back at Jess.

'I told you, I don't want anyone's charity.'

'And I ain't offering any,' Jess snapped back. Sarah's rudeness was starting to grate on her. 'But I bought it and it's no use to me, so if you don't want it I'll just give it away to someone else.'

Sarah's eyes fixed longingly on the jacket.

'Wait a minute,' she said, and disappeared inside the house, leaving the door ajar. Jess stepped inside, out of the cold.

The cottage was spotlessly clean and tidy, but rundown and reeking of damp. Ominous patches of dark mould blossomed along the skirting board. There was a bed in one corner, and an ancient stove and sink in the other. The only other pieces of furniture were a big scrubbed table and some chairs in the centre of the room, and a single armchair by the empty grate.

Sarah returned with her purse. 'Sixpence, wasn't it?' she said.

'That's right.' Jess watched her carefully counting out the farthings and halfpennies into her hand. She could see the girl could barely afford it and was tempted to ask for less, but she knew

Sarah would never accept the jacket if she did.

'Here you are.' Sarah handed her the money and took the jacket. She held it up to her cheek, and for a second Jess glimpsed an unguarded side to her as she pressed the soft lemon-coloured wool against her skin.

But then she noticed Jess watching her and the mask snapped back into place.

Jess waited a moment, then said, 'I'll be off.'

As she went to leave, Sarah suddenly asked, 'Why did you do it?'

'What?' Jess replied.

'Why did you buy the jacket for me? It's not as if you know me or anything.'

It was a question Jess had asked herself several times. And there was only one answer she could come up with. 'I suppose because I know what it's like to be an outsider,' she said.

'An outsider?' Sarah bristled. 'Is that what you think I am?'

'That's what you are, ain't it?'

Sarah stared at her so hard, Jess wondered if she had offended her again. Daisy was right, Sarah was a prickly character.

'Anyway, I'll be off.' She turned and started to walk away.

'I've just put the kettle on,' Sarah said suddenly. 'You could stay for a cup of tea, if you like?' She eyed Jess warily, as if she expected her to refuse. There was a proud tilt to her chin that Jess recognised all too well. It was the look of someone who expected to be rebuffed, and who had made up her mind she wouldn't care if she was.

'I'd love to, if you're making one.'

She sat at the table while Sarah put the kettle on and then built up the fire. She set it like an expert, Jess noticed. Then she remembered Daisy had said she'd been Mrs Huntley-Osborne's maid.

How had she put up with it? Jess wondered. The woman must have been insufferable.

As Sarah made up the fire, she said, 'What did you mean – about you being an outsider?'

Jess paused. 'When I started nursing, a lot of the other girls used to leave me out because I wasn't posh like them. I used to be a housemaid, and they didn't think people like me had a right to be a nurse.'

Sarah looked over her shoulder at her. 'You were a maid?'

'I went into service when I was thirteen.'

'Me too. I was sent to work straight from leaving the orphanage.'

'For Mrs Huntley-Osborne?'

Sarah sent her a sharp look. 'I suppose everyone's been gossiping about me?'

'If they have, I ain't been listening. I don't like gossip.'

'You're the only one in this village who doesn't, then.' Sarah stared into the flickering blue flames of the fire. 'And, yes, I worked for Mrs Huntley-Osborne. But only for the past three years.'

Sarah hauled herself to her feet wearily. She had the exhausted, heavy-bellied look of a young woman who was nearing her time.

'How long have you got before the baby comes?' Jess asked.

'A couple of months.' Sarah went over to the stove, where the kettle had started to boil.

Jess hesitated, choosing her words carefully. 'And the father?'

Sarah sent her a sharp look. 'What about him?'

'Does he know about the baby?'

'He's dead,' Sarah said flatly. 'He was killed by a U-boat in the Atlantic six months ago. But yes, he knew. He was going to marry me,' she said, looking defensive. 'He even gave me this ring. Look.' She showed Jess a grubby piece of string tied around her neck. Dangling from it was the most exquisite solitaire ring. It looked like an antique, ornate twisted gold surrounding a glittering chunk of emerald. A ring like that must have cost a fortune, thought Jess.

She looked at it, then up at Sarah. 'It's beautiful. But why don't you wear it on your finger?'

'I don't know ... it just doesn't seem right somehow, now he's gone.' Sarah gazed at the ring sadly, then slipped it back inside her jumper. 'Anyway, he was going to marry me,' she repeated firmly. 'He loved me. Whatever anyone else says about it,' she murmured.

Jess watched her making the tea. She couldn't imagine why everyone had turned against Sarah Newland. Yes, she was a bit of a spiky character, but who wouldn't be, in her situation? All Jess could see was a young girl who was down on her luck. She had fallen pregnant, but that wasn't the worst crime in the world. The rest of the village should have been giving her a helping hand, not condemning her.

'Why does everyone have it in for you?' she asked, as Sarah set the cups down in front of them.

Sarah gave her a resigned smile, as if she had

been expecting the question 'I can tell you that in three words,' she said. 'Mrs Huntley-Osborne.'

'But why?'

'She thinks I betrayed her.' Sarah stared down at her cup. 'As far as she's concerned, she took me in and gave me a roof over my head, and I repaid her by getting myself into trouble, as she called it.' Her mouth twisted. 'Mrs Huntley-Osborne likes to think of herself as the most respectable woman in the village, and having a pregnant unmarried maid would definitely give the wrong impression...'

'But that's no reason to turn everyone against you, surely?'

'She wants to drive me out. She's even tried to get the landlord to evict me, but thank God, he needs the rent more than he needs that woman's approval.' Sarah's mouth was a taut line. 'But I know her, and it's only a matter of time before she gets her way.'

Jess stared at her. 'But I don't understand. Why would it be any of her business what you do?'

'Because I'm an embarrassment to her, I suppose.'

'An embarrassment?'

Sarah shrugged. 'That's all I can think. But who knows what goes on in that woman's mind? Sugar?' she offered. 'It's only saccharine, I'm afraid. It's all I could get.'

'No, thank you.' Jess glanced across the table at Sarah. Her face was closed, deliberately expressionless. Jess had a feeling there was much more to the story, but if there was, Sarah Newland wasn't going to be the one to tell it.

Chapter Twenty-Three

That night, as the day staff were enjoying a New Year's Eve drinks party in the dining room, Jess was still stuck on nights in the Fever Wards. And it seemed as if fate had planned to make the last night of 1941 as difficult as possible for her.

'The night nurse in charge of the diphtheria ward has been sent off sick, so you'll have to go and cover for her,' Miss Tanner the Night Sister told Jess when she reported for duty. 'I've arranged for Nurse Frimley to take over your ward.'

'Yes, Sister.'

'Come with me, and I'll show you what needs to be done.'

Miss Tanner walked through the diphtheria ward with her, describing the various cases, and their stages of treatment. Jess had never imagined she'd miss the whooping cough ward, with its cacophony of coughing, retching and endless wet and dirty beds. But she feared the menacing silence of the diphtheria ward. All the patients were kept lying flat on their backs, too poorly to make a sound. And then there was the foul smell too; the sweet, sickly odour of the disease mingling with the sharp tang of disinfectant made her want to retch.

Miss Tanner pointed out a new patient, a four-year-old girl who had arrived that afternoon.

'Dr French has already increased her serum to twenty thousand units, but she seems to be deteriorating quite quickly, so keep an eye on her and call him if you think her dosage needs to be increased,' Miss Tanner instructed.

'Yes, Sister.'

As they returned to the sister's desk, Miss Tanner said, 'Are you sure you'll be able to manage, Nurse?'

'I'll do my best, Sister,' Jess promised.

Miss Tanner smiled. 'I'm sure you will, I know I can rely on you.'

Once the night sister had gone, Jess went through the ward, checking on all the children. She administered serum, swabbed throats with carbolic, gave strychnine injections and raised beds to stimulate failing hearts.

And all the while she was aware that Pamela Jarvis, the little girl in the corner, was getting steadily worse.

By ten o'clock, she decided to telephone Dr French.

'I'm worried about the new admission, Doctor. Pamela Jarvis. The little girl with faucial diphtheria? She doesn't seem to be responding to the serum.'

She could hear the sound of laughter in the background. He might have been on call, but it sounded as if Dr French was determined not to miss out on the fun of New Year's Eve. He had obviously sloped off to join the drinks party.

'She's very pale and restless, and she's having increasing difficulty swallowing,' Jess persisted. 'I wondered if we should increase her dosage?'

'We?' Dr French echoed coldly. 'When did you qualify as a doctor, Nurse Jago?' In the background came the sound of shattering glass, followed by a whoop of laughter.

Jess swallowed down her rising temper. 'I'm sorry, Doctor. I'm just a little anxious about her, that's all.'

He sighed heavily. 'Very well, I'll come as soon as I can. But I'm rather busy at the moment.'

I can hear that, Jess thought, listening to the voices in the background. 'But if you could...'

'As soon as I can, Nurse,' he said abruptly, and hung up.

Jess tried to stay calm, but she couldn't take her eyes off Pamela. She set up a steam tent but the little girl's breathing was laboured and noisy as she desperately tried to suck in the air past the dirty yellow, foul-smelling membrane that extended across her throat. If it spread any further, the child would suffocate.

After half an hour there was still no sign of Dr French. Jess tried to telephone him again, but there was no reply from the exchange. It was as if the whole world was off having a good time, leaving her to struggle alone to keep poor little Pamela alive.

But perhaps not the whole world.

A thought suddenly struck her, and she dashed down the corridor to the whooping cough ward.

'Will you listen out for my lot?' she begged Nurse Frimley. 'I just have to run and find someone. I'll only be a minute.'

Nurse Frimley, a nervous second year who was already clearly overwhelmed by the responsibility she'd been given, jumped to her feet. 'But what if–'

'One minute!' Jess promised, and darted off before Nurse Frimley could say any more.

Dr Drake was coming out of Male Medical when Jess caught up with him. He was clearly having as bad a night as she was. He looked utterly shattered.

He started off down the corridor but Jess called after him. 'Doctor?'

He swung round. 'Yes?'

'Can you come with me, please? I need you to check a diphtheria patient.'

His frown deepened. 'Dr French is covering that ward tonight. Call him,' he said shortly.

'But, Doctor–'

'Nurse, I'm far too busy looking after my own patients. Now, if you'll excuse me...'

'Dr French has buggered off with his friends. Please, Dr Drake!' Jess blurted out as he strode off.

He stopped dead, and for a moment she thought she'd gone too far. Jess tightened her fists at her sides and braced herself as he turned around slowly to face her.

'Show me this patient,' he said.

As soon as they arrived on the diphtheria ward, Jess knew she'd done the right thing. Pamela had got worse since she'd been gone. Her face was an ominous shade of purple, dark as a storm cloud.

Dr Drake put on an overall and examined her in silence for a moment.

'She needs a tracheostomy,' he said flatly. 'But we'll have to do it here. She's far too ill to be moved.'

'Yes, Doctor.'

Don't panic, Jess told herself as she arranged screens around the table in the middle of the ward and set up the trolley for the operation. He knows what he's doing.

She had never seen a tracheostomy performed before, and hoped her nerves didn't show as she wrapped little Pamela in a blanket and laid her down carefully on the table. Jess placed a sandbag under her frail shoulders so that her head tilted back, exposing the full arch of her slender neck.

Dr Drake's breathing was soft and slow behind his mask as he prepared to make the incision.

'Hold her head very steady, please, Nurse,' he instructed, his voice muffled behind the starched linen. 'We don't have a second chance at this.'

Every muscle in Jess's body went taut as she held on to little Pamela's head. She wanted to look away but she didn't dare. As Dr Drake lowered the scalpel to the child's tender throat she couldn't stop herself from yelping with fear.

Dr Drake's eyes met hers, stern over his mask. 'Trust me, Nurse,' he said.

He made the incision fast and decisively. There was a loud hiss of air, and immediately Pamela's colour returned to normal.

Dr Drake straightened up, the scalpel in his hand. 'Right,' he said. 'Let's get that dilator fitted.'

After Jess had put Pamela back into her bed and made sure her dilator was in place, she went off to wash up the instruments. She thought she was alone, so jumped in shock when she heard Dr Drake say, 'You did a good job, Nurse.'

She turned around. He was leaning against the doorframe, watching her.

'I'm sorry, sir. I didn't realise you were still here.'

'Just taking five minutes.' He took off his spectacles and rubbed his eyes. He looked utterly drained, Jess noticed.

On impulse, she said, 'I don't suppose you'd like a cup of tea?'

She hadn't expected him to accept. But he raised weary eyes to hers and said, 'Yes please, Nurse. That would be very nice.'

Jess began to wish she hadn't offered as they sat in awkward silence together at the ward table. She had never sat down and tried to hold a conversation with a doctor before, especially not one as stand-offish as Dr Drake. She had no idea what to say to him, and he didn't seem to know what to say to her, either, as he stared into the depths of his cup.

'Pamela seems a lot better,' she commented finally.

'Hmm?'

'The tracheostomy.' Of course he wouldn't know the child's name, she thought. The patients were just a set of symptoms to Dr Drake. Not like the charming Dr French...

But for all his charm, Dr French wasn't there when she'd needed him. And Dr Drake was.

'Oh, yes. Good.' He took off his spectacles again and polished them on the hem of his white coat.

Jess took a deep breath and tried harder. 'I've never seen a tracheostomy done before,' she said.

'I've never done one before.'

Her gaze flew up to meet his. 'You mean, that was your first time?'

The faintest hint of a smile appeared on his

lips. 'Did it show?'

'Not at all. I would never have guessed.'

'I wasn't sure if I should tell you.'

'I'm glad you didn't. I would have been even more nervous.'

'I think I was nervous enough for both of us!'

His smile widened and Jess suddenly realised that she had got him wrong. What she and all the other nurses had assumed to be arrogance was really just shyness.

From outside the window, far across the hospital grounds, came the sounds of laughter and singing.

'It sounds as if the party is livening up,' Jess said. 'And here we are, sitting like a pair of Cinderellas.'

He replaced his spectacles, pushing them higher on his long nose 'I don't mind. I'm not really one for parties.'

'Me neither.'

His brows rose. 'You surprise me. I thought you and your friends enjoyed a bit of fun? You certainly seem very lively on the ward.'

Jess immediately remembered the incident with the mistletoe. Poor Dr Drake. If he was as shy as she thought, he must have been utterly mortified. No wonder he'd flown off the handle like that, if he'd thought they were making fun of him.

He finished his tea and stood up. 'Well, I suppose I'd better be going,' he said. 'Thank you for the tea, Nurse. It was most welcome.'

As he went to leave, Jess happened to glance up at the clock on the wall. 'It's nearly midnight,' she said.

'So it is.' He smiled at her again. 'Happy New

Year to you, Nurse.'

Jess smiled back at him. 'Let's hope so, sir,' she said.

Chapter Twenty-Four

The first face Millie saw when she stepped on to the ward as a new nurse was Grace Maynard, coming out of the kitchen with a breakfast tray in each hand.

It came as a shock to see her former maid in her VAD's uniform, and Millie could tell from the other girl's expression that the feeling was mutual.

'Your ladyship! What are you doing here?'

'The same as you, I should think,' Millie said ruefully.

Grace stared at her uniform. 'Sister said we were getting a new nurse, but I never imagined–' Her mouth opened and closed again.

Millie read the expression in her hazel eyes. The poor girl looked completely at a loss, obviously wondering how she was going to deal with the situation.

'I know it might seem strange at first, but we're here to work together,' said Millie. 'And we can start by you not calling me "your ladyship" any more.'

Grace blushed. 'What else should I call you?'

'How about Nurse Rushton, since we're supposed to use last names?'

Grace nodded, but still looked decidedly uncomfortable.

'Can I help you with these?' Millie went to take one of the trays from her, but Grace held on to it firmly.

'I can manage, your – Nurse Rushton.' Grace looked flustered. Millie didn't blame her. The poor girl had spent the past ten years running about after the Rettingham family, and now here was Millie helping her.

'Please, Maynard?' Millie said, taking the tray.

Grace hesitated for a moment, then she nodded and handed it over. 'It's for bed six,' she said. 'His arm's damaged so he might need help cutting his food up. But don't fuss over him too much, it puts him in a bad mood.'

Handing out the breakfasts was a good chance for Millie to meet the patients. There were around thirty of them, with a variety of injuries, from dressed wounds on their heads and torsos, to splinted limbs supported by complex frames and pulleys. Many seemed quite well, sitting around the central table to eat their breakfast and chatting amongst themselves.

Grace explained that most of the men had come straight from field units or hospital ships, where they had received the emergency treatment they needed. They were then sent to the Nightingale for post-operative care or convalescence.

'Most of them have been injured in some way – gunshot or shrapnel wounds, or fractured limbs – but we also have some medical cases,' she said. 'Sergeant Powell in bed two, for example, was sent home with pneumonia.' She nodded to an older man, who was sitting up in bed quietly doing a newspaper crossword.

'What about those two?' Millie nodded to a dark-haired boy, who was patiently feeding a pale young man.

'That's Tommo and Alan. Alan had a terrible head injury, but he's getting better. Physically, at least,' said Grace. 'The doctors say there's no reason why he shouldn't start doing things for himself, but he seems to have lost the will... Sister has told us to keep an eye on him anyway.'

'His friend seems to be doing that already?'

'Tommo's a great help.' Grace smiled. 'Watch out for him, though, he can be a bit lively. He'll take advantage of you, if he thinks he can get away with it.'

'I'll remember that.' Millie watched the pair for a moment. Tommo was all solicitous concern, neatly wiping the other boy's chin with the corner of a napkin, then picking up the spoon to feed him again.

'Tommo's so protective of Alan, he never leaves his side,' Grace said. 'At least it gives the other men a rest from Tommo pestering them all the time!'

Miss Wallace came on duty as they were clearing away the breakfast dishes.

'Welcome back, Nurse Rushton.' She beamed at Millie. 'I see you've got stuck in straight away. That's good. It's just what we like to see, isn't it, Maynard? Someone who isn't afraid of hard work.'

'Yes, Sister.' Grace sent Millie a sideways look. She was probably thinking of all those times she

211

had fetched and carried for her, Millie thought. She hoped she would be able to prove that she wasn't afraid of hard work, as Miss Wallace had said.

She was determined to do her best and not to make any mistakes. But she had forgotten how much there was to good nursing. Even making a bed seemed beyond her. She could see the look of strained patience on Grace's face as she showed her for the third time how to smooth out the drawsheet so there were no wrinkles.

Desperate to impress, Millie then rushed through the bedpan round in record time, only to realise that she had forgotten to test and measure the patients' urine as Sister had specifically instructed her.

Miss Wallace was very good about it. 'Don't look so worried, Rushton. I'm sure it will all come back to you,' she reassured her cheerfully. But Millie was certain she must be furious with her.

At her break, she followed Grace down to the dining room. 'I know we're not supposed to talk to each other because of the silly rules, but can I just sit on your table?' Millie begged. 'I don't know anyone else and I'm a bit lost.'

'Of course,' Grace said. But there was something strained in her smile, and once again Millie worried that she'd made her feel uncomfortable.

She realised how little she knew about Grace Maynard. She had only found out recently from looking at the rent books for the estate that both Grace's parents were dead, and that she had been the breadwinner of her family for the past ten years. The poor girl had been through some hard times, but in all those years she had been nothing more than a shadow to Millie, flitting about on the edge of her life, quietly and efficiently serving her. It made her feel rather ashamed.

'How are you getting on at the Lodge, your lady– Nurse Rushton?' Grace made a faltering attempt to start up a conversation.

'I like it very much,' Millie replied. 'It's more practical for the three of us, and so much easier to keep clean.' She stopped, blushing furiously, re-membering that it was Grace who had kept Bil-linghurst Manor clean. Millie had never had to lift a finger.

If Grace noticed, she was too polite to remark on it. 'And how is Lady Rettingham?' she enquired. 'And Master Henry?'

'They're both very well, thank you. Although my grandmother misses you terribly,' Millie added. 'She was only saying the other day, you're quite the best maid we ever had...'

Grace's smile was strained, and once again Millie had the awful feeling she'd put her foot in it.

'Um... How is your family?' She desperately tried to change the subject.

'Very well, thank you. Walter and Ann have both had bad colds, but they're getting better now. And I had a letter from my brother Albie this morning. He seems to be doing well enough in the army, which is a relief.'

Millie pressed her lips together to stop herself from making another idiotic remark. She hadn't even known Grace's brother was old enough to be called up.

'And then there's my other sister, Daisy. She's over there, look.' Grace nodded over to the far corner of the room.' Millie looked over her shoulder at the pert blonde, chatting to a group of other staff nurses. Now Grace pointed it out, Millie could see a faint family resemblance. Although she took more pride in her appearance than Grace.

'Why don't you go and sit with her?'

Grace shook her head. 'Daisy says it's not allowed. She's a proper nurse, you see, not like me. Besides, she wouldn't want me hanging around with her friends.'

She said it so matter-of-factly, Millie could only stare at her. Daisy Maynard sounded like an even bigger snob than Millie herself was supposed to be.

After their break, she returned to the ward. Tommo called out to her straight away.

'Please, Nurse, I need a bottle.'

'Of course, Mr Thompson. I'll fetch one for you.'

She fetched a bottle from the sluice. As she pulled the screens around his bed, he said, 'Can you help me, Nurse?'

'I beg your pardon?'

'Can you – you know? Put it in for me? Only I can't manage it by myself.'

Millie looked at his face. His imploring expression would have melted a heart of stone.

'I thought it was your leg that was injured?'

'Yes, but my shoulder's playing me up too.' He massaged it, wincing at the pain. 'It's so stiff, I can hardly, move it. Pain shoots right down to my hand, it does. I can't hardly move my fingers.'

'Hmm.' Millie thought for a moment. 'Well, if

you really need help...'

'Oh, I do. I do.'

'Then wait here a minute. I'll just go and wash my hands.'

Millie could hear him chuckling to himself behind the curtains as she walked away. But his laughter stopped when she returned and he saw what she had with her.

'What – what are those?' he whispered.

'Rat-toothed forceps.' Millie advanced towards him. 'Come on, then, let's be having you.'

He shrank back, eyes still fixed on the shining, snapping jaws. 'It – it's all right, Nurse, I think I can manage by myself.'

Millie feigned a look of innocent concern. 'Oh, well, if you're sure?'

She was pushing back the screens as Miss Wallace whisked past.

'Ah, Nurse Rushton.' She looked from the forceps to Millie's expression. 'Let me guess – Mr Thompson?'

'Yes, Sister.'

'I trust you were able to assist him?'

'As it turned out, he didn't need my help, Sister,' Millie replied, straight-faced.

Miss Wallace smiled. 'You see, Nurse? I told you it would all come back to you.'

Millie went home at five o'clock, tired but happy. She had made some mistakes on her first day, but not nearly as many as she'd feared, and Miss Wallace had been pleased with her work.

She'd also managed to make a start on winning Grace over. By the end of their shift, they were chatting more like equals than mistress and former servant. Millie was pleased. She liked Grace and hoped they might become friends. Although she couldn't imagine what her grandmother would say about it.

There was a sleek black car parked outside the Lodge on her return. As Millie opened the front door, she could hear shrieks of childish laughter coming from the sitting room.

She put her head around the door. There, to her surprise, she found Lord Edward Teasdale scampering around the floor on all fours, Henry riding on his back. Her son was wielding a wooden sword.

'Teddy?'

He looked up, brushing a stray lock of hair out of his eyes. 'Hello, Millie.'

'I'm a knight, and he's my trusty steed!' Henry announced, waving his sword at her. 'And Nanny's a dragon!' he added.

She is indeed, Millie thought. She didn't dare look at Nanny Perks's face in case a prim display of disapproval made her laugh too much.

'I'm afraid your trusty steed needs to go back to his stable, old man.' Teddy gently disentangled himself from Henry and set him down on the floor. He stood up, brushing down the knees of his suit trousers.

Nanny ushered her charge out of the room, leaving them alone. 'What are you doing here?' Millie asked, looking up at Teddy.

'I was in the area, so I thought I'd drop in and say hello. Your grandmother invited me to tea, if you recall?'

Millie smiled. 'So she did. And why were you in the area? Have we had some Germans parachuting in that you need to question?'

He put his finger to his lips. 'Shhh! You know what they say ... careless talk costs lives. But no, actually it was just a very dull meeting of the top brass. Nothing remotely exciting, I'm afraid. Certainly no Germans marauding about the place.'

'So we can sleep soundly in our beds tonight?'

'Well, if you're terribly worried, I could stay with you and make sure?' His brows lifted hopefully.

'Teddy! What a suggestion!' Millie tapped his chest playfully. 'What would the lovely Miss Farsley say about that, I wonder?'

'The lovely Miss Farsley is no more, I'm afraid. Or rather, *we* are no more. As I predicted at Christmas, our love affair is over.'

'Since when?'

'Since she jilted me for a dashing guardsman.' He pulled a face. 'I suppose it must have been the uniform. Or the fact that his father owns most of Cambridgeshire.'

'You don't seem heartbroken about it, I must say.'

'Oh, well, you know what they say. *C'est la vie.*' Teddy looked her up and down. 'That's a rather attractive dress you're wearing. Is it from Paris?'

Millie looked down at her blue nurse's dress. 'Not quite. Surely you must know I've started nursing again?'

'Have you? Rather daring of you, I must say. What does your grandmother have to say about it?'

'Oh, she's utterly furious, of course. She can barely bring herself to speak to me. But I'm hoping she'll come round eventually.' Millie went over to the drinks cabinet and poured herself a sherry, then offered one to Teddy.

'Well, for what it's worth, I think it's a splendid idea.' He raised his glass to her. 'Here's to you, Millie.'

'Don't let Granny hear you say that!'

As she was about to sit down, she spotted the vase of flowers. 'Are these from you, too?'

'Much as I would like to lay claim to the idea, sadly not. They must be from one of your other admirers?'

'Oh, yes, of course. I have so many.' She picked up the card and read it.

'Well?' Teddy watched her over the rim of his glass. 'It's true, isn't it, I have a rival for your affections?'

'Actually, they're from Squadron Leader Tremayne. He's our Liaison Officer.'

'Liaison? That sounds rather racy. What kind of liaison?' He waggled his brows suggestively.

'Not the kind you have.' Millie read the message on the card again. 'He was just wishing me luck on my first day back at the hospital.'

'That was very nice of him.'

'Wasn't it?' Millie smiled at the card and put it back. 'I didn't think he'd remember.'

Teddy drained his drink and put down his glass. 'Well, since this Tremayne character has impressed you so much, I feel it only right that I should go one further by taking you out for the evening.'

'Really, I couldn't,' Millie started to say. 'I've

218

been on my feet all day and I'm so tired.'

'Nonsense, darling, I'm only suggesting dinner in Tunbridge Wells, not dancing all night at the Kit Kat Club. Go on, it'll do you good.'

'I really don't think so.'

'Some other night, then? Or better still, I'll take you and Henry out for lunch. What do you think of that?'

Millie considered it for a moment. She was determined after Seb not to allow herself to get involved with another man, whatever her grandmother might think. But Teddy was one of her oldest friends, and there was the added benefit of their not being attracted to one another in the slightest.

'I'd like that,' she said.

Chapter Twenty-Five

'Ready, steady ... go!'

Grace took off at a sprint, heaving the wheelchair in front of her. The sergeant was a heavy-set man, and pushing him wasn't easy. Millie, on the other hand, was wheeling a wiry young lance corporal, and managed to sprint ahead. She had reached the double doors at the end of the ward before Grace had even got so far as the table.

'I win!' Tommo crowed, his arms shooting into the air. 'That's two cigs you owe me, Pops!'

'Blooming cheat if you ask me,' Sergeant Jefferson grumbled, reaching into his locker. 'Poor

Nurse Maynard was hauling a sack of spuds. No offence,' he added quietly to the man in the wheel-chair.

'Oh, pipe down, you're just a bad loser. It ain't my fault if Nurse Maynard can't run for toffee, is it?'

'I heard that!' Grace, breathless and doubled over with a stitch, managed to gasp.

Tommo stuck a cigarette between his lips and carefully placed the other in Alan Jones's locker. 'Your share of our winnings, mate,' he said. 'You can keep it till later.'

Alan swivelled his eye to look at him, but said nothing.

'We took 'em good, didn't we?' Tommo cackled, nudging him. 'Wait till the next race, we'll really clean up then.'

'There isn't going to be a next race,' Millie said. 'Sister will be back soon.'

'Sister is already back,' came a voice from the doorway. 'Would somebody please explain what's going on here? Why are these men out of bed?'

Millie stepped forward. 'Um – I can explain,' she began. Poor Millie, Grace thought. She looked utterly mortified, a blush burning all the way up from her starched collar to her blonde hairline.

'We were just having a laugh, Sister,' Tommo butted in.

'I might have known you'd be involved, Mr Thompson. What have I told you about gambling on my ward?' Miss Wallace's stern brown gaze swept around the room. The men shuffled and stared at the floor like naughty schoolboys. Even Tommo looked slightly abashed.

Only Grace, standing close to her, saw the spark of mirth in the ward sister's brown eyes. Miss Wallace was a good sport, and anything that cheered up the men was usually all right with her.

'Now clear up immediately,' she instructed Grace and Millie. 'This is supposed to be a hospital ward, not a racecourse!'

'Can you let us know when you'll be taking your break tomorrow, Sister?' Tommo asked cheekily, as Grace and Millie set about pushing the tables and chairs back into place. 'Only Private Radley's got some humbugs I wouldn't mind winning off him!'

Miss Wallace glared at him. 'Don't push your luck, Mr Thompson.'

Once everything in the ward had been put back in its rightful place, it was time for the midday meal. Tommo was waiting as Grace brought over Alan Jones's tray.

'Not junket again?' he asked, looking down at the plate.

'What's wrong with it?'

'Alan doesn't like junket.'

Grace glanced up at Alan Jones. His blank face gave nothing away. 'How do you know?' she asked.

''Cos we're mates. I know these things.' Tommo leaned forward. 'I can see it in his face, see, when he likes and doesn't like things. Ain't that right, pal?' He grinned at Grace. 'He likes you, Nurse. I can tell you that. He thinks you're a right corker!'

Grace thought she caught the merest flicker of agreement in Alan's eye. But it was gone immediately.

'You're having me on,' she declared. 'Anyway, here's Mr Jones's dinner. I take it you want to feed him?'

'Yes, please.' Tommo moved to sit in the chair next to Alan's bed, set aside his crutches and lowered himself down carefully, then took the tray from her. 'He'll miss me doing this when I'm gone, won't he?' he said cheerfully.

'Have they said when you might be fit enough to leave?' Grace asked.

'Not yet. The doctor's still making a meal of this leg of mine, saying it ain't mended properly. But I'll be fit enough to go before long, don't you worry!' He reached over and gave Alan a spoonful of junket. 'I can't wait.'

Grace smiled. 'What's the matter? Don't you like the service here?'

'It ain't that, Nurse.' For once Tommo's face was deadly serious. 'I've never really had much of a family, growing up. My old man was a drinker, beat us all black and blue until I couldn't stand it any more and ran away from home. But when I joined up – I don't know, it was like I finally be-longed somewhere. I had a place to sleep, regular meals, a bunch of pals I could rely on, like brothers. It's the best life I've ever known, to be truthful.'

Grace felt a lump rise in her throat. 'I had no idea. I'm sorry.'

'Oh, don't be. Like I said, I've got a family now. And I'll be going back to them soon enough.' The next minute Tommo's cheeky smile was back in place and he held up the spoon. 'See? He hasn't touched this. I told you he didn't like it. Do us a favour, Nurse. Go and ask Sister if he can have a bit of that sausage and mash. You'll eat that, won't you, mate?'

After her shift finished at five, Grace cycled home. It was already growing dark, and as she skirted the airfield she could make out the looming outlines of three Halifax bombers being manoeuvred in from the dispersal areas. There were voices in the distance, people crossing the runway, guiding the planes into position for take-off.

To her other side, the field was covered in a drift of snowdrops, tiny beautiful flowers that heralded the coming of spring. It seemed almost like an omen to her. Perhaps it meant that soon they would win this war. People were talking about the coming of the Americans as if it changed everything, but they had been living under the shadow of war and death and shortages for so long, Grace had almost ceased to believe that things could ever be different.

She was so busy gazing over her shoulder she didn't look where she was going. She felt the front wheel of her bicycle hit something hard and heavy, and the next thing she knew she was sprawled on the ground.

For a moment she lay there, dazed. She had just started to pick herself up when she heard footsteps running towards her.

'Hey! Are you OK?' She recognised his voice immediately. It was Daisy's boyfriend Max.

He reached down and lifted her on to her feet. 'I heard a crash. Are you hurt?'

'Only my pride!' Grace brushed the dirt off her hands. 'I don't know what happened. One minute I was cycling along, the next I'd gone flying over the handlebars.'

'I guess you must have hit something.' Max bent down to examine the bicycle. 'The chain's broken,' he said. 'I could try to fix it for you, if you like?'

'It's all right, I can sort it out myself when I get home, or I'll get Walter to do it. I'll leave it here and collect it in the morning, when it's light.'

'Shall I carry it back for you now?'

'No, thanks all the same. I don't want to put you to any trouble.'

But as soon as she put her weight on her foot, it buckled beneath her.

'Here, lean on me.' Max's arm went around her, pulling her against him. Grace knew she wasn't the daintiest of girls, but he almost lifted her off the ground. The rough fabric of his flying suit smelled of engine oil. 'I'll walk you home.'

'Oh, no, I couldn't ask you to do that. I'm all right, honestly.' She took another step forward, gritting her teeth.

Max sighed. 'Come on, let me help,' he said. 'It'll only take ten minutes to walk you down to your cottage.'

Reluctantly, Grace allowed him to help her.

'I feel such a fool,' she said, as she limped along beside him. 'It's my own daft fault for admiring those snowdrops.'

'Huh?'

'They're my favourites,' she said. 'When I see them I always know better times are on the way.' Her mouth twisted. 'I suppose that sounds fanciful to you?'

'Not at all. We could use a little hope now and then.'

She glanced sideways at him. 'I saw the planes. Are you flying tonight?'

He shook his head. 'Not me. Not this time. I was up last night, so I've got some time off.'

They trudged along in silence, side by side in the darkness. She wished she didn't have to lean against Max for support. The solid heat of his body through his flying suit felt too intimate, too uncomfortable.

She tried to straighten up, cautiously testing her weight on her ankle. Pain shot up her leg and she had to grit her teeth to stop herself from crying out.

'I'm glad I ran into you,' Max said. 'I wanted to thank you again for Christmas Day.'

Grace laughed. 'I don't know why! Like I said then, we should be thanking you. You saved our bacon.'

'Pity I couldn't save your goose!'

Grace smiled back at him. 'You know, my offer of a proper dinner still stands, any time you want to call.'

'As long as I let you know I'm coming first next time?' Max asked.

Grace pulled a face. 'Oh, dear, was I that un-welcoming?'

'Put it this way, I've been less scared facing flak over the English Channel than I was when I saw your face!'

'I'm sorry, you just caught me on a bad day. I hope I didn't scare you off? Daisy would never forgive me.'

He went quiet until they reached the cottage and he set her down beside the front door.

'Would you like to come in?' Grace asked him. 'I think Daisy might be home...'

'No, thank you. I should be getting back.'

'Thank you for carrying me,' she laughed.

'Any time.'

She watched him sauntering off back down the lane, his hands in his pockets, then she turned and let herself into the cottage.

Daisy was laying the table.

'I thought I'd make a start, since I'm going out tonight, and – what happened to you?' She frowned as Grace hobbled over to the sink, clinging on to the stone edge for support.

'I fell off my bike.'

'Sit down and let me look at it.'

'It's all right.'

'I can see from your face it isn't. Now sit down.' Daisy guided her into a chair. Grace sank into it, grateful for the relief.

She winced in pain as her sister examined her ankle gently. 'Well, I don't think you've broken it,' said Daisy. 'But it's very swollen. I'm surprised you managed to walk all the way home. It must have been agony.'

Grace opened her mouth to say that Max had helped her, but something stopped her. 'Will it be all right, do you think?' she asked instead.

Daisy examined her injury again. 'I think it's probably just a sprain,' she said. 'I'll bandage it for you, but you'll need to get your feet up and rest tonight.'

Grace laughed. 'How can I do that? I've got to get tea ready for the kids.'

'I'm sure we can manage to put a bit of bread

and dripping on the table between us!' Daisy said. 'Anyway, I can help. I'm not going out until later.'

'Are you seeing Max?'

Daisy pulled a face. 'No, he's busy.'

'Is he? I thought...' Grace stopped herself.

'What?' Daisy frowned.

'Nothing.' Grace looked towards the window. Whatever was happening between Daisy and Max, it was none of her business. She just hoped her sister wouldn't get hurt. 'Let's see about that bread and dripping, shall we?'

By the following morning the swelling round her ankle had gone right down, and Grace could put her weight on it, if she was careful. She was getting ready for work when she remembered her broken bike.

'Could you be a love and go and collect it for me?' she asked Walter. 'It'll need fixing, but I'll do that when I get home tonight.'

Walter went out, and, fifteen minutes later she heard him trundling back across the yard, pushing her bicycle over the cobbles.

Grace went to the back door and looked out. 'You were quick,' she said. 'Did you manage to fix it?'

'You must be imagining things,' he said. 'There's nothing wrong with it.'

'Are you sure?'

'Come and see for yourself.'

She followed him out into the yard. Sure enough, there was her bicycle, as good as new. 'I don't understand,' she said, 'it was definitely broken last night.'

'Well, it isn't now.' Walter grinned. 'Maybe the fairies fixed it.'

'Maybe they did,' Grace agreed.

She wondered if the fairies had left the bunch of snowdrops in her front basket, too.

Chapter Twenty-Six

'Don't look now, Nurse, but your admirer's just walked in!'

Mrs Flynn looked up with a gaping grin, her false teeth in the bowl on Effie's lap.

She didn't need to be told. She had felt Connor Cleary's presence like a cold breeze on the back of her neck.

She tried to concentrate on the task in hand, swabbing Mrs Flynn's gums with a mouth mop. 'He's not my admirer,' she muttered. 'Rinse out your mouth, please.'

Mrs Flynn took a swig of Glycothylomine and spat it into the dish.

'I don't know how you can say that. He's always here, and he's always got his eye on you. Ooh, he's coming over. Quick, pass me my teeth, I don't want him to see me like this!'

She grabbed them and slipped them into her mouth just as Connor came over. 'Good morning, Mrs Flynn. How's my favourite patient?'

Effie busied herself collecting up the mouth swabs, determined not to meet his eye. Who did he think he was, swaggering round the ward like a doctor doing his rounds? He always did it, and it got on her nerves.

Mrs Flynn simpered like a schoolgirl. 'I'm very well, thank you, Mr Cleary.'

'How many more times do I have to tell you? It's Connor to my friends.'

Her smile widened. 'And you can call me Deirdre, if you like?'

'Deirdre, eh? Did you know, according to Celtic folklore, Deirdre was the most beautiful woman in the whole of Ireland?'

'Really?' Mrs Flynn looked entranced. 'No, I didn't know that.'

'Legend has it she was betrothed to a great king, but she fell in love with his nephew. The king got jealous and killed the nephew, so she threw herself under the king's chariot rather than live with a man she didn't love.'

Mrs Flynn clasped her plump hands together. 'Oh, isn't that romantic?'

'I'll tell you something else, Deirdre. On the spot where they both died two yew trees sprang up, and over the years they entwined together so the lovers were reunited in death.'

'What a lovely story.' Mrs Flynn turned to Effie, her face rapt. 'He's a gifted storyteller, isn't he, Nurse?'

'Full of blarney, more like,' Effie muttered under her breath.

'Your name's Euphemia, isn't it?' Mrs Flynn went on. 'Go on, Connor. What does Euphemia mean?'

Effie felt his gaze on her. 'Trouble, usually,' he said.

Mrs Flynn laughed. 'Oh, you are a card!'

Effie finished gathering the wash things on to the trolley and stood up.

'Sister will have your guts for garters if she catches you flirting with the patients,' she hissed to Connor as she walked away.

No sooner had she said it than Sister Allen appeared at the door to her office.

'Mr Cleary?' she called out.

Effie grinned. 'You see? Now you're for it!'

'We'll see about that, won't we?' Connor turned to face Sister as she advanced down the ward. Effie waited expectantly.

'Hello, Sister.' He sniffed the air. 'Is that a new scent you're wearing? It's gorgeous.'

Sister Allen blushed lightly. 'Why, thank you, Mr Cleary.' She patted her hair through her linen bonnet.

Effie stared in disbelief. Sister Allen's ice-cold heart was legendary, but somehow Connor's charm had managed to melt it. Why couldn't all these women see what Effie could see?

'Now I know what you're going to ask me, Sister, and the answer is yes,' Connor said. 'I've replaced all that old pipework, so you shouldn't have any more rusty water coming through the taps.'

'Oh, that's marvellous news.'

'And I put down some traps for the mice, too, so you won't have any more trouble there, either.'

'How splendid. Now I wonder if I might trouble you to look at that blackout curtain over there? The rail seems to be loose, and I'm worried the whole thing will come down one night.'

'I expect it's just a bracket needs replacing. I've

230

got my tools outside, I'll do it now.'

'Mr Cleary, I don't know what we'd do without you,' Sister Allen declared.

'You won't have to, Sister. I'm not going anywhere.' Connor winked at Effie as he said it.

He put her in such a bad mood she nearly crashed the trolley on her way back to the sluice. Once inside, she slammed the door shut, leaned against it and let out a scream through clenched teeth.

Daisy, who was scrubbing bedpans at the sink, looked over her shoulder.

'Let me guess?' she said mildly. 'Mr Cleary's here again.'

'He's driving me mad! Honestly, I don't know how much more I can stand of this.'

'You've got to admit, it is quite useful having him on the ward. I haven't seen one rat since he started working here.'

'Except for him,' Effie muttered. 'He's a great big stupid rat. I wish he'd go home.'

Not that there seemed to be much chance of that. In the two weeks he'd been working at the Nightingale, Connor had managed to make himself very much at home. He'd wooed and won over everyone with his twinkling Irish charm. He laughed and joked with the men, flirted with the women, and generally made everyone fall in love with him.

Everyone but Effie.

'He's persistent, I'll give him that,' Daisy said.

'Stubborn, more like.'

Jess considered it for a moment. 'You don't think there's a reason for it, do you?' she ventured.

231

'Yes! He wants to make my life a misery.'

'Are you sure he's not here because he's fond of you?'

The idea was so ridiculous, Effie snorted. She knew she could be fanciful herself at times, but Daisy Maynard took the biscuit! 'Connor? Fond of me? Don't make me laugh!'

She couldn't see the attraction herself, but she couldn't deny Connor Cleary was a hit with the women, and not just at this hospital. Why would he need to pursue her here when he had every girl in Kilkenny panting after him?

'Well, I reckon he's going to a lot of trouble just to provoke you,' Daisy said.

'You don't know Connor Cleary. He'd saw off his own leg with a rusty blade if he thought it would annoy me!' Effie shook her head. 'No, he's told me himself he's been sent over by my mammy to fetch me home. And I bet he couldn't wait to come over and start causing trouble!' she muttered.

'Perhaps you shouldn't have run away in the first place?' Daisy said.

'Don't you start! You sound just like Connor.'

The truth was, Effie did feel guilty for what she'd done. She loved her mother dearly, and had never set out to break her heart. She missed home, too. But even if she'd wanted to go back to Kilkenny she couldn't, because she didn't want to give Connor the satisfaction of thinking he'd beaten her.

All she could hope was that eventually he would get bored and go home to Ireland. But in the meantime, his looming presence was proving a real nuisance.

She was more worried about the effect it was having on Kit. She hadn't seen him for a few days now and she was sure he wasn't as keen on her as he used to be.

The few times they had seen each other had been a misery, thanks to Connor. If they met in the pub he would be in the corner, playing cards with his newfound friends. If they went for a walk in the moonlight Effie couldn't be sure Connor wasn't lurking in the bushes, ready to spring the minute Kit tried to kiss her. It was all very unnerving.

'When is he going to go home?' Kit kept asking.

'Don't worry, he'll give up soon,' Effie pleaded.

'Perhaps I should have it out with him…'

'Don't! Please don't.' She had seen Connor fight, and knew Kit wouldn't stand a chance. 'He's not worth it,' she added.

'It's a bit of a nuisance, you know.'

'I know,' Effie said. 'But it won't be for ever, I promise.'

'It'd better not be. My patience is starting to run out.' The note in Kit's voice frightened her.

When she left the sluice, Connor was up a ladder, replacing the curtain rail. Most of the patients had given up their books and their knitting and their crosswords puzzles to watch him in fascinated silence.

Effie could see how other women might swoon over him, what with those twinkling eyes, dark curls and rippling muscles. But Effie had grown up with him, and she knew he was actually the devil in disguise.

He was waiting for her when she left the hospital that evening, leaning casually against the gatepost, smoking a cigarette.

'If you're looking for the cart, it's already gone,' he said.

Effie looked up and down the road in frustration. She'd only been ten minutes late. 'But Sulley usually waits for me.'

'I told him you weren't coming.'

She turned on Connor. 'Thanks a lot. Now I'll have to walk home.'

'Or you could come for a drink with me?'

She stared at him. 'Why on earth would I want to do that?'

He shrugged. 'I thought you might want some company, as your boyfriend isn't around so much these days.' He blew a curling stream of smoke into the air. 'Has he gone off you?'

'If he has, it's all because of you!'

'Me? Why?'

'You make him nervous.'

Connor gave an insulting laugh. 'What is he, a man or a little girl?'

'Having you around would put anyone off.'

'It would take more than that to put me off, if I cared about someone.'

Now it was Effie's turn to laugh. '*You*, care about someone but yourself? I'd like to see that.'

'That's all you know, isn't it?' Connor's voice was low.

Effie stared at him. 'What's this? Have you got a sweetheart? Don't tell me Connor Cleary's actually fallen in love?'

'Shut up, Euphemia.' Connor's jaw tightened, but she could see colour creeping up his throat.

'It's true, isn't it?' she grinned. 'Come on, who is the poor girl? Do I know...'

Just then, as if by some miracle, Effie suddenly saw Kit striding down the lane towards them. She instantly forgot all about teasing Connor.

She heard Connor mutter something unpleasant under his breath as she ran down the lane to meet Kit. She was so thrilled she launched herself into his arms, hugging him fiercely and planting kisses on his face, for Connor's benefit as much as his.

'That's a nice welcome, I must say.' Kit held her at arms' length. 'I was worried I might have missed you.'

'The cart left without me. Thankfully.' Effie sent a meaningful look over Kit's shoulder to where Connor slouched against the gatepost. Little had he known he would be doing her a favour, sending Sulley away.

Kit glanced at him. 'I see you haven't managed to lose your shadow yet?'

'He'll go soon, I promise.' Effie threw her arms around his neck again. 'Oh, Kit, this is such a lovely surprise! Will we go out tonight?'

'Sorry, sweetheart, I can't. There's a briefing tonight, and I can't miss it.' He led her away, out of Connor's earshot. 'But I wanted to let you know, a few of us are heading down to the coast this weekend, and I wondered if you'd like to join us? On your own, of course,' he added, glancing back at Connor.

'I'd love to. If I can get the time off.' Effie had already decided she would do it, whatever happened. Nothing was going to keep her away from Kit.

'We're thinking of making a weekend of it, so you might want to sort out a staying-out pass too, if you can?'

He said it so casually, but his meaning was clear. Effie's heart swooped in surprise and alarm.

'I'll try,' she said quietly.

'Good girl. I know you won't let me down.' He kissed her passionately. 'I love you, and I'll see you on Saturday. Don't forget to bring an overnight bag with you.' He winked at her. 'But leave your friend Connor behind, all right? You know what they say, three's a crowd...'

Chapter Twenty-Seven

The Kent coast wasn't quite as picturesque as Jess had imagined it would be.

The beach was lined with sandbags and squat blocks of concrete to stop enemy tanks coming up off the beach in the event of an invasion. Ugly stretches of rusty barbed-wire fencing reached as far as the eye could see. Even the fresh sea air was tainted with the smell of cordite.

It was a cold, cheerless day, and the scene was bleached of colour. The iron-coloured sea blended into the grey sky, and the wind whipped at Jess's skirt and tried to tear the hat from her head.

'I guess no one's going to be getting a suntan today!' Harry quipped beside her, as they walked along the damp sand. In the distance, the clusters of sea forts looked like strange monsters wading in from the sea, the waves crashing around their long spindly legs.

'Doesn't look like it,' Jess agreed. 'But I'm just glad to be out in the fresh air, after all those nights on the Fever Wards.'

'Sooner you than me. I don't know how you can stand working in that place.'

Jess sent him a quizzical look. 'How can you say that? Your job's far more dangerous than mine.'

'All the same, I'd rather take my chances in the open skies than have to be cooped up with a bunch of sick folks night after night! How do you know you're not going to catch something?'

'Sometimes you can,' Jess admitted. 'But it's not a big risk if you're careful about keeping clean. And nurses are tested for immunity to certain diseases before they're allowed to work in the ward. I'm immune to diphtheria, for instance, so I can't catch it.' She picked up a pebble and aimed it into the sea. It fell short of the water's edge. 'Anyway, nights aren't too bad. At least it means I have my days free. Otherwise I wouldn't be able to come here, would I?'

Not like poor Daisy Maynard. As she and Effie were on the same ward, they couldn't both take time off. Effie had begged and pleaded with Daisy, and had ended up bribing her with her precious tin of scented talcum powder because she was so desperate to join the party.

Not that it was turning out to be much of a party. Daisy wasn't missing anything, Jess thought as she aimed another stone at the water. It landed with a plop.

'Here. This is how you do it.' Harry selected a

flat stone from the sand and sent it skimming across the flat, grey surface of the sea.

Jess looked at him admiringly. 'You're an expert!'

'I've had a lot of practice as a kid. Here, let me show you...'

As he rooted around in the sand for a suitable pebble, Jess looked down the beach at Max. He stood a few yards away from them, also aiming pebbles into the sea.

'Is your friend disappointed that Daisy couldn't come?' she said.

Harry laughed. 'Are you kidding?'

Jess frowned at him. 'What's that supposed to mean?'

'Nothing. I just get the impression she's keener on him than he is on her. Ah, this looks like a good one.' He picked up a stone and showed it to her, but Jess wasn't paying attention.

'What do you mean?' she said. 'I hope he isn't stringing Daisy along?'

'Believe me, that girl doesn't need stringing along!' Harry grinned.

Jess's mouth firmed. 'He'd better not be messing her about. She's my friend, you know.'

'And Max is mine.' Harry aimed the stone. It skittered across the surface of the water. 'Look, don't worry about Daisy. Max is a good guy. He'd never set out to hurt her. Unlike some people...' His gaze slid sideways to the distant sand dunes where Effie and Kit were sitting wrapped in each other's arms, oblivious to everything around them. 'That's the girl who should be careful. Kit has a bit of a reputation.'

Jess sighed. 'I've tried to talk to her, but there's no telling Effie anything.' She was glad in a way that Harry had confirmed her worst suspicions about Kit, although she worried for Effie. 'She's convinced he's in love with her.'

'Kit's good at convincing people.'

Harry took a bottle of ginger beer from his pocket and handed it to her.

Jess unstoppered the bottle, took a mouthful of ginger beer and gazed up and down the beach. They were the only three people on the lifeless promenade. 'Do they have nice beaches in Canada?' she asked.

'Sure, they have beautiful beaches right near where I live. We were always there when I was a kid.' He looked at her. 'How about you?'

She shook her head. 'If I ever did, I can't remember it.' She paused. 'I went to Southend with Sam, though. We went on a charabanc trip two years ago ... before he got called up,' she said.

It had been such a happy day. The weather was fine. They'd strolled on the pier, visited the amusement park, had fish and chips on the front and then caught a lift to the top of the cliff, trying to fit in as many happy memories as they could to carry them through the long separation that was to come.

As if he could read her thoughts, Harry nudged her and said, 'You'll be able to go again, when he comes home. Things will go back to normal soon, you'll see.'

Jess didn't reply. She turned her gaze to the ugly stretch of barbed wire. She couldn't imagine anything being normal again. The war had changed everything.

She forced herself to cheer up. The boys had been good enough to bring them all down here, the least she could do was enjoy herself.

'Are you looking forward to going back to Canada, once the war's over?' she asked Harry.

'You bet! I can't wait.' A broad smile lit up his lively face, making him look almost handsome. 'I'm going to have a huge party. And I'm going to hug that kid of mine so hard, I don't think I'll ever let him go.' He paused, then said, 'You know, it's his birthday today?'

'No! You didn't say. How old is he?'

'Three.'

He stared into the distance, and Jess could see his Adam's apple working as he fought down his emotions at the thought of his son. Poor Harry. She couldn't imagine what it must be like for a father to be separated from his son for so long.

'I know,' said Jess. 'Let's send him a message in a bottle.'

'What?'

'You can write a message, we'll stick it in that bottle and send it out to sea. You never know,' she grinned, 'it might make it all the way to Canada?'

Harry's mouth twisted. 'From the English Channel?'

'Oh, just try it!'

He shrugged. 'Hell, why not? I'm game.'

They finished off the bottle of ginger beer, then Jess found an old bus ticket and a stub of pencil in the bottom of her bag and Harry scribbled a message to his son. It seemed to distract him from his sadness for a while at least.

'We'll probably get arrested as spies,' Jess giggled as Harry took aim and tossed the bottle over the barbed-wire fence. It landed with a thud on the wet sand. Jess and Harry watched it, both willing the tide on as it inched towards it, then cheered when the bottle was finally claimed by a wave and began its journey.

'Happy birthday, son,' Harry murmured, a far-away expression in his eyes. Then he turned back to Jess, all smiles again. 'Now, how about we find a café? I don't know about you, but I'm freezing. I'll treat you to fish and chips and a nice hot cup of tea.'

'Tea?' Jess mocked. 'You're starting to sound proper English!'

'Well, we've got to drink something since the pubs keep running out of beer.' He called over to Max. 'What do you say, pal?'

'I guess so, if you're buying?' Max called back.

Jess nodded towards Kit and Effie, still snuggled together in the distant dunes. 'Should we ask them, do you think?'

'Hey, you two,' Harry called out to them. 'Do you want to come to the café with us?'

'You go on without us, old chap,' Kit called back, his voice carried off by the wind. 'We'll catch up with you shortly.'

'No prizes for guessing what they'll be getting up to, the minute our backs are turned!' Harry laughed as they trudged away.

Jess glanced back at Effie. She could just see the top of her dark head peeping out from behind the dune.

Poor Effie. She gave her heart far too easily, and

241

nearly always to the wrong man.

'I just hope she's careful,' muttered Jess.

Effie watched the others sauntering off, Harry's laughter drifting on the wind towards her.

'We should go with them,' she said.

'I'd rather stay here with you.' Kit reached up and twisted a curl of her hair between his fingers.

'It doesn't seem right to leave them on their own.'

'They'll be fine.' His fingers trailed along the arch of her neck. 'What's wrong, darling? Don't you like being here with me?'

'Yes, of course, but...' If she'd been honest, Effie had thought the seaside trip would be more of a laugh. She'd imagined them all eating chips on the beach, pushing each other into the sea and generally having fun.

But instead Harry, Jess and Max were having all the fun while she was stuck here in the sand dunes with Kit.

Not stuck, she reminded herself. This was what she'd been dreaming about, wasn't it? Just the two of them together, lying in each other's arms. Except in her dreams, Kit didn't kiss her so roughly, or keep trying to maul her through her clothes. She was exhausted from keeping him at bay.

'Anyway, it's not often we have any time alone these days, what with that ignorant oaf continually following you around,' Kit said.

'Connor's not an ignorant oaf!' Effie jumped to his defence, then wondered why.

'Darling, he's a potato farmer's son!'

'And I'm a potato farmer's daughter,' Effie

reminded him quietly.

'Yes, but you're different.'

'Am I? How?'

'Because I love you.'

He started to kiss her again but Effie shifted out of his embrace and sat up. She picked up a stick lying nearby and sketched out a heart in the sand. Inside, she wrote her initials – EOH – and was just about to write Kit's underneath when he said sharply, 'No, don't do that.'

The coldness in his voice startled her. 'Why not?'

'It's what the Canadians do when one of their crew is killed. They carve their initials on the fountain.'

Effie rubbed out the heart with her hand. 'I'm sorry,' she said. Then, seeing Kit's stony expression, added, 'But nothing's going to happen to you, is it?'

'Isn't it? I reckon I'll probably be dead long before the war ends.'

The matter-of-fact way he spoke shocked her. 'Don't say that!' she said.

'Why not? It's true.' He sat up, his gaze fixed on the horizon. 'Do you know how many bomber pilots don't make it back from each mission? Twenty per cent. That means every time I get into the cockpit of that plane, there's a one in five chance I won't come back.'

'I – I didn't know,' Effie murmured.

'I've lost count of the number of friends who've been killed over the past three years. One minute you're laughing and joking together, and the next–' He noticed her horrified expression and smiled. 'Don't look so shocked. I've been lucky so far. But I never know when my luck's going to run out, which is why I try to have some fun while I still can.'

He kissed her again, and there was something possessive about the way his mouth claimed hers, as if he was taking what belonged to him, what was due to him. Effie edged away.

'Don't,' she said. 'Someone might see.'

'There's no one around for miles. Just you and me.' His wolfish grin scared her.

'All the same, I don't want to.' She tweaked her skirt demurely over her knees.

'It's all right, darling, I'm not going to force you,' he said. 'After all, what's a few more hours when I've waited this long?'

Effie stared at him, genuinely puzzled. 'What do you mean?' she said, and then it dawned on her. 'You think we're spending the night together?'

Kit laughed harshly. 'Well, I didn't bring you all this way for the sea air, did I?'

Effie gazed out to sea, too embarrassed to look at him. 'I told you, I'm not ready.'

'So when will you be ready?' The impatient edge in his voice made her nervous.

'I don't know – soon,' she promised.

'You've been saying that for the past six weeks. I'm starting to get a bit tired of hearing it.' He looked at her. 'Don't you want me to make love to you, darling?'

Of course she did, Effie thought wretchedly. She wished she could be like the other nurses, merrily sneaking off for weekends with a borrowed wedding ring. But she was a good Catholic girl at heart, whether she liked it or not.

'I'm scared,' she said.

'I know, sweetheart, but I'll be gentle with you, I promise.'

'It's not just that. What if it goes wrong? What if I get pregnant?'

'You won't, I'll be careful.'

He pushed back the collar of her coat to nuzzle the tender skin of her neck. Effie felt a warm sensation uncurl itself in the pit of her belly as his lips moved up to nibble gently on her earlobe.

'You see, you like it, don't you?' he coaxed her, his voice husky with desire. 'I could make it really special for you, if you'll let me...'

She pushed him off so abruptly he almost fell backwards.

Kit's eyes narrowed. 'I hope you're not going to be a tease?' he accused her.

'I'm not a tease!'

'That's what it looks like to me. Giving me the signals, leading me on–'

'I'm not!'

'You're here, aren't you?' His eyes were cold. 'You're not that naïve, sweetheart. You must have known what was going on?'

Effie looked at the sand, her initials rubbed out.

'I wanted to wait,' she whispered.

'Save yourself for marriage, you mean?' Kit's mouth curled. 'God, now you really do sound like a potato farmer's daughter.'

Effie turned on him. 'That's not fair!'

'Neither is making me promises and then changing your mind.' Kit shifted towards her. 'I told you, I don't know how much time I have left. I want to have some fun while I can.'

He kissed her again, so hard she could barely breathe. She tried to push him off but he was too strong for her, pinning her to the ground. She heard the fabric of her skirt tear as his hand fumbled to get underneath it.

With her last bit of strength, Effie brought her knee up between his legs. It wasn't a hard kick, but it was enough to shock him into releasing her. As he jerked upright, she rolled away from under him and clambered quickly to her feet

'I – I'm going to find the others,' she said, brushing down her clothes.

Kit sat up. 'Don't bother coming back,' he muttered.

Effie looked down at him. 'Kit, please don't be like this. I love you...'

'Just go,' he cut her off, scowling at the distant horizon.

Effie paused for a moment, lost for words. Then, with a sigh of misery, she turned and started off down the beach.

Effie spent most of that night crying into her pillow.

She wished she'd caught the train home with Jess that afternoon, instead of hanging around with Kit, Max and Harry. But Kit had been in such a foul mood, Effie hadn't wanted to leave him until she'd tried to smooth things over.

Not that it had done any good. He had barely spoken to her since she'd rejected him. And the looks of silent sympathy that Max and Harry kept giving her hadn't helped either. In the end she'd slept alone in the room Kit had meant for the two of them, while he'd bunked in with Harry and Max.

She'd lost him for ever. Now the reality of what had happened had finally sunk in, Effie had begun to worry she had been too hasty. It was all her fault. She couldn't blame Kit for thinking what he did, when she'd given him the wrong signals.

'You mustn't blame yourself,' Jess had comforted her when Effie whispered what had happened, just before her friend went home. 'Don't you worry about it, love. You did the right thing.'

But it didn't feel like the right thing when she cried herself to sleep, or in the cold light of day when Kit ignored her all the way home.

She sat in the back seat of the car, staring at the back of his head. He was driving, but not once did he turn his head to look at her, or even catch her eye in the rear-view mirror. It was as if she had ceased to exist.

Effie slumped in her seat, too engulfed in misery to laugh at Harry's endless jokes. She kept replaying the events of the previous day, wishing she could have said and done things differently. If only she'd given in to him, they could all be happy now. She would be sitting in the front seat beside him, his hand stroking her leg, exchanging secret smiles, and basking in the afterglow of their love.

But now it was too late.

Kit stopped the car at the gate to the Nurses' Home. As she got out, Effie plucked up the courage to turn to him and whisper, 'When will I see you again?'

He didn't reply, but the dirty look he gave her

247

said it all. Without a word, he started up the car and drove off, leaving her standing there, alone and forlorn.

She was still staring down the empty lane when the heavens opened.

Effie looked up into the dismal sky. Rain spattered her face, the icy drops mingling with her hot tears.

She had lost Kit, and that wasn't even the worst of it.

Now she had to face the wrath of Connor Cleary.

Chapter Twenty-Eight

It had been a quiet night on the Fever Wards, but by the time the day staff arrived Jess was still bone weary and looking forward to her bed.

She also knew Effie would be coming home from the coast with Kit, Max and Harry that morning, and Jess was keen to find out what had happened after she'd left. Poor Effie had looked so anxious the previous afternoon, and even though Jess knew she'd brought most of her troubles on herself, she still couldn't help worrying about her friend. Jess was afraid Harry might be right about Kit's reputation. Seeing him with Effie was like watching a wolf playing with a kitten.

So she was dismayed when she was summoned to Matron's office just as she was going off duty. Jess racked her brains as she hurried across the courtyard towards the main hospital building. What could she possibly have done wrong now?

As usual, Miss Jenkins's forbidding expression gave nothing away.

'Ah, Jago.' Matron put down her pen and regarded Jess across the desk. 'I have some good news for you. I'm putting you back on to days.'

But before Jess had time to register the fact, Miss Jenkins added, 'I'm afraid one of the nurses on the Fever Wards has managed to come down with suspected scarlet fever. She is in isolation until Dr Drake can decide what's wrong with the silly girl.' Matron tutted, as if it was the poor nurse's fault that she'd fallen ill. 'Of course, it might all be a lot of fuss over nothing, in which case you'll be moving back to Female Medical. But for today you'll have to report back to Sister Fever.'

'Today, Matron?' The words were out before Jess could stop herself. 'But I've just come off night duty.'

Miss Jenkins raised her brows. 'I do know that, Jago. I'm not a simpleton. You must return to the Nurses' Home to sleep, then return for duty at noon.'

Jess glanced at the clock and did some frantic sums in her head. It was nearly eight now, which meant she had four hours to walk the two miles to the Nurses' Home, grab some sleep, then walk two miles back to the hospital. Was it worth even leaving? she wondered.

She was aware that Miss Jenkins was watching her through narrowed eyes.

'Well, don't just stand there, girl,' she said. 'You'd better hurry up, hadn't you?'

249

It was too much to hope that Sulley might be waiting at the gates in his cart. Jess pulled her cloak around her and started off up the track that led from the village. It was a grim, cold day, and the countryside was sheathed in grey. Rain drizzled down, insinuating its way inside her up-turned collar and turning the ground underfoot to churned mud that splattered over her feet and ankles. Jess sighed. She would have to polish her shoes and find a clean pair of black wool stockings before she came back on duty.

But at least there was one blessing. As it was Sunday morning Miss Carrington had gone to church, so the Nurses' Home was empty. Jess crawled into her bed, for once too exhausted to notice the hard, unyielding mattress or the thread-bare sheets. She pulled a pillow over her head to shut out the distant mooing of the cows in their barns. It sounded as if they were serenading her under her window.

And it seemed no sooner had she fallen asleep than she was woken up by the clatter of Effie re-turning. Jess had been looking forward to talking to her friend. But with the prospect of only an hour's sleep before she must return to work, it was the last thing she wanted to do now.

Jess tried to ignore her, but Effie made such a commotion moving around the room, unpacking her bag and throwing her things into drawers, shaking the rain off her coat and sighing heavily all the while, that Jess was dragged unwillingly from her sleep.

'Can't you be quiet?' she mumbled, the pillow still clamped tightly about her ears.

'Sorry,' Effie mumbled. The bedsprings creaked as she sat down, then promptly burst into noisy tears.

Jess threw off the pillow and sat up, rubbing the sleep out of her gritty eyes. 'What is it? What's wrong?'

'It's all right,' Effie sniffed, wiping her nose on her sleeve. 'You go back to sleep.'

'Not much chance of that now.' Jess looked at the clock. It was just turned eleven. 'I've got to be back on duty in an hour, anyway.' She got out of bed and went to sit beside Effie. 'What happened? Is it Kit?'

Effie burst into tears again, covering her face with her hands. 'Oh, it was awful!'

Jess was instantly alert, shaken out of her weariness. 'Why, what happened?' Coldness suddenly washed over her. 'He didn't – force himself on you, did he?'

'No!' Effie's reply was sharp with outrage. 'Kit would never do such a thing. He – he loves me. Or he did...' She broke into fresh sobs. 'But now I've ruined everything. I feel such a fool!'

Jess stood up, relieved now that she knew her friend hadn't been hurt. 'Look, we've both got to be on duty at twelve, so why don't you tell me all about it while we get changed?' she coaxed gently.

She listened as Effie explained how she had turned Kit's advances down and how angry and disappointed he had been. It was just as Jess had suspected.

'Now I've lost him and it's all my own fault. He's right, I was stupid and naïve, and now he's gone forever!' she wailed

'In that case he wasn't worth having in the first place,' Jess said stoutly.

Effie turned a reproachful gaze on her, blue eyes huge and puffy with crying. 'You don't understand, I love him.'

Jess suppressed a sigh. As far as she was concerned, losing someone like Kit was no loss at all. Hopefully Effie would see that eventually, if she didn't die of heartache in the meantime.

It was a long trudge back to the Nurses' Home, with Effie weeping silently beside Jess all the way, refusing to be consoled. It was a relief to be able to leave her at the door to the main building and cross the grounds to the Fever Wards.

At least Sister Fever seemed pleased to see her.

'I have some good news,' she said. 'It turns out Nurse Stone doesn't have scarlet fever after all.'

Jess smiled. 'I am glad to hear it, Sister.' Glad for poor Nurse Stone, and for herself, too. But before she could allow herself to hope that she might be allowed the rest of the day off, Sister continued,

'However, she's been told to rest for the day and come back tomorrow. So the patients will need feeding, and then the doctors will be doing their rounds. Then I want you to special the new pulmonary TB case that came in this morning. He's already had a severe haemorrhage, and he's on the Dangerously Ill List. I've asked the doctors to look at him when they come.'

Jess gave a last, yearning thought to her bed at the Nurses' Home, then straightened her shoulders. 'Yes, Sister,' she said.

Dr French and Dr Drake arrived on the ward just as Jess finished sterilising the dishes after lunch. Dr French was as genial as ever, pausing to flirt with Sister while Dr Drake twitched impatiently beside him.

'Do you think we could see the patient, since that's why we're here?' he snapped finally, his patience giving way.

'Oh, do calm down, old chap. I must apologise, Sister, for my colleague's lack of charm.' Dr French flashed another broad grin at Sister Fever, whose cheeks dimpled, even though she was in her late forties and easily old enough to be his mother.

They were just leaving when Dr French glanced over his shoulder, and said, 'Hello? Who do we have here?'

They all looked round. A young woman stood behind the window that separated visitors from patients, her pale hands pressed to the glass. She was anxious, but that didn't take away from the loveliness of her pale face, framed by thick honey-blonde hair. Her gaze was fixed on the doctors, as if she wanted to get their attention.

'That's Mrs Jarvis,' Sister said. 'Her daughter is Pamela, one of our diphtheria patients. The little girl who had the tracheostomy on New Year's Eve?' she prompted, as Dr French looked blank.

The one you couldn't be bothered to visit, even though she was at death's door, Jess added silently.

'She's rather early for visiting hour,' Sister frowned at the watch on her bib. 'If you'll excuse me, I'll tell her to come back later.'

'No, I'll speak to her,' Dr French said.

Sister and Dr Drake both opened their mouths to protest, but Dr French was already heading out of the door that led to the visitors' area.

'Hello there,' he said. 'It's Mrs Jarvis, isn't it? Little Pamela's mother?'

Mrs Jarvis blushed. 'You know who I am?'

'Oh, I never forget a patient. And I must say, little Pamela is every bit as pretty as her mother.'

'Oh!' Mrs Jarvis's colour deepened. Jess gritted her teeth so hard her jaws hurt. 'I'm very sorry to disturb you, Doctor. I just wanted to see how Pamela was getting on.'

'She's doing very well,' Dr French said, even though it was obvious he didn't have the first idea who or what he was talking about. 'I'm sure you'll be able to take her home in a couple of weeks.'

Mrs Jarvis looked up at him, her eyes sparkling. 'Really? Oh, that's wonderful news. I was so scared when Sister told me what had happened, I really thought we were going to lose her.'

Dr French looked mildly confused. 'Yes, well, she – um – gave us all a scare,' he said.

'Are you – the doctor who saved her?'

'Well, I wouldn't say that...' But the look of false modesty on Dr French's face told a different story. It was all Jess could do not to say something.

'I've been hoping to see you, ever since it happened,' Mrs Jarvis gushed. 'I wanted to thank you for bringing Pamela back to us. She's our only child and I – I don't know what we would have done if we'd lost her.'

Dr French lowered his gaze. 'My dear lady, I was just doing my job,' he murmured.

No, you weren't! Jess wanted to shout. You weren't doing your job at all. You were living it up at a party while poor little Pamela Jarvis was fighting for her life, and you couldn't even be bothered to come and look at her.

She glanced at Sister Fever. She was smiling benignly, because of course she knew nothing of that night's dramas. As far as she was concerned, Dr French might well have had a hand in saving the little girl's life.

The only other person who knew the truth was Dr Drake. But he was flicking through a patient's notes, staring down at the words with fixed concentration, as if his life depended on them. It seemed as if he hadn't even heard the conversation, but Jess could tell by the mottled flush that spread up his neck to his ears that he had.

She stared at him, willing him to speak up, to take the credit that was rightfully his. Finally, as if he could feel her gaze like a touch on his shoulder, he looked up at her. He glanced at Dr French, who was now explaining in detail to a breathless Mrs Jarvis exactly how heroically he had battled to save her daughter's life, then gave a slight shrug and looked back at the notes in front of him.

Chapter Twenty-Nine

Effie knew she would have to see Connor sooner or later.

When she went on duty at noon she was immediately tense and watchful, waiting for him to spring out at her at any moment like an avenging angel.

Connor would be angry, she had no doubt of

that. She had managed to give him the slip and go away with the others, and he would never forgive her for it. He would have to retaliate, his pride wouldn't allow him to do anything else. Dealing with Connor was like a sword fight, constantly parrying and striking at each other's weak spots.

She secretly quite enjoyed the constant battle of wits that went on between them, but not today. Today she was far too miserable over Kit to take pleasure in anything.

'You don't look your usual cheery self, dear?' Mrs Flynn observed, when Effie went to record her pulse and temperature after lunch. 'You haven't had a lovers' tiff, have you?'

Effie stared at her. 'How did you know?'

Mrs Flynn smiled. 'I thought as much. He was just the same first thing this morning. Turned up to bring the post with a face like thunder, he did. I said to myself, "Deirdre, something's not right with that young man." Because he's usually such a cheerful soul, isn't he?'

Effie realised what she meant. 'Oh, no, it's not Connor–'

But Mrs Flynn wasn't listening as she leaned forward and patted Effie's hand. 'Take my advice, love,' she said. 'Make it up with him. Life's too short for quarrels. Besides, you've got a good one there. You don't want to lose him, do you?'

Life's too short... Wasn't that what Kit had said to her yesterday? What if something happened to him? What if he was killed before she'd had a chance to tell him how sorry she was?

Mrs Flynn was right, she did have a good one there. She would never find another man like Kit, and she'd let him slip through her fingers.

Mrs Flynn looked over her shoulder. 'Here's your chance,' she said, nodding towards the door.

Effie turned round. Connor had come in, pushing an empty wheelchair.

'All aboard for the *Skylark*,' he started to say, then saw Effie and stopped dead. For a moment they stared, both eyeing each other warily.

'Ah, Mr Cleary.' Sister Allen came bustling down the ward towards him, breaking the tension. 'You've come to take Mrs Needham down for her X-ray? She's over there in bed seven. O'Hara, go down with her.'

'Me, Sister?'

'I don't see any other O'Haras around here, do you?' Sister's smile disappeared. 'Go on, girl, hurry along. And no sloping off for a cigarette while Mrs Needham is having her treatment,' she warned.

They travelled down in the rickety old lift together in awkward silence. They stood shoulder to shoulder, both staring at the metal grille across the lift door. It was strange, Effie thought miserably. Yesterday neither Connor nor Kit would leave her alone, and today neither of them would even look at her.

They made their way to the X-ray room, Connor striding ahead and Effie trailing behind. As they headed down the green-painted corridor Connor chatted to Mrs Needham, reassuring her about her treatment.

'It's nothing to worry about, Mrs N,' he said. 'They're just after taking some photographs. They want to make sure you're as good-looking on the inside as you are on the outside!'

'Oh, you!' Mrs Needham chuckled. 'You're such a charmer. Isn't he a charmer, Nurse?'

'If you say so.' Effie kept her eyes fixed on the wall, angry with herself for feeling so nervous. Why did she have to justify herself to Connor Cleary anyway?

Once Mrs Needham had been safely transported to the X-ray room, there was nothing for them to do except wait for her to come back.

'You can go if you like?' Effie offered. 'I'll let you know when we need to go back to the ward.'

'No thanks, I'll wait,' Connor replied stiffly.

The silence stretched between them, becoming more and more tense until in the end Effie couldn't bear it any more.

'Go on, then,' she said. 'Let's get it over with.'

He stared at her blankly. 'Get what over with?'

'The lecture. There's bound to be a lecture, isn't there? I expect you're just dying to tell me how irresponsible I am!'

'I've got nothing to say to you, Euphemia.'

It was the defeated way he said it that shook her. He sounded subdued, almost disappointed.

Effie rallied. 'That makes a change,' she snapped.

She hoped he might bite, but he didn't. She risked a sideways glance at him. His profile looked as if it had been carved from granite.

'I don't care anyway,' Effie went on defiantly. 'I'm allowed to do as I please. You're not my father, and I don't have to ask your permission!'

'Thank God for that,' Connor muttered. 'If your father were here he'd give you the belt for

258

what you did.'

Effie pulled a face. 'It wasn't that bad. All I did was sneak away for one night–'

Connor swung round to face her. 'You make it sound so casual,' he said. 'But I suppose that's the kind of girl you are these days, isn't it?'

'What do you mean?'

'That's the way you do things over here. Dropping your drawers for any man who shows an interest!'

Effie recoiled. 'But I didn't!'

'Of course you didn't.' Connor's lip curled. 'I daresay you stayed up all night playing Ludo, didn't you? Or did he give you a goodnight kiss and send you off to bed by yourself?'

That's exactly what happened, she wanted to say. But anger prevented her. She didn't have to explain herself to the likes of him.

'I haven't done anything wrong,' she said.

'Not by your standards, I suppose. But where I'm from, nice girls don't go around doing that. Or had you forgotten that?'

Connor sounded so patronising, Effie could feel her hackles rising.

'Why should I listen to you?' she derided. 'You're just – a potato farmer's son!' She repeated Kit's insult, forgetting how she'd stood up for Connor over it.

He flinched, and she knew her barb had hit its mark.

'Better that than a whore,' he hissed.

She'd slapped his face before she could stop herself. As soon as she'd done it she knew she'd made a terrible mistake. Her hand seemed to burn with the imprint of Connor's bristled jaw.

Her hand went up to touch the reddened patch on his cheek, but he jerked his head away, out of her reach.

'Do you really think Kit will still care about you?' His voice was low and full of contempt. 'Now he's got what he wants, he's probably forgotten about you already, moved on to the next girl...'

Effie didn't mean to cry. She had never, ever cried in front of Connor Cleary. But his words had opened up a wound in her heart, exposing her worst fears, and suddenly she couldn't stop the tears that spilled down her cheeks.

She looked away quickly, but it was too much to hope that Connor hadn't noticed.

'Wait... Are you crying?'

'No,' she mumbled

'Yes, you are. You're crying.' He sounded bewildered, and Effie didn't blame him. Even as a child, when he'd teased and tormented her, she had never let him see how much he'd upset her.

'What's wrong? Effie, talk to me.'

'Leave me alone.' The gentleness in his voice upset her even more. If he'd teased her now, perhaps she might have found the strength to fight back. But Connor being nice to her was more than she could cope with.

Fortunately, the door to the X-ray department opened then and the nurse announced that Mrs Needham was ready to be taken back to the ward.

Once again they travelled in deathly silence, the only sound the creak and rattle of the ancient lift as it rose to the third floor.

Effie stood as still as she could, every muscle in

her body rigid. Don't cry, she told herself over and over again. She'd already shown Connor more weakness than was good for her. He'd thrust at her heart and she'd been unprepared, hadn't parried fast enough.

But she would be ready next time.

Chapter Thirty

On a bright, cold Thursday morning in late January, they were halfway through Dr Drake's ward round when the telephone rang on Sister's desk. It was the Casualty department with an emergency admission, an injured aircraftman from the base at Billinghurst Manor. He had been badly burned in a petrol-can explosion while servicing one of the planes.

After the initial moment of shock, Miss Wallace swung smoothly into action.

'We'll put him in bed one,' she instructed Grace. 'Draw the screens round until we know the extent of his injuries. Rushton, please run a saline bath. He'll need to be treated before we dress his wounds.'

They hurried off to do as they were instructed. Millie was quite calm at first, moving automatically, her mind focused on the task. It was only when the patient arrived that she felt her self-control starting to slip.

It started with the smell: the horrendous stench of burned flesh and hair that went straight to her stomach until it was all Millie could do not to gag. She could see Grace felt the same even though, like Millie, she was trying not to show it. Only the whiteness of Grace's knuckles as she pressed her hand to her mouth gave away how she felt.

The orderlies carried the man, screaming in pain and swathed in blankets, straight into the bathroom. It was only when they laid him down and the blankets were removed that Millie saw how terribly injured he was.

His clothes had been cut off him in Casualty save for the large patches where the fabric of his overalls had stuck to his skin. His hands had been burned away to blackened claws, with bone showing through where the flesh had melted away. One side of his face was a blistered mess, his hair singed off to expose his burned scalp. The burns extended down one side of his body to the top of his right leg.

Millie's stomach clenched at the sight of him. Suddenly she saw, not a stranger but her own husband Seb, screaming out in agony.

She sucked in deep breaths through her mouth so she wouldn't have to smell the sickening stench. She must have breathed too hard or too fast, because the room began to spin. She planted her feet further apart to steady herself.

'Put him into the bath, quickly.' Even the calm, unflappable Miss Wallace had a tremor in her voice as she gave her order.

The orderlies carefully lifted him into the lukewarm water, and almost at once the man's screams began to subside to whimpers as the soothing saline did its work.

'There, that should do it.' Miss Wallace stood up. 'We'll leave him there to soak for a while, then hopefully we should be able to remove those bits of cloth that are still sticking to him... Rushton? Are you listening to me?'

Millie tried to focus on Miss Wallace's face, framed by her white linen bonnet, but black spots began to dance in front of her eyes, chasing each other across her vision. She heard the ward sister say her name, but her voice seemed to be coming from a long way away.

You will not faint. You will not faint, Millie told herself over and over. But already her head was growing heavier, pitching forward, taking the rest of her body with it.

The next thing she knew she was sprawled on the bathroom floor, the tiles cold underneath her, with the acrid smell of *sal volatile* being wafted under her nose.

'Nurse Rushton?' Miss Wallace's concerned face swam into focus above her. 'Nurse Rushton, can you hear me?'

Millie struggled to sit up. But Miss Wallace pushed her gently back down.

'No, you must rest there for a moment,' she said.

'But the patient—'

'Maynard is tending to him. Try to sit up and put your head between your knees for a moment. It might help.'

Millie felt foolish, sitting on the bathroom floor while Miss Wallace and Grace set about bathing the patient. She felt even worse after they left her sitting there while they dressed the aircraftman's wounds and got him into bed.

It should be me, she thought. I should be the one helping Miss Wallace with his dressings, not an untrained VAD. But instead she was slumped foolishly against the bathroom wall, as limp as a rag doll.

Once she had got herself to her feet and straightened her uniform, Millie reported to Miss Wallace's office.

'Ah, Rushton. How are you feeling?' The ward sister regarded her sympathetically across her desk.

'Better now, thank you, Sister. I'm terribly sorry.'

'These things happen, Nurse Rushton. But I think it might be better if you went home for the rest of the afternoon.'

'No!' The cry escaped her before she could check it. 'I need to be here, Sister. There's so much to be done.'

Miss Wallace raised a quizzical eyebrow. 'I appreciate you want to help, Rushton, but the last thing I need is one of my nurses fainting every five minutes!'

Millie blushed. 'But it won't happen again, Sister, I promise.'

'Won't it? Maynard explained to me that you'd lost your husband.' Miss Wallace chose her words delicately. 'Your reaction to the patient is completely understandable under the circumstances.'

Millie's face burned with shame but she said nothing.

'I think you should rest for the afternoon,' Miss Wallace said gently. 'Come back on duty at five o'clock if you feel you're able.'

Millie went home, feeling thoroughly ashamed of herself. Over and over again, she pictured herself sliding to the floor, and Miss Wallace's kind voice telling her to rest, as if she was one of the patients to be cared for, and not a nurse.

What had she been thinking? No wonder the ward sister had sent her home. 'The last thing I need is my nurses fainting all over the place,' she'd said. Millie had become more of a hindrance than a help.

She had pinned all her hopes on going back to nursing. Even when she was making a mess of everything else in her life, at the back of her mind she had always consoled herself with the thought that once there had been something she was good at, a place where she fitted in.

And now she realised she'd been wrong. She didn't fit in as a nurse, any more than she did running the estate. She was perfectly useless at everything. It was a joke to think she could ever be useful or needed.

Millie went through the gates of the estate, past the guards. But rather than heading for the Lodge she turned off the drive and walked up the narrow track that led through the parkland and up to the ridge above the airfield. It was her favourite ride, a place she loved to come when she needed peace and quiet to think.

Although being alone with her thoughts was quite possibly the last thing she really needed at that moment, Millie thought as she sat down on a mossy old tree stump.

She was tired of hearing the voices in her head condemning her, telling her she was useless, that she didn't fit in.

'You know, if you were a spy you'd have the perfect vantage point up here.'

She'd heard his footsteps approaching but didn't turn round until William stood behind her.

'What are you doing here?' she asked.

'Looking for you. I saw you walking up the road, and you seemed rather upset. Is everything all right?'

I do wish people would stop asking me that!' Tension made her snap. 'I'm not completely helpless, you know!'

'I didn't say you were.' William sounded hurt. 'I'm sorry. I'll leave you in peace...'

'Don't go.' Millie twisted round to look at him. 'I'm sorry. I've had rather a bad day. But I shouldn't have taken it out on you.'

She pulled her packet of cigarettes out of her bag and went to light one, but her hand was shaking so much she couldn't hold the lighter steady.

'Allow me.' William took out his own lighter and held it to the tip of her cigarette. Then he sat down next to her. 'Care to tell me about it?' he asked.

Millie kept her gaze fixed on the airfield below her. 'We had an injured airman in today. One of yours.'

William winced. 'God yes, I heard what happened. Poor blighter. How is he?'

'Not good.' Millie couldn't even begin to describe it. But every time she closed her eyes she saw those charred limbs and smelled that repugnant stench. It seemed to be on her hands, her clothes, every breath she took reeked of it.

'I fainted,' she said.

'Good God.'

'I kept thinking about Seb, you see. Seeing that poor man ... it made me wonder if that was what Seb looked like when they found him.' She took a nervous drag on her cigarette. 'I've always tried not to picture him – you know, like that. But ever since I saw that poor man, I can't seem to get the picture out of my head.'

'Millie–'

'And then I keep thinking that he must have been in pain,' she carried on, the words falling over themselves to get out. 'Silly, isn't it? Of course it was a horrible way to die, but I've comforted myself that perhaps he knew nothing about it, that at least it was quick...' She drummed restlessly on her knee with her fingers, too agitated to stay still. 'But now I don't know, do I? Now I've seen how much the human body can endure and still go on living, it makes me afraid that perhaps Seb suffered too...'

'Millie, don't. You can't torture yourself by thinking like that.' William's hand closed over hers, stilling her restless tapping.

'I know, but I can't help it. That's why I fainted, you see. I tried to cope with it, but in the end I couldn't even look at him. So silly of me really.'

'Not silly at all,' William said. 'Anyone would have reacted in the same way.'

'No, they wouldn't. Miss Wallace didn't flinch and neither did Grace. And she hasn't had any of my training.'

'Yes, but they haven't been through what you have.'

'That's not the point. The point is, I shouldn't have fallen to pieces like that. I'm supposed to be a professional nurse. I'm trained not to let this kind of situation get to me.'

'You're also a human being,' he reminded her. 'Don't be so hard on yourself.'

She heard what he was saying, but somehow couldn't allow herself to take in his words.

'I shouldn't have run away,' she said. 'I should have stayed strong, not let my feelings get in the way...'

'Your compassion isn't weakness, Millie. It's one of the things that make you such a good nurse.'

'But that man didn't need my compassion. He needed my skill and my care, and I was too weak and foolish to help him.'

'That's because you were in shock. You'll do better next time.'

'I don't think there's going to be a next time.'

Without thinking, she handed William her cigarette. He took a long drag on it.

'You mean to say you're not going back?' he said.

'I don't think Miss Wallace would want me anyway.'

'Don't be absurd. Of course she wants you. You're an excellent nurse.'

She turned on him. 'How can you say that, after what I've just told you? I'm a failure, and that's all there is to it.'

'The only way you can fail is if you give up completely.' He handed the cigarette back to her. 'Think about it, Mil. You made one mistake. Everyone makes them. The secret is not to allow them to get the better of you.'

She was silent, taking in what he'd said. 'I would miss it,' she admitted.

'And you would be missed, I'm sure.'

'Do you think so?' She looked at him. 'Do you really think I'm a good nurse?'

'One of the best,' said William.

Their eyes met and she felt a sudden, alarming jolt of attraction, a treacherous feeling she hadn't experienced in a long time. It suddenly occurred to Millie that they'd been sitting alone in the woods, sharing a cigarette and holding hands, almost like lovers. It would be too easy, she thought. Far, far too easy.

She stood up quickly, stubbing out her cigarette. 'I'd better be going anyway,' she said, suddenly brisk. 'Thank you for the pep talk.'

William looked up at her, and once again she found herself lost in his fathomless dark eyes. 'That's what friends are for,' he said softly.

Chapter Thirty-One

Kit was drunk.

The others had gone back to the base a long time ago, but he'd stayed after hours with the pub landlady. Not his usual type – she was thirty if she was a day, and hardly refined with her bleached blonde hair and dirty laugh – but she was up for some fun and that was what he needed. Especially after he'd wasted so much time on Effie O'Hara.

Oh, Effie. It was a pity, because he'd had such high hopes for her. She looked so wild and wanton, with that mane of dark curls. He'd seen a bit of naughtiness in those blue eyes, a reckless, impulsive side that he'd thought was like his own. But once it came down to business, she had turned out to be nothing more than a nice little convent girl, too terrified to let herself go. It was all very disappointing.

He paused for a moment, scanning the lane ahead of him. Was this the right way back to Billinghurst Manor? He was so bloody drunk, he had no idea. The only light was from the full moon high above him. A bomber's moon, as they called it.

Not that he was in any fit state to go up in a plane tonight! He laughed to himself as he weaved up the lane, crashing into bushes on either side.

Perhaps he should go back to the pub and ask to stay the night? He was sure the landlady would welcome him back into her bed. He struggled to remember the woman's name. Edna... Evelyn... No, it was gone. He couldn't remember anything except the way she'd writhed under him. Her husband was in the army and she missed the company, she said. That wasn't all she missed, he thought when she was wrapped around him up against the bar, urging him into her. He was looking forward to seeing her again. He wondered if he should book a hotel, perhaps the same B & B he'd taken Effie to. She'd be impressed by that, the silly little tart. But then again, why waste his money when he could get it for free anyway?

His thoughts strayed back to Effie. It was such

a shame she'd let him down. He would have loved to see her naked, sprawled out on that double bed, her dark hair spread over the pillow.

There was a rustle in the trees to his left. Kit stopped to listen. Nothing. Probably just his imagination playing tricks on him. That or the copious amount of whisky he'd had.

Lord, he was drunk! He'd pay for it tomorrow, he thought. What a hangover he'd have!

Glenys... Gloria... No, he still couldn't remember her name. But what did it really matter?

He looked sharply to his left. There was the sound again. A fox, he thought, or rabbits. Except he'd never met a rabbit who wore heavy boots.

'Who is it? Who's there?' He called out into the darkness. 'Max, Harry is that you? Very funny, I'm sure. If you think you can scare me creeping about in the–'

He slammed straight into the figure that stepped out into the road in front of him.

'Scare you?' a deep Irish voice said. 'Oh, fella, I haven't even started.'

Kit straightened up and nearly fell off balance.

Connor towered over him. Outlined against the moonlight, he seemed even more dark and menacing. If Kit was sober, he might have had the sense to be scared, but the whisky lent him a bit of bravado.

'Oh, it's you,' he said. 'What do you want?'

'A little bird told me you've been sniffing round the landlord's missus tonight?'

Kit grinned. 'Watching me, were you? You really ought to find a girl of your own, then you wouldn't have to spy on me. Oh, wait, I forgot. She doesn't want you, does she?'

That got him. Kit couldn't see the look on Cleary's face, but his silence spoke volumes.

'It isn't like that,' he bit out.

'Oh, no, of course it isn't. You just want to protect her, don't you?' Then Kit recklessly added, 'It's a shame. You don't know what you're missing...'

He didn't get to the end of his sentence before he felt himself lifted through the air. The next minute he was pinned to a tree trunk, his legs jerking uselessly, scrabbling to find the ground beneath his dangling feet.

'I could kill you and bury you right here, and no one would know,' Connor growled.

He was mad enough to do it, too. Even in the pitch-blackness, Kit could hear the threat in his voice.

Connor's grip tightened and Kit reached up, trying to claw the Irishman's hands away from his crushed windpipe. 'I don't think Effie would like that, do you?' he managed to gasp.

It worked. Connor released him abruptly. Kit stumbled to the ground, gulping in air.

'What happened?' Connor demanded.

'What?' Kit ran his finger around his collar to loosen it. 'What are you talking about?'

'You know. What happened – when you went away?'

It pained him even to say the words, Kit could tell. He smiled. So Effie hadn't told him the truth? This could be fun, he thought.

'Wouldn't you like to know?' he taunted him.

'That's why I'm asking you.'

Kit heard the ragged note in the Irishman's voice. It mattered so much to him, poor swine. Kit almost felt sorry for him.

Almost.

'Use your imagination,' he taunted. 'Although I daresay you already have, haven't you? I expect the thought of me making love to her is probably haunting your dreams every night...'

Connor winced. 'Don't push it,' he warned.

'Or what? What will you do, old man? Use your fists? I can't imagine Effie would be impressed by that, can you? She'd probably hate you even more, if that were possible.'

'Shut up,' Connor warned.

'What's the matter? Bit too close to the truth for you?' Kit laughed. 'It must kill you, to watch us together. Knowing you'll never have her.'

'I don't want her.'

Kit laughed. 'Now we both know that's not true. You watch her like a slavering dog. I'm surprised Effie hasn't realised it. But then, she's such an innocent, isn't she? Or she was,' he added, twisting the knife.

'I want you to promise that you won't hurt her,' Connor said gruffly.

'I don't think that's any of your business, do you?'

'I care about her.'

'Well, guess what? She doesn't care about you. Not a damn. And you can't make her care, even if you threaten me till Kingdom Come.' Kit circled him, enjoying his pain. 'And do you know why she doesn't care? Because you're just an ignorant farmer's boy. Why do you think she ran away from

273

Ireland, if not to get away from the likes of you?'

'Don't.' Connor's voice was low and threatening.

'I thought you wanted the truth?' Kit said. 'All right, I'll give you it, shall I? What do you want to know first? Do you want me to tell you how soft her skin was, or how her hair smelled of lavender? Or do you want me to tell you how she moaned my name in ecstasy when I took her–'

The fist came hurtling out of nowhere. Kit felt his jaw crack and the next second he was flying backwards. He slammed into the ground and lay there, winded.

Connor towered over him. 'Just don't hurt her,' he warned.

He strode off into the night, leaving Kit sprawled on the ground.

'You bastard!' he roared with rage, but Connor was already gone. 'I hope that made you feel better, because it's all you'll ever have,' Kit shouted after him. 'I'm the one Effie wants, not you!'

He nursed his jaw. It was already beginning to swell.

Hatred for Connor consumed him. Ignorant, uneducated oaf! Kit should have struck back, knocked him flat.

But even as he thought it, he knew that he was no match for Connor. Not physically, at least.

He got to his feet. There was more than one way to hurt a man like Connor Cleary. And Kit knew just the way to get to him.

Chapter Thirty-Two

'Hello, stranger. Remember me?' Pearl stuck her head round the back door. It was a Sunday afternoon, and Grace had the day off.

She looked over from where she stood by the stove, melting chocolate in a pan. 'Come off it, it's only been a couple of days since I last saw you!'

'More like a week. Come to think of it, I hardly see you any more since you started working at that hospital. And I've got no one to have a laugh with at the WVS.'

'Well, I'm here now, and the kettle's just boiled. You've got time for a cuppa?' Grace put down her wooden spoon and wiped her hands on her apron.

'I was hoping you'd say that.' Pearl came in and sniffed the air appreciatively. 'Something smells nice. What are you baking?'

'It's a birthday cake for Max. I've just taken it out of the oven.'

'Max, eh?' Pearl raised her eyebrows.

'I felt sorry for him,' Grace said. 'It can't be nice, can it, being so far away from your family on your birthday? I'd like to think someone somewhere might look after our Albie on his.'

Pearl dipped the tip of her finger into the chocolate mixture on the stove. 'This is nice. Is it for the icing?'

Grace nodded. 'I wanted to make ordinary icing, but you can't get sugar for love nor money.'

She poured the boiling water on to the leaves in the pot and gave it a stir.

'I didn't think you could get chocolate, either?'

'Max brought it for us. He seems to be able to lay his hands on anything through that PX store of his.'

'Max is quite one of the family these days, isn't he?' Pearl remarked, sitting down at the table.

'He comes round for his tea most nights.'

'You shouldn't be such a good cook.'

Grace smiled. 'It's Daisy he comes for, not my cooking. Anyway, I don't mind. He makes himself useful. He's fixed that leak in the roof we've had all winter, and he's done some other jobs.'

'Handy to have a man about the house, eh?'

'Isn't it?' Grace had never had anyone she could rely on before. For as long as she could remember she'd been the one up a ladder, painting or hammering or replacing loose roof tiles. She'd taught herself to do everything from decorating to plumbing, and she took pride in it. But it was a relief to be able to hand the toughest jobs over to someone else.

And it wasn't just that Max was useful around the house. He'd fitted right into the family, too. Walter and Ann adored him, and he was endlessly patient with them. Grace had become so used to having him around, she missed him on the nights he didn't call.

She poured out the tea, set a cup in front of Pearl and went back to her mixing. 'Come on, then. What's the news?'

'That's partly what I've come to tell you. They're having a Valentine's Day dance at the village hall, to raise funds for the prisoners-of-war. Mrs Huntley-Osborne's idea, of course.'

'Of course,' Grace agreed. 'She never stops, does she?'

'Anyway, she wanted me to let you know she's put us both on the refreshments sub-committee.'

'Has she now? Nice of her to ask me,' Grace said dryly.

'Oh, you know Mrs Huntley-Osborne. She never asks, always tells.'

'It'll make a nice change, I suppose. I expect Daisy will be pleased that there's a dance.' Grace went and fetched the cake from where it was cooling on the windowsill.

'That smells like heaven,' Pearl said, breathing in the spicy aroma.

'It's not much. I couldn't get hold of any mixed peel and there was hardly any sugar, so I don't know what it will taste like.'

'You never know, you might be making a wedding cake soon,' Pearl commented. 'For your Daisy and Max,' she said, when Grace looked blank.

'Oh, I don't know about that...' She spooned the chocolate carefully on top of the cake, but for some reason her hand was shaking so much, she barely had time to catch it with the edge of her knife as it spilled down the sides.

'Well, you never know, do you? If he's as keen as he seems... What's up?' Pearl asked with a frown. 'Have I put my foot in it?'

'Not at all,' Grace said. 'It just came as a shock to think that our Daisy could be getting married. The kids are growing up so fast, I don't know where the time's gone.'

'It can't go fast enough for me!' Pearl said with feeling. 'I can't wait for my little beggars to grow up, so I can get them off my hands!'

'I've looked after my lot for so long, I wouldn't know what to do with myself,' Grace admitted with a rueful smile.

'You could find a nice young man and think about having kids of your own,' Pearl suggested. 'I bet Daisy's airman could find a friend for you?'

Grace blushed. 'Get away with you! Who'd look at me?'

'Why not? You're a pretty girl, Grace Maynard. You just need to believe in yourself a bit more. It wouldn't hurt to get a bit of your sister's self-confidence.'

'I'll ask her if she can spare any!' Grace laughed.

She thought about it later as they all sat around the table, tucking into Max's birthday spread. As well as the cake, she'd made jelly with mock cream, and cucumber sandwiches, liberally covered in salt and pepper to disguise the taste of the margarine.

Pearl was right, the children were all growing up. Even Ann was no longer a baby. She was only a couple of years younger than Grace was when she'd taken over looking after the family.

She turned to look at Daisy and Max. Was Pearl right about that, too? she wondered. Would they end up getting married? She tried to think about her little sister as a bride, being carried over the threshold in Max's strong arms, and suddenly an overwhelming feeling of sadness hit her.

'Time for the cake,' Daisy said, breaking the spell.

'I'll fetch a knife.' Grace blundered to her feet, glad of the chance to get away. The room had suddenly become stiflingly hot.

As she handed the knife to Max, their fingers brushed and a jolt of electricity shot up her arm. Grace snatched her hand away and the knife clattered to the floor.

'Honestly, Grace, what's the matter with you?' Daisy tutted. 'You're as jumpy as a cat.'

'Sorry.' She pulled herself together. It was a mad moment, that was all. Nothing more than that.

She stood at the back of the room, trying to gather herself, as Max went about cutting his cake.

'Make a wish!' Walter and Ann shouted in unison.

Max's gaze sought out Grace at the back of the room. His eyes were quizzical, as if searching hers for the answer to an unspoken question. Grace could only stare back, struck dumb by an emotion she couldn't even name if she tried.

'I already have,' he murmured.

Chapter Thirty-Three

'Have you heard the news?' Daisy asked.

'Of course I have,' Jess replied. 'It was on the wireless last night. The Japanese have taken Singapore.' It was all anyone was talking about on the ward. 'It's terrible, isn't it? All those poor people. I wonder what will happen to them?'

Daisy screwed up her nose. 'Not that! They're having a dance in the village hall. What should I wear, do you think?'

Jess smiled to herself. Only Daisy Maynard could think her social life was more important than the progress of the war.

'Nurse! Nurse!' They looked at one another.

'Here she goes again,' Jess sighs.

'Do you want to go, or shall I?' Daisy said.

'It's my turn, I think.'

Mrs Flynn was sitting up in bed, propped against her pillows, with one of her favourite romance novels in her hand. She went through them voraciously. Her sister came to visit her twice a week, bringing yet more from the library.

'When's the doctor coming, Nurse?' she asked.

'Dr French isn't due to do his rounds until half-past ten, Mrs Flynn.' Jess fussed over her pillow. 'Why? Are you in any pain?'

'I might be... Yes, I think I've got a pain here.' She passed her hand over her flannel nightgown in the vague direction of her belly.

'I see. Perhaps you just need a hot water bottle?'

'No, I think I need to see the doctor,' Mrs Flynn declared firmly. 'Maybe you should get Sister to telephone him?' she said.

No sooner had she said it than the doors flew open and Dr Drake came flying through, white coat flapping, his long nose buried in his notes as usual.

'Well, that's a bit of luck, isn't it?' Jess smiled. 'He must be here to check on another patient. I'll fetch him for you...'

'No, don't.'

Jess frowned at her. 'But I thought you were in pain?'

'Yes, but I don't want to see that one. I want to see the other one. The nice one. The one who looks like Errol Flynn.'

Mrs Flynn spoke so loudly it would have been impossible for Dr Drake not to hear as he walked towards her. But he gave nothing away as he crossed the ward to talk to Sister Allen.

Poor Dr Drake, Jess thought.

'So will you ask Sister to telephone Dr French?' Mrs Flynn looked at her hopefully.

Jess tightened her lips before she burst out with something she'd regret. 'Let me fetch you that hot water bottle, and then we'll see how you are,' she muttered.

She went to the preparation room, where Daisy was putting together an ice cradle.

'Honestly, that woman is the giddy limit!' Jess fumed.

'Oh, dear, what's she done now?'

Daisy giggled when she heard the story. 'Well, you can't blame her, can you? I must say, I'd rather have Dr French fussing over me than Dr Drake!'

'Dr Drake is a good doctor,' Jess insisted.

'Yes, but he isn't nearly as charming as Dr French, is he?'

Jess thought about New Year's Eve, when Dr French had refused to attend poor little Pamela Jarvis. She had no doubt the child would have died if it hadn't been for Dr Drake's skill. She knew who she would rather have treating her, and it wasn't suave Martin French.

'Charm isn't everything,' she said. 'Besides, there's nothing wrong with Mrs Flynn. I'm sure she wouldn't have her mysterious pain if she didn't eat toffees all day long!' She was fuming as she set about making the hot water bottle 'I wouldn't blame Dr Drake if he prescribed her a strong aperient. That would teach her a lesson!'

Daisy sent her a knowing look. 'If you ask me, I think you've got a soft spot for our Dr Drake.'

'Don't be daft,' Jess dismissed this. 'I just feel sorry for him, that's all. Everyone prefers Dr French, and he doesn't deserve it.'

'Dr Drake shouldn't be so stand-offish then, should he?'

'He's just shy, that's all.'

Daisy laughed. 'I was right! You do have a soft spot for him. I'll have to write to Sam, tell him to watch out. While the cat's away...'

'Stop it,' Jess snapped. 'I'm not interested in him like that. But I reckon people would like him just as much as Dr French if they gave him a chance.'

'You should invite him to the dance then, if you feel like that?'

Jess knew Daisy meant it as a joke, but she said, 'Why not?'

Daisy laughed nervously. 'You're not serious? We wouldn't want a stuffed shirt like him hanging around. Besides, he'll only say no.'

'How do you know, if no one ever asks him?'

Daisy stared at her open-mouthed. 'Go on, then, ask him,' she said. 'I dare you!'

'All right, I will,' Jess replied. 'If he's still there when I've finished making this hot water bottle, then yes, I will ask him.'

Of course, she didn't really think he would be. So she was horrified when she returned to the ward with Mrs Flynn's hot water bottle, only to find Dr Drake filling in a patient's notes.

'Go on then,' Daisy hissed behind her. 'What are you waiting for?'

Jess thrust the hot water bottle into her hands. 'Here, take this to Mrs Flynn,' she said.

Dr Drake didn't look up from the notes he was scribbling as Jess tiptoed towards him.

'Yes, Nurse?' he enquired, head still bent.

Jess shot a quick look at Daisy. She must have told Mrs Flynn what was about to happen because they were both watching keenly. 'I – um–'

'Spit it out. What is it?' He finally looked up, his pale grey eyes fixed on hers. They were the colour of ice, thought Jess.

She took a deep breath. 'There's a dance at the village hall on Friday,' she said. 'I wondered if you'd like to come?'

The pale eyes narrowed to silver slits. 'Is that supposed to be a joke?' he said coldly.

'No! Honestly, I thought you might like to come.'

'I suppose your friends put you up to this again?' he interrupted her, looking around. His gaze fell on Daisy and Mrs Flynn, giggling together. 'Ah, yes, just as I thought. Well, I'm sorry, Nurse, but I'm far too busy for your pranks.'

'But it wasn't a prank,' Jess tried to say. He was already striding off. He walked so quickly that he tripped over his own shoelaces. Jess winced as Daisy shrieked with laughter.

'Oh, Jago, now do you see what a hopeless cause he is?' she said pityingly. 'Give up on him, for goodness' sake!'

Jess stared at the double doors. Daisy was right, of course. It was none of her business. She didn't even know why she'd taken it upon herself to try to help him, when he clearly didn't want it.

Poor Dr Drake. It might be better if she stayed out of his life, thought Jess. Every time she tried to bring him out of his shell, she only seemed to drive him further back into it.

Grace sat at the kitchen table, watching Max through the window. He was in the back yard, chopping firewood.

She couldn't take her eyes off him. He had stripped down to his vest, and the muscles flexed under his golden skin as he swung the axe, bringing it down on the block with easy strength. Sweat had darkened his blond hair, plastering damp strands to his face.

He looked up and caught her staring. Grace glanced away sharply, back to the hearts she was cutting from newspaper.

What was the matter with her? Ever since Max's birthday, she had suddenly become very conscious of him. She couldn't help herself. She couldn't even be in the same room as him without blushing like a schoolgirl.

She had never been so disturbed by a man's presence as she was by his. Her awareness of him crept under her skin.

He finished chopping the logs and carried them in armfuls to the woodshed. She heard him come into the kitchen but kept her head down, snipping away at the newspaper feverishly as he closed the back door.

'I've put the logs away,' he said.

'Thank you.'

'It's no problem.' He paused. 'What are you doing?'

'Making paper hearts. Mrs Huntley-Osborne wants them strung around the village hall for the dance, as it's Valentine's Day.'

She allowed herself to glance at him, and immediately felt her stomach tighten as she saw him shrugging on his shirt.

'Are you going to the dance?' he asked.

'I'll say.' Grace laughed a little too loudly. 'I'm helping to serve the refreshments.'

He didn't say anything. He was standing close to her, just behind her shoulder. If she breathed in, she could smell the musky male scent of him. She held herself tense as he picked up one of the paper hearts, turning it round and round between his fingers. The air between them seemed to swell, the pressure building.

He cleared his throat. 'Grace...'

'I suppose you'll be going to the dance with Daisy?' she broke in desperately. She had the horrible feeling that if she allowed him to speak, something would happen from which there would be no going back.

The door opened and Daisy walked in. Grace almost cried with relief.

'Max? What are you doing here?'

'He came to chop some wood for us,' Grace said. 'Wasn't that kind of him?'

285

The door hadn't been closed and a sudden gust of wind blew in, picking up the paper hearts in a little whirlwind.

'Daisy! Shut the door.'

'Sorry.' Her sister closed it as Grace scrabbled round on the hearth, gathering up the fluttering hearts. One drifted down like a snowflake and landed on the fire. Grace watched it curl up and blacken, consumed by the flames.

A heart, shrivelled to nothing. She knew how it felt.

Chapter Thirty-Four

Jess practically had to drag Effie to the dance. She trailed behind her and Daisy into the village hall with a face like a wet weekend.

'I wish we hadn't bothered to bring her!' Daisy complained. 'No one's going to ask us to dance with her hanging around. That face is enough to put anyone off!'

'Leave her be, she can't help it. You'd be just the same if your boyfriend jilted you.' Poor Effie, she'd been so down in the dumps after all that business with Kit.

In Jess's opinion, she was well rid of the selfish swine. But Effie was pining for him.

Harry came towards them, looking very smart in his Royal Canadian Air Force dress uniform. 'Hello, ladies,' he greeted them smoothly. 'You're all looking very beautiful tonight, I must say.'

'Where's Max?' Daisy asked.

'He's around somewhere... Oh, there he is. Over at the refreshments table.'

Jess peered through the crowd. 'Is that your sister with him, Maynard?'

'Yes, poor thing. Mrs Huntley-Osborne has got her running around as usual. I suppose I'd better rescue Max before Mrs H tries to take him over, too!'

As Daisy slipped through the crowd, Mrs Huntley-Osborne herself appeared, resplendent in a gold brocade get-up.

'So that's the famous Mrs Huntley-Osborne, is it?' Harry remarked as she swanned past. 'She doesn't look much like a dragon to me.'

'You wait until she starts breathing fire in your direction!' Jess said.

'I'm not sticking around for that.' He grabbed her hand. 'C'mon, let's dance.'

He started to pull her towards the dance floor, but Jess held back. 'I'm not really one for dancing. Why don't you dance with Effie instead?' She glanced at her friend, standing sullenly by. But Effie shook her head.

'Oh, don't mind me. I'm not dancing either.'

'Come on.' Harry tugged at Jess's hand. 'Live a little. Life's too short not to have fun.'

Harry was a very good dancer, and he whisked her around the dance floor to the fast music. Jess was glad he'd persuaded her to dance as he swung her round, lifting her until she was breathless with laughter.

Then the music slowed down and he pulled her closer, his arms circling her.

'I bet you wish you were with Sam right now, don't you?' he whispered.

Jess pulled away from him, staring blankly at his face. 'What? Why do you say that?'

'Relax, honey, I didn't mean anything by it.' He grinned. 'I just meant, I bet you'd rather be dancing with your boyfriend right now than with me?'

Jess blinked back the tears that suddenly sprang to her eyes. 'Yes, I do,' she whispered. 'More than you could imagine.'

'I wish you were my Hannah, too.' He pulled her closer, his hands around her waist. 'Tell you what, why don't we both close our eyes and pretend, just for a minute?'

'I'd like that.'

So Jess closed her eyes and suddenly she was in Sam's arms, swaying to the music and feeling the heat of his body pressed against her. And for a moment, everything was all right with the world.

Effie watched the dancers whirling around the floor and wished she could be one of them. She had told Jess she wasn't going to dance, but now she was here she realised how much she missed being spun around to a lively tune. And the band was playing all her favourites tonight, much to her annoyance.

Jess had insisted that coming to the dance would cheer her up. But Effie felt even more miserable if that was possible, surrounded by so many happy couples dancing and falling in love around her.

Kit was always such a good dancer, she thought with a longing sigh. So quick and graceful, all the girls wanted to be his partner.

She looked around the crowded village hall. She had half hoped he might be here, but there was no sign of him. Not that she really knew what she would do or say if she saw him.

And in a way, perhaps it was better that he wasn't there. Effie wasn't sure she would be able to face seeing him spinning another girl around the dance floor the way he used to do with her.

'Look at you, all on your own in the corner like a wallflower!'

She turned around slowly. Just as she'd thought the evening couldn't get any worse, there was Connor Cleary.

At least he was looking smart for once. He'd swapped his old work boots and trousers worn with braces for a suit, and his dark curls had been cropped.

'What are you doing here?'

'Same as you, I imagine. Except by the looks of you, I reckon I'm having a better time doing it. *Slainte.*' He raised his glass to her in mocking salute.

Effie glared at him. They had been avoiding each other for the past couple of weeks, which suited her very well. Mrs Flynn and the other women on Allen Ward might miss his constant presence, but Effie didn't.

'Where's your man this evening?' he asked, looking around.

So news of Kit jilting her hadn't reached him yet, she thought. That was something, at least. Listening to Connor teasing her about Kit would have been like a great big handful of salt rubbed into her wounded heart.

'He'll be here later,' she lied, not meeting Connor's eye.

'Liar. He's not coming, is he? You're here all on your own.'

'As a matter of fact, I'm here with my friends...' She looked around for them. Jess was still on the dance floor, and Daisy had disappeared with Max. 'Anyway, you're on your own too,' she accused.

'What do you mean? My dance card happens to be full for the whole evening, I'll have you know. But,' he leaned in confidingly, 'I could make room for you, since I feel so sorry for you.'

'Don't bother,' Effie snapped. 'It'll be a bad day indeed when I'm reduced to dancing with you, Connor Cleary!'

'Suit yourself.' He shrugged. 'Go on standing there like a wallflower.'

'Stop calling me that. I'm not a wallflower!'

Connor made a big show of looking around him. 'Well, I don't see many fellas queuing up to have a dance with you.' He grinned. 'Just like being in Kilkenny again, isn't it? Do you remember how none of the lads would dance with you because you were too tall for most of them?'

'How could I forget?' He had never missed a chance to tease Effie about it.

'I was the only one who could make you look dainty.' He held out his hand to her. 'Come on, let's take a turn around the floor for old time's sake, what do you say?'

She hesitated for a moment, then took his hand reluctantly. 'But you'd better not dance an Irish country jig and embarrass me,' she warned as she followed him.

'Oh, I think I can do better than that.'

He was a surprisingly good dancer. Not as good as Kit, but better than Effie remembered.

'Where did you learn to dance?' she asked, as Connor swung her round and dipped her low to the ground.

He gave her an enigmatic look. 'Oh, I'm full of surprises.'

'You're better than you were in Kilkenny,' she said.

'So are you.'

Her mouth twisted. 'Even for a big spindly wallflower?'

'Can I tell you a secret? I was actually glad you were so tall, because it meant I was the only one who could dance with you.'

Effie glared at him, bracing herself for the inevitable punchline. Any second now he would laugh in her face, tell her he was joking, make an eejit out of her again. But for once the look in his blue eyes was deadly serious.

Before Effie could take in that revelation, there was a tap on her shoulder and a familiar voice drawled, 'Excuse me, do you mind if I cut in?'

She looked over her shoulder, following Connor's stony gaze to where Kit was standing.

'Kit!' He looked so handsome, Effie could feel herself melt at the sight of him.

'Hello, darling.' He gave her a lazy smile, then turned to Connor. 'Do you mind, old chap?'

She felt Connor's grip tighten around her for a moment as he and Kit eyeballed each other. Then he released her abruptly.

There was so much Effie wanted to say, so much she knew she should say. She should muster her pride, turn her back on Kit. But she couldn't help herself. She abandoned Connor and slipped straight back where she wanted to be, in Kit's arms.

At the same moment the tempo of the music quickened.

'I haven't seen you for a while,' she said, over the jaunty sound of the brass.

Kit looked shame-faced. 'No,' he said. 'I was angry. I had to calm down for a while.'

'*You* were angry?' Effie stared at him in disbelief. 'What about me? You were the one who jilted me, remember?'

'I know, and I'm sorry.'

She had never heard him apologise with any sincerity before. It came as a big shock.

As if he could read her thoughts, Kit said, 'That's why I came tonight – to say I'm sorry. As I said to you once before, I never know how much time I've got left. And I didn't want to – you know – without making things right with you, telling you how I feel.'

His expression was so contrite, Effie couldn't stay angry with him. 'Go on,' she said.

He paused for a moment, then said, 'I should never have tried to force you. It was very wrong of me, and I bitterly regret it. But I couldn't help it,' he insisted, his expression pleading. 'I just adore you so much. And when you turned me down, it was as if you were saying – you didn't care.'

'But I do care,' Effie blurted out before she could stop herself.

'Do you, darling? Do you really?' His face brightened.

'Yes,' she said. She knew she probably should have played harder to get, made him work for her forgiveness. But it was so difficult when he was being so lovely and charming to her. Effie had never managed to master the art of being aloof.

'So will you give me another chance?'

Effie's smile was on her lips before her brain had had a chance to catch up with what Kit was saying. He was giving her another chance to prove how much she loved him. And this time she mustn't let him down.

'Oh, yes!'

Kit laughed. It was a loud, almost triumphant sound. He picked her up and swung her round, until she couldn't catch her breath. Effie tried to laugh but his movements were quick, nimble and daring; they thrilled her, and made her cling tighter to him.

'I'm so happy we're back together,' he breathed in her ear as he pulled her close. 'I was afraid that I'd ruined everything. These past couple of weeks have just been utter misery for me. I've missed you.'

'I've missed you, too,' Effie said.

'I never want us to be apart again, even for a second,' Kit said. 'However long I have on this earth, I want to spend every last second of it with you.'

A little spark of realisation flared in Effie's mind, and she started to tingle from head to toe with anticipation. 'What – do you mean?' She hardly dared whisper the question.

Kit smiled down at her. 'I mean I want to marry

you, darling – if you'll have me, that is?'

Jess sipped her glass of fruit punch and looked around the hall. It was warm, and the room was bathed in golden light, and all the girls looked so lovely in their pretty dresses, filling the floor with a whirling rainbow of colours.

In the middle of the dance floor, Effie was wrapped around Kit, looking so blissfully happy it was hard to imagine she was the same girl who had trailed in miserably a couple of hours before.

But now it was Daisy's turn to sulk. According to her, Max had barely spoken a word to her all evening, let alone asked her to dance, and she was bored and fed up.

'I've even danced with other officers all night, just to make him jealous, but he's hardly noticed,' she complained to Jess. 'If he hasn't bucked up his ideas in the next half an hour, I'm going to go home and see if he follows me.'

'I'll come with you,' Jess said. She had danced all the dances she wanted to, and now her feet were aching and she was tired and ready for her bed.

She was waiting by the door, already in her coat, when Mrs Huntley-Osborne sailed by.

'Oh, are you leaving already? Such a shame.' Her thin lips curved in a smirk. She clearly hadn't forgiven Jess for humiliating her that day on the ward.

But Jess had good reason to resent her, too. As Mrs Huntley-Osborne passed, she called after her, 'I met a friend of yours the other day.'

'Oh, yes? Who's that?'

'Sarah Newland.'

Mrs Huntley-Osborne's expression didn't change, but some of the colour drained from her face.

'Miss Newland was a former servant, hardly someone I would call a friend,' she replied contemptuously.

I'm sure you wouldn't, Jess thought. 'I've been round to visit her a few times, actually. Her baby's due next month.'

'Is it? I had no idea.'

'Poor girl, it isn't right that everyone's turned their back on her. But I don't suppose they'd dare do anything else, would they?'

'I'm sure I don't know what you mean.'

'Don't you? I suppose this isn't all your doing! You've turned everyone against her. No one would dare take her side against you.'

Mrs Huntley-Osborne's head reared back, nostrils flaring. 'Girls like Sarah have no place in a community like this,' she said shortly. 'There are good people living in this village, and we don't need the likes of Sarah Newland causing trouble among us. But I can see why she's made a friend of you,' she added, looking Jess up and down. 'It seems to me you're cut from the same cloth.'

'Good people?' Jess echoed disbelievingly, ignoring her insult. 'What kind of good person tries to drive a young girl out, just because she made the mistake of getting pregnant?'

A curious glint came into Mrs Huntley-Osborne's eye. 'Is that what she told you?'

Something about the way she said it made Jess wary. 'Yes. Why?'

Mrs Huntley-Osborne's mouth curved in a cold

smile. 'That just goes to prove my point, doesn't it? The girl is a born liar.'

'Then why do you hate her so much?'

'Because she stole from me. Something very precious. Something that cannot be replaced. She denies it, of course, but we both know the truth.' She looked at Jess. 'I don't suppose she told you that, did she?'

'No,' Jess said slowly. 'No, she didn't.'

A thought came into her mind, an image of something that wasn't quite right. Something that had struck her as odd when she'd first noticed it, but which she had since forgotten.

'So, you see, perhaps you should check your facts before you jump to conclusions?' Mrs Huntley-Osborne said, a hint of triumph in her voice. 'Look at Sarah Newland, Miss Jago, and then look at me. Who do you think is telling the truth?'

Chapter Thirty-Five

'Now that's something I haven't seen in a very long time,' William said.

Millie looked up at him as they circled the room with the other dancers. The band was playing one of her favourite songs, 'The Way You Look Tonight'.

'What's that?' she asked

'Your smile.'

She pulled a face. 'Oh, dear, am I usually so stern?'

'Not exactly. You smile quite a lot, actually. But it's never been a real smile. In fact, I've hardly seen you genuinely happy since we got here.'

'Yes, well, perhaps I haven't had much to be happy about.'

'And do you now?' he asked.

Millie looked around the dance floor, at the other couples swirling around them to the music. It might have been nothing more than the old village hall strung with a few fairy lights and chains of paper hearts, but it felt magical to her.

It was the kind of night that she could never have imagined herself having a few months ago.

'Yes,' she said. 'Yes, I do.'

Her heart felt as light as her feet as they skipped around the dance floor. Over the past few weeks, Millie felt as if she had stepped out of the shadows and started to walk towards the light of a new life.

'I'm glad to hear it.' William was dancing so close to her, she could almost feel the beat of his heart against hers. 'I feel as if you're back to being the old Millie again.'

'Goodness, I hope not!' She pulled back to look at him. 'I'd like to think I'm not that naïve and silly any more.'

'All right, you're allowed to mature a bit,' he said. 'As long as you keep the old charm.'

'Mature?' Millie laughed. 'Now you're making me sound like a cheese!'

William smiled. 'I'm afraid I'm rather out of practice with flirting.'

'That's not what I've heard!' she said. 'I've seen you with those WAAFs, don't forget.' Then she realised what he'd said and added, 'Is that what you're doing? Flirting with me?'

'Would that be such a bad thing?' he said softly.

She considered the question. A few months ago she would have rejected the idea out of hand, but now she was surprised to find she rather welcomed it. 'No,' she said finally. 'It wouldn't be such a bad thing, I suppose.'

'And if I were to take it further – perhaps suggest a night out together?'

'We're out together now, aren't we?'

'That isn't quite what I had in mind,' William said ruefully. 'I was thinking more of dinner or the theatre. Just the two of us?'

She looked up into his warm, brown eyes, like delicious pools of melted chocolate, and felt the same jolt of attraction she'd experienced the first time she saw him striding down the ward. She might not be a naïve little girl any more, but he still had the power to make her heart skip.

'I think that sounds delightful,' she said.

As the music finished, William lifted his gaze to glance over her shoulder. 'I think someone's looking for you,' he said.

Millie turned around. There was Teddy, weaving his way through the crowd, his gaze searching the room. She waved, and he made his way towards them.

'Hello, darling.' He leaned in and kissed her on the cheek. 'Sorry I'm late. Trains down from London were beastly, as per.'

'At least you're here now.' Millie turned to William. 'William, this is Teddy Teasdale, one of my oldest and dearest friends. You might have seen him visiting the Lodge? He often comes down to

298

see us.'

'Can't keep me away!' Teddy grinned.

'Teddy, this is William Tremayne. He's with the RAF squadron living up at the house.'

Teddy offered his hand to William. 'How do you do, old boy?'

William shook his hand briskly, then said, 'If you'll excuse me, I think the Wing Commander is leaving and I really should say goodbye to him.' He nodded briefly to Teddy. 'It was good to meet you.'

'Now why do I get the impression he didn't mean that?' Teddy said as they watched William threading his way past the couples on the dance floor.

Millie frowned. 'What do you mean? He seemed perfectly civil to me.'

'To you, perhaps. But I detected a definite *froideur.* I may be wrong, but I suspect your friend William sees me as a rival for your affections.'

'Don't be absurd!' Millie dismissed. 'Why on earth would he think that?'

Teddy sent her a withering look. 'Now you really are making me feel like a maiden aunt. Can't you just for once see me as the handsome rake I am?'

Laughter bubbled out of her. 'Oh, Teddy! You are funny.'

He sighed. 'For heaven's sake, let's dance before you destroy every shred of my masculine pride.' He held out his arms to her. 'Would you care for a turn around the dance floor, Lady Amelia?'

'Why, thank you, Lord Edward, I would love to.'

Millie danced more sedately with Teddy than she had with William. There was no pulsing attraction between them, no unspoken promises made with long looks. Instead Teddy carted her round the dance floor and told her about the recent grim talk he'd had with his parents.

'Sadly, news has reached them we won't be welcoming Georgina Farsley or her considerable fortune into the family. Needless to say, they're not best pleased,' he sighed.

'Poor Teddy!' Millie sympathised.

'I'm rather afraid I will be if they decide to cut me off as they're threatening to do. I can't even dangle the promise of a betrothal to you under their noses any more, since your affections clearly lie elsewhere these days.'

'What makes you say that?'

'My dear girl, you haven't taken your eyes off your friend William since he took to the dance floor with that rather cross-looking blonde.'

Millie dragged her eyes away from William and Agnes Moss and back to Teddy. 'I'm sorry,' she said.

'It's quite all right, my dear. Anyone can see you're utterly besotted. And if it matters to you, I would say the feeling is mutual.'

'Do you think so?' Millie felt a blush rising in her face.

'Most definitely. Makes me rather jealous, actually, seeing you make eyes at each other.'

'Then I'll have to find a nice girl for you, won't I?' Millie smiled. 'Is there anyone here that you like the look of?'

'Only one,' he said. 'And she's standing right in front of me.'

Millie laughed. 'Oh, do be serious!'

'I am serious.'

She waited for him to follow it up with one of his witty quips, but he didn't. He was staring down at her, and for once he wasn't smiling. 'Teddy?' she ventured uncertainly.

'I'm sorry, Mil,' he sighed. 'I know this is rather awkward, but I seem to have fallen in love with you.'

'Oh, Teddy!'

'It's my own silly fault,' he went on. 'I knew where we both stood when I started coming to visit you. But as time went by I started to enjoy seeing you and little Henry. And somewhere along the line I seem to have forgotten that we were just friends having some fun together, and well–' he shrugged expressively 'I realised I had these rather annoying feelings for you. It's all right,' he went on hastily, 'I know you don't feel the same. You don't, do you?' He stared into her face.

'I'm afraid not,' Millie said.

'I would have been surprised if you'd said yes. Delighted too, obviously, but very surprised. I promise I won't make any difficulties for you,' he said. 'I shan't be writing poetry to you, or standing under your window at midnight serenading you with love ballads I've composed.'

'I'm glad to hear it.' Millie smiled in spite of herself. 'You're tone deaf, as I recall.'

'Completely,' he sighed. 'Seriously, I don't mean to make you feel uncomfortable. Lord knows, I'll probably be in love with someone else by next week. You know how fickle I am. Unless, of course, you do decide you prefer me to your friend William, in which case I will be waiting for you with all the devotion of a pet Labrador.' He reached for her hand. 'Don't look so stricken, darling. I promise you, this changes nothing.'

He planted a kiss in her palm and Millie pulled her hand away gently. An hour ago and she would have thought nothing of such a gesture, but now it felt loaded with meaning

Teddy was wrong, she thought. Whether she liked it or not, his confession changed everything.

Sarah frowned when she saw Jess on her doorstep.

'It's a bit late for a visit, ain't it?' she said, pulling her cardigan around her expanded waistline. Her red hair was like a fiery cloud around her head. 'What is it? What's wrong?'

'Why didn't you tell me?' Jess said.

Sarah's expression grew wary. 'Tell you what? I don't know what you're talking about.'

'You could start with this.' Before Sarah could react, Jess grabbed the string around the other girl's neck. 'How about explaining why you stole this ring?'

Sarah snatched it back from her. 'I didn't steal it.'

'I think you did.' It had bothered Jess the first time she'd seen it. What was a girl living in a squalid little cottage doing with such an expensive piece of jewellery? But she'd pushed the doubts to the back of her mind, telling herself it was none of her concern. Until Mrs Huntley-Osborne's words had brought them bobbing back to the surface.

Sarah said nothing. She kept her gaze fixed on the ground.

'That explains why you never wear it, doesn't it? I should have known,' Jess said. 'I should have realised there was more to it than you were telling me. And to think I went in all guns blazing to have it out with Mrs Huntley-Osborne because I thought she was treating you unfairly!'

'I didn't ask you to.' Sarah found her voice.

'I did it because I thought we were friends,' Jess said.

It was hard for her, because she didn't let people in very easily. But she had seen something in Sarah that convinced her to let down her guard. It was difficult for her to believe that she had been so wrong.

'I don't have any friends.'

'I'm not surprised, if you go round lying and stealing.'

Sarah flashed her a furious look. 'I'm not a liar and I'm not a thief!'

'That's what it looks like to me.'

'Oh, well, that's it then, isn't it? You've obviously made your mind up about me, just like all the others.'

Jess stared at Sarah, unmoved. The self-pitying tactic wouldn't work on her now. 'So tell me the truth,' she said.

'Why should I?'

'Because I'm on your side.'

Sarah faltered, the fire fading from her eyes. 'It is her ring,' she admitted quietly. 'But I swear I didn't steal it.'

'So what happened?' The other girl's mouth firmed into an obstinate line, and Jess sighed. 'Look, I'm not having a go at you. But if you don't tell me the truth, I can't help you.'

Suddenly Sarah was defensive again, her shoulders taut, hackles rising. 'I'm not asking you for help. Just like I didn't ask you to come round here, bringing your clothes and your food parcels and everything else. I can manage by myself, thanks very much.'

'Fine. I'll leave you to it, then.' Jess was about to turn away when she saw the proud, defiant tilt to Sarah's chin. She recognised that look. She'd held herself like that many times, putting up a front so no one would know how scared she really was...

'All you have to do is give the ring back,' she said gently. 'I'm sure if you did Mrs Huntley-Osborne would–'

'No!' Sarah's hand tightened into a defiant fist around the ring. 'It's mine. Now I'll thank you to go,' she said stiffly.

'But I want to help.'

'I don't need your help, thank you very much. I managed without it before, and I'll manage again.'

Sarah closed the door in Jess's face before she could say any more.

Jess turned and walked away, annoyed with herself for blundering in. Sarah was right, it was none of her business. At any other time, she would have kept her nose right out of it.

Country life must have changed her, she decided. She'd turned into a busybody, just like everyone else in the village.

Chapter Thirty-Six

After the dance finished at ten o'clock, Grace and Pearl stayed behind to clean up the village hall on Mrs Huntley-Osborne's instructions. As the band packed up for the night on the stage, they swept the floor, carefully packed away the leftover food and went round putting anything they could find into boxes for salvage.

'You get off, I can finish here,' Grace said, when the band had gone home.

'Are you sure?' Pearl glanced towards the door. 'I did promise my mum I'd be back by ten for the kids.'

'Then go. It's fine, honestly. There isn't much more to do anyway. I've just got those paper chains to take down and we're all done.'

She surveyed the empty village hall, now looking rather forlorn with the lights and the music gone, and the refreshment table holding nothing more than empty plates and crumbs. It was sad to think it had been so full of life and colour and happiness just an hour ago.

She was up the ladder, unpinning the paper chains, when she heard the door open behind her. Thinking it was Pearl, she called out, 'What's the matter? Did you forget something?'

'Grace?'

She looked round so sharply she almost toppled off the ladder. Max was there in a second, standing below her, ready to break her fall.

'Are you OK?' he asked, his blue eyes full of concern.

'I'm fine, thank you. Just lost my balance for a minute.' She came down the ladder so that she was facing him. He was in his uniform, the slate-blue-coloured fabric taut across his chest and broad shoulders. All Grace's senses instantly flared into full alert at the sight of him, but she fought for control. 'What do you want?'

Max didn't answer her. Instead he nodded towards the ladder. 'Do you want me to get the rest of those decorations down for you?'

'There's no need, I can manage.'

'You don't have to manage when I'm here.'

She watched as he climbed the ladder. She knew she should move but she couldn't tear herself away. This was dangerous. All her senses were crying out, warning her. But she was deaf to them. She was willing to risk everything just for one more minute spent looking at him...

A moment later he was down again, his arms full of paper chains. As she went to take them, their eyes met. Warmth kindled in Max's blue gaze and she suddenly knew what was going to happen next.

'Grace,' he started to say, but she cut him off.

'I expect Mrs Huntley-Osborne will want to keep these for salvage.' She shifted her gaze to stare down at the paper chains in her arms as if they were the centre of her world.

'Grace, I need to talk to you.'

'I'll fetch a box. I'm sure I saw one in the caretaker's room.'

She started to move away but he grabbed her arm, holding her back. 'Grace, you can't keep walking away from me!'

Oh, yes, I can, she wanted to say. I can keep walking and walking and never stop, if it means keeping my family safe and happy. But at the same time she felt herself pinned to the spot, unable to move.

'What do you want?' she whispered

She wished she hadn't asked the question. She didn't want to hear what he had to say, because she had a dreadful feeling that it would change everything.

And she didn't want anything to change. She wanted the world to go on just as it always had, with her family at the centre of it and Grace always looking out for them, taking care of them.

Max looked down at his hands, suddenly bashful. 'I've just found out we're flying in the morning,' he said quietly.

Grace's heart hitched, as it always did when she learned Max was flying. She knew it was wrong, that she had no right to feel as worried as she did. But all the same, she could never rest until she knew he was safe again.

She told herself it was nothing more than the concern of one friend for another, but in her heart she knew it was more than that.

'It feels different this time,' Max went on. 'I don't know why ... but I didn't want to leave without telling you how I feel. Just in case...' The rest of his words hung unspoken in the air between them.

Don't say it, Grace begged silently. Don't say

307

anything. Then everything could stay as it was and everyone would be happy. There was no need to turn everyone's world upside down because of a few stupid feelings.

'I'm not good with words, but you know what I'm trying to say, don't you? God knows, I've not been very good at hiding it these past few weeks!' He smiled ruefully.

Grace couldn't speak. Her throat was so constricted every breath suddenly seemed painful, torn from her chest.

She stared helplessly at him, eyes fixed on his mouth. His perfect mouth...

'I love you, Grace.' He was smiling at her, not caring that he was throwing her carefully ordered world into chaos. 'I've loved you from the moment I saw you in your yard on Christmas Day, clutching that stupid goose carcass to your chest–'

'No!' She cut him off, shaking her head as if she could shake his words out of it. 'You can't!'

It made no sense. Of course she had noticed Max, been aware of his every move, his every breath. For him to notice her – it was impossible.

It was all a dream, she decided. In a moment she would wake up and everything would be back to normal and she wouldn't be standing here, her throat dry and her heart pounding like a sledgehammer against her ribs.

'I can't help it,' said Max. 'I never expected it to happen to me. This was just another posting, another tour of duty before I went back home. But then I met you, and...' He shook his head. 'I've wanted to tell you this for a long time, but I could never find the right moment. You were always so

308

busy, running around everywhere, looking after everyone else. But I think you feel it too, don't you?' he said, his earnest gaze meeting hers. 'I can see it in your face when you look at me.'

He reached for her but Grace backed away, colliding with the wall. 'What about Daisy?' she said. Just saying her sister's name felt wrong.

Max's face fell. 'Daisy is a sweet girl, but I just don't feel that way about her. I haven't been able to think of her in that way, not since the day I met you. I can't help it,' he said, his voice ragged. 'I didn't want this to happen, truly I didn't. I wouldn't have hurt her for the world, but–'

He gestured helplessly, wanting her to understand. Grace believed him. The anguish on his face told her he was speaking the truth.

'Daisy loves you,' she said flatly. 'It would hurt her so much if she knew about this.'

'So what am I supposed to do? Spend the rest of my life pretending to care for someone else, when all I want is to be with you? Don't you think that would hurt her more in the end?'

'I – I don't know.' Grace didn't know anything any more. Her mind was whirling with a confusion of ideas and thoughts.

'What if there was no Daisy?' Max said. 'If there was no one but you and me, would you want me then?'

'But there is, isn't there? That – that's an unfair question.'

'I'm just asking you how you'd feel?'

She stared down, knowing if she looked into his eyes she'd give herself away and all would be lost.

'What's the point of asking me that?' she whispered. 'There isn't just you and me, is there? And there can't be, not without my sister getting hurt.'

Max sighed. 'I don't want to hurt anyone,' he insisted. 'I never asked your sister to fall for me, any more than I wanted to fall for you. I certainly haven't encouraged her.'

'Yes, you did!' Grace challenged him, suddenly angry. 'You should have stopped seeing her if you didn't care about her.'

'Then I wouldn't have had an excuse to see you, would I?'

Grace stared at him, caught between pity for her sister and the yearning of her own heart. As usual, concern for her family came first. 'You used poor Daisy.'

Max shook his head. 'I made it clear to her we were just friends. If you feel I did wrong then I'm sorry for it. But I was desperate.' He ran his hand through his thick fair hair.

'I couldn't help myself. You understand that, don't you? Of course you do.' He answered his own question. 'I can see it in your face. You're blaming me because you feel just as guilty about the way you feel.'

'No,' Grace said, but she could feel the heat building inside her.

'Stop lying to yourself.' He reached out for her. 'You've spent so long doing what's right for other people, you've forgotten how to do anything for yourself.'

'That's not true–'

But her protest was lost as Max suddenly moved forward. He trapped her face between his hands. She could feel the heat of his skin seconds before he kissed her.

The moment that perfect mouth touched hers, she was lost. His kiss was gentle at first, almost tentative, his lips barely meeting hers. Then he tilted his face, his blue gaze staring down at her, full of wonder.

'Oh, Grace...'

She should have stopped it. All it needed from her was a word, a turn of the head to show his advances weren't welcome. But she was twenty-three and she had never been with a man, and she desperately wanted to know what it was like to kiss Max, just once, before she had to let him go for ever.

His strong arms went round her and she melted into his embrace, heat flooding through her.

So this was what it was like to kiss a man, she thought, before the dizzying sensations took her over, shutting out everything else.

Somewhere in the distance she heard the click of a door latch, but she was too lost in the moment to care, until a voice sliced through her befuddled senses with a loud, clear enquiry.

'What's going on here?'

Chapter Thirty-Seven

The sound of her sister's voice was like a bucket of icy water poured over Grace's heated senses. She sprang away from Max, releasing him at once.

Daisy stood framed in the doorway, her face expressionless with shock. She looked like a lost little girl and suddenly all Grace wanted to do was to protect her.

'It – it's not what you think,' she started to say, but Max interrupted her.

'Grace, don't.' His voice was deep and calm and measured. He turned to Daisy. 'I'm sorry, I never meant you to find out like this. I planned to talk to you, to explain everything...'

Daisy ignored him. Her eyes were fixed on her sister, cold and accusing. 'How could you? How long has it been going on?' she demanded.

'There's nothing going on,' Grace said, but the words sounded hollow, even to her.

Daisy laughed harshly. 'Do you think I'm a fool?' She looked from one to the other. 'I should have known you were up to something. All those private jokes, those sly little looks you kept giving each other when you thought I wasn't looking. You must have been laughing at me behind my back!'

'I wasn't, truly.'

Max stepped in. 'This is all my fault, it's nothing to do with Grace,' he said. 'Your sister didn't encourage me. I've been the one chasing her, not the other way round.'

But it was as if he hadn't spoken. Daisy went on staring at Grace with cold contempt in her eyes. Grace had never seen her sister look at her with so much hatred before.

But then, she'd never betrayed her before.

'I don't believe you,' Daisy said flatly. 'She did this, not you. She's always been jealous of me. She saw how much you loved me and she wanted to ruin it.'

312

'I don't love you, Daisy.'

Max's voice was gentle, but his words still had a devastating effect. Grace could feel her own heart breaking as she watched her sister's expression change from shock to disbelief before it finally crumpled in pain.

'You'd better go,' she told Max quietly.

'I'm not leaving you.'

'Please,' Grace begged, her gaze still fixed on Daisy. 'Just go. I need to look after my sister.'

Max looked from one girl to the other. 'I'll come and see you tomorrow, when we get back. We'll sort this out.'

'No, don't.' Grace stared at him, willing him to understand.

His expression faltered. He opened his mouth to argue but the fight seemed to go out of him. 'I see,' he said heavily. Once again, his gaze shifted to Daisy, still standing as if frozen in the doorway, then back at Grace. 'You know where I am, if you need me.'

He left, and it was just the two of them. Daisy stood framed in the doorway, her arms wrapped around herself in a self-protective hug. It was a habit she'd developed on the day their mother died. She had looked so lost and vulnerable then that Grace had promised herself she would go to the ends of the earth to protect her.

And now she was the one who had caused her sister pain, the reason poor Daisy was looking so lost.

'I'm sorry,' Grace said again, knowing how useless the words were.

'I came back for you,' Daisy said quietly, her

voice barely above a whisper. 'I was worried about you walking home on your own.' She looked at Grace with reproach in her eyes. 'How could you, Gracie? You knew how much I cared for Max. How could you do it to me?'

'It didn't mean anything,' Grace said. 'What you saw – it was a mistake. I wasn't thinking, I didn't know what I was doing...'

'I think you knew exactly what you were doing.' Daisy spoke in a low, flat voice.

Grace started. 'What do you mean?'

'You've always been jealous of me, haven't you? Always resented that I was the one with the education, the chances in life.'

Grace stared at her in shock. 'How can you say that? I've always looked after you. I've put you and the kids before everything. Why would I be jealous of the chances you've had, when I worked so hard to give them to you?'

'That's what you want everyone to believe, isn't it? You love it when they talk about you, the poor girl who gave up everything to look after her brothers and sisters. Selfless Saint Grace, always cheerful, always putting everyone before herself, willing to do anything for anyone.' Daisy's tone was mocking. 'But that's not it, is it? Deep down you're angry that you had to miss out.'

'That's not true. I'm proud of you, not jealous,' she tried to say, but Daisy wasn't listening.

'You can't let me have anything without wanting it too,' she accused. 'It's the same at the hospital, with you thinking you're a nurse!'

'I don't–'

'Don't deny it! I've seen you sucking up to Miss

Wallace and Lady Amelia, like you're one of them. And then trying to talk to me about the patients and their treatments, as if you know the first thing about it. As if you were the one with three years' training!' Daisy's green eyes glittered with malice. 'But you're not a nurse and you never will be. You're just – a glorified housemaid!'

'I – I know,' Grace faltered. She stared at her sister, scarcely able to believe the venom that was pouring from her. 'Daisy, stop, please.'

'And now ... as if it isn't enough that you've come to the hospital and tried to take all my friends away from me, now you've decided you want to steal Max away from me too.'

'I didn't... I don't...'

'Do you love him?'

The question was so sudden, it took Grace by surprise. 'I–' She hesitated a moment too long.

'You do!' Daisy accused.

'It doesn't matter how I feel,' Grace said quickly. 'All I want is my family. That's what's important to me, not Max. You, me, Walter, Albie and Ann, all of us together, just like Mum would have wanted.'

'Yes, but we can't have that now, can we? We can't be together any more. It can't be like that ever again, because you've ruined it!'

'It's not my fault Max doesn't love you!'

Grace realised she'd said the wrong thing as soon as she'd blurted out the words. 'I'm sorry,' she said, 'I didn't mean it to sound like that. Daisy, don't go!'

Her sister stared at her with hatred in her face. 'There's nothing more to say, is there? You've got what you wanted.' She turned to leave. 'I'll ask

Matron tomorrow if I can move into the Nurses' Home.'

'No!' Grace recoiled. 'You can't do that. We belong together.'

'Then you should have thought of that before you stole my boyfriend, shouldn't you?' Daisy turned on her viciously. 'You've destroyed this family, Grace Maynard. I only hope he was worth it!'

Back at the Nurses' Home, Jess was having a sleepless night.

She couldn't stop thinking about Sarah Newland. She lay staring up at the ceiling in the darkness, wondering how she could have misjudged someone so badly. She'd been sure she'd recognised a kindred spirit in the girl, someone who had been toughened by life but who deserved a second chance.

And in spite of what had happened this evening, she still wasn't sure she'd been wrong. Sarah didn't seem like a thief, although her defensive refusal to explain made her seem guilty.

Effie couldn't sleep either. That was another reason sleep eluded Jess: her room-mate insisted on chattering.

'Just think – I'm engaged,' she said for the hundredth time. Even in the darkness, Jess knew she was admiring her left hand, imagining a ring on her finger. 'I can't believe it, can you?'

'No, I can't,' Jess replied, and meant it. The story seemed fanciful, even for Effie. The boyfriend who had ditched her a couple of weeks before, suddenly turned up and popped the question. 'It seems a bit rum for Kit to change his mind like that, don't you think?'

'He realised how much he loved me,' Effie said simply. 'You know what they say – absence makes the heart grow fonder?'

More like out of sight, out of mind in Kit's case, Jess thought. He didn't strike her as the marrying kind somehow.

But then, she thought, she was starting to make a habit of misjudging people.

'Does your friend Connor know?' she asked.

'Not yet. I looked for him straight away, but he'd already gone. He didn't stay too long, come to think of it,' Effie said in a troubled tone.

'At least he'll be able to go home and tell your mum and dad that you're engaged,' Jess said.

'Hmm,' Effie replied thoughtfully. 'I'm not sure how my daddy will feel about me marrying an Englishman and a Protestant, too.' She blew out a heavy sigh. 'I'll be glad when I turn twenty-one in three weeks. Then I can do as I please.'

Jess smiled in the darkness. Effie O'Hara tended to do as she pleased anyway.

'Oh, I nearly forgot,' Effie changed the subject. 'You'll never guess who turned up to the dance after you left? Dr Drake!'

'What?' Jess sat bolt upright in the dark.

'Can you imagine? Talk about a fish out of water! He just walked in, stood there gawping around for a minute or two, then stomped out again. It was so funny. It's a shame you and Maynard weren't there to see it, you would have laughed.'

'I wish I'd been there,' Jess said quietly.

Poor Dr Drake. Shy as he was, it must have

317

taken a great deal for him to walk into that crowded dance hall. She couldn't imagine what he must think of her now...

Three dull thuds came out of nowhere, startling her out of her reverie. Effie squeaked in terror. 'What was that?'

'Sounds like someone knocking on the door.'

'In the middle of the night?' There was a rustle in the darkness as Effie pulled the covers up to her chin. 'You don't think it's the Germans, do you?'

'Germans wouldn't march up and knock on the door, would they?' Jess flung back the bedclothes and got out of bed.

She picked up her torch and went out into the hall. The beam picked out various other heads sticking out of bedroom doors down the length of the passage, most of them wearing crowns of spiky curlers.

At the far end of the passage, Miss Carrington emerged from her bedroom, swathed in a tartan dressing gown and looking cross.

'Who on earth is calling at this time of night, disturbing everyone's rest?' she muttered, heading for the door on slippered feet. 'Go back to bed, girls,' she instructed.

Most of the heads shot back into their bedrooms, but something made Jess hesitate. She heard bolts being drawn and keys jingling as locks were turned. And then, finally, Miss Carrington said, 'Yes? Who are you?'

'I – I'm looking for Jess Jago.'

Jess hurried up the passage until she could see the doorway. There, just visible beyond Miss Carrington, was Sarah Newland, wearing an old overcoat, doubled over in pain.

'Sarah?'

The girl looked up and spotted Jess. 'Help me,' she whimpered. 'I think the baby's coming!'

Chapter Thirty-Eight

Everything else was forgotten as they all rallied round to help.

Miss Carrington ordered two of the nurses to take Sarah into the sick bay, and another to run down to the telephone box in the lane and call for an ambulance.

'But the baby's coming!' Sarah wailed, struggling to catch her breath, gritting her teeth against the pain.

'Then we'll just have to do what we can, won't we?' Miss Carrington said grimly. 'Nurse Carr, go and fetch my medical bag from my room. Jefferson and Bevan, we'll need to make up the bed with a mackintosh sheet, and plenty of newspaper for the floor as well. Now, which of you girls has done her midwifery training?'

Two hands shot up. 'Excellent. One of you can prepare the room while the other prepares this – the patient.' She eyed Sarah dubiously.

The nurses set about boiling water and gathering up bowls, rubber gloves, cotton wool swabs, disinfectant and towels. In less than five minutes the sick bay was prepared and Sarah had been persuaded out of her overcoat, washed, and a clean nightgown had been found for her.

'Is there anything I can do, Sister?' Jess asked, as Miss Carrington emerged from her room, having dressed in her uniform.

'Are you trained in midwifery, Jago?'

'No, Sister.'

'Then it's best you stay out of the way.'

No sooner had she said it than Sarah screeched out, 'Jess! I want Jess.'

Miss Carrington lifted her brows heavenwards. 'It seems you're required after all,' she said.

Jess followed her into the sick bay, where one of the midwifery nurses was examining Sarah. She turned to Miss Carrington, eyes bulging in her pale face. 'Sister, I think the baby's coming.'

'Well, yes, that's why we're here, isn't it?' Miss Carrington washed her hands in the first of a line of enamel bowls that had been set out on the chest of drawers.

'No, Sister, I mean – look!'

Miss Carrington turned around in time to see the bloodied crown of a head appearing between Sarah's spread-eagled legs.

'Good lord!' she exclaimed, losing her composure for a fraction of a second. 'Come along, Nurses, there isn't a moment to waste!'

Jess barely had time to reach Sarah's bedside and grasp her hand before she screamed again. Jess's fingers were crushed in a vice-like grip until they lost all feeling, and a moment later a baby, bluish-red, smeared with blood and waxy vernix, slithered into the world.

'It's a girl!' Miss Carrington raised her voice over the baby's outraged cries. She looked dazed, poor woman. And no wonder – she hadn't delivered the child so much as caught it.

'A girl.' Sarah smiled dreamily. 'I've got a baby girl.'

Miss Carrington blinked hard. 'Let's cut the cord, shall we?'

They cut the cord and one of the nurses went off to wash the baby and find something warm to wrap her in, while Effie went to the kitchen to make a cup of tea for the new mother.

'I'm sorry – about what I said earlier,' Sarah murmured to Jess through dry, pale lips.

'It doesn't matter.' Jess squeezed her hand lightly. 'You were right, I shouldn't have interfered.'

'You were only trying to help. I suppose I'm just – not used to it.' Sarah's eyelids drooped and her head began to loll on her slender neck.

Poor girl, Jess thought. She was worn out. But then she saw the blood blossoming on the sheet between Sarah's legs like a giant crimson flower.

'Sister, she seems to be bleeding rather a lot... And she's gone very pale all of a sudden.'

'Let me see.' Miss Carrington remained utterly calm, but there was a slight tremor in her voice as she said, 'Yes, she does seem to be haemorrhaging more than I would expect. We'll try manual manipulation until the ambulance arrives.'

But nothing they could do would stem the tide that flowed out of Sarah.

'She must have torn an artery when she delivered so quickly,' one of the nurses, Janet Carr, whispered to Jess. 'I saw it happen once in training. It was awful.'

321

'What happened?'

'Well, she died, of course, but...' The nurse stopped herself, realising what she'd said. 'I'm sure your friend will be all right,' she said quickly.

I'm not, Jess thought. Sarah seemed to be fading before her eyes, her face taking on a worrying ashen look.

'I'm going to – die – aren't I?' she said to Jess, her voice barely above a whisper.

'Of course not,' Jess replied, giving her hand a little shake. 'Don't talk like that. Anyway, you can't die. You've got a daughter to look after, remember?'

The shadow of a smile curved the corners of Sarah's lips. 'I don't want her to grow up – in an orphanage,' she said. 'I don't – want her to be – like me.'

'She won't,' Jess said. 'She's got a mum who loves her.'

Sarah's eyes drifted closed, then snapped open again. 'I want you to do – something for me. The ring...' She lifted her hand and listlessly clawed at her throat, searching for it.

'It's here, ducks.' Jess picked it up from the bedside locker, where the nurse who had prepared Sarah had left it.

She tried to give it to Sarah, but she shook her head. 'Take it back – to her,' she murmured, eyes drooping again. 'Tell her ... tell her I'm sorry for everything...'

The ambulance arrived, and the next moment Jess was being ushered from the room as they got to work putting Sarah on a stretcher. The last thing Jess saw was her pale face, as cold and white as alabaster, as she was carried out.

Thankfully Sarah made it through the night, but the next morning she was still in a very bad way. Janet Carr had been right, she'd suffered a traumatic haemorrhage brought on by her baby's sudden and dramatic birth. Mr Cooper the Senior Surgical Officer had operated to stitch up the torn artery but Sarah had still lost a lot of blood, and no one seemed to know if she would pull through or not.

'It wouldn't be so bad if she weren't so weak and malnourished,' Janet Carr told Jess when she went up to the Maternity Ward to check on the patient during her break. 'I'm not sure she's got any fight left in her.'

'Oh, she's a fighter, all right,' Jess said. 'Don't you worry about that.'

'What about the baby? Have you seen her?'

Jess nodded. 'I popped down to the nursery before I came up here. She's doing well.' Considering the child was a month early she was already as bright as a button, with her shock of black hair and her mother's green eyes.

'Well, I hope she pulls through, for the baby's sake,' Janet said. But she didn't seem convinced.

Jess thought about the ring in her pocket, and the promise she had made to Sarah.

If anything happens to me…

Perhaps Sarah felt the ring was cursed, she thought. After all, she hadn't had much luck since she'd stolen it. Perhaps that was why she wanted to give it back, in the hope that her fortunes would change.

Mrs Huntley-Osborne lived in a grand Georgian

house at the far end of the main street, with a commanding view of the village. So she could keep an eye on her subjects, Tess thought.

Jess wasn't looking forward to seeing the woman again. But she had made a promise to Sarah, and she meant to keep it.

The maid showed her into an elegant drawing room with pale lemon walls and dove-grey silk upholstery. A grand piano dominated the room, its polished ebony surface covered with a forest of photographs in silver frames. There were pictures of Mrs Huntley-Osborne as a young girl, playing tennis and sitting astride a horse. There was a wedding photograph, and various pictures of a timid-looking man Jess took to be the late Mr Huntley-Osborne.

But most of the photographs were of the same subject: a handsome dark-haired boy. There were pictures of him as a baby in rompers, of him as a schoolboy winning a prize, in a student's cap and gown. The biggest was one of him looking smart in a Royal Navy uniform, smiling at the camera, a proud glint in his dark eyes.

Jess picked it up and studied it. This must be Mrs Huntley-Osborne's son, she decided. Now she came to look more closely, she could see he had his mother's prominent brow and long nose. But somehow it looked better on him.

'Put that down!'

Mrs Huntley-Osborne's cry nearly made Jess drop the photograph. She stood in the doorway, her steely gaze fixed on Jess.

'I was only looking.'

'I'd rather you didn't touch anything.' Mrs

324

Huntley-Osborne advanced into the room and took the photograph from her. She wiped an invisible mark off the silver frame with her sleeve, then replaced it carefully on the piano, in exactly the same position. 'My maid said you wanted to see me. You'll have to make it quick, I'm due at a committee meeting in half an hour.'

'I won't keep you. I only came to give you this...'

Jess handed her the ring. Mrs Huntley-Osborne stared down at it, a curious look on her face.

'Where did you get this?' she asked.

'Sarah gave it to me. She said she wanted you to have it back.' Jess looked at her. 'It is the one she took from you, isn't it?'

'It's my mother's ring.' Mrs Huntley-Osborne didn't take her eyes from it, turning it round and round in her fingers. 'And she told you to give this to me, you say?'

Jess watched her warily, a thought occurring to her. 'She won't be in any trouble, will she? Not now she's given it back?'

Mrs Huntley-Osborne looked up at her blankly. 'But I don't understand ... why would she return it?'

Jess shrugged. 'I don't know. Just wanted to make amends, I suppose.' She paused. 'She's in hospital. She gave birth to her baby last night.'

The other woman frowned. 'But surely the child wasn't due for another month?'

'She was born early. Took us all by surprise, she did.'

'She?' Mrs Huntley-Osborne interrupted. 'It's a girl? How is she?'

'She's very well. I just wish I could say the same

for her poor mother.'

'Why? What's wrong with her?'

Jess stared at her, surprised. For someone who loathed Sarah, this woman was taking a great interest in her suddenly. 'She's fighting for her life. The birth was very traumatic... We still don't know if she's going to pull through or not.'

'How very – unfortunate.' Mrs Huntley-Osborne's stiff mask was back in place.

'Yes, it is,' Jess agreed. 'If Sarah dies, that baby won't have a soul left in the world.'

'I suppose not.' Mrs Huntley-Osborne's gaze shifted to the photographs on the piano. She seemed lost in thought, oblivious to Jess and everything around her.

Jess followed the other woman's gaze towards the photograph of the good-looking sailor. 'Is that your son?' she said.

Mrs Huntley-Osborne nodded. 'Clifford.'

'He's very handsome.'

Mrs Huntley-Osborne gave her a sad smile. 'He was. He was killed in the North Atlantic six months ago.'

Jess looked at the young man in the photograph and then back at Mrs Huntley-Osborne. And suddenly everything clicked into place.

Chapter Thirty-Nine

'It wasn't the ring,' she said.

Mrs Huntley-Osborne shot her a sharp look. 'I beg your pardon?'

'It wasn't the ring that Sarah stole from you, was it? It was him. Your son.'

Something very precious, she'd said. Something that could never be replaced. At the time, Jess had assumed she was talking about a valuable piece of jewellery. But now, seeing Mrs Huntley-Osborne's face, she realised that the ring meant little to her compared to the loss of her son.

'I don't know what you're talking about,' Mrs Huntley-Osborne said, but her face betrayed her.

'What happened?' Jess said. 'Did he fall in love with Sarah?'

'I think it's time you left.' She reached for the bell to summon the maid, but Jess didn't move.

'I suppose that must have been difficult for you to accept, your son falling in love with the house-maid.'

'He didn't fall in love with her!' Mrs Huntley-Osborne snapped. 'If you must know, Sarah trapped him. Clifford was an impressionable young man, and she managed to twist him round her little finger. By the time I realised what was going on, she was pregnant. And of course, just as she'd planned, Clifford felt he had to do right by her.' Mrs Huntley-Osborne's mouth was a tight, bitter line.

'So he gave her the ring?'

'He had no right to do that – and she had no right to take it. Scheming little minx!' Her face was taut. 'Sarah knew exactly what she was doing. She stole my son from me.'

'Has it ever occurred to you that he wanted to marry her because he loved her?'

Mrs Huntley-Osborne turned on Jess, temper flaring. 'How could he possibly be in love with that – that creature?' Her mouth curled. 'I brought him up better than that. He was well educated, cultured. I made sure he went to the best school and the best university money could buy. He had ambition, he was going to be a doctor. How could someone like my son ever fall in love with a workhouse girl who could barely write her own name?'

Mrs Huntley-Osborne had answered her own question, Jess thought. If Clifford Huntley-Osborne had grown up being pushed through life by an ambitious, forceful mother, he might well be attracted to a girl who was completely the opposite.

'Sarah might not have been educated, but she wasn't stupid,' Mrs Huntley-Osborne went on. 'Oh, no, she was as cunning as a sewer rat. The way she pursued him... Clifford had another girlfriend at the time ... Evelyn Allen, the ward sister at the hospital? But once Sarah Newland got her claws into him, he dropped poor Evelyn completely. And she was such a nice girl, too.'

There was nothing nice about Sister Allen, Jess thought. Poor Clifford had had a lucky escape. But Sister Allen and his mother were both cut from the same cloth. Mrs Huntley-Osborne had probably hand picked his wife-to-be for him, the way she'd picked his expensive education.

And perhaps Clifford had been willing to go along with it, until Sarah Newland came along and showed him there might be a different way to live his life. She was his last, bold bid for freedom.

Jess could understand why Mrs Huntley-Osborne might dislike the girl so much. Not only did she have to cope with the shame of having a housemaid for a daughter-in-law, and a pregnant one at that, but Sarah was a free spirit, who wouldn't be controlled like Evelyn Allen.

'None of this would have happened if Clifford had taken my advice,' Mrs Huntley-Osborne continued. 'I said we could make other arrangements. I even offered the girl money to go away and have the baby quietly, then give it up for adoption. I told him: just because you've made a mistake, it doesn't mean you have to spend the rest of your life paying for it.'

'And what did he say to that?'

Mrs Huntley-Osborne's nostrils flared. 'He told me he had no intention of turning his back on his child or the woman he loved. But that was Sarah talking, not him,' she said. 'She got inside his head, made him think differently.' Mrs Huntley-Osborne swallowed hard. 'We were estranged when he died. I didn't get the chance to say goodbye.'

She stole from me … something precious. No wonder Jess had thought Mrs Huntley-Osborne was talking about a ring. She talked about her son as if he were a possession.

'Perhaps he loved her?' Jess said quietly.

Mrs Huntley-Osborne sent her a cold stare. 'I

know – knew – my son,' she said. 'He would have grown bored with her eventually. But as it is...' Her voice faded. 'He died before the situation could resolve itself.'

'And so you threw Sarah out. I bet you couldn't wait to do that, could you?'

'What else could I do? Besides, I only had her word for it that Clifford was the baby's father. For all I knew it could have been any one of a dozen men.' Her lip curled. 'You can hardly trust the word of a common maid, can you?'

Jess's hands balled into fists at her sides, and it was all she could do not to launch herself at Mrs Huntley-Osborne's smug, superior face. But she kept her temper with a supreme effort.

'Your son is the father,' she said, glancing at the photograph on the piano. 'If you saw the baby, you'd know she was the spitting image.'

'I don't want to see her!' There was real panic in Mrs Huntley-Osborne's voice. 'I don't want to have anything to do with her or her mother.'

'Is that why you've been trying to drive Sarah out of the village? Because you didn't want to see your own grandchild?'

Mrs Huntley-Osborne winced at the word. 'I want nothing to do with either of them,' she repeated. 'I loathe that girl for what she did to my family. She took my son away from me, drove a wedge between us during the last few precious months of Clifford's life. I'll never forgive her for that.'

'And now she could be dying,' Jess said. 'I'd say you've more than had your revenge, wouldn't you?'

'That's very unfair,' Mrs Huntley-Osborne said. 'I didn't cause her illness, did I?'

'No, but you could help her.'

'How?'

'By taking in her child if anything happens to her.'

Mrs Huntley-Osborne reared back in her seat. 'Certainly not! How could I possibly do that, without giving people cause to talk?'

'Let them.' Jess shrugged.

'That's very easy for you to say, I'm sure,' Mrs Huntley-Osborne snapped. 'But I have my position in this village to consider. People look up to me...'

'And that's more important than your own flesh and blood, is it?' Jess said. 'Look at yourself. You live in one of the biggest houses in the village, and you have no one to share it with. You spend all your time on committees and everything else just to keep busy and stop yourself being lonely. Don't deny it because it's true,' she added, seeing Mrs Huntley-Osborne opening her mouth to protest. 'But in spite of all that, you would rather see your own granddaughter sent to an orphanage than claim her!'

Mrs Huntley-Osborne looked scornful. 'They're not my family.'

'No, but they could be,' Jess tried to reason with her. 'I know Sarah might not be the girl you'd choose as your daughter-in-law, but she was the girl your son fell in love with, and surely that should be good enough for you? Besides,' she went on, 'I think you'd actually like her if you stopped seeing each other as the enemy and took

331

the trouble to get to know one another.'

Mrs Huntley-Osborne laughed harshly. 'I can assure you, that will not happen! Hell would freeze over before I ever accepted that woman in my house.' She reached for the bell, ringing it in agitation.

'If that's how you feel about it, there's nothing else to be said, is there?' Jess said. 'But just think about this. Sarah kept your secret all these months. She didn't even tell me, and I'm supposed to be her friend. She did it for your sake, out of love for Clifford.'

The maid appeared at the doorway. 'Miss Jago is leaving,' Mrs Huntley-Osborne said. But she sounded less sure of herself than she had a moment before.

Jess followed the maid to the door, then turned to look back. 'At least go and see them,' she pleaded. 'Talk to Sarah, while you can, for your son's sake. And your grandchild's.'

Chapter Forty

Effie sat at a corner table in the Keeper's Rest, watching her future husband flirting with the woman behind the bar.

Kit was supposed to be buying their drinks, but he'd been chatting to the landlady for ages. He'd spoken to her longer than he'd spoken to Effie all evening.

She turned her gaze away to look around the

bar. It was crowded with airmen and WAAFs as usual, as well as a few locals. There was no sign of Connor, thank God; the last thing Effie needed was him making fun of her.

She looked over at Kit, willing him to return to her. But his back was turned so she couldn't catch his eye. All she could see was the way the landlady ran the tip of her tongue over her parted lips as she looked him up and down, like a lioness sizing up her next meal.

Don't be daft, Euphemia, she warned herself. The landlady could flirt all she liked, but Effie had no reason to fear. Kit was her fiancé. She was the one he had chosen to marry, not a brassy barmaid with hungry eyes and a dirty laugh.

Except Effie didn't feel very engaged. She looked down at her bare left hand, still bereft of a ring after nearly a week. The other girls were beginning to ask questions.

'Are you sure you're really engaged?' Janet Carr had asked her with a mocking smile. Janet had also got engaged on Valentine's Day and now she was sporting a very nice diamond and sapphire ring from her airman fiancé.

Effie had made the same excuse Kit had given her, that he didn't want to buy her any old ring– 'I have to choose one that's absolutely perfect, darling' – but she'd reached the point where she would have stuck an old curtain ring on her finger just to make herself feel better.

No more, she thought. Tonight, she was determined to pin him down to a date, at least.

Finally Kit returned to the table with a lemonade for her and a whisky for himself.

'Can you believe they don't have any beer?' He nodded to a sign hanging above the bar.

'It took you long enough to find that out,' Effie murmured under her breath.

Kit put her drink down on the table and sat down opposite her. Over his shoulder, Effie could see the landlady smirking at them as she polished glasses behind the bar.

Effie turned her gaze away, ignoring her. 'Kit, we need to talk about the wedding,' she said.

He took a gulp of whisky and put down the glass. 'What about it?'

'There are things we need to sort out. When we're getting married, for a start. I was thinking the spring is a good time.'

'This spring?'

'Why not?'

'But it's February now. Surely that's too soon?'

Effie frowned at him. What had happened to the young man who lived like there was no tomorrow?

'I don't think so. Janet Carr and her fiancé have already booked their church for late April.'

'Not Janet Carr again!' He rolled his eyes. 'That's all I ever seem to hear about these days. "Janet Carr's booked the church, Janet Carr's chosen her bridesmaids, Janet Carr's done this and that" – I pity her poor fiancé!'

'At least her fiancé wants to get married,' Effie shot back, hurt. 'I'm beginning to think you're getting cold feet.'

'I told you, darling, there's plenty of time.' Kit rested his hand on hers, reassuring her. 'Of course I want to marry you, more than anything in the world. But I want it to be really special.'

Like my ring? Effie thought, looking at her left hand again.

'I suppose so,' she agreed with a sigh. 'I expect my mammy will want to help me decide all the details anyway.' She smiled across the table at him. 'I can't wait for you to come to Kilkenny to meet my family,' she said. 'My daddy might be a bit difficult at first, but I'm sure he'll come round when he—'

Kit blinked at her. 'You want me to go to Ireland with you?' he said slowly.

'Of course.' Effie frowned at him. 'Why? Don't you want to meet my family?'

He looked as if he was about to say no, but then to her surprise he grinned and said loudly, 'If that's what you want, darling, then that's what we shall do.'

His sudden change of attitude startled her, until she looked at the door and realised Connor Cleary had just walked in.

Effie's heart immediately plunged. She hadn't told Connor about the engagement yet. She told herself it was because she didn't want him to rush off and tell her parents before she did. But if she was truly honest, it was mainly because she was a coward.

He approached their table and she waited tensely for him to throw one of his usual sarcastic comments her way. But to her surprise he walked straight past and joined his friends who were playing cards on the other side of the bar.

Effie let out the breath she had been holding ever since he walked in.

Kit watched him over the rim of his glass as he took his seat. 'Your friend doesn't look very happy tonight,' he remarked.

'As long as he's quiet and doesn't bother us, I don't care,' Effie said. 'Let's just ignore him, please?'

But Kit seemed too fascinated to ignore him. He watched Connor as he studied his hand of cards. 'Maybe he's upset about the engagement?'

Effie looked down at her drink. 'He doesn't know yet,' she admitted quietly.

Kit frowned. 'Why not?'

'I don't know... I didn't want him to make any trouble for us, I suppose,' she said.

'Well, let's tell him now, shall we?'

He rose from his seat but Effie grabbed his arm. 'Please don't,' she begged, but Kit had already shaken off her grasp and was making his way across the sawdust-covered floor to where Connor sat, still studying his cards.

Kit cleared his throat. 'I say,' he said in a loud voice, 'I want to buy you a drink.'

Connor didn't look up from his cards. 'No, thanks.'

'I insist. After all, we're celebrating.'

Connor laid a card down silently in the middle of the table He looked particularly dark and menacing tonight, his jaw shaded with stubble and his curls hanging in his navy blue eyes.

'Don't you want to know what we're celebrating?' Kit prompted. He was goading Connor, Effie realised. It made her cringe to watch him. Kit was like a small boy poking at a wasps' nest with a stick. He had no idea what he might unleash.

Finally Connor raised his gaze to him. 'If I ask, will you promise to go away?' he growled.

Kit reached back and grabbed Effie's hand, dragging her forward. 'We're engaged to be married!' he announced.

Connor's gaze flicked to meet hers. It was like a bolt of electricity going straight through her, rooting her to the spot.

'Engaged?' he said.

'That's right, old man.' Kit looked pleased with himself. 'What do you say to that?'

Connor's gaze never left Effie's face. 'Congratulations,' he said quietly. 'I hope you'll both be very happy.'

Kit gave him a mocking smile. 'I thought you'd be pleased that I was making an honest woman of her at last,' he said.

Effie didn't understand the look that passed between the two men. All she knew was that if the pub hadn't been full of people, there was a good chance Kit would have been dead.

Instead, Connor said evenly, 'And why would that be my business?'

'Why indeed? But you seem to have made it your business lately.'

They stared at one other in silence for a moment, and Effie could feel the tension rise in the room. Other people noticed it, too; around them conversations ceased and drinks were lowered.

To Effie's surprise, it was Connor who looked away first. 'Not any more,' he said brusquely. 'She's your problem now. So if you don't mind?' He indicated his cards. 'I'd like to get on with my game in peace.'

'Well, I think he took it rather well,' Kit said, when they returned to their table. 'Another drink, darling?'

As he went to the bar, Effie looked back at Connor. He was still concentrating on the game, but there was something about his expression and the way he threw down his cards that told her he hadn't taken it well at all. It made her uncomfortable to watch him.

Kit noticed it, too. But unlike Effie, he seemed to take great delight in it. He kept smiling over at Connor, as if there was some great private joke between them that only they understood.

'I wish you hadn't told him,' Effie said.

'Why? He had to know sometime.'

'Yes, but not like that. You were trying to provoke him.'

'So what if I was?' Kit looked petulant. 'He's provoked me enough times.'

Kit was at the bar again when Connor laid down his last hand, scooped his winnings from the table, drained his drink and got up to leave.

Effie glanced towards the bar. Kit was deep in conversation with the landlady again, laughing with her over something. On impulse, Effie grabbed her bag and her coat and slipped outside.

'Connor, wait!'

He stopped and turned to face her. It was a full moon, and the bright silver circle illuminated his rugged, unsmiling face.

Seeing his grim expression, Effie blurted out the first thing that came into her head. 'I'm sorry, I was going to tell you. I just thought–'

He shook his head. 'You've surpassed yourself this time, Effie O'Hara. I know you can be a bit away with the fairies at times, but I didn't think even you would be this stupid!'

Effie stared at him, taken aback. 'What?'

He came towards her, his arms flung wide. 'Can't you see what he's playing at? He's got no more intention of marrying you than I have of cycling to the North Pole. This is all a game to him.'

Effie stared at him, bewildered. 'Why would you say something like that?'

'Because I know his sort! Don't you see, he's only doing it because he knows I–' He stopped, his mouth closing like a mantrap.

'He knows what?' Effie prompted.

'Nothing.' The moonlight cast harsh shadows on the planes of Connor's face. 'But think about it, Effie. Does Kit seem like the marrying kind to you?'

She had thought about it. Doubts rippled beneath her excitement like sinister dark shapes lurking in the depths of a pond. She had managed to push them down so far, but Connor was dragging them to the surface, forcing her to confront them.

And she hated him for it.

'People can change,' she insisted.

'Not him.' Connor's mouth curled with contempt. 'He's playing with you,' he said. 'And when he feels like it, he'll drop you like a stone.'

Effie stared at him. She could feel her fragile confidence crumbling, and all her hopes with it.

'Have you ever thought he might be marrying

me because he actually loves me?' she whispered, her voice clogged with tears.

Emotion flickered across his face. 'Effie? Are you crying?'

'No.'

'You are.' He reached out for her, but she wrenched herself free from his grasp.

'Go away, Connor,' she said. 'If you really care about me, just go away and leave me alone!'

She fled back to the pub before her tears started to fall. The last thing she wanted to do was give him the satisfaction of seeing her upset.

Chapter Forty-One

'Don't look now, fellas, but we've got another popsy on the ward!'

Daisy was conscious of the men's eyes following her as she walked the length of the ward to report to Sister's desk. Usually she would have enjoyed the attention, but today she was just angry.

Of all the wards she could have been transferred to, why did it have to be the Military Ward? It was only temporary, Matron said, but Daisy knew her time spent here would feel like a lifetime.

Grace was already waiting at Miss Wallace's desk to receive her list of jobs for the day. Lady Amelia, or Nurse Rushton as she called herself, was with her. Daisy deliberately didn't look at her sister as she took her place beside her.

'Good morning, you must be our extra nurse,'

Miss Wallace greeted her. 'What's your name?'

'Maynard, Sister.'

'Nurse Maynard?' Miss Wallace frowned from Daisy to Grace and back again. 'You're related, I presume?'

'We're sisters, Miss Wallace,' Grace replied for them. Daisy pressed her lips together and said nothing.

'I see. Well, I hope you'll be as much of an asset to the ward as your sister is.' Miss Wallace smiled at Grace. 'Now, I see you've come from Female Medical, but I daresay you've done some surgical nursing too?' She looked enquiringly at Daisy, who nodded. 'That's good. You'll need experience of both with our boys.'

She went through the morning's work list, issuing them with their tasks for the day. Daisy was charged with looking after a wounded airman with severe burns who had been admitted a month earlier.

'He's making very good progress, but he still needs a saline bath and his dressings changed every day,' Miss Wallace said. 'See to it, please, Nurse Maynard. Your sister can assist you.'

Over my dead body! Daisy thought. But she managed to smile sweetly, and say, 'Yes, Sister.'

As they walked away, Grace said, 'Would you like me to run the saline bath for you?'

Daisy glared at her. 'I'm perfectly capable of running it myself, thank you very much.'

'But Sister said—'

'You don't have to tell me how to give a patient a saline bath, Grace. I am a trained nurse, after all,' Daisy added. Her barb hit its mark as Grace blushed a deep crimson.

'I was only trying to help,' she murmured.

'Well, don't.'

Grace hesitated. 'So what do you want me to do?' she asked.

'Stay out of my way!' Daisy closed the bathroom door on her sister's hurt face.

She deserved it, she thought. She knew Grace was desperate to make amends, but Daisy couldn't bring herself to look at her, let alone speak to her. She had managed to avoid seeing her for nearly two weeks, and didn't want to spend any more time than she had to in her company.

In spite of her confidence, it took Daisy a while to run the saline bath. Everything was in a different place here from in the Female Medical ward, and it took her a while to find all she needed. But she was utterly determined not to ask for any help, especially not from her sister.

Grace must have been waiting for her, because when Daisy emerged from the bathroom to collect her patient her sister fell into step beside her.

'How long is this going to go on for?' she said in an undertone. 'I've said I'm sorry.'

'Sorry isn't good enough.'

Daisy wasn't sure she would ever get over the shock of her sister's betrayal. Every time she closed her eyes, she saw herself walking into the village hall and finding Grace wrapped in Max's arms.

Grace sighed. 'I wish you'd come home, Daisy. I miss you.'

'You should have thought about that before you did what you did, shouldn't you?'

'Walter and Ann really miss you too. They keep

asking after you, and I don't know what to tell them.'

'How about the truth? That you stole my boyfriend and ruined my life?'

Grace winced. 'I didn't steal him. He came to me.'

'Yes, but you encouraged him, didn't you? Making eyes at him, inviting him round for tea, getting him to help around the house just so you could be alone with him.'

'That's not true!'

'Nurses?' Miss Wallace's voice rose behind them. 'Keep your family tiffs off my ward, if you please!'

'Yes, Sister,' they chorused dutifully.

'Now see what you've done!' Daisy hissed. 'Just leave me alone, Grace. I don't want anything more to do with you!'

She watched her sister walk away, her head hung low. She was upset, but she deserved to be. In the past two weeks, everything in Daisy's life had gone wrong, and it was all Grace's fault.

Moving into the Nurses' Home wasn't what she'd thought it would be. There was no room for her at the hospital Home, so she'd had to move out to the old farm buildings where the London nurses lived. She had imagined it might be fun, but that illusion was quickly shattered when Miss Carrington the Home Sister roused them all at six o'clock and they had to queue for the bath-room in a cold, dark passageway. And then there was the awful ride in Sulley's stinking old cart up to the hospital. After two days, Daisy had begun to think longingly of waking up to one of Grace's home-cooked breakfasts and then strolling down the lane from their cottage to the hospital.

She missed home, and she missed her family. But she couldn't go back, not after what Grace had done to her.

The airman's wounds were awful, far worse than Daisy had imagined. He sighed with relief as she helped him into the saline bath.

'That's better,' he said. 'You know, this is the only time in the whole day when I'm not in agony.'

Outside the bathroom, she could hear Sister and Grace laughing and talking with one of the other patients as they did the dressings round.

I hope you'll be as much of an asset to the ward as your sister is, Miss Wallace had said. It was all wrong. Daisy was supposed to be the clever one, the pretty one, the one who got all the praise. Grace was supposed to be the solid, dependable one. The one no one noticed.

But all of a sudden everyone seemed to be noticing her. She was gaining confidence, coming out of her shell. It wasn't fair, Daisy thought. She wished none of this had happened, that they could have gone on as they were, with Grace tucked away at home, running the house and looking after the family, the way she always had.

Daisy stopped short as a thought occurred to her. She had accused Grace of trying to be like her because she was jealous. It came as a shock to realise that Grace wasn't the jealous one at all.

Sister wasn't pleased with the job Daisy had done on the airman's wounds.

'Really, Nurse, you should have trimmed the tulle gras dressings to fit,' she'd said. 'Supplies are

344

so scarce these days, we have to make economies where we can.'

'Yes, Sister. I'm sorry.'

Grace saw her sister's bowed head and knew poor Daisy was mortified. She wished she could do something to make it better.

But as Daisy had made clear, nothing Grace could do would help. She was the cause of all her sister's misery. Grace despaired of making things right with her. She had hurt Daisy far too badly.

At the end of her duty, Grace went back to the cottage with a heavy heart. It didn't even feel like home now that Daisy wasn't there. She dearly missed her sister's laughter, and her scandalous stories about the other nurses and patients she'd met. She even missed their sisterly bickering. Grace had given up her life so that she could keep her family together, and now she was the one who had driven them apart. The guilt was almost too much for her to bear.

It was raining heavily, sheets of water gushing from the leaden sky, turning the rutted path under her feet to a slurry of reddish-brown mud. Grace kept her head down to avoid the puddles, so she didn't see Max until she was almost at the gate.

He was drenched. The rain had soaked through his leather jacket and flying suit, plastering his blond hair to his head. But he seemed oblivious to it as he walked towards her.

She hadn't seen him since that night at the village hall. For a split second her heart lifted at the sight of him, but she fought down her feelings of joy.

'What are you doing here?' She tried to keep her

voice even. Looking at him, so big and blond and handsome, it was all she could do not to launch herself into his arms. 'You're soaked to the skin!'

'I hadn't heard from you... I wanted to make sure you were OK?'

The look of tender concern in his aquamarine eyes nearly undid Grace. She swallowed hard. 'I thought it would be better if we didn't see each other,' she murmured.

'Better for who?' he asked. 'Not for me. Or you either, I'm guessing?'

Grace looked away in case her eyes betrayed her. Of course she was wretched without Max. She loved him. She hadn't wanted to put a name to her feelings until that night in the village hall, but now she realised that she had been falling in love with him since the first time they'd met on Christmas Day.

Not that she would ever have done anything about it. She had buried her feelings for Daisy's sake, told herself it was nothing more than friendship. But that night when he'd kissed her and told her he loved her, Grace had caught a tantalising glimpse of what her life could be like. It wasn't easy to forget.

But she had to forget it, if she wanted to put her family back together.

She moved past him, through the gate. The chickens in the coop clamoured at the sight of her, and the bedraggled cats wound themselves around her legs in greeting.

Max followed her across the yard. 'Can I come in?' he asked.

She looked at him, the rain dripping off his

346

hair. The idea of being alone with him terrified her, but she couldn't leave him standing out in the rain, either.

'I suppose you'd better, before you catch your death,' she said.

His presence seemed to fill the house. She was aware of nothing else but him, the rain dripping off his jacket, pooling in puddles on the stone-flagged floor at his feet.

'Get that wet coat off, I'll fetch you a towel,' she said. She started for the airing cupboard but Max stopped her.

'Never mind that,' he said. 'Grace, there's something I need to tell you.'

He sounded so serious, she stopped in her tracks. 'What?'

'I'm going home.'

'Home? You mean back to Canada?'

He nodded. 'My pal Harry and I have just found out we're being shipped back once this tour's over.'

'And how long will that be?'

'Depends. Most likely a couple of months.'

Panic washed over her, but she fought to control it. 'Well, that's good news, isn't it?' she said brightly.

'Is it?'

'Of course. You'll be able to see your family.' Once again, she found she couldn't meet his eye. 'I'll go and fetch that towel.'

'I want you to come with me.'

She swung round to face him. 'Me?'

'I told you, I love you. I can't stand the thought of leaving without you, of never seeing you again.'

347

He took a step towards her, his face bright with hope. 'I want to marry you – if you'll have me?'

The shy way he looked at her from under his lashes nearly tore her heart out. 'Me? Go to Canada?'

'You'd love it,' he promised her. 'And my family would love you, too. Well?' he said. 'What do you say?'

What a question! A million things were racing through her mind, and she didn't know what to say first.

But one question was uppermost.

'What about the kids?' she asked.

'They could come too,' Max said. 'Walter and Ann would love it out there. We could stay on my family's farm until we get a place of our own.'

'What about Daisy?'

He stifled a sigh. 'Daisy is old enough to take care of herself.'

Grace shook her head. 'I couldn't leave her.'

'Grace, she's not a kid any more. She doesn't need your protection.'

She thought about Daisy, so angry and defensive on the ward that afternoon, lashing out in pain. She had seen the hurt in her sister's eyes, and knew that being separated from her family was killing her as much as it was killing Grace.

If Max thought that Grace would just abandon her, then he didn't know her very well.

'I can't,' she said.

'Why not?' There was an impatient edge to his voice. 'I'm offering you the chance of a new life, Grace. The two of us, starting out together. Why won't you take it?'

She wanted to. God knows, she couldn't think of anything she wanted more than to be with Max, wherever in the world it happened to be.

But she had made a promise to her mother on the day she died that her family would always come first, no matter what.

'I'm sorry.' It was all Grace could manage. If she'd tried to say any more she would have started to cry, and she didn't want that. She had to stay strong.

Max looked at her, his face full of sorrow. 'So am I,' he said.

Chapter Forty-Two

It was good to see Sarah Newland looking so much better.

The colour had returned to her freckled cheeks as she lay propped against the pillows in the maternity ward. She was holding her baby daughter in her arms, her hard features softened by maternal pride.

'The midwife says she's doing well, considering she was born so early,' she told Jess when she went to visit her.

'She was certainly in a hurry to get here.' Jess put out her finger for the baby to grasp. 'Once she'd made up her mind, there was no stopping her!'

'She's determined, like her mum!' Sarah smiled down at the infant.

'Have you thought of a name yet?'

'I thought I might call her after you?'

Jess stared. 'Me?'

'It's the least I can do. You've been such a good friend to me, helping me out.' Sarah lowered her gaze. 'I know I didn't deserve it, after the horrible things I said to you.'

'It's all forgotten,' Jess said. 'I'm just glad we were there to help. Although I'll never forget Miss Carrington's face when you turned up on the doorstep!'

'I didn't know where else to go,' Sarah said. 'I knew if I tried to make it to the hospital, this little one would probably be born in the middle of the road!'

Jess looked at the baby's tiny starfish hand, clamped around her finger. Little Jess. The thought touched her.

'Have they said when you might be able to go home?' she asked.

'The end of the week, if I'm lucky. I can't wait. No offence to this hospital, but there's nothing like being in your own place, is there?'

Jess pictured Sarah's rundown little cottage. Beauty really must be in the eye of the beholder, she thought.

Then her thoughts turned to Mrs Huntley-Osborne's grand house. It was so warm, and spacious, the perfect place for a baby...

'No word from her grandmother, I suppose?' She hadn't mentioned it before, she had wanted to wait until her friend was well enough. And she had also hoped that the pair might sort out their differences by themselves.

Sarah's gaze shot up to meet hers. 'How did

you know?'

'It wasn't difficult to work it out when you asked me to take the ring back, and I saw all those photographs of Clifford...' She looked down at the baby. 'She looks just like him.'

'Doesn't she?' Sarah's fond smile hardened. 'But no, Mrs Huntley-Osborne hasn't been in touch. I can't say I expected her to be. She'd already made her feelings plain enough the day she threw me out of her house.'

Jess said nothing, but deep down she felt disappointed. She had seen a different side to Mrs Huntley-Osborne, a glimpse of humanity under that stiff mask she wore. The way she'd asked about Sarah and the baby, with so much genuine concern, Jess had been convinced she would offer an olive branch to the girl.

But no such luck. Mrs Huntley-Osborne had obviously decided that saving her own face was more important than saving her family.

'Anyway, we don't need her,' Sarah went on defiantly. 'Little Jess and I will be all right by ourselves. Ain't that right, love?' She kissed the top of her baby's head.

Jess smiled. I hope you're right, she thought. But she couldn't help fearing for her friend. If Sarah had felt isolated by the community before, how would they treat her now she was an unmarried mother in their midst?

No sooner had Jess arrived back on the ward, than Sister Allen sent her straight off to see Matron.

'Oh, dear, what have you done now?' Effie grinned at her.

'Search me.' Not that she had to do anything wrong to be in Miss Jenkins's bad books. Her very existence seemed to be enough of a crime. 'But knowing Matron, I expect she's got some nice surprise lined up for me,' Jess added grimly.

And she was right. 'Ah, Nurse Jago.' Miss Jenkins regarded her across the desk. 'I'm putting you back on the Fever Wards for night duty as from this evening. Go back to your ward until midday, then return to the Nurses' Home and report for duty at eight.'

She didn't see fit to explain why, and Jess knew better than to argue. But she was still put out about it when she returned to the Female Medical ward.

'That's not fair!' Effie was outraged on her behalf. 'You only finished a stint there a few weeks ago. Why is she sending you there again?'

'I don't know, do I? Ours is not to reason why, as they say. Although if you're that upset about it, you could always go to Matron and volunteer yourself?' Jess suggested.

That shut her up. Effie kept her sympathy to herself until Jess went off duty at twelve.

But for once, it seemed as if Miss Jenkins wasn't simply being deliberately spiteful. When Jess reported for duty that night, she found the ward in chaos. An epidemic of diphtheria had broken out in the village, and every bed was full.

'We've had six new cases in the last two days,' Miss Tanner the Night Sister explained. 'Then this morning the nurse on night duty started complaining of a headache and sore throat. It may be nothing, but she's been put into isolation for a

352

couple of days to be on the safe side. I assume you've had a negative Schick test, as you've worked on this ward before?' she asked Jess.

'Yes, Sister.'

'All the same, you must take extra precautions. We don't want another nurse falling ill, do we?'

She gave Jess specific instructions about a couple of the worst cases, then left her alone.

Once again, she was struck by the hideous silence of the ward, with all the patients flat on their backs, too poorly to move. And the smell – the foul, sickly stench coated her own throat and nose every time she breathed.

She went around the ward, checking on the patients, swabbing throats with carbolic and administering serum. One of the patients seemed particularly weak and poorly, so Jess raised the end of his bed to help strengthen his heart.

Just before midnight, Dr Drake arrived to do his round. He seemed taken aback to see her.

'Oh, Nurse Jago. I didn't realise you'd be here,' he said coolly.

They conducted the ward round even faster than Dr Drake's usual rapid speed. Jess had the distinct feeling he couldn't wait to get away from her.

She wasn't surprised; he had been offhand with her ever since the dance at the village hall.

How was she supposed to know he was going to turn up out of the blue like that? He hadn't given her any clue he was going to come to the dance. Exactly the opposite, in fact; from the contemptuous way he'd dismissed her invitation, she'd thought it was the last thing on his mind.

Of course she would have stayed at the village

hall if she'd known he was going to be there. But as it was, he seemed to think she had set out to play another prank on him. As if she had the time or the energy to devote herself to humiliating him!

She tried to make amends by offering him a cup of tea after the round, but Dr Drake refused abruptly. Jess wanted to grab him by the lapels of his creased white coat and shake him. Why did he have to be so cold all the time? She understood he was shy, and she had even caught the odd glimpse of a nice man underneath that chilly exterior, but shyness was no excuse for rudeness in her book.

Midnight struck as he was leaving. Jess did another quick round of the ward, taking temperatures, checking pulses and swabbing throats. Then she made herself a cup of tea and went outside to catch her breath.

The cold February night air felt fresh and untainted after the cloying, sickly reek of the diphtheria ward. Jess wrapped her hands around her hot cup to keep herself warm as she stared up into the starry night sky. In the distance, she heard the heavy thrum of approaching planes as the bombers returned home from another mission. She found herself counting the planes as they passed overhead, the way Harry and his pals always did. He'd told her how they ran up to the roof of the manor house to watch them come home safely, no matter what time of day or night it was. Jess had no idea how many planes there were supposed to be, but she counted them anyway.

It was a quiet night, thank God. But by the time Jess had woken the patients, offered them their morning tea and done the bedpan round, she was wearily ready for her own bed.

Night duty took a lot of getting used to, she decided as she trudged the long path from the Fever Wards to the main hospital building in the grey dawn light. She hoped it wouldn't be too long before the night nurse came out of isolation and Jess could be allowed to return to the land of the living.

She turned the corner of the hospital building, hoping against hope that Sulley would be waiting at the gate with his horse and cart. Perhaps if he was he would be in a good mood and give her a lift back to the Nurses' Home. She didn't fancy the two mile trudge in cold, wet drizzle.

Her luck was in because Sulley was there. He'd just arrived with the last of the day nurses. Jess could see Effie and Daisy, one tall and dark, the other small and blonde, climbing down from the back of the cart.

'Wait!' Jess hurried down the drive towards them, desperate to reach the cart before it left. 'Don't go without me!'

At the sound of her voice Effie and Daisy both looked up. Then, suddenly, they were running towards her.

Jess stopped. This wasn't right. Nurses weren't allowed to run, except in case of fire and haemorrhages. They would catch it from Matron if she noticed them.

Then Jess saw their faces and forgot all about the cart she was supposed to be catching. Effie was as pale as milk, and Daisy's eyes were swollen and red-rimmed from crying.

'What is it?' she said, staring into their stricken

faces. 'What's wrong?'

They looked at each other, then back at her. 'Haven't you heard?' Daisy said.

'Heard what?' A trickle of fear began to work its way down her spine. 'What are you talking about?'

Effie reached out and put her hand on her friend's arm. 'Oh, Jess,' she said, her voice barely above a whisper. 'It's Harry...'

Chapter Forty-Three

The plane had been on a training flight with others, but had encountered some flak over the French coast. The last the radio operator had heard was just after midnight when they had reported two of their engines out, and the loss of their tail fuselage and rear gunner. They were making their way home but two hours later still hadn't returned.

Millie had woken up in the early hours with a horrible sense of panic, knowing something was wrong. Without thinking, she had got up, put on her coat over her nightdress and slipped out of the Lodge.

Up at the airfield she had found dozens of people on the runway, scanning the skies, counting the planes as they came back. They all talked about the possibility of the crew escaping safely, using their parachutes, until the news they had been dreading came through just before dawn. The plane had crashed on the Kent coast with the loss of all crew.

Millie returned to the Lodge to dress, then went to look for William. She found him in the rear gunner's room, packing up the airman's belongings into a brown leather suitcase. The bed had already been stripped down to the iron frame, the mattress segments stacked neatly on top.

'We have to get rid of everything quickly,' he explained in a quiet, flat voice that Millie scarcely recognised. 'It's bad for morale otherwise. And the bed will have to be moved, too, so the men don't have to see it...'

He picked up a battered old cap from the chest of drawers and stared at it, lost in thought.

Millie took it from him gently and put it in the suitcase. 'Let me help you,' she said.

Together they packed up the airman's belongings, moving in silence, unpacking drawers and folding clothes. In his bedside locker, Millie found a half-empty packet of Canadian cigarettes, a bundle of well-thumbed letters, and a photograph.

She stopped for a moment, staring at the pretty woman nursing a plump, smiling baby in her arms. Once upon a time, a stranger must have packed a similar photograph of her and little Henry, sending it back to her in a cardboard box with the rest of Seb's belongings.

'Will you write to his wife?' she asked.

William nodded. 'She'll be informed by telegram, of course, but I'll also write and explain exactly what happened.' He sighed. 'I just wish I knew what to say.'

Millie thought about the letter that had come for her. It had been two weeks before she could bring herself to read it.

'It doesn't matter what you write,' she said quietly. 'It won't mean anything to her, except that her husband is dead and her world has fallen apart.'

William stared at her, realisation dawning on his face. 'Oh, God, Millie, I'm so sorry. I didn't think.' He looked around at the room. 'You shouldn't be doing this. You shouldn't have to see it.'

'I want to,' Millie insisted. Unlikely as it seemed, she liked to think that another woman, a wife and a mother, had packed Seb's things for him. That someone had cared, even at the very end.

William ran his hand through his dark hair. 'I know I should be used to doing this. God knows, I've done it enough times. But every time it's just so damn hard...'

'And so it should be,' Millie said. 'This isn't just a death to be processed and packed away. This was a real person, someone with a life and a family. It's only right they should be mourned. The day you get used to it is the day you lose your compassion.'

'You're right,' William said heavily. 'It was the same when I was a doctor. I never got used to losing patients, either. But at least then I knew I'd tried to help them, not just sent them off to their death–'

He sank down on the iron bedframe, his head in his hands. 'Oh, God, this is just such a waste, isn't it? Those young men going off to die, leaving their families behind. And I can't help feeling it's all my fault.'

Millie dropped the shirt she had been folding

and went to sit beside him. 'How can you say that?'

'I was supposed to be training them. If they got into trouble it must mean I've failed them in some way...'

'You can't think like that. You weren't responsible for what happened.'

'Then perhaps I should have been there in their place?'

'Then you would have been dead instead of them.'

'But would it have mattered?' He took the photograph from her hands and stared down at it. 'I don't have a wife or a child to leave behind. I don't have anyone–'

'You have me,' Millie said. 'You matter to me.'

William's eyes met hers. 'Do I?' he said hoarsely.

Her gaze trailed over the angular planes of his face, with its straight dark brows and sharp cheekbones, then his mouth. The next moment she was kissing him, her hands buried in the silky thickness of his dark hair.

It took them both by surprise and afterwards they sprang apart, neither of them knowing what to do next. Millie stared into William's eyes. She had forgotten how the dark brown irises were flecked with so many colours, from amber to deepest black. Today they were red-rimmed from exhaustion.

'Millie?'

There was a question in his voice that she couldn't answer with words. She put her hands up to his face, feeling the roughness of his unshaven jaw under her fingers. Then slowly, deliberately, she allowed her lips to meet his. She hoped that would be answer enough for him.

'What did you think?' Daisy said, as they watched Jess walking away. She seemed unnaturally calm for someone who had just been told her friend was dead.

'She didn't seem to take it in, did she?' Effie agreed.

'Poor girl, she was closer to Harry than the rest of us were.'

'Perhaps one of us should stay with her?' Daisy suggested. 'In case shock sets in later?'

'Better not. You know Jess, she likes to keep her feelings to herself.'

Daisy watched her friend climbing stiffly on to the back of Sulley's cart. She wasn't sure it was such a good idea to stifle emotions like that. Sooner or later they would have to come out.

'I can't believe it,' Effie said as they climbed the stairs to their respective wards. 'When I heard it was D-Dragon that had crashed, I was so sure–'

'I know,' Daisy said. They'd talked about little else since they'd heard the news that morning.

She got to the ward, and the first person she met was Grace. She rushed up to her sister, white-faced.

'They're all talking about a plane crashing,' she blurted out. 'Is it true? Was it D-Dragon?'

Daisy nodded. Grace let out a moan of anguish. 'Max ... is he–?'

Daisy stared into her sister's pain-filled face. In spite of her anger, she couldn't help but feel compassion for her.

'No,' she said. 'Kit and Max were told to make way for a pair of rookie pilots.'

'Oh, thank God.' Grace closed her eyes. Tears squeezed through her closed lids and spilled down her cheeks.

Daisy was about to open her mouth to speak when the doors opened and Miss Wallace arrived on the ward. Immediately they abandoned their conversation and hurried to gather around her desk.

Daisy watched her sister, surreptitiously wiping her cheeks with the sleeve of her dress. She realised with a shock that when she'd first heard about D-Dragon crashing, it hadn't occurred to her to think about Max.

What did that say about her love for him, she wondered.

Millie was shocked by how quickly things returned to normal after the aircraft crash. At dawn, everyone had been devastated. They had stumbled around, hollow-eyed with shock, barely able to speak. But by the time she returned to the house that evening, the daily routine had reasserted itself and people were going about their business as if nothing unusual had happened at all.

Perhaps that was the way they learned to cope with it, Millie thought. In the same way that nurses hardened themselves to the loss of patients, perhaps the crews had to close their minds to the risks that awaited them and their friends every day.

But in spite of their brave faces and determination to carry on with business as usual, she was sure that they felt the loss of their comrades very keenly. Millie had been racking her brains all day to come up with a way she could help them, and she'd finally had the idea of allowing the men to hold a service of remembrance in Billinghurst's private chapel. It wouldn't bring their friends back, but it might help if they were allowed to show their respect properly.

Millie went up to the house to see William and tell him about her idea. But it wasn't just the memorial service that was on her mind. All day long she'd been thinking about their kiss. She wanted to find out if it had been just an impulse brought on by the heat of the moment, or if, as she hoped, it was the start of something more serious.

Jennifer Franklin and Agnes Moss were typing away at their desks when she walked into the hall. They greeted her in their usual way, Franklin with a polite smile and Moss with a scowl.

'Where is Squadron Leader Tremayne?' Millie asked.

She caught the sideways look Agnes Moss gave Jennifer Franklin, but this time she had too much confidence to let the girl's sly attitude bother her.

'He's on the airfield, Lady Amelia,' Franklin said. 'Would you like to leave a message?'

'Thank you, there's no need. I'll walk up there and see him myself.'

'You'll have to be quick,' Agnes Moss muttered, not looking up from her typing. 'He's due for take off in ten minutes.'

Millie looked at her, not sure if she'd heard properly. 'He's flying tonight?'

'According to the schedule,' Agnes shrugged. 'He's co-pilot of G-Grasshopper.'

Millie ran all the way up to the airfield. She reached the guardhouse just in time to see the planes taxiing into position on the runway. There were six of them lined up, one after another.

One of the ground crew was passing, and lifted his hand in greeting.

'If you're looking for Tremayne, he's just taking off,' he shouted over the deafening sound of half a dozen Halifax engines roaring into life.

Millie watched the planes soaring into the sky, her heart in her mouth. It was an awesome, terrifying sight.

She went back to the Lodge, but couldn't rest or eat. She tried to play with Henry to distract herself, but she kept looking out of the window.

Of course her grandmother commented on it. 'Really, Amelia, will you sit still? You're up and down like a Jack in the Box. What are you looking for anyway?'

'Nothing, Granny.' But she kept her nose pressed against the glass, straining to hear the tell-tale sound of aircraft engines telling her William had returned safely.

It was exhausting. Every nerve in her body seemed stretched to breaking point, just waiting for news.

It was nearly midnight when she heard the roar of the planes overhead, by which time she had lain awake for several hours, imagining flak storms and diving German fighters, and burning planes crashing into the sea. She got up and dressed quickly, throwing on her coat against the chilly February night.

William was climbing down from the cockpit

by the time she reached the airfield. He'd taken off his helmet and his dark hair was ruffled. His flying suit emphasised the long, lean lines of his body.

He saw Millie standing at the end of the runway and strode towards her. 'Hello, what are you doing here?'

'Waiting for you.'

'That's nice.' He opened his arms to her, but Millie held herself back.

'Why didn't you tell me you were flying?'

'I didn't know myself until this morning. A few of the rookie pilots were a bit unnerved by what happened last night, so I was told to take a couple of them up and show them how it's done.' He was smiling, but Millie's face was too rigid to respond.

'And will you be flying again?'

'Probably. We've been losing so many men lately, I'm likely to be back on active service within the next month, if not sooner.' He tugged at the straps of his gloves with his teeth to loosen them. 'Why do you ask?'

'I don't want you to fly.'

He stopped, halfway through peeling off his gloves, and stared at her. 'What?'

'I don't want you to fly. It's too dangerous.'

He smiled uncertainly, as if he wasn't sure if she was joking or not. 'I don't think I've got much choice in the matter!' he said. 'Besides, I want to go. It's my duty. How can I send those boys up if I'm not willing to go myself?'

He was talking but Millie wasn't listening to him. She was thinking about the hours she'd just spent lying awake, her heart pounding with fear, waiting for him to come home. She couldn't put herself through that again, night after night. Not after losing Seb the same way.

'What if something happened to you?' she whispered.

'Nothing will happen, I promise.'

'How can you say that? How can you make a promise like that after what happened last night?' Her voice shook.

William looked at her for a long time. 'You're right, I can't,' he said flatly. 'But as I said, I don't have a choice in the matter.'

'No, but I do,' Millie said quietly.

'What do you mean?' He frowned.

'I mean I can't allow myself to – be with you if this is the kind of life you lead. I don't want to get hurt again. I don't think I could bear it.' She lowered her gaze. 'I think we should end this before it goes too far.'

William stared at her. 'You don't mean that,' he said flatly.

'I do. I'm sorry, William, but I've already been through enough heartache. I can't do it again. I'm not strong enough.'

'Or you don't care enough?'

His words lingered in the air behind her as she walked away.

Oh, William, she thought. Couldn't he see, she already cared far too much?

Chapter Forty-Four

The tiny chapel at Billinghurst Manor was full for the remembrance service. The pews were a sea of slate-blue uniforms, while more airmen crowded in at the back with the locals. It seemed as if everyone in Billinghurst had come to pay their respects to the airmen they had taken to their hearts.

Squarely at the front of the chapel, as usual, sat Mrs Huntley-Osborne, surrounded by her cronies. She bristled with self-righteousness, as if the entire congregation was there for her benefit. The rest of the village filled the sides of the chapel.

Daisy sat at the back with the other nurses. Many of her friends were sniffing back tears, handkerchiefs pressed to their faces. At the far end of the row, Janet Carr sat with her back perfectly straight, staring unblinkingly ahead of her. Her fiancé David had been navigator on the ill-fated D-Dragon flight that night.

Max sat a few rows in front of her, his head bowed. Daisy fixed her gaze on the shorn blond hair at the back of his neck. She felt so sorry for him, she couldn't hate him any more. He had lost his best friend, and anyone could see it had drained the life from him.

She wasn't the only one watching him. On the other side of the chapel, Grace sat perfectly composed, staring at Max. There was a raw yearning in the way she looked at him, her hands folded in her lap as if to stop herself reaching out for him.

As if he knew he was being watched, Max turned his head slightly and caught her eye. Both of them looked away sharply, their gazes dropping to the ground.

Daisy felt a pang. She tried to tell herself it wasn't her doing, but she couldn't fight the feeling of guilt that overwhelmed her. There was already too much unhappiness in the world, and she couldn't help feeling as if she'd brought about even more.

The chapel door opened behind her, and a sudden hush fell over the congregation. Turning round, Daisy saw why. Sarah Newland had walked in, her baby in her arms. Her pale face and fiery red hair contrasted dramatically with the shabby black coat she wore.

The silence lasted a second or two, then broke into a hubbub of whispers.

'Look at her!'

'What's she doing here? She should know better than to show her face.'

'Bold as brass, that one.'

'Fancy bringing that child into a house of God.'

The tide of whispers followed her, but Sarah seemed determined not to be aware of them as she made her way to the far side of the chapel, head held high, baby clasped to her shoulder. But Daisy could see the scarlet flush rising up her neck.

She reached the area where the villagers stood, packed shoulder to shoulder, almost as if they were forming a wall against her.

'May I find a space, please?' Sarah's voice was quiet and clear, making a challenge.

Everyone ignored her. Then, suddenly, a voice rang out from the front.

'Here, you may take my seat.'

A collective gasp echoed around the chapel. Even the British and Canadian airmen who knew nothing of village life seemed to be aware that something interesting was happening as Mrs Huntley-Osborne rose from her place on the front pew and stepped aside.

Sarah stood frozen, her expression wary. For what seemed like an endless moment, the two women stared at each other across the width of the chapel. Then, slowly and cautiously, Sarah moved towards Mrs Huntley-Osborne.

'Thank you,' she whispered.

'We can't have you standing with a baby, can we?'

Almost immediately, both of the people beside Sarah jumped to their feet to offer Mrs Huntley-Osborne their seat. She placed herself down on Sarah's right. The two of them sat side by side, neither of them speaking or even looking at each other. But Daisy was aware, as were most of the villagers, that a momentous shift had occurred.

She glanced across at Grace to see if she'd noticed it too, before she remembered that they weren't on speaking terms. A cloud of loneliness settled over her then. It was at times like this that she missed her sister more than ever.

After the service, Grace slipped quickly out of the chapel. Daisy saw Max looking for her. He stood like a mighty oak, his big frame towering above the rest of the congregation as they filed past him towards the doors.

Daisy wormed her way through the crowd until she was standing behind him.

'If you're looking for Grace, she's already left.'

'Oh.' His broad shoulders slumped in dejection.

Daisy hesitated, not sure what to say next. She had always struggled to make conversation with Max. Not like Grace, who seemed to be able to chat away to him for hours...

'I'm sorry – about Harry,' Daisy ventured. 'It's such a terrible thing for his wife. She must be heartbroken.'

'He was due to go home next month.'

'No! How awful.'

Max nodded. 'Just a few more weeks and we would have been safe and sound in Canada.'

It took a moment for Daisy to register what he'd said. 'We? Are you going back to Canada too?'

'Yes.' For the first time, his frowning gaze flicked to meet hers. 'I thought Grace would have told you.'

Daisy lowered her gaze. 'Grace and I aren't on speaking terms. Told me what?'

'So you won't know that I asked her to come with me?'

Daisy's mouth fell open with shock. She'd had no idea that Max's feelings for her sister ran so deep. 'What did she say?'

'What do you think?' His eyes turned to chips of ice. 'She turned me down. Said she couldn't leave her family.'

Daisy was silent, shaken by his revelation. 'But I don't understand,' she said. 'She could have had a new life...'

'I guess she prefers her old one.' Max shrugged.

Daisy pictured her sister's yearning face as she'd watched him in the chapel. It was exactly the same expression she saw on his face now.

Jess couldn't face the service in the chapel. She'd woken up on Sunday morning with the same pounding headache behind her temples that she'd had ever since the day Harry died. It wouldn't go away, even with the aspirin Miss Carrington had given her.

Even so, she'd tried to go, for Harry's sake. As soon as her night duty finished, she'd walked up the lane to the tiny stone-built chapel in the grounds of Billinghurst Manor. But as soon as she walked in, she realised she couldn't do it. It was too hot and too crowded, and she could feel clammy perspiration blossoming all over her body just from being there, crushed in by people on every side. As everyone else took their seats, Jess had slipped outside, gulping in the cold, fresh air as if her life depended on it.

Now she took refuge by the ornamental fountain, soothed by the bubbling water and the darting fish in the pond's murky depths.

There were six new sets of initials carved into the stonework, the letters fresh and white against the mellow grey stone. Jess quickly found the one she was looking for: HT. Harry Turner. And there, underneath it, was the date the plane had crashed, 28 February 1942.

Jess traced the letters with the tip of her finger, but they still didn't seem real to her.

Why have a tribute at all? she wondered. Why constantly remind themselves he was dead?

Wasn't it easier to keep him alive in their minds, as if he'd just popped outside for a smoke? Then they wouldn't have to face the unbearable pain of knowing they would never see him again.

Either that, or they should forget him completely. What was it Christina Rossetti said in her poem? 'Better by far you should forget and smile/ Than that you should remember and be sad.' It would make no difference to Harry whether they mourned him or not, and it was surely easier for everyone than sobbing in the chapel, wringing their hands and feeling sorry for themselves.

As she had written in her last letter to Sam, it was far better to try and put it behind them and get on with life. That's what Harry would have wanted, and that's what Jess was trying to do. But her friends wouldn't have it. Daisy and Effie followed her around, watching her closely, as if they expected her to break into hysteria at any moment.

'Are you all right?' Effie kept asking her, anxiously.

'Yes, of course I am. Why shouldn't I be?' she snapped back.

And if they weren't watching her, they were sighing over their memories.

'Do you remember when we all went to the coast?' they would say. Or: 'Just think, it was only a couple of weeks ago we were at that dance in the village hall...' As if they could make themselves feel better by dwelling on how much they missed him. It made no sense to Jess.

For once, she was relieved that Matron had kept her on nights during the diphtheria epidemic, and didn't have to listen to them going on, wallowing in their misery and memories. She didn't have time to think about Harry's death because she was so busy trying to look after her living patients. The diphtheria outbreak was spreading, and every day seemed to bring more cases to the already over-crowded fever ward. Jess spent her nights running from bed to bed, swabbing throats, setting up steam tents and administering serum.

But if she worked hard, then Dr Drake worked even harder. He seemed to be a permanent fixture on the ward since the outbreak had started, and Jess got used to working alongside him. They rarely spoke, but she liked the reassurance of having him there. The ward seemed strangely empty without him on the rare occasions he was called away to an emergency elsewhere in the hospital.

But even working as hard as they did, they still couldn't save everyone. The night after Harry's remembrance service, a boy called Toby died. He was sixteen years old and delivered groceries for the village shop until he was taken ill.

Dr Drake came to fill out the paperwork and sign his death certificate, then Jess set about performing last offices. She washed Toby's body carefully, combed his hair and wrapped him in a shroud ready for the orderlies to collect. She tried to work quickly and efficiently, but her aching limbs seemed to defy her, growing heavier and more difficult to move the faster she tried to work. All the while her headache was pulsing behind her eyes until she had to stop and close them for a moment just to ease the pain. She could feel a sheen of sweat on her brow.

When she emerged from the room where she'd laid out the boy, Dr Drake was still on the ward. He was making a great show of checking a patient's notes, but Jess had the feeling he'd been waiting for her.

'Are you all right, Nurse?' he asked.

Usually Jess would have answered him politely, but her weariness and aching head made her snap. 'Why do people keep asking me that?'

Dr Drake blinked owlishly behind his spectacles. 'I couldn't answer for anyone else, but you seem rather unwell to me.'

Jess forced herself to calm down. It wasn't Dr Drake's fault. The poor man must have been wondering what had hit him.

'I'm sorry, Doctor. You're right, I am a bit under the weather. I think I might have a cold coming.'

'Yes, I can see you have a fever.' His pale gaze searched her face. 'Perhaps you should go to the sick bay?'

'Oh, no, I'm far too busy for that.'

'No one is too busy to be ill, Nurse. Tell me your symptoms.'

His authoritative tone stopped her in her tracks. 'I have a headache and my limbs ache,' she admitted.

'Any sore throat?'

Jess paused. 'A bit,' she said. 'But it isn't what you think,' she went on in a rush, seeing his face. 'I had the Schick test, remember?'

'Test or not, let me see your throat.'

She sighed heavily and sat down at Sister's desk, tilting her head back so he could examine her by the light of the green-shaded lamp. She had never been so close to him before, and found herself swivelling her gaze so she wouldn't have to look so closely into his pale silvery eyes behind his spectacles. He smelled of coal tar soap.

Finally he released her and she straightened up, massaging her neck. 'As you can see, I'm fine,' she started to say, but he cut her off.

'Nurse Jago, you are far from fine,' he said shortly. 'I want you to report to the sick bay immediately. I will telephone Night Sister and inform her.'

The serious expression on his face worried Jess. 'What is it, Doctor?' she asked.

But deep down she already knew the answer.

'Diphtheria?'

'That's what Miss Carrington says. Apparently Dr Drake noticed Jess was ill when she was on duty last night and sent her straight to isolation.'

Effie rubbed the sleep out of her eyes. The Home Sister had roused her even earlier than usual that morning with the news that Jess had been taken to the sick bay. She had stripped Jess's bed and told Effie to get dressed and then pack up some of her room-mate's toiletries and nightclothes for her.

She was now trying to do just that while Daisy sat on the bare frame of Jess's bed.

'How bad is she?' Daisy asked.

'I don't know. But she must be bad to be in isolation, don't you think?' Effie packed Jess's toothbrush, tooth powder and a clean flannel, towel and soap, then deliberated over the few items of make-up set out on the dresser. She couldn't imagine that her friend would need lipstick and powder while she was in isolation. She hardly ever wore them anyway.

'Should someone tell her family?' Daisy said.

Effie shook her head. 'I don't think she has any. Not that she's close to, anyway.' She knew Jess's mother was dead, and that she came from a desperate, rundown part of Bethnal Green. She also knew Jess loathed her father and stepmother and never spoke to either of them. But apart from that, Effie was surprised to realise that she knew next to nothing about her friend's family. Effie had told Jess everything about her own life growing up in Kilkenny, her mammy and daddy and four sisters. She'd even told her the name of their parish priest! But she couldn't remember Jess ever telling her anything in return. When it came to talking about herself, Jess was as closed as the many books on her shelf.

'I wonder if she'll want any of these?' She ran her gaze along the leather spines. *David Copperfield ... Great Expectations ... Jane Eyre...* Jess always had her nose in one of them. Effie could never understand why. It took all her time and concentration to read one book, let alone all these, over and over again.

'I can't imagine why,' Daisy said. 'If she's that poorly, she won't feel much like reading, surely?'

'But she'll need to do something to pass the time,' Effie argued. 'Poor girl, if she really has diphtheria she'll be flat on her back for weeks, not seeing a soul. Maybe I'll put a couple in the bag, just in case.' She chose *Great Expectations,* because it was Jess's favourite – she knew that about her, at least. Jess was always willing to talk about her favourite books, if nothing else.

'Should someone tell Sam, do you think?' Daisy asked.

Effie considered it. 'I don't know,' she said. 'He's bound to wonder what's going on when he doesn't get a letter from her. Especially as she writes to him practically every day.'

'I think we should write to him,' Daisy decided.

'But how do we find out his address? He could be stationed anywhere.' Effie racked her brains to remember if Jess had mentioned it. But her relationship with Sam was something else she never talked about.

'Have a look for one of his letters. It might give you an address.'

Effie recoiled from the idea. 'I couldn't do that! Jess wouldn't like it. You know how private she is about her things.'

'Then I'll do it.' Daisy slid off the bedframe. 'Where does she keep his letters?'

'In that box under her bed. But I don't think you should touch it,' Effie added. 'It's not right to go spying in her personal business.'

'I'm not going to read them, am I?' Daisy got down on her knees and rooted under the bed, groping for the box. 'I only want to look at one to get the address – ah, here we are.'

She pulled the cardboard box out from under the bed. 'Blimey, it's heavy,' she said, lifting it on to the bare mattress. 'Sam must be an even bigger letter writer than Jago!'

'He can't be. She never seems to get any letters from him.' Effie frowned. 'Come to think of it, I can't remember her getting a single letter from

Sam in the whole time I've been here...'

'And I think I know why – look.'

Daisy pushed the box towards Effie, and she peered inside. The box was full of letters, all in thin blue envelopes, all sealed – and all addressed to Sam in Jess's neat handwriting.

Chapter Forty-Five

'I say,' said Teddy. 'Isn't that your friend William down there?'

Millie averted her gaze from the airfield below them. She had already picked out William's tall, lean figure, with a sheepskin jacket over his blue flying suit, striding across the runway towards the plane.

'Yes, it is,' she said, tight-lipped.

Seeing him had quite spoiled her day. Up until then, she had been enjoying a pleasant Sunday afternoon ride with Teddy and Henry. Teddy was riding her father's handsome old hunter, Samson, while Henry sat sturdily astride her own childhood pony, a fat piebald called Mischief. Millie was riding Aphrodite, a slender and rather excitable chestnut.

They had ridden around the park, and Teddy had very patiently taught Henry to trot. Then, at her son's insistence, they had taken the path up to the ridge to look down over the airfield. Henry rode between them, Mischief's fat flanks grazing their horses'.

It had been such fun, having Teddy there to share the day with them. Henry adored him, and insisted on showing off all his tricks. And Teddy, as usual, made a very patient audience.

He was looking at Millie now, eyebrows raised. 'What's this?' he said sharply. 'A lovers' tiff?'

Millie busied herself leaning down to adjust Henry's stirrups, hoping Teddy couldn't see her face. 'Whatever there was between us is over,' she stated firmly.

It had been a week since Millie had delivered her ultimatum. And even though she realised with hindsight she might have been unfair to make demands that William couldn't possibly meet, she still stood by every word.

'What did he do wrong?' Teddy asked.

'Nothing. I just realised that it would never work between us, that's all.'

Teddy pulled a face. 'Oh, my dear. Did you find out something truly shocking about him? An unforgivable skeleton in his closet?'

'Nothing like that.' Millie smiled in spite of herself. 'If you must know, I realised I couldn't possibly allow myself to fall in love with another pilot.'

'Ah. I see.' Teddy considered this for a moment. 'Yes, all becomes clear to me now. You can't face the prospect of those sleepless nights, worrying if what happened to Seb will happen to him?'

'Exactly.' If Teddy could understand how she felt, why couldn't William? Millie wondered.

But he plainly didn't. And things had become strained between them since that morning. Now, if they happened to meet in the grounds or near the house, William simply ignored her.

'Anyway, whatever there was between us is well and truly over now,' she said firmly. She eyed the planes as they taxied down the runway. 'Shall we turn back? I can see they're about to take off, and Aphrodite is easily spooked.'

No sooner had she said it than one of the bombers suddenly picked up speed and took off. It roared low over their heads, almost brushing the tops of the trees, casting them into deep shadow.

Millie fought to keep Aphrodite's head as she skipped and shuffled sideways away from the noise, but it was Mischief who panicked. He reared up on his stubby hind legs and then took off, galloping into the trees carting Henry with him.

Millie screamed, but Teddy's reflexes were faster. He jabbed his heels into Samson's flanks and took off after Henry.

'Hang on!' she heard him yelling to her son. 'Hang on until I catch you.'

Aphrodite was still dancing on the spot, spooked by all the excitement. Millie wheeled her round and urged her on, following Henry and Teddy.

She was barely into the trees when she spotted Mischief, chomping on the grass. Samson was with him, looking around warily. Then Millie saw Teddy, crouched over the small body that lay on the damp, mossy ground under a tree, and her blood turned to ice.

'Henry!' Millie was off Aphrodite before she had even stopped. She dropped to her knees beside Teddy, her heart in her mouth. 'Is he–'

'He's breathing,' Teddy said, one ear pressed to Henry's chest. 'I think he must have hit one of those low-hanging branches.'

'Henry?' Millie took over, gently trying to rouse her son. 'Henry, can you hear me? It's Mummy.'

It seemed like a very long moment before Millie heard her baby boy groan. Relief flooded her body, and she burst into tears. 'Oh, thank God!'

Millie watched as Teddy tenderly examined the boy, reassuring him softly as Henry whimpered. She knew she could have done it herself, but was too paralysed with shock to move. At least Henry had stopped crying, although he was staring up at Teddy with round, dazed eyes.

'Well, there don't seem to be any bones broken, but I'm no expert,' Teddy said finally, sitting back on his heels. 'But we'd better get him back to the house and call a doctor, just in case.' He took charge, gently gathering the boy up in his arms. 'I'll take him, shall I? I think Samson will be a safer bet with precious cargo.'

'Thank you.' Millie kissed the top of Henry's blond head, smiling through her tears as he squirmed away from her. He was already getting back to normal, she thought with relief.

At the Lodge, there was a long, anxious wait while the doctor examined him. Millie sat in the drawing room beside Teddy, clutching his hand so hard she carved half moons in his flesh with her nails. The calm manner she used on the wards seemed to have completely abandoned her.

'It will be all right,' Teddy kept telling her. 'He'll be fine.'

'What if he isn't?' she whispered. She had been a nurse too long not to realise that the simplest fall could have dire consequences. Consequences that weren't always immediately apparent.

'Stop it, darling. You saw him when we brought him into the house. He was practically his old self.'

She was quiet for a moment and then she was on her feet again. 'Do you think that doctor knows what he's doing?' she said. 'He's only a locum, not our usual GP...'

'Nevertheless, he still has a medical qualification.'

Millie allowed Teddy's calm voice to wash over her, soothing away her fears. Just his presence was like balm, comforting her. She was sure he was right, But at the same time, she couldn't help feeling anxious.

'Thank you for being here,' she said. 'I don't know what I would have done without you. Gone quite mad, probably.'

'That's what friends do, darling.'

Millie smiled gratefully. Teddy had been more than a friend. He had been a hero. Without him, she was certain she would have fallen to pieces.

More importantly, he was there when she needed him, not several thousand feet up above the English Channel.

The doctor appeared and pronounced Henry none the worse for his adventure.

'You'll need to keep an eye on him for a few days, just to make sure he doesn't develop any nasty symptoms,' he advised. 'Watch out for any nausea or vomiting, or if he seems dizzy at all.'

'I know what to look for, Doctor,' Millie assured him. Now she knew Henry wasn't in terrible danger, she could finally allow herself to relax.

Teddy showed the doctor out while Millie went

in to check on Henry. He seemed fine despite has accident, although the scowling look Nanny Perks gave her said that she wouldn't forgive Millie in a hurry.

When she returned to the drawing room, Teddy had poured them both a large whisky. 'I think we need it, don't you?'

'Thank you.'

As she sat down, Teddy told her, 'You know, the doctor said the most extraordinary thing as I was showing him out. He told me I had a delightful little boy. You don't think he imagined we were a family, do you?'

He looked so taken aback by the idea Millie laughed. 'Would that be so terrible?' she said.

'Not at all.' He shook his head. 'In fact, I don't think I could think of anything more perfect.'

Millie looked at his kind, handsome face. Teddy would never let her down. He had a heart of gold. He would always keep her safe.

'Neither can I,' she said.

Chapter Forty-Six

It was a chilly March morning, and the ward was still in darkness, huddled behind blackout curtains, as Grace lit the fire, piling up the kindling and lighting the paper. The warmth of the flames made her chilblains tingle. She sat back on her heels and examined the skin on her fingers, tight, red and throbbing with pain. Even though March was here, there was still no sign of spring. Winter held on grimly, casting its grey shadow everywhere.

She thought about the winters in Canada. Max had painted such a vivid picture of the cold beauty of the landscape, everything blanketed in thick, sparkling snow, the whiteness so blindingly brilliant it hurt to look at it. Sometimes, he said, the snow was so deep it drifted right up against the windows. Then they would have to put on special shoes that helped them walk on the snow's surface. Grace could hardly believe such a thing was possible, but Max had assured her they worked very well.

She often found herself thinking about Canada, daydreaming about what it might be like to go there and see it for herself. Max had told her all about the mountains, their peaks tipped with snow all year round, even in the summer. He'd told her about the pine forests, the vast lakes, and the ocean where you could go out on a boat and see whales and dolphins, close enough to touch. She couldn't imagine how wonderful it must be.

Daisy whisked past, lifting Grace out of her pleasant daydream. She had just come on duty and as she hurried down the ward, Grace could see her shivering inside her cloak, her face pinched and white with cold.

'I've got the fire going, if you want to warm yourself for a minute?' she offered. Daisy looked at her for a moment, then gave the slightest shake of her head and moved on.

Grace sighed. She desperately wished her sister would forgive her, and that everything could go back to normal. She dearly wanted to take care of her again. Poor Daisy looked so lost.

She had been a little better towards Grace since the crash that had killed poor Harry and the others. Sometimes Grace caught her sister watching her, and fancied that she might even want to speak to her. But somehow pride always stopped her. It was almost as if Daisy couldn't allow herself to be friendly.

Grace tried to forget about it as she helped to serve the breakfasts.

'Morning, Gracie!' Tommo greeted her cheerfully when she brought Alan's tray over. He was sitting up in bed, all smiles.

'What have I told you about calling me that?' Grace warned. It was a bad day for her when Tommo had found out her Christian name. Now he insisted on using it all the time.

'Aw, don't be like that, Gracie. I'm in a good mood today.'

'Oh, yes? And why's that?'

'I'm getting a visit from my CO, to be told when I can rejoin my regiment. I can't wait!' He rubbed his hands together in glee.

'Nor can we, mate!' Sergeant Jefferson muttered from the next bed. 'Can't wait to see the back of you!'

'That's good news.' Grace set Alan's tray down. 'How is your leg healing up?'

Tommo stared down at the injured limb, still propped up on its frame, and his face clouded over.

'It's a bit stiff,' he admitted. 'But I'll be right as rain soon. And it won't stop me firing a gun, will it?' He cheered up. 'I'm telling you, Gracie, I can't wait to get back to my old pals.'

'Well, I'm very pleased for you,' she said. 'Now, do you want to help Alan with his breakfast, or shall I do it?'

'No need for that, Nurse.' Tommo looked across at Alan in the next bed, his eyes twinkling. 'I've been teaching him how to feed himself. He can almost manage it now.'

'Never!' Grace looked from one to the other. 'When did this happen?'

'Oh, we've been practising for a while, haven't we mate? We wanted it to be a surprise for you.' He winked at Alan. 'What do you say? Do you want to show Grace how you're getting on?'

Tommo got out of bed and carefully positioned the bowl of porridge in front of Alan, then placed the spoon in his hand. Grace sat at the bedside, watching as the spoon wobbled in Alan's shaky grasp. It was painful to watch, and she had to lace her fingers in her lap to stop herself moving to help him as he lowered the spoon slowly into the porridge, then lifted it to his lips.

Grace and Tommo both watched him. Grace silently willed him on as the porridge slopped off the spoon, Alan's head still craning forward, mouth open. But finally he captured it between his lips and sat back, a look of triumph in his eyes.

'Oh, that's wonderful!' She clapped her hands. 'Well done, Alan. And you too, Tommo, for teaching him.'

Tommo looked proud. 'I did a good job, didn't I?' He preened himself. 'Now all I've got to do is teach him how to stand up and walk by himself.

You'll have to do that, won't you, mate? When I leave, I mean?'

Alan gave him an awkward sideways smile, as he lowered his spoon shakily into his bowl again.

Grace sat there until he'd finished every painstaking mouthful. She was tempted to seize the spoon and do it for him, but Tommo was very strict about that.

'No, Grace,' he insisted. 'Leave him be. He's got to learn to stand on his own two feet.'

'You're right,' she said, but she still felt sceptical. There was no doubt Tommo had done a good job; when Grace had first seen Alan, no one had imagined he would ever do anything more than stare into space. But she doubted if even Tommo's determination could make his friend stand on his own again. Even if he could manage it physically, he lacked the strength and the will to help himself.

Once breakfast was over, and Grace had washed up the dishes, it was time to get on with all her other jobs. She ran baths, set trolleys, scrubbed and cleaned, handed out and collected bedpans and straightened beds. Sometime in the middle of the morning, she saw a tall, uniformed officer striding down the ward, flanked by Miss Wallace and Dr Pearson. Grace watched Miss Wallace setting up the screens around Tommo's bed, and smiled. Poor Tommo had waited weeks for this moment, and she was pleased it was finally happening for him.

'The patient in bed seven has just vomited. Clean it up, *stat*.' Grace started at the sharp sound of Daisy's voice. But before she could react her sister was already walking off down the ward, her spine stiff and straight.

'Someone's in a funny mood?' The kindly corporal whose bed she had been straightening grinned up at her.

Grace smiled. 'Only with me.'

Sometimes she wondered why she didn't accept Max's offer, and just up sticks and go off to Canada. It wasn't as if Daisy wanted her around any more. And even though she was trying to keep her distance from Max, the idea of never seeing him again was almost too painful to bear. She knew it would be a good life for Walter and Ann there, far better than the life they had at the moment.

But she couldn't think about leaving Daisy, not while they were still at loggerheads. Grace had looked after her younger sister for so long, she couldn't imagine not being there to watch over her.

And if she was honest, Grace was also afraid of the idea of making a new start. She had spent her whole life at the beck and call of others, and wasn't sure she would even know how to live her life for herself.

When she emerged from cleaning up around bed seven, Miss Wallace called her over.

'Maynard, could you keep an eye on Mr Thompson?' she said. 'He's had some rather bad news. His CO has just told him he won't be going back into the army. His injuries are too severe.'

'Oh, no! Poor Tommo!'

'Quite. He's very upset about it, as you can imagine.' Miss Wallace glanced over her shoulder towards him. 'He's refusing to eat his lunch. I wonder if you could try to persuade him?'

'I'll do my best, Sister.'

As Grace went off, Miss Wallace called after her, 'Be careful, Maynard. He's in a rather difficult mood.'

Tommo didn't even look at Grace as she brought his tray over to him. He lay on his back, staring up at the ceiling with glassy, vacant eyes.

'You can take that away, I don't want anything,' he grunted.

'But it's pease pudding, your favourite.'

'Are you deaf? I told you, I don't want it.'

Grace ignored him as she set the tray down on his locker. 'You have to eat something, to keep your strength up,' she said briskly.

'What for?' He turned his head to look at her. Grace was shocked by the hopeless expression in his eyes. For a moment she was at a loss for words.

'So you can get better,' she said stoutly.

'What's the point in getting better? It don't matter what state I'm in, it ain't going to make any difference. I suppose you've heard they don't want me back in the army?'

Grace lowered her gaze. 'Sister told me. I'm very sorry.'

'Much good sorry will do!' His mouth was set in a bitter line. 'I dunno why they bothered patching me up. It might have been better if they'd left me to die out there.'

Grace gasped 'You can't say that!'

'She's right, you ungrateful little sod,' Sergeant Jefferson broke in.

Tommo turned on him. 'Oh, yeah? And what have I got to be grateful for?'

'You're alive, ain't you? Some boys weren't that

lucky.' He nodded towards Alan. 'Look at that poor devil. He's in a worse state than you, and you never hear him feeling sorry for himself.'

'That's 'cos he ain't right in the head!' Tommo snapped back. 'It would have been a mercy if they'd let him die, too.'

Grace and Sergeant Jefferson stared at each other, shocked. 'That's a terrible thing to say!' Grace said.

'Why? Look at him. He's never going to be any use to anyone. He's like me – on the scrap heap.'

Grace shot a look at Alan. He was propped up as usual, staring straight ahead of him with his single glassy eye. It was hard to know if he'd taken in what Tommo had said. She hoped he hadn't.

'Any life is better than no life at all,' she hissed. 'I bet Alan's family is thankful that he's come through it.'

Tommo turned bitter eyes to hers. 'That's the difference, ain't it? He's got a family to care about him. All I had was the army. And now I ain't even got that...'

He dashed his hand across his face, but not before Grace caught the glitter of a tear escaping from the corner of his eye.

'You've still got friends here,' she tried to reason with him.

'No, I ain't. None of them could give a stuff about me.'

'Alan cares about you.'

'Alan don't know what time of day it is half the time. What use is he to me?'

Grace opened her mouth to speak, but Tommo cut her off. 'Look, Nurse, I know you mean well, but just do me a favour and push off, will you? I don't want to talk to you, all right?'

Grace glanced across the ward at Miss Wallace, who was watching them. She gave a little shake of her head.

'All right, I will leave you alone,' she whispered, picking up the tray. 'But you're wrong, Tommo. People do care about you.'

She fetched Alan's tray and sat down beside his bed. He looked up at her enquiringly.

'Right, let's get you something to eat, shall we? Do you think you can manage this by yourself?' She picked up the spoon and tried to put it into his hand, but Alan's slack fingers wouldn't grip it. He looked over at Tommo, wanting his encouragement.

'Just leave him be,' Grace whispered. 'He's only lashed out because he's scared and angry. He'll calm down soon.'

She tried again to get Alan to take the spoon, but his fingers remained slack and inert. In the end Grace picked it up and started to feed him herself. All the while, Alan's sad gaze stayed fixed on his friend in the next bed. Tommo kept his own eyes averted, staring up at the ceiling with studied indifference.

Poor Alan, Grace thought, simmering with fury. He understood more than anyone imagined, and Tommo's cruel comments must have hurt him deeply.

When lunch was finished and the dishes were cleared away, Grace had to take Tommo's neighbour, Sergeant Jefferson, down to the X-ray department. Usually they would get an orderly to do it, but as they were few and far between, more often than not Grace had to do it herself. She didn't mind too much. It did her good to get off the ward for a while, and she enjoyed chatting to the wounded soldier as she wheeled him down the passageways.

Of course Sergeant Jefferson wanted to discuss Tommo.

'I'm not surprised that lad doesn't have any mates,' he grumbled. 'He's his own worst enemy.'

'I suppose it's the way he was brought up,' Grace said. 'Growing up in a workhouse, you're bound to feel as if all the world's against you.'

'No one's against him,' Sergeant Jefferson insisted. 'We're all in this together, and we'd all give him a chance, if he didn't go round putting people's backs up.' His mouth set in a grim line. 'Not sure anyone will give him the time of day now, though. Not after what he said about poor Alan.'

'Hmm.' Grace agreed with the soldier, but she couldn't help feeling sorry for Tommo, too. She knew that underneath his tough exterior he had a good heart. He liked Alan, and once he'd got over his upset and disappointment, he would be sorry that he'd hurt his friend.

When they returned an hour later, Grace was aware of a change of atmosphere on the ward. She paused in the doorway, frowning. Something had happened, but she wasn't sure what.

It was Sergeant Jefferson who noticed it first.

'Will you look at that?' He nodded towards Tommo's bed.

Grace looked, and for a moment she couldn't

believe her eyes. Alan was sitting – actually sitting – at Tommo's bedside. Tommo was lying there, facing in the opposite direction, staring into space, seemingly unaware of his friend's hand resting on his shoulder.

'How did he get there, I wonder?' She spoke her thoughts aloud.

'Someone must have helped him,' Sergeant Jefferson replied.

'Actually, they didn't,' Miss Wallace said as she hurried past. 'Would you believe, he walked those few steps by himself? We were all speechless. It was like witnessing a miracle.'

'I'll bet.' Sergeant Jefferson shook his head. 'Would you credit it, Nurse? That's the first time I've ever seen him get out of bed.'

Grace watched Alan, tenderly patting his friend's shoulder, his expression full of concern. 'Perhaps he's never had a good enough reason before?' she said.

Chapter Forty-Seven

'Married?' her grandmother said flatly. 'You're getting married?'

'You don't look very pleased about it,' Millie said.

'Yes, of course I am, my dear. If that's what you want. I'm just rather – surprised, that's all.'

'I don't know why. You know how often Teddy's been calling lately.'

'Yes, but I didn't realise things had progressed this far. Not to the point where you've discussed marriage.'

'Well, they have.' Millie reached for Teddy's hand, for reassurance as much as anything. He smiled encouragingly back at her. He was going to be her husband, she thought with a slight sense of shock. She had been engaged for less than twelve hours, and she was still getting used to the idea.

'So I see.' Lady Rettingham looked from Teddy's face to Millie's and back again. 'Well, in that case, I'm delighted for both of you.' She gave Millie one of her rare smiles of approval. 'When were you thinking of getting married?'

'As soon as possible,' Millie said promptly. 'Next week, perhaps?'

'Next week?' Her grandmother's smile froze. 'Oh, no, my dear, I don't think so. These things take time to arrange if they're to be done properly. It will take at least a month to arrange for the banns to be read in church...'

'Yes, but we don't need to do all that, do we?' Millie said with a touch of desperation. 'Surely we could just get a special licence at a register office? Couples do it all the time these days.'

'Only if they're in a particular hurry,' Lady Rettingham said. 'If they're called up for service, or if they – have to marry.' Her lip curled with distaste. 'And I'm sure we don't want anyone thinking that there's a reason for you to marry in such indecent haste.'

Her questioning gaze fell on Millie's waistline.

'Of course not!' Millie laid her hand over the flatness of her stomach. 'I just thought it would

393

be best, that's all. We don't really need a lot of fuss, do we?'

'It's your wedding. Why shouldn't you make a fuss?'

Millie frowned at her grandmother. Wasn't it enough for her that they were getting married, without having to go through all this rigmarole, too?

She glanced at Teddy for his support, but he simply shrugged and said, 'Your grandmother is quite right, darling. Why not wait and make an event of it? After all, it's not every day one gets married, is it? And I'm sure my mother and father will want to make something of the day, especially as they probably never thought it would happen!'

His expression was so bright and hopeful, it took a moment for Millie to remember that this was her second marriage but Teddy's first. Of course he would want a big wedding.

She had been looking at it all wrong. It wasn't just rigmarole, it was a cause for celebration.

'Of course,' she said, summoning a smile. 'We'll wait, and make it a day to remember.'

Millie was grooming her horse in the stable yard. William watched her from the window of the briefing room, drinking in the sight of her. There had been times during the previous night when he wasn't sure he would ever see her, or anyone else, again.

He had already closed his mind to what had happened. He'd already had to relive it once before his superiors in the briefing room, going through the technical details of the incident: the flak that tore

394

the heart out of the plane, how they'd limped back over France, before he'd managed to bring her down in a field, by sheer luck as much as skill. There had been a couple of broken limbs and a head injury among the crew, but at least they were all alive.

And now it was over. William wasn't interested in the Wing Commander's praise or his promise of a commendation. All he wanted to do was forget it.

He would never fly again otherwise. Every time he climbed into a cockpit, he had to clear his mind of every near miss, every exploding fuselage and failing engine, every friend and comrade he had ever lost.

It was the only way he could get through it.

There had been some ribbing in the officers' mess about his brush with death. But William was more interested in hearing about what had been going on while he'd been away.

'You've heard about the little boy – Lady Amelia's son?' one of the other officers said, as William tucked into his bacon and eggs. It was every airman's reward at the end of a mission.

William dropped his knife and fork. 'No? What happened?'

'Horse got spooked by the planes and carted him off into the woods. Knocked himself clean out, apparently.'

'Is he all right now?'

'As far as I know. But you should probably expect a visit from Her Ladyship shortly, asking if you could take off and land more quietly!'

The officer guffawed with laughter, but William

didn't join in. He knew how much Millie adored her little boy. She must have been utterly terrified, he thought.

He had made up his mind to see her, even though they hadn't spoken since the day she'd told him she wanted nothing more to do with him. He'd been angry and hurt, and had done his best to stay out of her way. But he knew she would be upset about Henry, and he cared too much to ignore her pain.

Millie looked up briefly when he came out into the yard, then went on with her grooming.

'I hope I'm not in the way?' she said. 'I meant to finish the job last night, but I – had an emergency to deal with.'

'I heard what happened to Henry. How is he?'

She paused, then went on brushing down her horse's gleaming flanks. 'He's fine,' she said. 'No sign of concussion, thank God. But I'm keeping an eye on him.'

'The horse was spooked by the planes taking off, so I'm told?'

She nodded. 'But it was my own fault. We shouldn't have been up there, but Henry so wanted to see them.'

There was a long silence. William wondered whether he should leave, but his feet were rooted to the spot.

'I'm sorry I wasn't there,' he said quietly.

'Why should you be?'

'Because I care about him – and you.' William took a step forward. 'You needed help, and I couldn't be there.'

'You can never be there. That's the trouble,'

Millie muttered under her breath.

Her comment hit home. 'You make it sound as if it's my choice,' he bit out. 'As if I decide to get into a plane and fly into enemy fire, night after night, just to provoke you.'

I almost died last night, he wanted to shout. But he pushed the memory to the back of his mind. He couldn't bring himself to say the words.

Millie went on brushing her horse, long unhurried strokes over the gleaming chestnut flanks.

'Anyway, I wasn't on my own,' she said, not looking at him. 'Teddy was here. He stayed the night, actually.'

William bristled. He wasn't sure if Millie was trying to make him jealous but it had worked. 'I'm glad,' he forced himself to say.

As he turned to go back to the house, she said, 'I think you should know, Teddy and I are engaged.'

William swung round to face her. 'Since when?'

'Yesterday.'

He paused, struggling to get his thoughts in order. 'Do you love him?' he asked.

She stopped brushing and straightened up to face him. 'Yes,' she said.

'But you're not in love with him, are you?'

Delicate colour rose in her face. 'Of course I am,' she said. 'Why shouldn't I be? He's kind, thoughtful, he adores Henry—'

'And he has a nice, safe desk job,' William finished for her. 'That's the most important thing, isn't it? Never mind if you truly love him or not, as long as he comes home to you every night?'

Her chin tilted in defiance. 'So what if it is

important to me? What's wrong with not wanting to live in fear for the rest of my life? Oh, I know other women have to put up with it,' she said as he opened his mouth to speak. 'And I put up with it too once, remember? I put up with it every day until that telegram arrived.' She pointed the brush at him. 'Do you blame me for not wanting to live through that moment again? For wanting to protect myself, and my son?'

William stared at her, and his mind was suddenly filled with a horrific image from the previous night – a splintering crash, the smell of burning gasoline mingled with sweat and panic as half a dozen young men stared death in the face.

He knew in that moment that she was right. He loved her too much to want to put her through that kind of hell. Far better that she be with someone else than suffer that.

'No,' he said wearily. 'No, I don't blame you at all.'

Chapter Forty-Eight

Jess was with Sam in Victoria Park. It was a perfect summer's day and they were on the boating lake together. Sam was rowing, shirt sleeves rolled up to reveal his muscled forearms, while Jess lay back, eating an ice cream and enjoying the warmth of the sun on her face and the sound of the brass band playing on the band stand.

Sam was fooling about the way he always did,

pretending to drop the oars and making the boat wobble from side to side until Jess had to hang on for dear life and beg him to stop. Even though she was terrified, she was still helpless with laughter.

As they floated past the boat shed, Jess heard someone calling her name. She sat up.

'Who's that?'

'It's no one,' Sam said. 'Take no notice. Here, look.' He distracted her, putting down the oars to skim a stone across the water.

Jess smiled as she watched it skipping across the water, shattering the mirror-calm surface. Then she raised her gaze and saw a young man standing on the opposite bank. Tall and lanky, with a shock of brown hair, he was polishing his spectacles on the hem of his white coat.

'Dr Drake?' she said his name aloud.

Sam looked up. 'I don't see anyone.'

'You must see him. Look, over there.' She pointed. Dr Drake was waving to her, calling out her name.

'Nurse Jago? Jess? Can you hear me?' His voice drifted across the lake, mingling with the soft splash of the oars in the water and the quacking of the ducks.

Jess looked away, annoyed. 'I wish he'd go,' she said. 'I don't want him here, spoiling our day. What's he doing here, anyway? He shouldn't be here.'

Sam smiled at her sadly. 'I think he's come to take you back.'

Jess sat upright. 'What do you mean? I don't want to go anywhere. I'm happy here with you.'

'I know. And I want you to stay, truly I do.' He

was staring down at the space between her feet as he said it, his face downcast. 'But you've got to go, Jessie.'

'I don't want to go!' Jess heard the panic in her own voice.

The sun drifted behind a cloud, casting a dull grey shadow over the surface of the water. A chill breeze came out of nowhere, pimpling the bare skin of her arms.

The boat was drifting towards the bank where Dr Drake was standing, stretching out his hand to her.

'Come on, Jess,' he was calling. 'You can do it. Come on!'

She turned to Sam accusingly. 'Row away,' she said. 'Don't go towards him. Go the other way!' She tried to grab the oars but Sam held them out of her grasp.

'I'm sorry, Jess,' he said. His smile was the sweetest, saddest thing she'd ever seen. 'You know I'd let you stay if I could, but it's not your time. You've got to go back.'

Dr Drake was closer now. She could see the light glinting off his spectacles. He was teetering over the water, still reaching for her.

'Go to him,' she heard Sam's voice say in her ear. 'Just go to him, Jess. Trust me, it's the right thing to do.'

Jess looked at Dr Drake, then back at Sam. 'If I go, will I see you again?'

He grinned at her. 'One day,' he promised. 'When the time's right, I'll come back for you.' He nodded towards the man on the bank. 'But he'll take care of you for now.'

'Jess?' Dr Drake's voice was desperate. It seemed closer to her now, filling her ears. The gentle lapping of the water, the quacking of the ducks and the sound of the brass band seemed to recede into the distance, becoming hushed until she could barely hear them.

Jess looked back at Sam, one last glance. 'Are you sure?' she whispered.

He winked at her. 'Go on,' he said.

Jess turned to Dr Drake, screwed her eyes tight shut, took a deep breath and thrust out her hand to take his.

Chapter Forty-Nine

Alan was going home.

More precisely, he was being transferred to a convalescent home in Wales, closer to where his parents lived, so he could receive the long-term care he needed.

''Course, you know the nurses at the convalescent home won't be a patch on our lovely lot?' Tommo lounged on his bed, watching Grace pack Alan's suitcase. 'They keep the pretty ones to work in the hospitals. The ones at the convalescent home all look like Old Mother Riley!'

'Take no notice of him, he's only teasing you,' Grace said to Alan. But she was pleased to see Tommo more like his old cheeky self. After a few days of sadness, he had finally pulled himself round.

Alan had helped. While Tommo had been depressed, Alan had never left his side. He said nothing, but his calm, reassuring presence had somehow been just what Tommo needed to make him realise that he wasn't on his own against the world after all.

And it had had a remarkable effect on Alan, too. Somehow, being useful and needed had dragged him out of his own dark, enclosed world. In the past few days he had started walking a few halting steps, and was even trying to speak, although he could only utter sounds rather than words.

But now the friends were being separated. And even though Tommo was trying to put on a brave face, Grace could see he was troubled by it.

'I'll be sorry to see you go,' he admitted gruffly to his friend, staring down at his hands. 'You're the only one worth talking to in this place.'

'The only one who'll listen to you, you mean?' Sergeant Jefferson chimed in. But he was smiling as he said it.

'Never mind,' Grace said. 'It won't be long before you're going home, too.'

Tommo's face clouded. 'Much good it'll do me,' he mumbled.

'Have you thought about what you'll do?' she asked.

He shrugged. 'Well, I did reckon I might become a footballer, but I don't suppose that's going to happen now...' He stared disconsolately at his leg. 'Either that or a ballet dancer.'

Alan gave one of his shy, crooked smiles, and made an explosive sound that might have been a laugh. Grace rolled her eyes. 'Honestly, you're as bad as each other!' she sighed.

The double doors opened, and Alan's parents entered. They had been to see their son a couple of times but always looked ill at ease on the ward, their arms firmly linked and gazes turned to the ground, as if they feared the horrors they might see if they looked around.

Miss Wallace intercepted them and guided them over to her desk. Tommo watched them talking, their heads close together in conversation. Every so often they glanced over at Alan and him, then back at Sister.

'Oh, dear,' he teased Alan. 'Looks like they don't want you, after all. If you ask me, I reckon Sister's having a hard job persuading them to take you home.'

'Tommo!' Grace warned.

Finally Mr and Mrs Jones came over. They greeted Alan, his mother moving forward to envelop him in the usual hug. She smelled of lavender water.

'Oh, son!' She finally pulled away from him, her eyes full of tears. 'I never thought the day would come when we'd be taking you home, I truly didn't.'

'And we know who to thank for it, don't we?' His father nodded stiffly to Tommo. 'Sister's been explaining how much you've done for Alan. She wrote and told us all about you, didn't she, Gwen?'

'She did.' His wife beamed at Tommo. 'We knew you two were friends, but we didn't realise how much you've helped pull him through.'

Tommo shrugged, embarrassed. 'He's my

mate,' he said quietly.

There was a brief silence as Alan's mother and father looked at each other. Then his father said, 'Sister also told us you don't have anywhere to stay when you leave hospital?'

Tommo looked away, his face flushed. 'I expect I'll find somewhere,' he mumbled.

'My wife and I wondered if you'd consider coming to stay with us?'

'We've got plenty of room, and I'm sure Alan would like it if you were close by,' his mother put in eagerly.

Tommo stared from one to the other of them, and Grace could see that for once he was lost for words. 'I – I dunno what to say,' he muttered, his colour deepening.

'Think about it, anyway.' Alan's father cleared his throat. 'I could fix you up with a job too, if you like? I've got a shortage of workers at my engineering firm. You never know, perhaps one day you and Alan might work together...' He glanced at his son, hope and sadness in his eyes.

'I'll think about it,' Tommo said. But even though he was doing his best to appear nonchalant, Grace could see the look of dazed wonder in his face. It was as if all his Christmases had come at once.

It was Grace who spoke first. 'Right, let's get you ready, shall we, Alan? Have you brought a coat for him, Mrs Jones? It's cold outside, and he won't be used to it. We don't want you catching a chill, do we?'

As his mother busied herself helping Alan into his coat, his father collected up the suitcase. Grace went off to fetch a wheelchair, but Alan shook his head.

'You want to walk?' Grace flashed a look at Miss Wallace, but she was busy with another patient. 'Well, I'm not sure–'

'Let him walk, if he wants to,' Tommo broke in. 'Lazy devil's been lying around too long, it'll do him good to get some exercise.'

Alan's parents looked startled by Tommo's bluntness, but Alan gave another of his crooked smiles. He lurched forward and rested his hand on Tommo's shoulder.

'My ... mate.' The words were slow and slurred, but unmistakable.

They went off slowly, Alan walking between his parents. Each step was slow and halting, but determination was written all over his face.

'Reckon I might have to take them up on their offer, just to make sure they don't mollycoddle him,' Tommo said with an air of studied casualness. He watched Alan go. 'That's right, mate,' he murmured. 'You stand on your own two feet.'

'Who is responsible for this?'

A deathly silence fell over the Military Ward. Miss Wallace was such a cheerful soul usually that when her voice took on that icy tone, everyone knew it meant trouble for someone.

She was standing at the bed of their latest patient, a delicate-looking young lieutenant. He was supposed to be being treated for eye injuries and a septic gunshot wound in his thigh, but looked as if he was having an asthma attack. He was grey in the face and struggling for breath.

Daisy felt her heart sink to her stout black shoes.

'Whoever attended to this patient has cleaned his wound with perchloride of mercury,' Miss Wallace said. 'His notes specifically state that he has a severe allergy to mercury, and that only Lysol or carbolic is to be used.' The sister's dark gaze swept the room. 'Someone has failed to read the notes correctly, and as a result they have subjected this poor man to a great deal of misery and discomfort. I would like to know who did it?'

Daisy felt sick. She should have read those notes, but she had been so busy that morning.

But she knew no excuse would wash with Sister. Better to admit her guilt and suffer the punishment.

'It was me, Sister.' Daisy looked up sharply as Grace stepped forward. 'I'm sorry,' she murmured. 'I know I should have checked the notes. I – I didn't think.'

Miss Wallace turned to her. 'Really, Maynard, I'm very disappointed in you,' she said. 'You're usually such a conscientious girl, I don't understand how you could have made such a silly mistake.'

'I'm sorry, Sister.' Grace hung her head, her hands locked behind her back, every inch the contrite VAD.

Daisy opened her mouth to speak, but Grace shot her a silencing look.

'I'm afraid I can't allow a mistake like this to go unnoticed,' Miss Wallace said, with genuine regret in her voice. 'I shall be putting you in my report.'

'Yes, Sister.'

The report was a written record of the events that had happened on the ward during the course of a day or a night. It included details of nurses who had particularly shone during their duty, as well as those who didn't. Too many black marks on the ward report could mean dismissal. It would certainly make it hard to get a good reference.

As Miss Wallace walked away, Daisy sidled up to Grace. 'What did you do that for?' she hissed. 'You know I treated that patient, so why did you tell her it was you?'

'I didn't want you to get into trouble.'

'But it was my fault!'

'Yes, but a bad ward report would reflect poorly on you.'

'It will reflect badly on you, too.'

'Yes, but I'm only a VAD. I don't matter.'

Daisy stared at her. That was Grace's attitude towards everything, she realised. She didn't matter. Whether it was sharing out food at the dinner table or deciding who was to get a new pair of shoes, Grace automatically put herself last.

And now she had landed herself in trouble to save Daisy's skin.

But it wasn't only the thought of her sister's punishment that troubled Daisy as she went about her morning routine of taking temperatures and pulses, and administering massage and medicine.

She couldn't forget what Max had told her: how Grace had turned down the chance of a new life in Canada with the man she loved because she needed to put her family first.

The reason Daisy had been able to become a nurse was because Grace had given up her own chance of an education to look after her brothers and sisters. While Daisy, Albie, Walter and Ann had gone off into the world, Grace had stayed humbly in the background, taking a quiet pride in their achievements. If Daisy soared, it was because Grace had given her the wings.

She watched her sister at the far end of the ward, quietly going about her work. Now it was time to give her some wings, too.

Miss Wallace was surprised when Daisy approached her just before lunch.

'Yes, Nurse Maynard?' Now her temper had calmed, she was back to her pleasant self.

'Please, Sister. I used the perchloride of mercury on that patient, not Grace.'

Miss Wallace frowned. 'But I don't understand. Why would she take the blame for you if she didn't do it?'

'I don't know, Sister.'

'I see. I must say, I did think it was rather out of character for her to be so careless.' Miss Wallace considered it for a moment, then said, 'Well, thank you for owning up, Nurse. I appreciate your honesty.'

'Thank you, Sister.'

Grace was waiting for her sister in the kitchen. She was supposed to be making beef tea for one of the patients on a liquid diet, but the moment Daisy came in she turned on her.

'What were you saying to Sister?'

'I told her I used the perchloride of mercury, not you.'

'But why?' Grace looked anguished. 'Now you'll get into trouble.'

'Yes, and I deserve it,' Daisy said. 'You can't keep protecting me for ever, Grace.'

She was silent, staring at the kettle, waiting for it to boil.

'I spoke to Max,' Daisy broke the silence. 'He told me he'd asked you to go to Canada with him.'

Grace's expression darkened. 'He shouldn't have said anything,' she said.

'Why did you say no?'

Grace looked round at her. 'How can I go to Canada when I've got you and the kids to look after?'

'He told me Ann and Walter could go with you. Don't you think they'd enjoy that?'

'Yes, but what about you?' Grace's face was pinched with anxiety.

'What about me? I'm old enough to look after myself. And I've got used to living in at the Nurses' Home.' Daisy touched Grace's arm so she turned around to face her sister. 'You've been so good to me, Grace. I haven't wanted for anything since Mum died, thanks to you. But I'll never grow up unless you stop protecting me, like you just did with Sister.'

'Perhaps you're right.' Grace smiled ruefully. 'It's a hard habit to break, that's all.'

'So where better to break it than the other side of the world?' Daisy paused then went on, 'Look, I know I was selfish about you and Max, but I can see now you two are made for each other. You love him, don't you, Grace?'

'I hardly know him,' she mumbled, colour flooding her face. 'What if it doesn't work out?'

'You won't know until you try, will you? And be-

409

sides, I have a feeling it will work out very well.'

As Grace turned away to make the beef tea, Daisy saw a slight smile curving her lips. She was already daring to consider the possibility of a new life.

But by the time she finished preparing the drink, her old doubts were back in place.

'I can't go,' she said. 'It's not right.'

'So what are you going to do? Stay in the village for ever? Ann isn't a baby any more, Gracie. Soon we'll all have grown up and left, and then where will you be? Stuck in that cottage with no one for company, wishing you'd taken the chance when it was offered to you.'

Grace smiled shyly at her. 'I wish I had your confidence, Dais.'

'Then let me give it to you,' Daisy urged. 'You take my wings and fly, Gracie. Fly as far away from here as you can.'

Chapter Fifty

'Happy birthday to you, happy birthday to you. Happy birthday, dear Effie, happy birthday to you!'

Effie sang grimly to her reflection in the scrap of mirror above the sluice sink. What a way to spend her twenty-first birthday, she thought, scraping vomit off a sheet down a plug hole.

It wasn't even as if she could have a laugh today. It was lonely on the ward without Jess and Daisy around. But with Jess still recovering in isolation, and Daisy on the Military Ward, that only left sour-faced Sister Allen to share her birthday with.

As if she had somehow summoned her with her thoughts, the sluice door suddenly flew open and Sister Allen appeared, hauling a bag of soiled dressings.

'These need to be taken down to the incinerator and disposed of immediately,' she instructed. '*Stat!*' she added, when Effie didn't move straight away.

The incinerator was kept away from the main hospital building, in a squat brick-built shed called the Furnace Room. The gigantic incinerator filled the small room, its gaping, fiery maw like a portal to hell. The orderlies manned the furnace in shifts, stripped to their vests, feeding the beast with soiled dressings, amputated limbs and any other ghastly detritus that the hospital wished to be rid of. Because of the stench and the roaring, uncomfortable heat it belched out, very few of the senior staff ever ventured down there. Which made it a popular hiding place for the junior nurses and medical students.

Just Effie's luck, it was Connor who was on furnace duty today, shovelling rubbish from a heap into the burning jaws with a pitchfork. Silhouetted against the bright circle of fire, with his dark colouring and the red glow of the furnace reflected on his skin, he couldn't have looked more like one of the devil's minions if he'd tried.

Effie watched him unseen for a moment. Even though she didn't like him, she could appreciate what a perfect specimen of manhood he was. His

411

vest clung to him damply, outlining every muscle of his toned, broad-shouldered physique.

He stopped for a moment to push a damp curl out of his eyes, and caught her watching him.

'Enjoying the show?' he said quietly.

Effie cleared her throat. 'Sister Allen told me to bring these dressings down to you.' She shoved the sack at him, not meeting his eye. He picked it up and swung it easily into the furnace, where it was swallowed by the leaping flames.

As Effie turned away, he said, 'Happy birthday, by the way.'

She stopped. He was the only person who'd wished her that all day. 'I didn't think you'd remember.'

'How could I not remember you turn twenty one today?' His mouth twisted. 'You've been counting the days ever since I arrived, haven't you?'

'And now it's here,' she said. 'I'm a free woman, I can do as I like.'

'God help us all,' Connor muttered. He leaned on his pitchfork. 'So what has your fiancé bought you for your birthday? Not an engagement ring, by any chance?'

His mocking gaze fell to her left hand. Effie hid it in the folds of her skirt. 'Even if he had, I wouldn't be wearing it on duty, as you well know,' she said.

'I'll take that as a no, then.'

Effie lifted her chin. 'As a matter of fact, I won't know what he's bought me until I see him tomorrow. He's taking me up to London for dinner,' she announced proudly.

'London, eh?' Connor sounded impressed, but

412

the teasing glint in his eyes told a different story.

Effie turned away, irritated. Why did he manage to get under her skin so easily?

As she went to walk away, Connor called after her, 'By the way, I've got a present for you, too.'

'Have you? Where?' Effie looked around warily. She wouldn't put it past Connor to present her with a severed leg and think it was hilarious.

'It's more of a surprise,' he said.

'A nice surprise?'

'I think you'll like it.' He paused for a moment then said, 'I'm leaving.'

Effie stared at him. 'You're going back to Ireland?'

He nodded. 'I can't stay here for ever,' he said. 'Summer's coming and I'm needed on the farm. I've already stayed away far too long. Besides, what's there to keep me here, now you're making your own way in the world?'

What indeed? He was watching her face closely, waiting for her reaction. But Effie didn't quite know how to respond.

'What will you tell Mammy?' she asked.

'I'll tell her the truth, that you're of an age now to do as you please.'

'Will you tell her about Kit?'

He smiled. 'I think that's best left to you, don't you? Although I'd like a front seat when you finally pluck up the courage to tell your father you're marrying an English Protestant!' he laughed.

Effie sighed. She'd had more than a few sleepless nights over it herself.

As if he could sense her troubled mood, Connor said, 'Are you sure you're doing the right thing?'

413

Effie was instantly defensive. 'Not again! When are you going to stop interfering, Connor Cleary?'

'When that eejit proves he's good enough for you.'

She laughed, taken aback. 'I didn't know you had such a high opinion of me.'

Connor didn't crack a smile. 'You'd be surprised,' he said seriously.

Their eyes met. Effie's skin prickled with heat, but she put it down to the warmth belching from the furnace.

'When are you going?' she changed the subject.

'I'm booked on the boat from Holyhead on Thursday morning. I'll be catching the train from London tomorrow night.'

'I'll miss you.' The words were out before she could stop them.

Connor laughed. 'Euphemia O'Hara! Have you just forgotten yourself and said something nice to me?'

'No!' she denied it, staring at the floor. 'I just mean you're the closest thing I've got to family over here. Like a brother.'

His dark brows rose. 'Is that what you think? That I'm like a brother?'

'What's wrong with that?' she asked.

He dropped the pitchfork with a clatter and before Effie knew what was happening he'd crossed the room in a couple of strides, cupped her face in his hands and planted a kiss on her mouth. Effie braced herself, expecting him to try and dominate her the way Kit did. But even though he was physically much stronger, Connor's kiss was the gentlest she'd ever experienced. He barely brushed

414

her mouth with his soft, dry lips, but it was enough to send a dart of pleasure right through her.

He pulled away and smiled at her. 'Did that feel like a brother's kiss, Effie?' he said softly.

After she'd come off duty, Effie went to visit Jess in the sick bay on her way back to the Nurses' Home.

Jess was lying flat on her back, supported by pillows on either side to keep her still. It upset Effie to see the scar at her throat where Dr Drake had performed the emergency tracheostomy.

But at least Jess was well enough to be bored.

'I don't know how much longer I can put up with this,' she complained, her voice husky. 'Dr Drake said I might have to stay here for five weeks. It's not been five days and I'm fed up already!'

'I borrowed a magazine off Mrs Flynn for you, so that might help,' Effie set the copy of *Woman's Own* down on the bedside locker. 'Can I get you anything?'

Jess managed a smile. 'It's all right, Nurse O'Hara, you're not on duty now. You don't have to attend to my every need! Sit down and tell me what's going on in the outside world. Happy birthday, by the way. Your card's on my dresser if you want to find it.'

'Thank you.' Trust Jess Jago to be organised, thought Effie. Only she could get rushed to sick bay and still deliver a birthday card on time!

Effie sat down beside the bed. 'You gave us all quite a scare.'

'Did I? I don't remember much about it.'

'You went downhill so quickly you took us all by

surprise. One minute you were protesting that you were fine, the next you were delirious with fever, and couldn't breathe for the wretched membrane in your throat. We all thought we'd lost you, until Dr Drake did that tracheostomy. He practically brought you back from the dead!'

A strange, faraway look crossed Jess's face. 'I remember him bringing me back,' she said. 'I didn't want to come at first, but Sam made me–'

She stopped dead, her ashen cheeks suddenly stained with hectic colour.

'It's all right,' Effie said gently. 'I found the letters under your bed. I wasn't snooping, honestly,' she said quickly, seeing the stony expression on Jess's face. 'I was only looking for Sam's address so I could write and let him know you were ill.'

She paused, trying to choose her words carefully. It had been such a shock, finding all those carefully written letters. There had been a letter from Sam's mum, too, passing on the terrible news that he had been killed during the siege of Tobruk. 'Why did you go on writing to him, Jess?'

She turned her face slightly, so Effie couldn't see into her eyes. 'I – I don't know,' she said. 'I kept meaning to stop, but somehow I couldn't. I thought if I carried on writing to him it would mean he was still out there, reading them. In the end my letters turned into a kind of journal. I could pour out all my troubles to Sam, and imagine what he might say about them It made me feel – I don't know – closer to him.'

'But it wasn't just the letters,' Effie said. 'You talked about him as if he were still alive, too.'

The scar at Jess's throat bobbed as she swallowed hard. 'I couldn't help it,' she said. 'You started talking about him, and I thought if I told you what had happened, you'd start asking questions, and I'd have to drag it all up again... But then the longer I kept up the pretence, the worse it got. It reached the point where I couldn't tell you. I was afraid you'd think I'd gone mad.' Jess turned her dark eyes to Effie's, pleading for understanding.

Effie didn't reply. She didn't like to say so to Jess, but she feared her friend had been gripped by a kind of madness, denying the truth of what had happened to her boyfriend. It had taken Harry's death and her illness to bring her to crisis point.

Perhaps now the crisis was over and the truth was out, Jess could slowly start to rebuild her life.

Dr Drake came into the sick bay, carrying a book.

'Here's that Wilkie Collins novel I was telling you about,' he said. 'I thought you might like to–' He looked up and stopped dead when he saw Effie sitting there. 'Oh, I'm sorry. I didn't realise you had company.' A vivid blush flooded his face.

'Dr Drake was telling me about an author he thinks I might like,' Jess told Effie.

'Is that right?' Effie looked up at Dr Drake, then back at Jess. She was blushing too.

Chapter Fifty-One

That afternoon, Jess was surprised to get a visit from Sarah Newland.

'I heard you were ill,' she said. 'Makes a change, doesn't it? Me coming to visit you in hospital, instead of the other way round?'

Jess smiled. 'I'm not a very good patient, I'm afraid. I'm not really used to being waited on.'

'I know what you mean.' Sarah grinned. 'But from what the doctor says, you're going to have to get used to it.'

'I know!' Jess closed her eyes. She couldn't imagine lying still for five weeks. 'How are you, anyway? How's little Jess?'

'Getting bigger every day!' Sarah beamed with pride. 'Oh, Jess, I'm so lucky to have her. She's like a miracle.'

'I'm glad things are going well for you.' Jess frowned. 'But who's looking after the baby today?'

A blush rose in Sarah's cheek. 'Her grand-mother,' she said quietly.

She spoke so softly, Jess wondered if she'd heard correctly. Then, as Sarah reached up to brush a stray lock of red hair from her face, Jess noticed the emerald ring sparkling on the third finger of her left hand.

'You're wearing your ring?'

'Mrs Huntley-Osborne gave it back to me.' Sarah blushed. 'She said Clifford meant me to have it.' She smiled. 'Between you and me, I think it makes me look a bit more respectable. You know what she's like!'

'I do indeed,' Jess agreed. Which made her change of heart all the more mysterious.

Sarah seemed to read her thoughts. 'I know,' she said. 'I don't really understand it either. But ever since that day in the chapel, at the memorial service – oh, you won't know about that, will you?' Jess shook her head. 'It was the strangest thing. She just gave up her seat for me, in front of everyone. The whole village was watching. I was so surprised, I nearly fainted on the spot, I can tell you!'

'I don't blame you.' Jess was stunned, too. She couldn't imagine what had brought on Mrs Huntley-Osborne's change of heart. Perhaps her own words had sunk in after all, thought Jess.

Or perhaps Mrs Huntley-Osborne finally realised that pride could make her into a very lonely woman.

'Anyway, after that she asked if she could come and see the baby. Asked, mind – not her usual way of giving orders.' Sarah shook her head, still marvelling over it. 'And you should see what she brought for Jess. Matinee jackets, mittens, bootees – I reckon she'll be the best-dressed baby in Billinghurst at this rate!'

Sarah looked stunned, as if she couldn't quite believe her luck. Jess didn't blame her. Only a month ago she had been an outcast, living from hand to mouth. And now this.

'Did she see her granddaughter?' Jess asked.

Sarah smiled. 'She couldn't leave her alone! Says she looks just like Cliff did when he was a baby.'

419

'She's admitted he's the father, then?'

Sarah nodded. 'She always knew it, deep down. But you know Mrs Huntley-Osborne. She wanted better things for her son. I don't blame her,' she added. 'I'm sure I'll be just as protective when Jess grows up.'

Jess looked at her. People thought Sarah Newland was a troublesome girl, but she had a big heart. Mrs Huntley-Osborne could not have found a better daughter-in-law.

'Can you forgive her for what she did to you?'

'There's nothing to forgive.' Sarah shrugged. 'She was hurt and angry after Cliff died, and lashed out at me because I was an easy target. And, I must admit, I did the same to her. We were as bad as each other, really. Anyway,' she went on, 'the most important thing is that little Jess has a proper family.'

'I suppose you'll be moving in with Mrs Huntley-Osborne next?'

Sarah laughed. 'You must be joking!'

'Hasn't she offered? I thought she might, as she has that big house...'

'Oh, she's offered, all right, but I said no. Can you imagine the two of us living together? We'd drive each other mad in no time!' Sarah grinned. 'No, I think we're better off taking things gradually to start with. Although I've told her, I wouldn't say no to her paying for someone to fix the damp and the loose roof tiles in my cottage...'

Jess smiled. No one could ever accuse Sarah Newland of being a fortune hunter.

'And you're wearing that, are you?'

Millie caught her grandmother's flinty expression in the looking glass. It came as no surprise to her that her grandmother was dissatisfied with the outfit she had chosen for her wedding. Lady Rettingham had been dissatisfied with everything lately.

Millie stifled a sigh. 'What's wrong with it, Granny?'

'Nothing at all. It's a perfectly serviceable outfit – for one of Mrs Huntley-Osborne's fund-raising committee meetings, or perhaps afternoon tea with someone you're not particularly fond of. But surely not as a wedding outfit? Why can't you have a proper wedding dress?'

Millie regarded her own reflection. The dove-grey two piece was very becoming, she thought. And the little velvet hat perched at an angle on her blonde curls finished it off nicely.

'A proper wedding dress, as you call it, would cost a fortune in clothing coupons,' she said. 'And what's the point in squandering all that just for one day?' She tilted the hat to a more rakish angle, and stood back to assess the effect. 'This is far more practical, because I can wear it again after the wedding.'

'You can take practicality too far,' her grandmother said darkly.

Millie turned to face her. 'I'm surprised to hear you say that, Granny,' she said. 'I thought you valued practicality over everything?'

The dowager pursed her lips but said nothing. Millie couldn't help feeling irritated by her grandmother's change of attitude. Wasn't she the one who'd urged Millie to remarry for the sake of the

Billinghurst estate?

'It's hardly practical if it isn't a good fit,' Lady Rettingham muttered.

'It seems to fit well enough to me.' Millie half turned, smoothing the skirt over her hips.

'That's because you can't see it from where I'm standing.'

Millie caught her grandmother's eye in the mirror. She suddenly had the feeling they were no longer talking about her outfit.

She stifled a sigh. The last thing she wanted was to have this conversation, but it had been hanging over them like a storm brewing for several days.

'What is it, Granny? Don't you want me to marry Teddy?'

'Of course I do – if he makes you happy.'

Millie smiled. This was another idea her grandmother had never entertained before. 'Happiness comes a long way after duty, Granny. Isn't that what you've always taught me?'

Lady Rettingham's mouth pursed in frustration. 'Is that what you think you're doing? Acting out of duty?'

'No, of course not – not entirely, anyway.' Millie considered the question. 'I – care a great deal for Teddy. He's loyal, loving, and he makes me feel safe.'

'Do you love him?'

Millie paused, surprised by the question. 'Yes, I do love him – in a way,' she replied carefully. 'And that's enough, isn't it? It's more than many women in my position can say, anyway. Haven't you always told me you loathed Grandfather for at least the first year of your marriage?'

It was one of her grandmother's favourite homilies. She regularly held herself up as a shining example of someone who had bravely upheld family duty, carrying out her father's wishes that she should marry well.

'Yes, well, you and I are very different people,' Lady Rettingham replied quietly, looking at her hands.

Millie stared at her grandmother's reflection. This was yet another revelation. Could it be her grandmother was finally acknowledging that Millie might have a mind of her own?

'What on earth makes you say that?'

'Because I've seen you lately ... since you began working at that hospital.' The words seemed to be dragged out of her. 'I have to admit, you've been a different girl. You've had more energy, a greater sense of purpose. It's made me realise that perhaps I've been wrong, forcing you down a path you were never meant to take.'

Millie turned back to her reflection, too shaken to reply. Was her indomitable grandmother really admitting she might have been wrong about something? She waited for the earth to rock to its foundations, and was surprised when the ground stayed still beneath her feet.

Millie met her own gaze in the mirror. A pair of steady blue eyes looked back at her. It was no longer the bright, hopeful gaze of a young girl full of optimism for the future. It was the measured look of someone whose life had been shadowed by grief and loss. Someone who had experienced enough of life to know that playing it safe was better than risking everything for higher stakes.

'I appreciate what you're saying, Granny, but this is my path, whether I like it or not. And I think it's about time I started thinking with my head, and not my heart.' Millie looked at her grandmother, her smile tremulous. 'Don't look so unhappy, Granny. Things will work out for the best, you'll see.'

Chapter Fifty-Two

It was one of the swankiest restaurants in London, and as Kit kept reminding her, Effie was lucky to be there.

'I've never brought a girlfriend here before, let alone bought her champagne,' he told her. 'You should feel honoured.'

'But I'm your fiancée, not just any girlfriend,' Effie reminded him.

'So you are.' He raised his champagne glass to her.

He had pulled out all the stops, Effie had to admit. The restaurant was so stylish, filled with the crème de la crème of London society. Not that Effie recognised a single soul, but Kit kept pointing out various politicians and famous beauties. He'd splashed out on champagne and oysters and steak, and Effie knew she should be having the time of her life.

But all she felt was – flat.

All evening, she found she couldn't keep her eyes

off the clock on the wall. She didn't want to do it, but she couldn't stop her gaze creeping up to check it, counting the minutes as they ticked by.

In the end, Kit grew annoyed. 'Do you have an urgent appointment somewhere?' he snapped. 'Because I'd hate to feel I was keeping you...'

'It's not that,' she hurried to reassure him. 'Connor's train leaves at nine.'

A smile of pure relish spread across Kit's face. 'Good riddance,' he said. 'I can't wait to see the back of him, can you?'

'No,' Effie agreed. But her words sounded hollow, even to her.

The truth was, after less than a day she was already beginning to miss him.

Worse still, his absence had made her realise how little she and Kit actually had in common. When Connor was around, they were united in their dislike of him. He gave them something to talk about, someone to plot against. Effie had quite enjoyed playing the thwarted lover, and she had a feeling Kit did too. But with Connor not around to add a spark to it, their romance felt disappointingly flat.

'I'm sure he'll be happier when he's back wallowing in the peat bogs, among his own kind,' Kit said dismissively.

'They're my kind, too,' Effie reminded him.

'Yes, but you're different, aren't you, darling? You wanted more out of life. You'd never settle for an ignorant farmer's boy.'

'Connor's not ignorant.'

Kit's brows rose. 'Oh, so you're defending him now, are you?'

'No, but I don't think it's fair to call him names.

425

Especially when he isn't here to defend himself.'

Kit retreated into sulky silence. 'I couldn't see Connor Cleary bringing you to a place like this,' he said finally. 'The only time the likes of Connor would come in here is if he was working in the kitchens!'

Effie pressed her lips together to stop herself speaking out. He's your fiancé, she reminded herself. You don't owe Connor Cleary any loyalty. If it had been left to him, you'd be on that boat back to Ireland by now...

She was shocked by how much she suddenly missed her home. How much she longed to see her mammy and daddy, and to walk in the fields with her dog, with no barbed wire anywhere or fighter planes circling overhead.

'You know he was in love with you, don't you?' Kit said casually.

Effie laughed. 'Come off it!'

'I'm serious, darling. Connor was absolutely besotted with you. Of course he was desperate to hide it – those strong, silent types always are – but I spotted it straight away. Why do you think he was so keen to keep us apart? He wanted you for himself.'

Effie stared at Kit.

'Connor has no interest in me,' she said. But the memory of his kiss was still imprinted on her lips. She had been trying to tell herself he didn't mean it, and it was just another way for him to torment her.

Kit sent her a pitying look. 'Do you really think he'd come all the way over to England in the middle of a war just to torment you?'

'My mammy sent him.'

'I very much doubt it, darling.' Kit leaned forward. 'Do you know, he came to see me after we came back from the coast? He laid in wait for me in the dark – it was quite menacing, actually.'

'What did he say?'

'He was utterly convinced that I'd besmirched your honour. Kept telling me I shouldn't hurt you. It was comical to watch, really. Him virtually pleading with me to make an honest woman of you, when really he was desperate to have you himself.'

Effie looked at his arrogant face and realisation dawned. 'Was that why you asked me to marry you?'

Kit nodded. 'Well, he wanted me to do the right thing by you, so I thought I'd take it one step further.' He laughed. 'Wasn't it priceless, the night he found out we were engaged? You had to see the funny side, didn't you? I'm so glad you didn't tell him, sweetheart. If you had I would have missed out on the pleasure of seeing his expression!'

He'd tried to warn her, Effie thought. Connor had told her exactly what game Kit was playing, and she'd refused to believe him. She cringed to think of the harsh things she'd said to him that night.

Connor Cleary, defender of her honour and keeper of her heart.

She stood, pushing back her chair. Kit stared up at her. 'Where are you going?'

'I need to see Connor before he leaves.'

His face changed. 'Oh, no, you don't. You're not walking out on me.'

'But I need to apologise–'

Kit's hand flashed out, grabbing her wrist. 'You're not going,' he said flatly. 'I'm not letting that oaf think he's won...'

Effie stared at him, realisation dawning. 'That's all this is to you, isn't it?' she said, pulling herself free from his grasp. 'A competition. This isn't about me, it's about getting one over on Connor.'

'That's not true!'

'And what about our engagement? Was that all part of your game, too?' Kit said nothing, but his face gave him away. 'It was, wasn't it? Connor was right, you had no intention of marrying me.' She rubbed her wrist where he'd grabbed it.

Kit lowered his gaze. 'Sit down and we'll talk about it,' he muttered.

'No.' Effie shook her head. 'I've fallen for your lies often enough. I don't need to listen to any more.'

Connor stood at the far end of the train platform, smoking a cigarette. Effie picked out his tall, broad-shouldered figure in the crowd straight away, but paused for a moment before she approached him. She could be on the verge of making the biggest mistake of her life.

But if she let this moment slip by, she could be making an even bigger one.

She was almost behind him and he still hadn't noticed her.

'Connor?' she said quietly.

He swung round, surprise written all over his face. 'Effie? What are you doing here?'

'I came to see you off.'

'Make sure I was really leaving, you mean?' His brows lowered, and she saw the light disappear from his blue eyes. 'Don't worry, I won't be back.'

'That's not why I'm here. I came to ask you a question.'

'Oh, yes? And what's that?'

'Did you go and see Kit after we came back from the coast?'

His brows drew together again, and for a moment it looked as if he might deny it. Then his shoulders slumped in defeat.

'I might have known the little weasel would go running to you,' he muttered, his voice full of contempt.

'Why did you do it?'

Colour rose in Connor's face. 'Because I wanted to make sure he treated you right.'

Kit had been telling the truth: Connor cared about her, Effie realised.

'And what about what you want?' she asked softly.

He flicked her a quick look. 'What do you mean?'

She looked down at her hands, suddenly unable to meet his eye. 'I just wondered why you'd try to push me to be with someone else when you want me for yourself?'

A stunned silence followed her words, and for a dreadful moment Effie wondered if she'd got it horribly wrong. What if he laughed at her? She didn't think she could bear the humiliation.

'Where did you get that idea?' he said gruffly.

'I'm right, aren't I? That's the real reason you came over to England looking for me.'

She forced herself to look up at him, and almost immediately Connor turned away from her. 'Your mother sent me to find you,' he insisted stubbornly, but she knew he was lying.

'Why didn't she send my father, or one of my sisters, or my cousins, or–'

'All right,' he cut her off impatiently. 'You're right, I asked to come.'

'Because you like me,' Effie said.

Connor glared at her. 'What do you want me to say?' he snarled. 'Yes, I like you. Is that what you want to hear? Jesus, Effie, why are you doing this to me?' There was a pleading note in his voice. 'You've got the man you want. Now just leave me alone, all right?'

The train was approaching. People started to gather up their belongings.

'Don't go,' Effie said.

Connor's mouth twisted. 'Why? So you can use me to make your fiancé jealous whenever you feel like it?' He shook his head. 'Sorry, Effie, I'm not interested in playing those games.'

'I'm not playing games.'

'Effie O'Hara, you've been playing games with me since the day you were born.'

The train was drawing closer, emerging from a cloud of dirty steam as it rolled into the station. Effie's heart rate speeded up; she knew she didn't have much time left.

'I honestly didn't realise you cared for me,' she blurted out.

'So why else did you think I came all the way over from Ireland? Why do you think I've been hanging around for weeks?'

'I don't know... I thought you wanted to torment me. It's what you've always done.'

'You mean I didn't fall under your spell the way every other boy in Kilkenny did?' He shook his head. 'Well, I've got news for you, Effie. I did. Only I had too much pride to tell you, because I knew it wouldn't get me anywhere.'

'What makes you say that?' she asked.

'Because I know you. No one in Kilkenny would ever be good enough for you, you made that clear. You didn't want to stay in a sleepy corner of Ireland. You wanted to follow your sisters to London and make something of your life. Don't you remember, you were constantly telling us about all the big plans and dreams you had? Kilkenny was never going to be good enough for you, and neither was anyone in it. I didn't want to be trampled under your feet in your rush to get away.'

The train came to a halt and doors started opening and closing as people got on. Connor froze for a moment, not moving, his eyes searching her face. Effie tried desperately to read his expression.

'Why did you come here, if you felt like that?' she asked.

'Because I had to see you. Poor simple fool that I am, I couldn't stop myself.' He smiled ruefully. 'But from the minute I got here, I realised I'd made a mistake. I've spent the last few months torturing myself, but I can't do it any more.'

He picked up his bags and started moving down the platform towards his carriage. Effie followed him.

'I don't want you to go,' she pleaded.

'Sorry, Effie. You can't twist me round your

431

little finger for ever.' He jerked his head down the platform. 'Go home. Your fiancé will be waiting for you.'

Effie watched him loading his cases on to the train. The guard was moving down the platform closing the doors. She could feel her chance of happiness slipping away.

'He's not my fiancé,' she said.

Connor pushed down the window. 'What?'

At the far end of the platform the guard blew his whistle. 'I've left Kit. I broke off our engagement.' Such as it was, she thought bitterly.

'Why?'

The train belched steam, enveloping Effie in a choking, bitter cloud that stung her throat.

'Because I love you, you eejit!' she shouted, her voice lost in the hiss and grind of the train's engine. Someone had to say it, and she didn't think Connor would ever admit it.

But it was too late. The train was already pulling out of the platform, disappearing into a cloud of steam. Effie watched it go, and could almost feel the pull in her chest as it took her heart with her.

Why had she been so stupid? As usual, she'd been so wrapped up in chasing her own silly dreams, she hadn't seen that what she really wanted was right under her nose, waiting for her.

But now it was too late.

She set off down the platform dejectedly. But she hadn't reached the gate before she heard a voice behind her.

'Effie O'Hara?'

She swung round to see Connor's tall figure emerging from the fading steam. Effie ran to him and launched herself into his arms, feeling herself being whisked up into the air effortlessly.

'You'd better not be messing with me, Euphemia O'Hara, because I've left half my worldly possessions on that train!' he warned sternly, when he'd set her down again.

'Oh, no!' Effie stared at the train, receding into the distance. 'We must get your case back.'

'No need.' Connor reached for her hand. 'I've got everything I need right here.'

Chapter Fifty-Three

On the day Lady Amelia Rushton was marrying Lord Edward Teasdale at Billinghurst chapel, William was surprised to receive a visit from the Dowager Countess.

He couldn't quite believe it when the elderly lady swept into his office, tall and ramrod straight, her iron-grey curls perfectly set around her unsmiling face.

'Lady Rettingham, what a pleasant surprise.' He rose from behind his desk to greet her. 'I must say, I didn't expect to see you'

'I don't have all day, Squadron Leader,' she cut briskly through his pleasantries. 'There's something I would like you to do.'

'Oh, yes? And what's that?'

'I want you to stop my granddaughter's wedding.'

William froze, still halfway up from his seat. 'I

beg your pardon?'

'You heard me, I want you to stop the wedding.'

He straightened up. 'You want me to ruin the happiest day of your granddaughter's life?'

'Oh, please!' Lady Rettingham dismissed. 'If it was the happiest day of her life, do you really think I would be here? You and I both know Millie is making a terrible mistake. I'd speak to her myself about it, but I know she won't listen to me.'

'And what makes you think she'll listen to me?'

'Because she loves you. And you love her, if my eyes don't deceive me,' she added.

Lady Rettingham faced him squarely. 'Do you want to see Amelia throw her life away?' she asked bluntly.

'She won't,' William said. 'She's made her choice and I happen to think it's a good one. Teddy Teasdale will make her far happier than I ever could.'

'If you believe that then you're a fool!' Lady Rettingham snapped. 'I'm not saying Teddy isn't delightful in his way, and I'll admit he's tried very hard to make Millie content, and will continue to do so to the best of his ability. But he'll never make her truly happy. Only you can do that.'

William sank back down behind his desk. This was all a dream, he decided. It wasn't possible that he and the austere Dowager Countess could really be in his office discussing the intricacies of the heart.

'Well?' Lady Rettingham's gaze fixed on him. 'Will you talk to her, make her see sense?'

William shook his head. 'I'm sorry,' he said, 'but unlike you I won't interfere in Millie's life.'

Lady Rettingham sighed impatiently. 'Oh, for

goodness' sake, why does everyone keep going on about interfering as if it's a bad thing? It's only by interfering that we get anything done in this world!'

'I'm sorry, but I won't help you.'

She regarded William consideringly. 'You know, I disliked you from the moment I saw you,' she said.

'Thank you.' The feeling was mutual, he thought.

'I disliked you, but I also respected you. I could see you were committed and passionate, that you were someone who would fight for what he believed in. You took me on, and there are not many people who would do that.' She tilted her head questioningly. 'So let me ask you this, Squadron Leader. Is my granddaughter not worth fighting for too?'

Billinghurst chapel was decorated prettily for a country wedding. But the cloying scent of the freesias that bedecked it made Millie feel sick.

Was it natural to feel this nervous, she wondered as she prepared to walk down the aisle. She couldn't remember feeling so many butterflies in her stomach before she'd married Sebastian. But she was younger then, and carefree. She'd had the confidence of youth, that nothing could possibly go wrong. Now she was older, and wiser, and it was surely only right that she should be having doubts...

The pews were packed. Millie's glance picked out Teddy's parents, her in-laws the Duke and Duchess of Claremont, and Mrs Huntley-

Osborne. Her grandmother sat in the front row, looking solemn in stiff pewter silk.

And there, at the front, stood Teddy, waiting for her.

Everyone was watching her, all faces turned expectantly. She couldn't let them down, even though every fibre of her being was suddenly telling her to turn tail and run.

You're doing the right thing, she repeated over and over again in her head. You love Teddy. He'll look after you and Henry, and keep you safe for ever.

It was such a short walk down the tiny aisle, but it seemed to take for ever as she forced herself to put one foot in front of the other. Somehow she reached the altar and there was Teddy, beside her.

'You look beautiful,' he whispered.

'Thank you.' Millie's smile was pinched. Don't do this, she kept telling herself. If you run away now, you'll ruin everything. Poor Teddy would be utterly humiliated, and he didn't deserve that. And her grandmother would probably never speak to her again.

The vicar started the ceremony. Millie tried to concentrate on what he was saying, but she could hardly hear him over the clamour of voices in her head. She didn't know what was happening until a silence fell and she realised all eyes had turned to her expectantly.

'I'm so sorry, could you repeat that?' she whispered.

The vicar sent her a frowning look. 'Will you, Amelia Charlotte, take this man, Edward Charles, to be your lawful wedded husband?'

436

A ripple ran through the congregation, and Millie realised she had hesitated a fraction too long. 'I will,' she said finally, and heard the collective sigh of relief.

The vicar turned to Teddy. 'And will you, Edward Charles, take this woman, Amelia Charlotte, to be your lawful wedded wife?' he intoned.

Millie smiled up into Teddy's face. His lovely, sweet face. How could she ever think she didn't love him?

'No,' he said.

A tide of shocked whispers broke out behind them. Millie stared at him in disbelief.

'Teddy?' she said.

'I'm sorry,' he shook his head. 'I can't.'

On the front row, Teddy's parents were shifting in their seats. It seemed to be all his mother could do to stop his father storming the altar.

Millie couldn't take her eyes off Teddy's face. 'But I don't understand ... I thought you loved me?'

'I do, darling girl, with all my heart. That's why I can't marry you.'

As Millie stood there, rooted to the spot with mortification, Teddy turned to the congregation. 'I'm terribly sorry, but there isn't going to be a wedding today,' he said. Then he turned to the vicar and said, 'Would you excuse us for a moment? I need a quiet word with Lady Amelia outside.'

Millie still didn't know what was going on as he pulled her from the church into the cold, fresh spring air. This all seemed so unreal, like a terrible dream.

'Teddy, what's going on?' she begged. 'None of this makes any sense...'

He held on to her hands. 'Millie, I love you,' he said. 'But I know you don't love me. That's why I can't marry you.'

'I do love you!' she protested.

'Darling, I could see it in your face as you came down the aisle. You looked like a lamb going to the slaughter.'

'I – I was just nervous, that's all.' She reached desperately for his hands. He took them, wrapping his warm fingers around her cold, stiff ones.

'Nervous because you knew you were doing the wrong thing. Because you're in love with someone else. It's true, isn't it?' he prompted her. 'You're still in love with William Tremayne.'

She opened her mouth to deny it, then closed it again.

'I don't ask for much in a wife,' Teddy said. 'But I do think it's fair to expect her to put me first. I think I deserve that, don't you?'

'I would put you first.'

'Not in here.' He pressed his finger to her heart. 'Not where it counts.'

He was right, she realised. No matter how much she might wish things to be different.

'I'm so sorry,' she said.

'Darling, you have nothing to apologise for. I'm the one who jilted you, remember?'

She smiled shakily up at him. Now her shock had abated, she could see he was right. 'And I think that might be the nicest thing anyone has ever done for me.'

He grimaced. 'I hope you get the chance to tell

that to my parents. I suspect my father is in there organising a lynch mob as we speak.'

They both looked round at the sound of pounding footsteps and a moment later William appeared, running up the path towards them.

He stopped dead when he saw them standing there, holding hands.

'Am I too late?' he said.

'No, old man, you're not too late.' Teddy looked from him to Millie with amusement. 'Typical RAF, cutting it fine,' he said dryly.

Chapter Fifty-Four

The bomber squadron was being relocated to an airfield in Lincolnshire, which meant the RAF was moving out of Billinghurst. Perverse as ever, the Dowager Countess wasn't pleased about it.

'After all the fuss they made about moving in, they only stay for a matter of months,' she complained. 'Was it worth all the disruption, I wonder?'

Millie looked at William. 'I think so,' she smiled.

'Hmm.' Her grandmother glanced at Millie's wedding ring, but said nothing. She had been very tight-lipped since Millie and William had insisted on getting married quietly in the register office in Tunbridge Wells. 'Although I suppose it was for the best, since we're all still trying to live down your last wedding,' she had said.

'So what will happen now?' Lady Rettingham

wanted to know. 'Will we finally be allowed to move back into our own home, do you suppose? And what on earth will we do with that runway at the bottom of the garden?'

'I expect it will come in useful when the Americans arrive,' Millie said casually.

Her grandmother turned pale. 'Americans?'

'Oh, didn't I mention it? We've had another letter from the Ministry. A squadron from the American Air Force is looking for a base, and they think Billinghurst will be ideal.'

'Do they indeed?' Lady Rettingham's brows arched. 'We shall see about that.'

'I think it sounds like an excellent idea,' William said. 'Think of the advantages, Lady Rettingham. You'll never want for a pair of nylons or a stick of chewing gum again.'

Millie stifled a laugh by pretending to blow her nose. Her grandmother sent William a withering look.

'Of course,' Millie said, 'there might be a way to prevent it...'

'What's that?' Lady Rettingham pounced eagerly.

'I've been thinking of opening up the house as a military hospital. I've realised from working at the Nightingale that they need more specialist hospitals. I'm sure the Red Cross would be willing to supply nurses, if we can offer them a suitable base.'

'And who would run it?' her grandmother asked.

'I would.' Millie met her gaze steadily, bracing herself for the stinging retort.

Lady Rettingham paused. 'I think that would

be a splendid idea,' she said. Millie stared at her. She had expected to have a fight on her hands.

'Really?'

'Why not? You're a very resourceful and capable young woman, Amelia. I don't think you give yourself enough credit.' Then, just as Millie was beginning to swell with pride, her grandmother added, 'At any rate, I imagine anything would be preferable to Americans.'

'You know, she's right,' William said later, when they were in the bedroom changing for dinner. 'You are a very capable young woman. Capable of great deceit, that is.'

'Me?' Millie pulled an innocent expression in the mirror as she applied her lipstick. 'I'm sure I don't know what you're talking about.'

'There are no Americans, are there? There was never any letter, either.'

Millie grinned. 'All right, perhaps I did embellish the truth a little. But it worked, didn't it? Granny would never have agreed if I'd approached her with the hospital idea straight out.'

'Very shrewd,' William commented.

'You have to be, if you want to stay one step ahead of my grandmother.' Millie smiled. 'I'm so glad we'll be opening a hospital here. It will give me something to occupy my mind while you're up in Lincolnshire.'

The thought of being separated from him after so long together cast a shadow over their relationship. But Millie was determined not to let him see how upset and worried she was. She had to try to learn to let tomorrow take care of itself.

'Of course,' William said, 'if you're opening a

hospital then you're going to need doctors, aren't you?'

'I was thinking of applying to work for the Red Cross myself,' he said. 'I think I've pushed my luck far enough with flying.' He sent her a wry look. 'I don't suppose you'd consider me for a position, would you?'

Millie pretended to think about it. 'Well, you'd have to pass a very strict selection process,' she said.

His brows rose. 'Oh, yes? How strict?'

'Extremely.' She allowed her gaze to trail down his long, lean body. After three weeks of marriage, she was still very much enjoying her honeymoon. 'And it would involve a very thorough physical examination...'

On a damp day in April, Grace married her airman.

It wasn't a grand wedding by any means, but Grace was overwhelmed by the way everyone in the village had come together to make it special for her. Friends and neighbours had contributed ration coupons for the wedding breakfast. Mrs Huntley-Osborne commandeered the village hall for the reception and mustered the WVS to prepare a spread of potted meat and fish paste sandwiches, and a variety of cakes and fancies. The centrepiece was an impressive wedding cake, covered in what looked like ornate royal icing, but was actually a simple fruit cake inside an elaborate cardboard façade.

Grace had already bought herself a nice two-piece costume from Waymarks in Tunbridge Wells but on the morning of the wedding her friend Pearl had surprised her with the most beautiful dress, sewn from a length of parachute silk her farmer husband had found in one of his fields.

'I might not be as good a cook as you, but I'm handy with a needle,' she'd said with a smile.

'Oh, Pearl, it's smashing!' Grace smoothed her hand over the delicate fabric. She had never worn anything so beautiful in her whole life.

'It's not all my own work,' her friend admitted. 'Miss Pomfrey did all the beading and embroidery. You know I haven't got the patience for all that fiddly work.'

Daisy, her bridesmaid, did Grace's hair for her. She'd taken great pains with it, pinning and curling it into a halo of soft fair waves around her face. Grace scarcely recognised herself when she looked in the mirror, especially after Daisy had applied some powder and mascara and a soft pink lipstick.

'Oh, Dais, you've made me look really pretty!' she marvelled.

'You *are* pretty,' Daisy replied. 'You just need to take a bit more time and trouble with yourself, instead of worrying about other people all the time.'

With everyone working together, the wedding day was wonderful. Not least because Grace was marrying Max. He looked so handsome in his uniform, she almost had to pinch herself before she could believe he was her husband.

She wasn't the only one admiring him. 'I wish I'd waited for a handsome Canadian, instead of marrying a fat farmer!' Pearl complained. 'Just think, not only are you going to live in the mountains, you're also going to wake up next to that lovely-looking man for the rest of your life!'

'I know! Some people have all the luck, don't they?' Grace looked across the room at Max.

'You deserve it, love. It's about time you had a bit of happiness.' Pearl gave Grace a wobbly smile. 'But I'll miss you,' she said. 'Who's going to protect me from Mrs Huntley-Osborne if you're not here?'

'I think Mrs Huntley-Osborne is too busy with her new granddaughter to give you much trouble,' Grace said, glancing across to where she sat contentedly nursing the baby in her arms.

For once, the village busybody had found herself the topic of gossip when it came out that her son Clifford was the father of Sarah Newland's baby. But talk had soon died down, and now Mrs Huntley-Osborne could be seen proudly pushing her grandchild up and down the village in her new Silver Cross pram, forcing people to stop and admire her.

'She's beside herself now Sarah's working for Lady Amelia,' Grace said. Millie had taken Sarah on as a nanny when Nanny Perks left. Grace had never got on with Perks, and suspected Her Ladyship wasn't sorry to see her go, either. Now Sarah brought her baby daughter to Billinghurst whenever she could wrestle her from her grandmother's clutches, and Mrs Huntley-Osborne went around bragging to all and sundry that little Jessie Elizabeth and Lord Henry were playmates.

'I'll miss this place,' Grace sighed, looking around her.

'Get away with you! You won't give us a second

444

thought once you're over in Canada, with all that fresh air and lovely scenery.' Pearl looked meaningfully across the room at Max when she said it.

'You will keep an eye on Daisy for me, won't you?' Grace said anxiously.

'I said I would, didn't I? Don't worry, I'll make sure she stays out of trouble. But she's a big girl now, don't forget. She can look after herself.'

'I suppose you're right,' sighed Grace. But it was still difficult to admit it.

All too soon, it was time for them to leave. Grace hugged her sister fiercely. 'I wish you were coming with me,' she cried.

'So do I,' Daisy mumbled into her shoulder as she clung to her. 'But maybe it's time we both learned to stand on our own two feet, don't you think?'

'You're right.' Grace pulled away, holding her at arm's length. 'Now you will remember to feed the chickens, won't you? Make sure you keep the coop locked at night, so the foxes can't get in. And you'll make sure you eat properly?'

'Grace! What did I just say about standing on my own two feet?'

Grace sniffed back her tears. 'Old habits die hard.'

Daisy smiled. 'It won't be for ever,' she said. 'You go and find me a nice Canadian lumberjack to marry, and I'll be over there like a shot.'

'It's a promise.'

They looked into each other's eyes for a long time. 'Goodbye, Daisy.' Grace could hardly manage the words. She stared at her sister, as if she could somehow force into her all the wisdom and knowledge she felt Daisy needed to survive without her.

'Goodbye, Gracie.' Daisy was looking back at her, and Grace had the feeling she was doing just the same.

Peter Drake was at the wedding reception, looking like a fish out of water as usual. He seemed even more awkward out of his white doctor's coat as he stood in the corner, polishing his spectacles.

He always did that when he was nervous, Jess thought. It was one of the things she'd had time to notice during the five weeks she'd spent in isolation.

Jess had hardly seen him since she'd returned to work. She had been moved up to Female Surgical, which brought her more into contact with the Senior Surgical Officer Mr Cooper than with the physicians.

Feeling sorry for Dr Drake, Jess went over to say hello.

'Oh, hello, Nurse.' He fumbled to put his spectacles back on. 'How are you? Feeling better, I hope?'

'Much better, thank you, sir.'

'Splendid. That's – er – splendid. And the scar?'

'Almost healed.' Jess arched her neck so he could see the faint pink line on her throat.

'Yes, that all looks very good.' He turned his gaze towards the cardboard wedding cake in the centre of the table. 'You gave us all a bit of a fright there, Nurse.'

'So I heard, sir. You saved my life, by all accounts.'

'Oh, I wouldn't say that.' Colour rose in his face and he took off his glasses again, polishing them feverishly on the hem of his jacket.

Jess wondered what he would say if she told him how he had come and rescued her in her dream. She had been poised in the moment between life and death, and it had been his voice, his presence, that had brought her back.

He probably would have told her what she already knew. That it was only a dream, a trick of her imagination brought on by the fever. But Jess was still comforted by the idea that Sam was somewhere out there waiting for her, and that she would see him again one day, when the time was right.

In the meantime, she had to go on living her life as best she could, for Sam's sake as well as her own.

'How are you enjoying the Female Surgical ward?' Peter Drake asked.

Jess looked at him in surprise. How did he know where she had been sent? 'It's very interesting,' she said. 'But I might not be there too long. Miss Fox has said I can go back to London, if I want to.'

Dr Drake looked dismayed. 'And will you go?'

'I don't know. I don't think so.' Jess smiled. 'I'm quite enjoying it here.'

She'd never thought she'd hear herself say it, but she'd got used to the countryside, and the people in it.

She was grateful for the wisdom of Miss Fox. The Nightingale's matron had realised, even if Jess hadn't at the time, that she needed time and space to come to terms with what had happened to Sam.

'I hope you stay,' Dr Drake said, then added quickly, 'you're a good nurse and they're hard to find.'

'In that case, I'll definitely have to stay, won't I?' Jess smiled at him. He promptly dropped his spectacles in his confusion.

As he bent down to pick them up, something fell from his jacket pocket.

'Looks like you've dropped something–'

'I'll get that–'

Dr Drake went to snatch it up but Jess got there first.

She stared down at the twisted fragment of paper in her hand. It was a little more tattered than it had been, but it was unmistakably the spring of paper mistletoe that Daisy had put up in the ward at Christmas. The one Dr Drake had later taken down in a fit of embarrassed pique.

Had he really kept it all this time? Jess wondered.

'I don't know how that got there,' he said, blushing furiously. But at the same time, Jess caught the slightest hint of a shy smile on his lips.

He'll take care of you, Sam had said in her dream. She looked down at the paper mistletoe in her hand. It was going to be slow going, she thought. But perhaps, by next Christmas, they would be ready to put it to good use.

This Large Print Book for the partially sighted, who cannot read normal print, is published under the auspices of

THE ULVERSCROFT FOUNDATION